WALK TO PARADISE GARDEN

John Campbell

Ocean Highway Books T.M.
Independent Publishing Consultants

ISBN: 9781470140670

Acknowledgements

Warm and special thanks go to: Wendy Bertsch, Robert Davidson, Richard Sutton, Genevieve Graham-Sawchyn, Kathy Vorenerg, Val-Rae Christensen, Debbie Girardi and her illustrious book club, Valerie Tate, Caroline Hartman, Jake Barton, Richard Allen, Clark G. Vanderpool, Fontaine, Mary Enck, Nicole Dweck, Mary Vensel White, Marge McRae, Roberta Winter, Elizabeth Matson, Iva Polansky, Marssie Mencotti, Johanna Stephen-Ward, Alverne Ball, Kay Christina Fenton, John Breeden, Barbara Jurgensen, Caleb Engel, Mike Dewey, Bridget Dunn, Christina Naftis, Wangari Mathenge, Meredith Rackley Stoddard, Emmett Delaney, Andrew Wright, Frank Laurie, Bill Clark, John McGrosso, Pamela Campbell, John and Betty Campbell, Vicktoria Jimenez, Saundra Verstrate, Tanya McCulloch, Evelyne Keith, James Protsman and many patient friends and colleagues.

Chapter One

1915 – Flanders

"My father is a butcher in Chicago," John Armitage informed the lorry driver. The man ground the gears and grunted, his yellowed teeth threatening to sever the stub of a rank cigar.

John shrugged and gazed out over the desolate Belgian landscape. The overcast sky offered nothing but monotonous gray, save for two dark buzzards circling over a dip. Even the muddy crossroad before them lacked a signpost, as if no one could possibly want to know what lay ahead.

The gears shifted with a lurch. Albert, the driver and John's only companion, sniffed. "Well, no disrespect, young man, but I can see and hear you're a nob through and through. Lemme just tell you what ol' Albert saw back there." He turned toward his window and spat the butt through the opening. "When you tried to get in the transport wagon, you looked right indignant when they blocked yer way an' was tellin' you as it was full up. And you and I both knows it weren't that full. They'd read you as a toff, same as I did."

"Your perception is admirable."

"Prob'ly thought you was a surgeon or sumfink, if not a proper toff." Albert added with relish, his tone affable.

"Ha! Far from it."

"Now, don't you take it personal. Them boys are out of sorts. Scared, they is, 'bout goin' to the Front, and they prob'ly just wanted to go this last stretch wiv their own company o' mates. But that's not all I heard outta you. No sir. Thing is, you don't talk like any butcher's son I ever met. Me ear tells me there's more than Yank in you. I detect a bit o' West End—Mayfair or maybe up by Highgate." Albert pointed a gnarled and grimy finger his way. "And yer hands is soft."

"I can see, Albert, that you're a real Sherlock Holmes," John said stiffly, slightly annoyed at being read correctly. Nonetheless, he was thankful for the opportunity for some banter. It would help dispel, at least for the moment, his mounting anxiety as they drew closer to the battle zone.

"Ta, very much. That means you credit me my intelligence. Yep, Ol' Albert can read well enough, both books and folks. But now, don't go takin' any offence. I'm happy to see an American cross the high seas and volunteer to help our boys. Lord knows as they needs all the help they can get." Albert dropped his voice to a low whisper. His playfulness evaporated as quickly as would laughter at the crack of close gunfire. "It's hell out there, I'm sorry to say. You, my friend, are in for the shock of yer life."

John frowned, surprised at his companion's sudden change of demeanor. He turned and scanned the disheartening view again. Dismal fields stretched in all directions. The few trees dotting the land looked as if they had died of despair.

A dark shape on the other side of the road caught his eye, materializing as a lone boy. The dejected figure trudged southward, bent under a bag slung over his shoulder. Albert paid scant attention to the lad despite the fact that the young face watched them. The driver's attention was elsewhere. For a long moment, the boy's sad gaze locked with John's, twisting and weighing down his heart. An orphan? His family and home destroyed by war? Heading for Calais or some other city to live off the streets?

John checked Albert's expression and wondered why the man still wouldn't look the boy's way. It was deliberate, he could tell. John considered saying something, then thought better of it. If some personal pain forced his companion's gaze straight ahead, better to let it be.

A pent-up breath escaped John's lips. Everything about this war upset him. He silently fumed, feeling helpless. All he could do was wish the insanity throughout Europe would end. He was about to set into a tirade over the pompous old fools who had allowed this whole mess, those who had weakly chosen violence over diplomacy. But the tension still emanating from Albert convinced him to swallow his complaints.

"Got a bit to go yet," the driver said with a hollow lift to his voice. An effort, possibly, to compensate for ignoring the boy.

They had jolted over the lonely stretch for some time before a Red Cross wagon pulled by two dray horses approached, most likely heading back to Calais. Perhaps they would encounter the child along the road and offer him a lift to town. As the two vehicles passed, each going its own way along the pitiful road, the drivers traded somber waves.

"There goes some lucky lads. Goin' for a Blighty. Tha' means a bit o' rest at home. O' course, 'lucky' means they're less a limb or two. I heard abaht one poor boy went back without 'is face. Got mostly blown off from an explosion. Woulda been more merciful had he died."

John's skin felt suddenly cold and clammy and he swallowed down nausea. The relentless jostling in a truck that reeked of petrol and sweat was bad enough. Now, with images of irreversible injuries and ruined lives floating through his mind, he had to summon up control with a concerted effort. He wiped damp hands on his trousers and tried to think of something else.

But he couldn't. And he craved conversation. "Uh," John said, clearing his throat. "I can only guess morale must be pretty low these days."

"Sumfink turrble, it is. But the boys love their homeland. Just let anyone talk against what they're fightin' for and the bloke's in fer a beatin."

"Right," John said, his mind filling with frightening scenarios. He didn't subscribe to blind patriotism, and in John's experience, speaking his mind often got him into scrapes.

For a second, John was back to that cold day, standing on his soapbox in front of Lunt Library. Incensed at hearing of Roosevelt's intention to run a third-term campaign, John had begun his own address and began speaking out against reneged promises. Many in the gathering crowd were his fellow footballers. The tension was palpable. Edwina had done all she could to doctor his cuts and bruises after that rigmarole.

John had always been determined to be his own man. His mother would have pampered him into a feckless fop, had it not been for his British nanny, and later his governess, Edwina Pitt, who had emigrated to live with the family in Illinois. Edwina had the gonads of a Royal Navy admiral. While his father neglected him, Edwina went out on the Lake Forest estate grounds in her skirts and kicked the soccer ball around with him on numerous occasions. The spry woman had guided his masculine development and fostered not a few of his ideals.

John could never imagine himself killing anyone, but he was no coward. His decision to serve in the Royal Army Medical Corps was accomplished in phases. After leaving the Midwest in a huff, he had taken a steamer from New York to England. With rumors flying about

German U-boats on the prowl, that had proven to be a brave step. In London he had preferred not to stay at his mother's Mayfair house, because his cousin Basil was residing there. John found the man insufferable. Instead, he rented rooms in modest Lambeth and considered his next move.

One dreary day, as he was crossing Cavendish Road, a Red Cross poster had caught his eye. It read *Ease Pain; Save Lives; Join the Red Cross.* Soon after, John saw a recruiting station advertising their need for stretcher bearers for the Royal Army Medical Corps,. He marched directly in and volunteered.

He had considered this kind of field service before, after he'd read an article about the fate of the wounded on a battlefield in Solferino, Italy, some fifty years before. The article had been presented in his European history class and it told of 40,000 injured soldiers who had been abandoned on a mountainside without any help.

"...smell your own flesh rotting." John jolted straight. Had he said that out loud?

"Aye. That's a nasty problem," Albert replied. "Trench Foot, mostly."

"Oh, no. I...I was thinking back to something I'd read about injured soldiers in Italy. There was no Red Cross or RAMC there. I've often imagined what it must've been like for the wounded left behind, smelling the gangrene before sinking into death."

Albert shot him a sideways glance. "That's pretty morbid for a lad just startin' out his duty."

"Uh, sorry. That's why I volunteered. To help, I mean."

Albert grunted his reply.

In hindsight, John admitted his decision to volunteer came in part from the unattractive wish to spite his father. He also conceded that he yearned for adventure. But something else had niggled at the back of his mind, and he now saw clearly what it was. By doing this, for the first time in his life, John felt needed.

He was told that as a stretcher-bearer, he would be facing the same dangers as those in combat. But helping the wounded was how he had chosen to serve. He couldn't help the dead, but sometimes even dragging their bodies out of No Man's Land seemed of some value.

"Can ya smell it? O' course ya can," Albert said, speaking not of his truck nor of death in Italy, but to introduce the conditions into which John would soon be submerged. The stench from the Front at the

Ypres Salient carried for miles on the stale breezes. It caught in John's throat as they approached Vlamertinghe, the small village west of Ypres that would serve as his base. And the smell was undeniably getting stronger.

"Ye'll get used to it, mate."

Though he tried not to, John burst into a coughing fit, trying not to give in to the waves of nausea threatening from lower down. As he gained command of himself, the truck pulled up in front of what looked like a warehouse. Albert ground the gears and floored the brakes, and the lorry lurched to a halt.

"That'd be your barracks, sir."

John scrambled out, grabbed his suitcase, then stood at mock attention, albeit a bit stiffly after the long ride. With a sincere grin, he ceremoniously saluted his driver.

"Thank you, sir," John barked in friendly mimic.

Albert pointed across the street. "The pub fare is better at that Signee Nory."

As the lorry pulled away, the engine backfired and chugged so loudly John could only wave and nod appreciatively for the advice. He looked down the lane, hunting for the suggested tavern. "Oh, *Le Cygne Noir*. The Black Swan," John said to himself. He chuckled, reflecting both on Albert's pronunciation and on his company. In a way, he was almost grateful there had been 'no room' for him in the transport wagon, back in Calais.

Turning toward his destination, John considered the building that would house him when he wasn't risking his life at the Front. For a utilitarian commercial building, it looked quite smart, with its symmetry and large windows. The brickwork offered a smattering of ornamentation. The RAMC sign announcing the structure's new official purpose did all it could to dress the building down.

He was just about to enter when a powerful shoulder struck him from behind, shoving him against the doorframe. A British soldier, a bear of a man, towered over him. "Are you a bloody journalist, come to write lies?"

Reining in his anger, John straightened. "No. I'm here with the RAMC to help get you boys patched up."

"Then you're a bloody conchie." The man's breath was nasty.

John enunciated as if to a dim child. "I am an American, offering to carry a carcass like yours off the battlefield."

"Hmph. Well, you best watch where you're goin', mate. There's one thing I can't abide and that's a conscientious objector." The soldier spat to the side and walked around him—a victory in itself—then lumbered down the street.

Pleased to note his hands weren't shaking, John took a deep breath of relatively fresh air and entered the barracks. He reported in and was subsequently deposited in a second-floor wing. There he washed, put on fresh clothing, and tried to settle his nerves. Tomorrow would begin his baptism by fire. Shaking off a chill that ran the length of his body, he sat on his bunk to unwind, propping his feet up, pressing his shoulder blades against the cool brick wall. The air in the large room was heavy with the scent of a recently washed wood floor, mixed with a muskiness which clung to the blankets and folded clothing of other men. More than a dozen bunks lined the walls of his section, all unoccupied at the moment, except for one in which a young man snored.

Some distance outside the village, rumblings and cracklings of artillery fire echoed over the flatlands. How many lives had been snuffed out just then? John closed his eyes and sighed, doubting himself. How would his heart survive observing firsthand, repeated tragedy?

A more immediate confrontation broke out just below his window. John got up and peered out, then realized it was just boisterous bantering. A handful of British soldiers were walking with a nurse, each man jockeying for her attention, all of them juddering past like chickens in a yard. John reached for his satchel and pulled out a book, but after several minutes of effort even Plutarch failed to calm him. With a vague sense of relief, he got up, checked his reflection in the mirror and that of his unknown roommate, and left the building.

Chapter Two

As old taverns go, *Le Cygne Noir* was unexceptional from the outside. John had just reached the other side of the lane when a man dressed like a local stumbled out of the place, offered a slurred salutation and bowed to him in jest. John nodded, determined to be one of the fellows, and then stepped into a warm welcome of lantern light and laughter.

Closing the door with the back of his heel, he stood for a moment on the plank floor, waiting for his eyes to adjust to the smoky room. Along the far wall he spied Eddie Thompson, whom he had met back at the Lambeth office. John had been told before crossing the Channel that he and Eddie would likely be partnered as stretcher-bearers. He didn't know how long they might work together, peons in the RAMC, but he found it slightly amusing that he again had an Eddie in his life. He doubted, however, that many men could match the spirit of the formidable Edwina Pitt.

As he meandered between tables, John was almost hit in the gut by a drunken Belgian, flailing his arms as he made fun of something. The soldier apologized, looking somewhat sheepish, but John patted him on the back and continued navigating his way toward Eddie's table. He pulled out a chair. "Mind if I join you?"

"I'd be 'onored." Eddie's tone and expression were welcoming. The young man had told him he had been a cobbler in Wapping before he'd signed up. Like John, he was just twenty. Unlike John, he looked as if he were fifteen, a lanky youth with tousled sandy hair. John angled a chair so that as he sat he could lean against the wall, his right elbow on the table.

"They're outta whisky, I'm sorry to tell ya," Eddie drawled. "I 'elped them with tha', which I'm not sorry to tell ya. The wine's not bad, though."

Eddie signaled to the older couple tending the bar and the woman came over promptly, setting a sparkling clean glass before John. "For Monsieur." Her posture told him she was proud of her well-kept establishment, neat and efficient when everything around them was in war-torn shambles. Her expression, however, expressed concern, as if she realized she had yet another young man to worry about.

John stood and made a quick bow. She giggled at this special treatment and returned to the bar, still smiling. Eddie poured, filling both glasses.

Lifting his by the stem, John gazed through the red liquid. "I don't know how I'm going to get any sleep tonight with all that rumbling from the Front. It must be maddening to realize each volley brings misery and bloodshed." He took a sip, swallowed hard, and grimaced. The wine was a touch too bright, carrying an essence of vinegar, but it was drinkable. He was glad to have it.

"You'll get used to the noise. Daown't take too long. I've been 'ere for over a week now, almost two. Sleep like a baby most times, when I gets to." Eddie held up his glass. "Here's to ya," he said, and tossed back a gulp.

They talked about the cobbler business then went on to discuss eel pies, which were sold on the occasional East End street corner. It was a delicacy on which they disagreed; John was not a fan of eel pies.

Eddie's face suddenly lit and he nodded toward the door. "Ah, look at what just came in, will ya? Two nice lookin' nurses. One fer you and one fer me."

John smiled appreciatively at the ladies, letting his gaze linger. They glanced his way only briefly before sitting at a table closer to the bar. "I don't think they're quite taken with us, old man."

"Don't underestimate our charms." Eddie shook his head and stifled a belch. "They're T.F.N.S., if I heard c'rectly."

John closed his eyes, grappling to come up with words for what that meant. British officialdom's acronyms were fast becoming annoying.

"It stands for Tuff Nurses." Eddie barked out a laugh, sounding pleased with himself. John hoped the ladies hadn't overheard them and forced himself not to look their way. Eddie sat straighter. "Sometimes they assist at the Casualty Clearing Stations. So, we, my good gentleman, might just get to ride out there in their company."

John frowned at this revelation. "They have ladies near the Front?"

"Only the trained and the brave. A special lot, them." With his elbow propped on the table, head in his hand, the cobbler beamed a dreamy gaze at the women.

"That brown-haired lass sits right like a toff. Back straight. Lovely. Now there's a match fer ya. Me, I like 'em plump, like blondie there. I've seen 'er around but 'aven't yet 'ad the pleasure."

John slapped the table as the meaning finally came to him and Eddie jumped, almost knocking over his glass. "Territorial Field Nursing Services. Ha!"

The wine bottle before Eddie was empty, so John got up to get another, keeping his eyes casually on the brunette as he negotiated his way around tables. There was something about her that pulled at him, as if there were a new energy in the room, a tension which heightened his senses. It couldn't be from the wine; he'd only had a few sips. When he reached the bar, John tried to shrug off the uncomfortable sensation that the entire place was watching him. He gave a quick glance around, but no one was paying the least attention.

The elderly publican behind the bar leaned closer and smiled, ears pricked, as if ready to decipher something other than French or Flemish. The woman beside him, wiping glasses with a white towel, glanced over her shoulder and gave John a familiar smile.

John spoke in formal French. "It's my first evening here and I'm grateful to find such a pleasant establishment so handy."

"Merci, monsieur. I am Jacques, and this here's my wife, Amelie. Welcome to *Le Cygne Noir*. This is my family's business."

Letting his eyes wander, John admired the crafted detail of the cabinetry. "How old is the building?"

"Oh, more than two hundred years. I hope it survives." A shadow of doubt crossed the man's amiable features, then disappeared beneath his ready smile.

Amelie came to stand by her husband. "I hope you survive, too, young man. So many nice boys we meet and never see again."

As fascinating as it was to get the pulse of the area through these folks, John was still distracted by the lingering sensation of being watched. The assessing gaze bored into his back, and he imagined—hoped—it was from the women behind him. Leaning his elbow on the bar, he casually turned as if admiring the room while still conversing. He hoped he was placing his words in the right order as he stole a quick glance at the ladies. The brunette remained attentive to her companion's conversation. John couldn't help thinking that were her profile minted on a gold coin, it would be more than appropriate. The blonde's eyes shifted, catching his. She winked.

He turned back, his pulse internally audible. Smiling at Jacques and Amelie, he felt sure they could read him. Without missing a beat, however, he added, "I can't imagine what it must be like for you to see the surrounding area ruined as it is."

"It's hardly recognizable," Jacques agreed, his voice resigned.

Amelie clucked her tongue and looked away. Her hazel eyes might have held a sparkle once, but not now. She began wiping down the bar, despite its already pristine finish. John bought a bottle of the only red they had left, a claret. Returning to the table, he filled Eddie's glass and settled back in.

Eddie's one-sided conversation ran on, contentedly detailing life in Wapping and the East End in general. It was obvious the young man was homesick. John nodded and grunted in response as needed, but his attention shifted back to the T.F.N.S. ladies. The blonde, evidently dominating the conversation, was taking care of what looked like a bottle of Pernod, an ambitious project for one. The brunette held a teacup and listened politely. Her rich, dark hair was pulled up in a neat topknot bun, accentuating her elegant neck. She was slender with delicate features, the epitome of femininity, and yet here she was, in a war. He considered the courage and compassion it must have taken for her to volunteer. The suggested depth of character attracted him.

The next thing John knew, Eddie's conversation had ceased. The young cobbler's head had lowered to the table and he had begun to snore.

Recognizing opportunity, John rose and approached the ladies. With a slight bow he asked, "Mind if I join you ladies for a bit?"

"Owh, we don't mind at all, do we, Evie?" the blonde said, puffing out a breathy perfume of anise liquor.

"Please do," the brunette said. A slight smile spread across her face, hinting at amusement. John pulled a chair to their table, noticing how large her exquisite hazel eyes were. These, too, revealed humor, as if there were something comical about his joining them. He wondered fleetingly if the blonde had made some kind of bet about his doing so.

"Oi'm Liz and this here's Evie. Her real name's Evelyne, but she lets me call her Evie. Can't say if she'll be as nice to you." Liz licked her lips and looked him up and down. "But Oi reckon she might. Go ahead and sit. You just get in, did ya?"

He slid into his chair. "First day on the job's tomorrow. Stretcher-bearer. I'm nervous, of course." He looked at Evelyne. "How about you?"

"Lucky fer you they just got in some new ambulances," Liz chipped in.

Evelyne nodded, agreeing with Liz' contribution. "We received a Rolls and a Sunbeam last week, and I understand a Star lorry is due here any day." She lifted her cup and sipped her tea, ignoring his question about her time at the Front.

Liz continued, chatting on and on about horses for some time before John realized he had been staring at Evelyne's delicate hands: a lady's hands, worthy of jewels and caresses. With a start, his mind raced to catch up, registering a moment's eye contact as Evelyne set down her cup. She lowered her hands smoothly back to her lap when her efforts to restrain a smile succeeded. John mumbled some nonsensical reply to Liz's comment, all the time wondering how the war conditions might affect this brave young woman before him, this lady who sat with the air of a grand duchess.

Liz's grating voice finally grabbed his full attention. "Owh, Oi been here just three weeks. Evie's been 'round for some time now. Ridin' in them ambulances can about break your bum. New or not, this area's rough on 'em, ambulances and bums. Roads are nuthin' but ruts most the time. Poor horses were scared to death of the gunfire and flares. These horseless ones break down, and they usually do that in the worst o' places," she said, indicating the Front. "Wheel'll come off now and then."

"You're American," Evelyne said, matter of fact. Her words slipped in naturally, as if she'd meant to include them initially, as if Liz's conversation hadn't interrupted at all. He read kindness and frankness in her expression, a forthrightness that was refreshing.

"Yes, from Chicago," he replied. "I have dual citizenship, though. My mum is British." He affected an imitation of her accent and grinned.

She laughed with him and the conversation shifted to what she and Liz had experienced thus far. After hearing their accounts of assisting medics and surgeons in primitive and dangerous conditions, John was amazed at how they appeared relatively unscathed. The evening passed too quickly. The women said they had to get back and John jumped up to pull Evelyne's chair back as she stood.

Liz glanced over at Eddie. "Should we wake him?"

John shook his head. "Oh, I'll come back and collect him after I get you two ladies safely home." John grinned and so did they, as if realizing that he'd meant "safe" from Eddie, too.

Outside, Evelyne took Liz's arm. In the dark a foot might slip or an ankle give on the slick cobbled lane.

John found it remarkable that Evelyne didn't appear shackled by the rigid social stricture of her obviously upper class British roots. Before the war it had simply not been done for even a modestly titled young woman to keep company with the likes of Liz. The women spoke softly to one another, unaffected by the dark and sporadic barrages of distant gunfire, and he couldn't help admiring her courage. Would he be able to acclimate and assimilate as well as she had in so short a time? He felt as if he had done nothing all day but fail at exactly that.

Around the corner, someone sang a bawdy song. Horse hooves lazily clomped from behind, heading toward the Australian camp, and the delicate fragrance of Lily of the Valley wafted from Evelyne's hair. Passing through lamplight, John admired her graceful carriage and was startled when her lovely eyes met his gaze. Awash with exhilaration, he barely resisted reaching out to touch her. *You're an impetuous lad*, Edwina reminded him. He sunk his hands safely in his pockets.

"Here we are," Liz announced. Disappointment soaked through him. "One of us will prob'ly ride out with ya tomorrow," she added. "Won't know till we report in."

Evelyne said, "It was nice meeting you, John."

He wished them goodnight and gave a salute before Liz latched the door behind them.

Try as he might, John could not fall asleep. A familiar aching in his chest overwhelmed rumblings from the Front, thoughts of the dreamy-eyed Evelyne, and the general noise. His mind buzzed, busy with old arguments and counterarguments. He thought of his father and how, after so long, the old man had stepped in from out of nowhere, planning to steer John's life. He had wanted his son to come work for him, at the Armitage Meats Company. But John had refused to set foot in the building.

I know all about outfits like yours and their exploitation of workers, he'd said. *Yes, I read Upton Sinclair. Fiction or not, everybody knows those conditions are real.*

He had stood unflinching as the old man flung accusations, but John was determined. He'd thrown it all back in his father's scowling face. *No, I'm not a blasted socialist, I'm a humanitarian, unlike you.*

John had shaken with rage after that conversation, though he'd done it behind closed doors. Not that it mattered. His father had disappeared yet again.

Where were you before now? I didn't have a father growing up, I had a nanny. Where were you? At that stinking plant!

Then came the remorse. After a tirade, John was always riddled with guilt. And no one could make him fly off with rage like Chicago's great Franklin Armitage.

Chapter Three

Brisk breezes slapped at John's face as he headed outside to report for duty. Dawn had just arrived and moody clouds painted everything gunmetal gray. It was cold for April, but even more chilling was the coming confrontation with real war conditions. His focus was on the base, so he only vaguely noticed the haunted look of the few villagers he passed along the cobbled lane. The ambulance base was housed in a stable yard, next to a large building constructed of fieldstone. This home served as the infirmary. Just before entering the base, John inhaled the heady aroma of baking bread. Despite having eaten, he wished he had time to investigate. Turning from the comforting sensation as if he were leaving behind the last vestige of civilization, he stepped into the stable yard and shook the chill off his back, ignoring his growling stomach.

He had been awake all night, alternately fuming about his father and regretting harsh words. It shouldn't have surprised him that the tentacles of pain and the guilt Franklin Armitage could inflict reached so far from home. Now he was angry with himself over his weakness of mind, for not having the control to dispel his old demons. As a result, he was setting out on his first day—at the Western Front, of all places—with an exhausted mind and body.

Learning that Liz, not Evelyne, was joining his ambulance run to the Casualty Clearing Station did not lighten his mood.

Eddie moved about like an old man as he loaded the vehicle, paying the price for having sought consolation in drink. The surgeon, who needed to be driven to the Front, was a somber Scotsman named Alistair MacLeod. He was a small man in spectacles who wore the serious expression of one who had been there for some time.

MacLeod rode up front with the driver, a middle-aged volunteer from Wales. In the back Liz clung to the edges of the bench, trying to keep from sliding off at each curve and bump. Eddie was nursing his hangover, head between his knees for most of the trip. The ambulance lurched over a rut, and the cobbler cursed.

"See what Oi mean?" Liz said good-naturedly. She placed her hand on Eddie's back and murmured something soothing to him. They'd just met, officially, in the stable yard, but she was quick to sympathize. "Ya need a tough bum to ride in one o' these things." She released a hearty laugh.

Gunfire barked back and forth across the lines of the fast-approaching Front. John's stomach knotted and his hands felt clammy. He would have given in to the urge to retch from nerves had it not been for the calming presence of Liz. If she and Evelyne could put up with the conditions of war, he should be able to as well.

They pulled up to the Casualty Clearing Station, otherwise known as the C.C.S., and John hopped out, his new boots landing in a sucking puddle of mud. He studied the large tent structure, noting the Red Cross insignias displayed front and side. Without a word, MacLeod strode past him, heading in to confer with the other surgeons. Eddie picked up a stretcher, clumsy from nerves or inexperience, and then followed the surgeon. John grappled with another, but stopped before entering.

He propped up his folded stretcher like a staff and surveyed the scarred earth stretched between the C.C.S. and the trenches. The firing had subsided during their approach and an eerie silence pressed against him. Stronger waves of stench arose, flowing from the tent, and he fought nausea again. He wondered if he would ever get used to the smell, then wondered if that would be a good thing or a bad one.

It was hard to envision the land's pastoral appearance before the insanity. When he squinted, he could make out the barbed wire. With a little more yardage and elevation, he imagined he'd be able to see the Germans if they came up to fire. He swallowed involuntarily and went in search of Eddie.

Within the Red Cross tent, misery and concern hung like smoke, suspended in a veil over the occupants. John set the stretcher against the side of a cabinet and spotted Liz and Eddie talking in low tones with two orderlies. MacLeod was to the side, nodding and evidently getting direction from his superior. John made his way toward Eddie. Walking past a latrine, John breathed through his mouth, trying to ignore the stink of blood, urine, effluvia. He kept on, now moving between rows of cots.

He inadvertently met the gaze of a young soldier who began struggling to sit up. It was as though the lad wanted to get up on John's account. Was he in need of reassurance? Diversion? His brow was bandaged, as was his right hand. John smiled with something he hoped gave strength. The answering smile on the lad's face stretched in a controlled manner, evidently defying pain. His front two teeth were missing. In the silent interchange, the soldier's expression spoke. *I'm one of the lucky ones.* John nodded acknowledgement then turned and walked on, afraid to look too closely at some of the others, particularly those who moaned under blood-soaked sheets and others who were inanimate. He approached the surgical station desk and waited for instructions.

An orderly was speaking to Eddie, who looked even paler than he had during the ambulance drive. "Ronnie Dunn's bought it, poor lad. Hardly nineteen, he were," the orderly said, his voice shivering. He stood with his arms akimbo as if holding himself steady. "Suffered somethin' terrible at the end. I held his hand. Called for his mum, he did."

MacLeod motioned John and Eddie away from the orderly and read their list of duties, pointing to this cot and that, as though the human factor didn't exist. John imagined war left little time or energy for sentimentality and wondered how he would view all the carnage after being here for weeks. The Scotsman then handed John the list as if appointing him in charge of something more than moving the injured. Having time before her duty, Liz offered to help, as did the troubled orderly. Stone-faced, Eddie fell in next to John, and they went in search of the first patient.

"Here we are," John said, trying to sound both sympathetic and encouraging. The soldier in cot number fourteen had both of his legs broken. He would spend some time in the infirmary before heading home to recuperate. Having shifted him onto one of the stretchers, John and Eddie began carrying him to the ambulance.

The man looked up at Eddie, eyes big in his grimy face. "Ya heard they got Ronnie, yeah? How's his poor mum goin' to take the news?"

Eddie didn't reply. John couldn't see his expression. He sensed his partner's hangover had dissipated and had likely been replaced by raw emotion. Ronnie had evidently been a school chum or, if not that, at least close to Eddie in some way.

The injured man went on, not seeming to care if anyone listened. "Me, I get to go home while I get me legs to walk again. Only I don't got a mum to go home to. Just me Da. Me and Da, that'll be nice while I mend. Have a pint and some pie, we will."

Gravel crunched under John's feet as they made their way to the vehicle. They got the soldier into the ambulance and slid him next to the side, away from the bench.

"I'll be back here, though," the soldier assured them. "Gotta do it for Ronnie, I do."

Just before Eddie jumped out of the ambulance, he turned back. "Daown't go anywhere for now, mate," he said wryly. The soldier laughed, but the sound was hollow.

They turned toward the C.C.S., passing Liz and the orderly as they made their way with their charge. John recognized the patient as the lad he had smiled at earlier and felt compelled to see if they needed a hand. Blood seeped through the head bandage, causing John a pang of concern. He watched Liz climb in first as the orderly did a careful hoist. The young man had the use of his legs, though they shook as if he suffered with tremors. Liz guided him to a corner and had him slide down to the floor where he could be propped up. The young man smiled his thanks and Liz gently patted his cheek before returning to the tent.

That day they made three trips, transporting fifteen wounded men to the infirmary, four of whom would be transferred home for long-term recuperation. For hours at a time John's mind was filled with sharp impressions of the soldiers he had helped. If he hadn't had the image of Evelyne visiting his thoughts, he would have wished to get well and truly soused that night

It was early for camaraderie at *Le Cygne Noir*, but John had been too restless to sit in his room. After washing, he had come straight over. He sat at a table by himself, yearning for the company of Eddie and the two nurses. Amelie set the stew he'd ordered before him, and he used his fork to search for pieces of meat. He found only two small bits. The vegetables, at least, were tasty. As his plate was cleared away, a few soldiers filtered in, their conversations somber. John listened to their voices, feeling a similar need to talk about his day, to somehow meld his experience into a universal purpose. He smiled with relief when Eddie appeared at the door. Together they drank a bottle of claret before Liz and Evelyne arrived and joined them. Though Evelyne was polite and seemed glad to see him, sadness clouded her expression.

In short order Liz had her Pernod and was raising a glass in John's direction. "You did good on yer first day. Pleasure workin' with someone who's got more manners than Eddie 'ere."

"What d'ya mean?" the cobbler demanded, but the question was rhetorical and they all knew it. Liz ruffled his hair. Evelyne forced a courteous smile.

At a nearby table, a ruckus broke out between some soused soldiers, loud and physical. Just as quickly, it settled down, though tension lingered.

"That edgy lot is from Manchester," Eddie explained, careful not to be heard beyond their own table. John recognized one of them from his arrival, the man who had purposely knocked him against the doorframe. Liz unabashedly gave the rowdies a disdainful glare, then, as if she were taking credit for handling the matter, belted down a shot of Pernod and smiled with satisfaction. John made no comment about the quick dispute or about his amusement over nervous Eddie and spirited Liz, but Evelyne's eyes met his in unspoken agreement.

Despite the pleasant companionship, pent up feelings about the day overtook John and the claret encouraged him to speak. "It's infuriating," he said, "seeing Britain's young men decimated like this. And for what?"

As if he had spoken with a bullhorn, tension engulfed the table and filled the entire pub. Conversation ebbed. John sat frozen, wondering if it were only his imagination, or if everyone had stiffened at hearing what they considered to be treasonous talk. Instead of looking around, though, he kept his gaze locked with Evelyne's. He was surprised at how much her opinion mattered to him, and he worried she might take him for a radical, or worse, a coward. He had no intention of compromising his feelings, but was relieved to see warmth in her expression, brightening her eyes and smile.

The lapse in conversations ended, which was also a relief. John had been worried the edgy lot might leap to their feet, countering his question. *For God and Country, man!* Instead, one by one folks fell back into their private discussions. John's peripheral told him some might even agree.

"What's wrong with diplomacy?" he asked, keeping his voice low this time. "Why must our military leaders sit back and play war games while young men, little more than boys, get blown to bits?" He cleared his throat and gulped a swallow of wine. "It's, uh, well, it's a nasty state of affairs." Again silence ensued, but this time there was less tension. He chuckled self-consciously. "But listen to me going on. What do I know? You three have been a part of this for what? Weeks already, right? Uh, more than that for the ladies."

Liz perked up at this reference to her being a lady. "Actually, Evie's been here for several months, haven't ya, pet?"

Evelyne nodded, her expression quiet.

Eddie shrugged, his gaze on his empty glass. "Even though, we're still all wet behind the ears, we are."

Liz seemed to notice John's concern for the silent Evie. She patted his hand. "Evie here's had a bad one today, poor thing."

Evelyne gave an apologetic half-smile. "A young man died in my arms this afternoon. He was due to go home with a blighty wound." Her eyes blinked quickly. "He looked so lively when he came to my ward today. We changed the dressing on his head. It was a surface wound, but needed attention again. Nothing serious, from the look of it. They thought he would make it home, at least."

John grimaced. "He wasn't missing teeth, was he?" he asked, hoping it wasn't the youth he had noticed earlier.

"Yes," she said quietly. "Toby Phelps. Later in the day he complained of a severe headache as I passed by his bed. I sat with him, thinking at first he just needed to be comforted. Next thing I knew, he lost consciousness. And then he died."

"The doctor said it musta been a brain hemorrhage," Liz said.

John yearned for whisky, for something stronger to dull the pain he felt for Evelyne, and for dead boys like Toby Phelps. He reached across the table and took Evelyne's hand, finding it hard to imagine these delicate fingers changing bloody bandages. He imagined how angelic she must seem to near-delirious patients in her nursing duties.

She withdrew her hand before he'd even registered it. Without word or gesture, she got up and strode hurriedly to the door. John glanced at Liz, his heart full of questions and emotions.

"Poor little dove," Liz said and clucked her tongue.

"It's bound to wear ya daown, all this is," Eddie agreed, his expression clouded. He pressed his lips together as if trying to decide how to say something. Then he apparently changed his mind. He gulped the last of his wine and stared at his hands on the table.

"I'm going after her," John announced as he got to his feet.

"Ugh, naow wait a bit, lovey." Liz reached out to grab his arm, possibly intending comfort rather than restraint, but he slipped from her grasp. Eddie sucked in air but said nothing. Other patrons watched John as he went after Evelyne, their prurient suggestions sticking to him like gnats in humidity. He zigzagged his way through them, avoiding the legs of empty tables and chairs, ignoring the few mocking comments at his back.

He stepped out in the night and looked down the lamplit lane but didn't see her. The openness and quiet was like a breath of relief, removing some of the annoyance he'd picked up from the crowded room. The way was empty. If Evelyne wasn't heading to her dormitory, where was she?

Chapter Four

"I'm here," she offered from the shadows.

He made out her silhouette where she sat on one of the empty crates at the far end of the Black Swan. She and everything around her were bathed in midnight blue.

A wall of tension stood between them, as tangible as coolness rising from a river. Even so, he couldn't help but approach. He lowered himself onto one of the crates and said nothing when she turned her face away.

A scraping noise cut through the night air as a small cart came around the corner, its wheels grinding on the cobbles. The old woman pushing it trudged along, eyes downcast, too tired to bother scrutinizing them.

Evelyne spoke, her voice husky with restrained emotion. "It's funny how something I read long ago suddenly springs to mind. Seems relevant." Her hands fidgeted in her lap. Was she meaning to communicate or mystify ? "When I was reading Pushkin, the world was entirely different." She looked at him, her expression masked. "He wrote in verse, you know. Perhaps that explains the durability of the lines. Certainly their power." She stood. "I should go."

He shot up. "Was it something I—"

"No." She turned away. "Pardon me please, Mister Armitage." He could feel the heat of her emotion from where he stood. "No need to escort me back." She walked away, her skirts swishing. He came up abreast, but she faced him, her hand pushed against his chest. "Please. Go back inside." Tears glistened on her cheeks and he involuntarily reached out to console. She drew away. "You cannot be this nice," she finally said, then ran down the lane, her steps echoing off ancient stone walls.

Liz and Eddie were the only folks in the tavern who noticed his return. The mocking soldiers, even the edgy Manchester lot, ignored him, their focus now on slurred diatribes and stories. Returning to his friends' table, John was unable to rouse himself to be better company. He barely heard the few words his companions offered.

Eventually, Liz stood to leave. "Daown't worry, love. Won't help. Things'll straighten round." She patted his shoulder, nodded to Eddie with a meaningful look, then headed out.

After a moment, Eddie leaned forward, his eyes intent. "I need to tell ya sumfink I didn't know till today. Well, 'ow could I, as I didn't really know Liz till today?" He glanced down at his fingers and tapped a tattoo on the weathered tabletop.

"What?!"

"She's married. That nice-lookin' Evie's already married."

Chapter Five

The canteen, used both by soldiers and medical personnel, had been a cheese factory before the war and was as large as a barn. The inside had been stripped of its equipment and filled with rows of tables and benches. Its whitewashed walls and ceiling, now colored with a patina of dust, sometimes echoed nervous laughter, sometimes sheltered a morose silence. Today, John felt the numerous conversations revealed a rawness of emotion.

In the past, rumors claimed the war would end before Christmas. They were long past that now, with no sign of victory anywhere in sight.

A company of Algerian infantrymen huddled together along the wall farthest from John. His gaze settled surreptitiously on them, feeling both admiration and pity. Forced into service by the French, the Algerians were often sent to the front lines and suffered heavier casualties than their Imperial masters. It wasn't only their exotic features and uniforms that drew his attention. It was more how they carried themselves with a kind of dignity in the face of this injustice.

Eddie broke into his thoughts. "I used to think I could eat a horse if I was hungry enough, but this stuff is awful." His face twisted with disgust.

"Hmm? Oh." John glanced at the table in front of his mate: a tin of processed meat, a few biscuits and a mug of tea. "See that?" He pointed to the side of Eddie's meat tin, indicating the name Ballantine. "That's my uncle's meatpacking business in Limehouse."

"Oh, sorry."

"Don't be. He's a nice enough man but, like my father, who is also in the meatpacking business, profits are more important to him than people. Especially his own workers."

Eddie frowned, looking interested, and John took this as encouragement. "You can't imagine the conditions of working with animal products. Meat is the mainstay, but byproducts from things like hoofs turn into buttons and soap and such." John leaned toward Eddie. "You know what happened after the war began? Women started taking jobs in place of all the men who'd come here, and my uncle had the audacity to cut wages. Can you believe that? He was already paying precious little and having them work under terrible conditions. 'Nobody pays women as much as men,' he told me. What does their being women have to do with anything?" John stabbed his fork into a hunk of jellied meat and held it up like a weapon. "In my opinion, men like my father and my uncle too readily accept the plight of the poor and exploit it for their own gain."

Taken aback at the vehement speech, Eddie looked down at his tin and chuckled nervously. "Yer'd think with a woman's touch, this stuff would taste better than it does."

"I tell you, Eddie, this isn't how I'd expected to spend the twentieth year of my life." John shook his head, giving a derisive laugh. "I apologize. That sounded self-centered. What do you think you'd be doing now if the war hadn't broken out?"

Eddie pushed his plate aside, lowered his head into the axis-frame of his thin hand and looked pathetic. "I like makin' shoes, that's all well and good, but right now, I could go fer me mum's cookin', and havin' a pint with me da at the Rusty Hen, or playin' a bit o' football with me mates."

"I hear you, Eddie," John said with a grin. "That would be grand. At Northwestern University we played the American game, but I prefer British football. I'm grateful I could play at all, because the school directors had previously banned the sport for five years."

Eddie didn't hear him. His eyes had glazed over, as if he saw the East End along with all of his memories.

John went on, talking to himself more than to Eddie, because he needed to. If he didn't get his thoughts out, he would go crazy, "They said they banned the game due to violence. Ha! Too bad the pompous fools of the world couldn't ban war due to violence."

Eddie sighed. "And then there was Maggie. I always was wantin' to ask her out, but never got up the nerve. Wish I had."

John patted his friend on the shoulder, letting his own thoughts drift to Evelyne.

He had been an eligible bachelor on Chicago's North Shore, and several fine young ladies had been paraded past him by eager mothers. But never had a woman captivated him so completely as had she, and there hadn't been the slightest intention on Evelyne's part. It wasn't only her beauty, but her noble spirit and self-sacrifice that made her so highly attractive to him. Then to learn that she was taken—blast! This vexed him to no end.

Movement among the Algerians caught his eye. One of them had collapsed in evident grief, dropping his head into his hands as he sobbed in silence.

John sat up straight, then surprised even himself by raising his voice and demanding, "What are we here for? Europe's finest young men are being mowed down and it's all over a crazy Serb and a dead Archduke. Everyone's gone mad! We shouldn't even be here!"

That was all he got out before someone grabbed him from behind. Powerful arms went through his, lifting his frame and pinning his arms up and out. Eddie looked on, frozen with stunned horror.

Hot, rancid breath tickled John's ear. "I've heard enough from you, conchie." The soldier jerked John's arms back, shooting pain up his neck. From the voice, John knew it was the man that had accosted him on that first day in front of the barracks. "A man not willin' to fight fer God and Country ain't in no position to complain."

"God has nothing to do with this bloody war!" John bellowed.

"Now ye're accusin' me o' blasphemy, are ye?" the man asked, mocking him. "Come on, boys. Let's teach this bloke a lesson."

John strained to free his arms as men from the Manchester regiment scrambled to their feet, fists clenched. Fortunately, only one could come at him at a time, because the row between tables was so narrow. John kicked out at the first assailant, hitting the man squarely in the sternum and knocking him back into the throng. Before John could kick again, two men came over the top of the benches. The first fist caught John solidly in the jaw, almost ripping his head from his neck. The second landed in his gut, stealing both breath and strength.

Next thing he knew he was dragged to the wider aisle. He tried to muster strength but couldn't get his breath. At the first slackening of the grip on his arms he freed himself and crouched in a fighting position, backing up against another table. He managed to ward off the next attacker, almost deafened by the jeering of the men in the room, but his peripheral vision was darkening. Fearful he might faint and die under the barrage, he forced himself upright, took a deep breath and struck out. He took down a man but stumbled over him, unable to stop his fall. He swore as hands pushed under his arms again. Just as he was being hoisted in that dreaded familiar hold, a captain strode up, red-faced and barking orders. Behind the officer, large eyes anxious, was Evelyne. Embarrassment swept over him as their gazes locked. Another punch caught him in the gut, and he blacked out.

John lingered in the ethereal comfort of near-oblivion, safe within his mind. Yet despite his resistance, dawning alertness drew him to the surface. He lay on his back, eyes closed. His tongue slid over his teeth, checking and rechecking, searching out any sharp edges that hadn't been there before. Various sensations began nagging him, each fighting for dominance: upper back, shoulders, neck, jaw and stomach. When he tried to take in a deep breath, another agony joined the ranks, a dull, almost restrictive one, telling him his chest must be badly bruised. Ah yes, he thought. The fracas.

He didn't regret a word of what had inflamed the testy Manchester bunch, but he cursed himself regardless. When would he learn discretion? He tried to open his eyes, but the glare of the room pressed them closed. The glare and…a silhouette stationed close to his bed. *Please heaven, not Evelyne.* Not with humiliation stuck to his face like scabs.

He forced his eyes open a slit and saw it was indeed Evelyne in her uniform, her lovely eyes searching for his. Her gaze commanded him to open his. He tried to mask his embarrassment, but in that instant she read him, and he knew she understood. He considered feigning a drift back to unconsciousness, but thought better of it. He tried to smile, but his swollen jawline quickly put a stop to that.

"John."

In that syllable she communicated a book of sentiments: honesty, understanding, a little judgment, perhaps? Concern, certainly. And could it be…affection? With complete focus, he studied her face, but she averted her eyes toward the small table next to his infirmary cot. Her chair stood next to the mattress, within reach. He sensed movement, then felt her hand settle on his arm. Her cool, soft fingers calmed his jagged breathing, helping him to think more clearly.

"I, uh…" It hurt to move his mouth. His right hand went to his jaw and carefully explored the damage. His puffy skin felt like an overripe tomato. "I, uh, must look a fright."

She nodded, eyes still locked with his.

"I'd fancy some water."

"I have some right here. Can I help you sit up?"

"Uh, no, no." His stomach felt like jelly. He tried to push with his hands against the mattress to raise himself, but could barely clench his teeth to fight the pain. Once up, he needed to catch his breath.

After a moment she said, "Now, as you try to sip, don't be alarmed if some drips down your chin. You'll find your lips are clumsy yet."

He frowned, feeling vaguely pleased that at least he could frown without pain. He couldn't help but remember all the times Edwina had ministered to him like this.

"I'll hold it," she said. "Keep your hands on the bed to steady yourself."

She placed the tin cup against his bottom lip and tilted it. He tried desperately to sip without mishap, but water came around and over his lame lips, dribbled down his chin and onto his lap. He almost cursed. She could easily read his frustration in his face, but he was relieved she didn't change her facial expression or say a word. What he could swallow refreshed his throat.

He took a shaky breath. "I feel like a baby."

"That's rather appropriate."

Ah, there was judgment there after all.

"Sorry." Her expression pinched with remorse. "That was unattractive. I know you were only trying to be true to your ideals." She smiled for reassurance. "Ideals that I agree with, by the way."

After setting the cup down, she took his hand in both of hers. This time it was his turn to look away, away from this married woman.

Chapter Six

After two days of convalescence John returned to his duties, though still stiff and sore. He was relieved his workmates for the day were Liz and Eddie. Underlying every activity and conversation, every wounded soldier lifted and carried, John felt burdened with a heavy, almost sick feeling in his gut. He was also relieved that every minute he was at the Front was another minute he could postpone his next encounter with Evelyne.

Eddie had been quiet, as if nursing some pain of his own. After they had loaded those they could from the C.C.S., he pulled John aside. They stood by the broken stump of an old oak. Sky, earth and tree were all muted in lifeless grays.

Eddie stared at the ground. "I can't tell yer 'ow sorry I am." Shame flushed up Eddie's cheeks. "Shoulda been with yer the other day. I, uh, I just couldn't make myself jump into that mob." He looked up, seeking reassurance.

John felt immediate sympathy for him, but couldn't find the words he wanted.

"Forgive me?" Eddie asked, his voice slightly panicked.

"Of course." John reached out and gripped Eddie's thin shoulder. "Of course."

The next afternoon, before an ambulance run, John found Evelyne standing in the stable yard, her arms wrapped around herself despite the sun's warmth. The wall around her was up again, keeping him at a distance. John talked of his morning, feeling stupid because of the awkward stiffness in his voice. She employed polite smiles and graceful acknowledgements while they waited for the driver. Before long his mind went blank, useless when he most wanted conversation to cover those uncomfortable pauses. Eddie arrived, and he didn't seem to know what to say either.

The driver arrived and John helped Evelyne into the back of the van. Eddie, trying to lighten the air, raised the hem of an imaginary skirt and lifted his wrist, as if he should be assisted next. John chuckled and cuffed him on the back of his head, then got in behind him, sliding next to Evelyne on the bench.

They jostled against each other for what seemed like a long time, but they probably weren't more than two miles out of the village when he spoke. "Where is your husband?"

She didn't answer right away. It was too dark to see clearly, but her expression seemed unsure for a moment. He wondered briefly if it was regret he saw, then cursed himself for his own arrogance. If he saw anything at all, it was most likely concern for her husband.

"He's Russian. We met while my father was in diplomatic service under George Buchanan in St. Petersburg. I had lived there since I was sixteen. When the war broke out I happened to be in Paris with a dear friend, an older Russian princess. The conditions of war separated me from my husband. He's now an officer in the Czar's army."

The ambulance jutted back and forth, causing Evelyne to land in John's arms. Every muscle wanted to hold on to her, but he reluctantly helped her sit up again.

"Miraculously, he survived the slaughter at Tannenberg." She glanced at him, wanting to explain. "That's in East Prussia. You probably haven't heard about the loss because the British press hasn't said much about it. I suppose they want to keep a German victory quiet for the sake of morale, but it angers me that it's been swept under the carpet. So many Russian soldiers died. Almost a hundred thousand were taken prisoner."

She sighed and he feared she would stop speaking. He loved hearing her voice, her intelligence. Fortunately, she had more to say. "Before that, we had thought his brigade would go to France and then come here, which is why I volunteered for Belgium. But his last letter said he was to remain at the Eastern Front. Hard to imagine, but they say it's almost more chaotic there than it is here. Some Russian troops are traveling from Vladivostok to Marseilles to help in this theatre, if you can believe it. It seems crazy. But the end result is Pavel can't make it west."

Somehow it was worse now that she had said his Christian name. John made a conscious effort to loosen his facial muscles after he realized his lips were pressed together, his jaw clenched. He was having trouble adjusting his feelings and viewing Evelyne as a mere colleague.

He cleared his throat. "I can't imagine what it must be like for you."

She gave a slight shrug. "We just have to roll up our sleeves and get through this mess." She met his gaze, looking serious. "The world is changing so fast it makes my head spin. But I can't let myself worry. I'm simply not the type to sit by the fire and fret and do needlepoint." She paused, as if unsure of her phrasing, or perhaps of his opinion. "Perhaps my father's diplomatic travels helped me see a larger picture."

It was no good. He lost himself in the depths of her eyes, envisioning their lives intertwining, rising above the chaos, feeling her warmth, yes, but also being freed somehow by her spirit.

She turned away.

The van came to a sudden stop and John put out a hand to steady her. She thanked him, but a coolness—propriety—returned, along with reality.

Eddie spoke then, his kind intentions evident. "Well, let's see what we 'ave to face this time."

MacLeod, the surgeon, marched directly into the tent. The three others gathered in front of the ambulance and gazed into the distance.

"Every day stuck in those stinkin' trenches, those poor sods," Eddie said under his breath.

John grappled for something to say to Evelyne, hating the awkwardness of the moment.

"What's that?" Eddie cried, pointing toward the Front.

A greenish, gray cloud slithered toward them, rolling eel-like over the lines. John heard Evelyne's sharp intake of breath.

"Lord in heaven," she whispered. "It's, it's—"

"Blimey, it's gas." Eddie took a step forward. "Those bloody Germans!"

Retching and strangled cries spewed from the distant trenches. Soldiers climbed out of them like ants from their hill, a few at first, then more, running to escape, stumbling, falling, writhing. Then the guns began barking, relentless rhythmic staccatos from the German line.

John was struck dumb with horror, transfixed as the poisonous cloud undulated over the bodies and drifted toward them. Men came out from the clearing station, then stopped and stared in disbelief.

Along the line, where the cloud was thickest, the Allied defense abruptly disappeared. Moments later, dark figures danced in the smoky mass.

Someone shouted, "The Germans have broken through!"

John's mouth went dry. There were only a handful of soldiers here at the rear who could hold them off.

Another voice, shrill with panic, screamed, "What's happening out there?"

"Stupid Germans advanced into their own poison."

"They have gas masks," Eddie yelled back.

"But some of them are falling." Macleod pointed to the stick figures, some of whom flailed in the dark. He stared at them, evidently thinking hard, then ran to the tent.

Gunfire and chaos continued around the trenches. The land between John and the Front was cluttered with falling, and fallen. soldiers trying to retreat. Helpless, retching, wounded boys.

"Come on, Eddie," he said. "Let's get out there." Eddie stood and stared, rooted. John turned, impatient. "We've got to bring back those we can."

"They're still shootin'," Eddie said, stalling. "We should wait for an order."

"Hold on, you two," MacLeod yelled, running back from the C.C.S. He flung damp cloths at them. "Cover your nose and mouth, both of you."

Eddie looked doubtful.

"They're soaked in…em…ammonia," MacLeod explained, his features creased with concern. "It might help." He looked at Eddie. "Now here's your order: Keep those on and go."

John secured his makeshift mask, trying not to gag. If he could avoid becoming one of the victims of what was going on before his eyes, he would breathe through anything MacLeod told him to. He tied it behind his head then set off in the direction of screams and panic. Eddie ran alongside, grappling awkwardly with the stretcher under his arm.

Most of the gunfire sounded distant, the trenches still far off. John couldn't tell if the Allies had regained control of the line. His throat burned and he coughed violently, bending over almost double until the suffocating sensation cleared, then he moved on. He passed those who looked as if they could make it back on their own, then knelt beside a young man on the ground, sobbing with pain. His arms thrashed wildly and blood soaked his torso.

"I think he's hallucinating," he said to Eddie. He leaned closer to the suffering man. "Come on now, mate. We're here to help you." A weak punch glanced off John's jaw and he shook it off. "Yep, he must think he's got a German coming at him. Probably can't hear us, either."

The man grew weaker, as did his cries. They eased him onto the stretcher and headed back.

The greenish cloud began to dissipate as a breeze blew in, but John's breathing labored. He felt compelled to yank off his cloth mask but forced himself to leave it in place. He nearly tripped into a crater, but righted himself quickly enough. He moved on, with Eddie keeping up the pace behind him, though they both gagged a number of times. Then John saw Evelyne helping a soldier hobble back toward the tent and almost dropped his young charge. He hoped she had the sense not to advance into the gaseous vapors and gunfire.

Victims of the gas attack darted around outside the tent like rabid animals, flailing arms and legs, screaming in agony. He and Eddie dodged them and entered the hazy realm within the tent. All the commotion sounded farther away than it looked and all the movement seemed to slow into some kind of lugubrious modern dance. They lowered their man onto a cot. John then stood straight and shook his head, clearing away the odd sensations. With the cots all taken, MacLeod began directing everyone else to the far side of the C.C.S.

John stepped outside, tears streaming from his burning eyes. He squinted against the pain, desperate to find Evelyne. He wanted to tell her to stay well back from the danger, and he didn't care if she took him as a presumptuous fool. But she was nowhere to be seen.

"Let's go," Eddie cried.

More ragged soldiers scurried here and there, helping their mates. One yelled out, "They got the lines secured again. We're back in business, men."

"Let the Hun feel the pain!" another cried.

Intense gunfire erupted at the trenches, but John and Eddie continued moving toward the noise. John's mind clouded again while he stepped around several still bodies. He couldn't bring himself to look at those who had succumbed to the poisonous gas. But there were so many of them, their bodies curled or stretched in their final poses. After a few more steps, he stopped and looked. The face of a young, dead soldier by John's feet was contorted, his parted lips dark with a bloody froth. The man had died with his eyes wide open, terrified even in death.

John scanned the mayhem and swallowed hard. He was paralyzed by the horror of the bloodbath and his own outrage overtook him, followed by a sweeping wave of weakness. He sank to the ground while chaos ripped the world apart.

A shell exploded nearby. Another one hit and bits of earth pelted the ground to his right, showering John and snapping him back to attention. Somewhere deep in his mind he heard Eddie's bleating voice, rising and falling against the cacophony. He felt himself fading away again, losing himself in the nightmare. A sudden pull at his shoulder startled him awake.

"That soldier. There!" Eddie yelled into his ear as though he thought John had fallen deaf. "Let's go!" John struggled to his feet and began running alongside his companion. He stumbled, rolled, got back up. As he approached a corpse, John slowed and stopped again, startled to realize he was about to step over his first German. The lifeless body belonged to a handsome young lad with blond hair, whose vacant blue eyes stared to the heavens. Another boy, dead. Sticky dark blood had oozed through his uniform. Someone had probably taken the gas mask from him after he'd fallen.

Eddie yanked John's arm again. Just as they reached the British soldier on the ground, the man quit squirming.

"He's either died or passed out," Eddie cried.

John knelt and touched the side of his neck. "He's got a pulse."

They eased the man onto the stretcher. Lifting the dead weight had become awkward this time, now that John's arms shook and his knees wobbled. He set his gaze on the C.C.S. and forced his exhausted legs forward, trying to narrow his vision so nothing would interfere. The give and take of their movements finally fell into sync. A bullet hissed past John's ear, adding urgency to his steps. Off to his left someone screamed for help, but he had to keep going.

When they got to the tent a medic immediately attended to their unconscious charge, while John paused to catch his breath. Someone offered him a canteen and he lifted his damp mask so he could pour the warm, stale water into his mouth. After several gulps, he discovered it wasn't helping to quell the burning in his throat and lungs. A fit of coughing erupted, which he managed to control, but he felt even weaker afterward. With tears stinging his eyes, he handed the canteen back.

Where was Evelyne?

A rasping voice from near the tent made him turn. Prostrate on the ground lay the Manchester soldier, John's nemesis. A number of other bodies lined up beyond him, all inanimate and gray. The soldier's eyes were wild. John approached and knelt beside the bear of a man. He was suffocating, his lips the color of plums. Between rasps, he whimpered, "I can't die. I'm 'ealthy and strong. Not a bullet in me."

John took his hand and gripped it hard. "Try to relax. It might help your breathing." They locked eyes as mayhem continued around them. The man nodded almost imperceptibly, keeping his streaming eyes on John.

"Armitage!" MacLeod called.

Muttering an apology, John got up, stumbled and came up to the surgeon.

"He won't make it," MacLeod explained, out of the soldier's earshot. "It's going to suffocate him. No way to help. Damn those Germans."

MacLeod turned away, his expression defeated, and wandered back into the tent. John would have argued that the soldier needed to be comforted, at least, but he had no strength to utter the words.

"What a bleeding nightmare." It was Eddie, standing beside him now, his voice dispirited.

"Have you seen Evelyne?"

"Uh, not for some time."

John yanked off his mask, ignoring the pulling of his hair at the back of his head.

"This is like Dante's Inferno." He heard her voice behind him and spun to face her. The soft lines of her face were smudged, and her eyes carried a lost, dazed look in them. Whatever resolve she had garnered during the day left her when she saw his expression. It was as if she had held on until she had someone to hold onto her. She crumbled into John's arms and wept, her slender body heaving and trembling with grief.

"It's too much. It's too much," she cried.

His head throbbed, his eyes, throat and lungs burned. His ears ached from the constant noise, his knees almost gave way from exhaustion, but he held her tight.

Chapter Seven

Liz worked the ambulance for the next two days. She said Evelyne was needed at the infirmary, but her words sounded hollow. Apparently, Evelyne was physically all right, but John worried about her spirit. Experiencing the insidious slaughter would have devastated a general, let alone a lady of fine breeding. Or was it something else? Was he to blame for her sudden disappearance? Had his embrace revealed too much?

He couldn't get her out of his thoughts. Images of her helping evacuate the wounded from between the lines and the Casualty Clearing Station replayed in his memory. There followed the almost tangible memory of her in his arms. She had felt perfect there. As if she belonged. Yet he didn't even know her last name.

"It's Dolgorukov," Liz said that night. Evelyne had stayed behind to rest. The flickering shadows from the candlelight gave Liz the look of a blonde Roma fortuneteller. "Or, you know how they do for ladies: Dolgorukova. Those Ruskies like their snappy syllables. Dol-gor-uuu-ko-vahhh."

"Easy enough fer you to say," Eddie mumbled into his glass.

"I seen his picture," Liz continued, looking more at John than Eddie. "Right handsome bloke, he is. A bit older, but looks as if he has his charms." She pressed her lips together in a sympathetic expression. "She's worried about him. Russians are dropping like flies at the Eastern Front."

John felt weak with disappointment and angry with himself for falling so quickly for this married woman. He had no right. Misery tugged at him, tempting him to recede into himself as he had for most of the day. Then Edwina's voice came to him.

Remember, Master John David, it's important for other people to feel comfortable in your presence. You can't allow your moods to carry over to them. It's not your comfort that matters when you mix with Society. A true gentleman is charming, even when his heart's broken.

He tried to remember what he had done to bring on that lecture so many years before. He had probably said something unkind to Wilhelmina Burton at her birthday party when she had displayed her preference for James McGowan. He could have been no older than fourteen at the time.

He wouldn't have minded having Edwina join him at the Front. She'd probably have the war all sorted out within a week.

He felt like a fool, and he could see his mood was making his friends uncomfortable. At least Jacques and Amelie had gotten in a shipment of whisky today, though it wouldn't last long with all these thirsty lads, these desperately sad young men, including himself. He forced a smile and lifted his glass in toast.

"To friends," he said, saluting Liz and Eddie while silently honoring Edwina back in Illinois. He drank it down and set the glass on the table. Eddie was quick to get them each another.

The next night Evelyne entered *Le Cygne Noir* unaccompanied. John noticed her immediately when she came into the lantern-lit room. He had just finished his dinner of potato soup and bread. He was about to stand and gesture for her to join him at his table, then realized his presumptuousness. He was pleased, however, when she chose to approach him, and immediately stood in response, trying not to look too eager. He set his napkin on his chair and gestured for her to sit opposite him.

"No Liz tonight?" he asked, trying to rein in the boyish grin that he was sure dominated his face.

After having endured all the misery and muck of the Front, her movements were still elegant. She sank onto her chair and shook her head with a shrug. "No." She brought her hand to her collar, a modest gesture, and he noticed her fingers caressed a necklace or pendant beneath her blouse.

Amelie came to take her order. The only meal available was soup and bread, which Evelyne requested, along with tea.

John said, "I haven't seen you since ..." He stopped, regretting what he'd been about to say. Since when? Since the gas attack? Since he had held her in his arms? He cleared his throat. "How are you?"

She looked across the room, her expression unreadable. "Oh, I'm all right." An awkward silence hung between them. "And you? How are you faring?" she asked. The lightness of her voice sounded forced, born of societal discipline. Amelie set a steaming cup of tea before Evelyne. "Oh, thank you, Amelie."

For the first time in his life John wondered if he were an idiot. Evelyne was a married woman, and obviously a lady of principle. Yet sitting across from her both soothed and uplifted him. They talked of their backgrounds. He mentioned Edwina, and she told him about the death of her mother during their first year in Russia. In time, she also discussed that part of her life, her marriage, all six weeks of it, before the war started.

She touched her napkin to her lips. The plates had been cleared.

"Would you like a Cognac?" John offered, hoping she would linger.

"Yes, please."

He got the bottle and glasses from the bar and returned to the table, feeling almost giddy as he served her.

She savored her first sip. "Hmm. That's lovely. Thank you."

He smiled and she leaned back in her chair, looking thoughtful. "When I left London for Russia, it felt like an emancipation of sorts. I found our British social strictures terribly oppressive. Fortunately my father allowed me to read newspapers and attend lectures." He nodded, encouraging her. "On the other hand," she added, "I do look back on that time as remarkably peaceful." She shook her head and gave a wan smile. "We'd taken so much for granted."

"What was it like, living in St. Petersburg? I've seen a few pictures of it. The city must be full of architectural gems."

"Oh, it is." She leaned forward with enthusiasm. "Riding home on a snowy night in a sleigh, gliding alongside icy canals lined with palaces, snug under sable coverlets—it was like a fairyland." Relaxing, she looked off into a shadow. "Well, that's the girl in me talking. It wasn't always so nice. The worst event I witnessed was the assassination of Pytor Stolypin at the opera. Fortunately, I didn't see him actually get shot, but I felt the fear in the place, the horrified energy after we all realized he'd been killed. I really liked him. And there were strikes now and again, which made all of us rather nervous."

She smiled, gracing him with a flash of pale hazel eyes, and sipped at her drink. "I became good friends with an older princess, Princess Irina Ivanova Belovskaya. I believe I've mentioned her before. She still has a palace just off Nevsky Prospekt and she keeps a suite of rooms at the Hotel Ritz in Paris. I was her guest in Paris when the war broke out. She and I agreed on so many things, in particular about music. We loved the beauty of Tchaikovsky, the power of Mussorgsky." She chuckled, but the sound was thin and shaky, uncharacteristic for her usually confident voice. It gave John the impression that she was barely managing to hold her composure together. He wanted to touch her hand, but refrained. "We both found Verdi's La Forza del Destino absurd, everybody wreaking revenge against everyone else."

"But we mostly loved Verdi's music. Especially 'Pace, Pace.' Do you know it?"

"Uh, no, I can't say that I do. My family and I went to the symphony quite regularly. His words felt as inadequate as an umbrella during a hurricane. He grinned. "Please go on."

She shrugged. "Mother found Verdi and Puccini to be too earthy for her refined taste. She used to say the Italians just ran around the stage, screaming. That's why I so enjoyed being with Irina Belovskaya. She's so open-minded. After her husband, Prince Sergei, died, she became even more socially involved. She invited poets and scholars to her soirées. Women in Russia were able to have more intelligent conversations than back home. And that's where I met Pavel, at Irina's."

"Yes, Pavel," was all he said. He groped desperately for his manners. "I can't imagine how you feel," he managed. He felt clumsy, grappling with how to handle the topic, but he wanted to show her he cared. "I've never really been attached to anyone, but I am sure I'd be rather hopeless, knowing my beloved was in danger and far away. Would you prefer not to discuss it?"

"Honestly, I'd prefer to talk about it. That is, if you don't mind."

He nodded and smiled his assent, but unease swirled in his belly. They had been having such a comfortable, intimate discussion and now it felt as if she had invited her husband to join them.

"It helps, somehow," she explained.

Sounds of thunder rolled in the distance. After the relentless gunfire, he'd almost forgotten how pleasant the natural rumbling could be.

She sipped her Cognac. "Pavel was quite the dandy when we met. An excellent horseman. I was rather taken when I saw him in one of his parades. We became better acquainted at a ball the week following the soirée. It's a little funny, actually. The ball was at Prince Glazunov's palace. The place was grand, opulent … and freezing. My neck and shoulders were bare, so I danced all night just to keep warm. Pavel sought me out and after what might have been fifteen waltzes, we became very well acquainted." Her eyes shone at the memory. "He talked of Pushkin with such adoration. How I wished he could read English well enough to enjoy Wordsworth. I am, I modestly admit, better at languages then he. I became fluent in Russian. I like hearing it sung more than Italian. Anyway, I began reading Pushkin and Tolstoy so we could discuss them at length."

Despite talk of Pavel, John enjoyed hearing her voice. It was like drinking a heady wine, and he couldn't get enough. She was so alive, so rich with varied interests. And her beauty was enhanced by her capacity for showing love and kindness.

And she was leaving.

"What?" The room suddenly lost its warm glow. "You're leaving? For how long?"

"I don't know," she said, her expression pensive, as if she just realized she would be missing something. "I got word that Irina is poorly. Her only daughter is in St. Petersburg and can't get to Paris. She needs me."

"You'll come back when she's better?" He had to stop his hand from reaching for hers.

"I don't expect so. Pavel will remain at the Eastern Front. He doesn't want me to go there. He says it's utter chaos. I don't know what I'll do, except help Irina in Paris for the time being."

He swallowed involuntarily. "If I can take leave, and if I happen to be in Paris, may I look you ladies up? I, uh, would like to meet this sage princess."

Her eyes laughed at him, as they had when he'd first met her, but he didn't care.

"That would be nice." She got up to leave and he stood along with her. "I'll be thinking of you and Eddie and Liz every day. Take care of yourself, John Armitage." She took his hand in hers, then said she wished to walk back to her room on her own.

He tried to object, but she shook her head. She placed her hand lightly on his chest and gave a gentle nudge, signaling goodbye. He watched her turn, slide smoothly between the tables, and reach the door. The image of her slipping out into the night stayed in his mind for the rest of the evening, and for days and weeks and months after that.

Chapter Eight

1917 - Paris

John Armitage got off the train at Gare Saint-Lazare, recognizing it more from Monet's painting than he did from the childhood visit to Paris he had made with his parents. As a five-year-old boy, the painting of a train had naturally been his favorite. As with most of the family vacations before he was in his teens, the bulk of John's time was spent in the hotel with Edwina. She read to him and told him stories of her own, then indulged him with the occasional walk around the block.

Now that he was back, he could almost sense Edwina taking his hand. *Paris is a city of dreams, Master John David. You should come here after you're all grown up. Then you'll see what I mean.* He had attributed more than one distinction to his old governess, but imagining her as a prophetess made him smile as he walked through the station.

It would take something significant, however, for him to view the war-weary place as a city of dreams. A pall of dreariness hung over Paris, as bleak as fog. Vapors of steam hissed from the train, clouding and settling around the platform. Metal clanked, porters called out, with background sounds accompanying the din of passengers coming and going. Anxiety drained the color from the waiting faces of shabby-looking Parisians who crowded the platform. Amidst the grays, John saw stubborn flashes of color in the station's terminal: a stylish hat, an outrageous one, a beaver-trimmed coat, a man in a shiny, black top hat. Each semblance of normalcy was comforting.

Out on the curb he was fortunate enough to find a hansom cab and was surprised to see horses still in service, as opposed to in the stables near the Front, or lying dead in No Man's Land. He tossed his suitcase into the cab, noticing that the driver seemed disinclined to assist. When he announced his destination, the Hotel Ritz, he saw surprise in the man's expression. Evidently, he looked no less shabby than the others did. No matter. He was here on leave and he was going to enjoy himself.

An old footman at the Ritz promptly relieved John of his suitcase. After tipping the cabbie, John entered the opulent lobby and was relieved to see at once the spirit of the Old World still intact. A string trio sat inconspicuously in one corner of the lobby, playing what he thought might be Brahms. Fashionably dressed patrons sat amongst potted palms on richly upholstered settees, reading newspapers or talking together in low tones. The only clue to the current state of affairs was the absence of any young men. Just women of various ages and goateed older gentlemen, mingled.

After checking in, he asked the clerk, "Is Madame Dolgorukova still receiving mail here?" He knew she was, but he didn't want either his knowledge or his interest to seem blatant.

"Yes, sir," the clerk replied. "Would you like to leave a message?"

"Yes, thank you." Consciously controlling the excited tremor in his hand, he wrote out a quick salutation along with a request for her to meet him in the lobby that evening. He tipped the clerk and followed the bellman to the lift.

John was painfully aware that he shouldn't be floating on air at this moment. He should at least pretend to be somber, sorry for the grief which Evelyne no doubt was experiencing. But he couldn't help himself. He almost sang as the lift carried him to his room.

Evelyne had gotten word to Liz that both her husband and the princess had died. She'd said she would remain in Paris only long enough to tidy up the old woman's affairs. John had immediately written her and tried to be delicate about the possibility of his coming to Paris. How does one suggest a visit while not presuming upon a woman so recently widowed?

Until now, he had stayed away from Paris, living through the hell of the Front for two long years. He had taken most of his leaves in Calais. Once he'd spent a few weeks in London.

He had received her reply two days ago and had come as swiftly as his legs would carry him.

As the bellman departed, closing the door with a gentle click, John surveyed the room with its fine furniture and richly curtained windows. He didn't have the best view; in fact, half of his view was of an alley. He obviously hadn't impressed the desk clerk, but then he hadn't tried. No doubt the suite of rooms kept by Princess Irina Ivanova Belovskaya had a prime Parisian vista.

He didn't care. And he couldn't get the ridiculous grin off his face. He would wash, have his shirts pressed, and arrange to have money wired in from Chicago. On his way to the bathroom, his feet danced a quick jig.

He literally ran into Evelyne on the stairway. After dressing, he had gone downstairs, then realized he'd left the letter from Liz in his room. He had been jogging back upstairs to retrieve it when he'd collided with her. She had just rounded the corner to descend the steps. His momentum was the greater, allowing him to catch her, saving her from a fall on the hallway carpet. He fell to his knees with her in his arms.

"Oh! Mr. Armitage!"

Though thrilled to have her there in his arms, John was horrified. After all this time, all the dreaming and planning he had done, had he already ruined everything by offending her? Her flushed face showed obvious surprise, but he couldn't help wanting to kiss her. When an unexpected smile spread across her face, relief flowed through him.

They walked downstairs and, after being seated at a linen-covered table in the hotel restaurant, she offered a wry smile. "I'd planned on making an entrance, you know. I didn't take the elevator because I'd worked it all out, coming down the marble steps, pausing dramatically just as you caught sight of me …"

She was the epitome of elegance, sitting still with her small hands in her lap. She was dressed tastefully yet enticingly in a dark, plum-colored coat dress with black velvet lapels and trim. A black and plum velvet hat perched stylishly on her head, displaying an opulent peacock feather front and center. His gaze slid from her bright and happy eyes to some of the most stunning diamonds he had ever seen. Earrings, necklace and brooch. She wore no rings.

She noticed his appraisal and touched an earring self-consciously. "A gift from the princess."

"I regret I didn't get to meet her," he said. "Not just because of her generosity and good taste. She sounds like she was interesting and fun." He stumbled through an obligatory statement of consolation about the death of her husband. She thanked him briefly and the topic turned to Eddie and Liz.

"I'll have to get that letter from Liz for you. I forgot it in my room," he said. "She sends her love and hopes you'll come back but wouldn't blame you one bit if you didn't."

After dessert, the conversation returned to the late princess.

"I'm certain learning of the revolution killed her," Evelyne said. "Well, it would be a shock, wouldn't it? Losing her palace probably meant little. She had enough here to live out her days in comfort. Naturally, she was worried for her daughter, who would be forced to live like a peasant. Marie may now never be able to leave the country. I don't even know whether she received word of her mother's death. Oh, when I think about such people, trapped like that…" Evelyne shook her head and looked off toward one of the dazzling chandeliers, her features creased.

She cleared her throat and continued, "But Irina was such a believer in the human spirit that even concern for Marie paled compared to the trauma of seeing a whole world pass away so violently."

"I hope she didn't suffer too much."

"It was hard to tell. She never seemed to be in physical pain, but her mind began to go. Not madness. Senility, I suppose." She stirred her coffee. "That's why I had to come back. This last time, every now and then, when I looked hard, I could see the Irina I knew. Eyes reveal so much. When I told her the extent of the revolution, I saw her understanding. I wish now I had kept it from her, but with Marie in St. Petersburg I thought I should tell her. Then a day or two later, something in Irina gave way. Her heart? Her will?" Evelyne gave a delicate shrug.

John noticed the waiter for the first time when the bill arrived. As he paid, he caught a look of disdain in the older man's eyes. Was it because John was not in uniform? Was it his awful French? Nonetheless, after settling the bill with a generous tip, John was content to linger over coffee. Evelyne led the conversation to lighter topics, away from the dead princess, away from the war, and for the time being, away from the late Lieutenant Pavel Andreyevich Dolgorukov.

Chapter Nine

The next day they strolled down Rue de Rivoli and into the Jardin des Tuileries. Each statue in the sculpture garden stood heavily protected, caged by wood girders and banked by sandbags; lovely stone ladies shielded from the Hun. Despite this reminder of war and the damp dormancy of the season, the bones of the place were still lovely.

"Someday soon this garden will be beautiful again," Evelyne said, as if reading his mind. He liked it when wistfulness crossed her features. "Not all that long ago our Jardin des Tuileries breathed so much life into the city, with its vibrant flowers, its acrobats and puppet shows."

"I'm not one for formal gardens myself," he admitted. "I like them more intimate and mossy. But there's something comforting in the openness and symmetry here, even as it is."

"Yes. I do love gardens. Of all kinds, really."

A mist pervaded the cool spring morning, settling in with a bone-deep chill. Evelyne wore an ankle-length black coat with a sable collar and a black hat, its modest brim sweeping diagonally up and arching over her right brow. Winking from within the sable were two strands of fine pearls. Her shoulder brushed his as they meandered, a companionable silence overtaking them.

An elderly gentleman, slightly stooped, passed them on the path, his arm linked through that of a similarly aged woman. The couple moved as one, despite their arthritic difficulties. John watched the woman look at her companion, a smile of complete contentment evident.

"Poor Pavel," Evelyne whispered. "He was a nice man."

All morning John had regretted his failure to properly address the death of her husband. If they hadn't collided on the stairs, which had disheveled their composure as much as their clothing, his social training would have compelled him to say something more substantial so he could be done with it. He had grappled with a way to introduce the subject, to deal with the matter with due propriety.

Now he was relieved. He wouldn't have to start the conversation after all. "I apologize for not mentioning my condolences properly yesterday."

"Oh, I never felt what you'd said was in any way remiss." She seemed to consider this, then added, "Perhaps if you hadn't needed to catch me on the stair, our conversation would have more naturally lent itself to protocol." She smiled from under her hat brim. Her candid intuitiveness made her even more desirable.

John swallowed a flutter of excitement. "Nonetheless, please allow me to sincerely convey my condolences. We have both of us seen far too many men die at the Front and cannot pretend that his death was an easy one. I can't imagine how you must feel."

She sighed. "I don't know if he died at the hands of the Germans or his own men. With the revolution, some have turned on their own commanders. No one brought me any of his personal things. Sometimes a widow receives her husband's medals, his sword, something. But it's chaos out there, especially now."

"But you have reason to believe the report is true? How did it come to you?"

"Well, I suppose I never questioned it. I received a telegram from a colonel who is recuperating in Smolensk. Surely if there were any doubt, he wouldn't have sent it."

She looked shyly at John, giving him a smile that hinted at embarrassment. "I'm sad for Pavel," she said, "but for some reason I can't bring myself to mourn or even observe mourning. Some women might lie awake at night and tell themselves their husband will survive all odds, that she hasn't heard a reliable report, that he'll come home someday. Pavel's dead. I can feel it. All I want is for someone to tell me he didn't suffer."

They walked without speaking for a few steps until he forced himself to ask a question which had been burning in his throat. He tried to sound nonchalant. "What do you plan to do now?"

"I haven't decided. I have independent means, so I don't have to run to my father's house. I feel I should be of help to our men, but I haven't been able to drum up the drive to go back to the Front." She stopped and frowned expectantly at him. "Am I terrible?"

"Not at all," he answered immediately. "Most women have stayed at home all along. You gave of yourself for how long at the Front? And before that?"

She shrugged. "At the time I found escape in the work. Surrounded by Hell—pardon my language, but I still say there's no other name for it—I didn't even care about being dirty." Her hand brushed her fur collar. "It's been glorious, wearing nice things again, being back in civilization, however battered Paris is. Oh, how long will this insanity go on?"

A young girl with a grime-smudged face appeared out of nowhere and stopped beside Evelyne, holding out a small hand and asking in French for money to buy bread. Before John could say anything, Evelyne handed the girl some francs. He almost said what he was thinking, that if she continued that way they'd soon have much of Paris lining up for a handout, but when he noticed the satisfaction on Evelyne's face, he was glad he had been slow to speak. Her gaze followed the girl's back as she skipped away and disappeared into the crowd.

"You just gave her enough to buy meals for a week or more," he noted.

Her eyes danced. "What of it?"

"Don't think I'm callous. It's only that, one day in Lambeth, I gave a boy a few shillings and within seconds I found myself mobbed. I couldn't help them all and I barely got back to a main street with clothes on my back." He flushed, not meaning to have drawn attention to himself. "I wouldn't wish to see you mobbed. Just tripping over my practicality, I guess."

"I know you have a good heart, John Armitage.

"If I allow myself to think about the children throughout Europe, how many have become orphaned, it gnaws at my heart," she said as they started walking again. "Who's caring for these damaged children?" She looked suddenly stern. "And don't tell me the church. They're too busy blessing arms, encouraging young men to kill for the 'Fatherland' and becoming as guilty as anyone else. How ironic that we have Catholics killing Catholics and so on. How many families have been devastated? Countless." She stopped walking again and stamped her foot. "If I weren't a lady, I would scream or … or spit." She met his bemused gaze and laughed at herself. "Just listen to me," she said, still grinning. "You must think me far too outspoken."

"I like what I hear. And what I see."

The smile faded from her lips and she looked more deeply into his eyes, searching his face. "Do you, John?"

There was nothing John could do. He was undone by her eyes, her voice, by everything about her. He lifted one hand, touching his fingertips against her cheek. She blinked with surprise. "I'm sorry, Evelyne, but I'm afraid I've fallen in love with you. It happened the moment I first saw you, I believe. Forgive me for being rash. All the chaos around us has broken down barriers, social strictures. I'm sure you must find me impertinent, but I couldn't keep quiet another moment."

As he watched, her face softened, all the worries seeming to drain from her expression. Her eyes twinkled, then lit with joy. "Oh, John. I love you, too."

John swallowed, paralyzed by hope. He stepped back, out of the way as two newsboys ran past, chanting some slogan or rhyme he couldn't make out, and she moved with him, taking his hand in both of hers.

"Maybe world events will steer our course again," she suggested, nodding toward the boys.

A shout from across the street caught their attention. "Look at the crowd gathering around that kiosk," John said. "Something really big must have happened."

She dropped his hand and instead tucked hers inside the crook of his arm. "Come along," she said, the tone of her voice warm and intimate. "Let's go see."

They stepped off the curb and headed across the street, the heels of her boots clicking as she tried to stay abreast of him. The people around the kiosk were animated, announcing the headlines loudly to one another and discussing the ramifications. A few were practically jumping up and down like children.

"U.S. Enters The War!" one of them cried.

The news hit John like a bucket of ice water. That meant he—

Tears streamed down Evelyne's cheeks. Her eyes searched his face, as if to memorize it, as if she expected to lose him already. Might he be conscripted? He had no idea. Desperate days, these.

"I want you, Evie. Will you marry me?"

She paled yet a hunger remained in her gaze. "I'm not the angel you think I am."

"I want you, as you are."

She took his hands, her clasp ardent as she raised them to her lips.

When John awoke the morning after their civil wedding, he opened his eyes and watched a hazy ray of sunlight warm his wife's sleeping figure. Evelyne lay surrounded by a geometric glow, cast over her from a window frame.

The moment evoked in him a memory of sitting in church. The irony of this made him smile. John was not religious, but when, years before, the minister at the Lake Forest Presbyterian Church had quoted something about a joyful bridegroom coming from his nuptial chamber, John had sat straight up in the pew.

Now he sat up in bed, in his own nuptial chamber. The scent of roses filled the room—he had ordered twelve dozen yesterday for the occasion. John floated, feeling happier than he had ever been. And, for this all-too-short window of time, he almost forgot that an ugly war raged on. He inhaled the flowers' scent, warmed his face in the early morning sun, then reached to touch Evelyne's shoulder.

Chapter Ten

1919

Moss-framed flagstones led him along a meandering route within the walled garden at the rear of the Mayfair residence. Despite the hot day, coolness emanated from the stone, more a sense of color than touch: blues and grays sedate under the shade. Dappled sunlight danced along the west end, while the gentle buzzing of a few bees came from the Gipsy Boy roses beyond the reflecting pool. John leaned back in the wicker chair, his finger tracing the smooth rim of his tumbler of whisky and soda, his gaze fixed on the figure in the sun.

It was a sculpture. Evelyne had commissioned it and later placed it on a pedestal in the center of the small pool: a boy sitting crossed-legged on a bench, reading a book, lost in the imaginary world within the pages. She adored the little boy, often pausing to gaze on his childlike expression of innocence. She told John it brought to mind all children in need of care.

He crossed his legs and breathed in. The scent of damp earth and cool stone mingled with the heady aroma of blood-red roses wafting across the pool. Even the whisky, though diluted, offered a gentle bouquet, one with hints of walnut and butter. Part of him settled into a serene joie de vivre but, like the distant rumbling of gunfire he'd known in Belgium, a vague discontent nagged at him.

A horse whinnied from the mews beyond the back wall. Someone in the Blixen home struggled unsuccessfully to master a Chopin polonaise. Out on Bourdon Street, a vehicle backfired—

As if the sun were suddenly blocked by clouds, John's mind went dark. Triggered by the backfiring vehicle, soldiers fell, blasted apart on the gray cratered field before him. Rifles barked and shells exploded, flinging bloodied limbs from erupting earth.

"It's a bit early for whisky, isn't it?" The voice jerked him back, prompting both irritation and relief.

He looked into Evie's smiling, knowing expression. She didn't seem to be criticizing, only observing, which steadied him. He stood to greet her.

"Mind if I join you?" she asked.

They settled into the wicker chairs, side by side. She took his hand while he tried to gather his thoughts. After a few moments of easy silence, Evie waved toward the house. Within a minute, little Elspeth came out and walked toward them, carrying a tea tray. Once the clatter of ceremony was done, tea poured, milk added and stirred, Elspeth retreated back into the kitchen.

"I don't know what I'd do without your Thomas," Evie said. "He keeps your mother's garden looking like paradise."

"It's as much your garden." He let his fingertips caress hers.

After a few moments, she added, "It's nice of your family to let us live here."

He nodded. She didn't require a reply. A butterfly fluttered through a stream of sunlight and lit on a shaded shrub. When John spoke, his voice was a mere whisper. "One could almost imagine sitting here at an earlier time. Before the war. As if life could then possibly have taken a different course. No war. No tragedies."

She offered an understanding smile and allowed the serene sounds of the garden time to do its consoling.

After a bit, she set her cup and saucer purposefully on the tray, as if she wanted to speak of something important. She nodded toward the old oak in the corner. "I imagine you climbed that many times as a boy."

He eyed the tree's familiar boughs. "Hardly ever. I was very young when we left here for America. Only made it to that first branch, then Thomas had to help get me down. I was brought back to this home only once, just prior to our family vacation in Paris. Mother made a few trips here on her own from time to time." He took a slow sip of his whisky. "I climbed plenty of trees at our Lake Forest estate, though. It was just me, Eddie—I mean Edwina, my surrogate parent—and my own devices in those days."

Chopin colored the air again, but this time it was played properly, with smooth running lines and even rhythm. John reckoned the new pianist must be Lady Eleanor Blixen rather than her adolescent daughter.

Gripping the arms of his chair, John turned to his wife. "If we had a son, would you allow him to climb the old oak?"

She laughed, a light throaty sound that was rich and charming, and one which still thrilled him. "Even if we had a daughter, I would."

"You'd allow her to become a tomboy?"

"Of course, within reason."

John thought about this, his mind floating from happy images of his own son or daughter to the agonized faces of so many slaughtered young men on the battlefields of Europe, leaving behind fatherless children around the globe. Melancholy pulled at his heart, the lack of solution began twisting it tight.

Shadows lengthened and birds sang without a care, almost in time with Chopin. John breathed deeply and locked away visions of hell. He reached for Evie's hand, lingering with her in a garden of paradise and, within moments, accepted its pleasure.

Chapter Eleven

Evie announced her pregnancy with such glee that John could barely control his own tears. He broke out the champagne, then they danced around their living room to an imaginary orchestra. Before the week was out, Evie began decorating an adjacent bedroom as a nursery. They spent many evenings in jovial argument over names for their child.

With encouragement from his mother, they had settled in more permanently at the Mayfair house, adding to it by purchasing a few of their own pieces. Cousin Basil, having avoided service of any type during the Great War, had died of the Spanish Flu. The number of fatalities from influenza was alarming. Basil had been away from the Mayfair house at the time of his infection and death, and they'd had to travel to Sussex to attend the funeral.

The footmen and other male servants at John's mother's house had all disappeared during the war. The only servants now were Thomas the gardener, Mary the cook and Elspeth. John suggested Evie get a lady's maid, but she declined, stating that if she could take care of herself at the Front in Flanders, she could do so in London.

Two months later their dreams were dashed when Evie lost the baby. What could John say to console her? She suffered episodes of hysterics, depression, then dismal resignation while he fumbled through the reasoning that early-term mishaps were not uncommon, that many child-producing years lay ahead of them. None of his words made any impact on her. She was so upset she didn't speak at all for two days.

On the third morning John carried a tray into their bedroom, bringing tea and breakfast to Evie. He set it on a small table then slowly pulled back the heavy curtains and turned to her prone figure. He held his breath, waiting, knowing there was little chance he'd say the right thing. The best decision was to wait for her to speak.

The sheets rustled. Then, just as the soldiers had thrown down their guns in the trenches when the sunlight vanquished the clouds and streamed down upon Flanders, Evelyne, the stoic woman that he knew and loved, finally rose from the ashes. She sat up, arranged her pillows and looked at him with a resolute smile.

John was jolted from sleep when the mattress heaved and the entire room shuddered. A thud, then another, rumbled up from the floor beneath the bed.

"Lord in heaven!" Evelyne cried from beside him.

He strained to look around; the room was dark as pitch. But the fierce, howling wind revealed that the disturbance was a storm, and not…not exploding shells. Bright flashes were instantly followed by cracks of thunder as furious as any artillery assault. He reached for his bedside lamp and turned it on. They sat up, quick and clumsy.

"It's just a storm," he said unnecessarily.

She pointed across the room. "I have never known a storm to knock pictures off the wall before."

Footsteps tapped down the attic stairs at an excitable pace and John stood, struggling into his robe and slippers. "Either Elspeth is scared silly or there's some damage to the house," he said, then flung open their bedroom door and walked down the wide hall, past the dim light on the hall table, to the stairs. Elspeth's voice carried up the servant's staircase from the kitchen, despite the continued crashing of the storm.

John passed the main staircase and ran down the hall toward her voice. At the top of the back steps, he called, "Are you all right, Elspeth?"

"Oh, Mister Armitage, I'm all right. But my, oh my! What a mess!"

He rounded the bottom landing into the kitchen, squinting as the brightness from three hanging bulbs glared into his eyes. As his vision adjusted, he surveyed the room and gasped at the sight of gnarled, finger-like branches stretching through one of the windows as if reaching to grasp Elspeth. Leaves, twigs and shards of glass lay scattered at her feet.

"I'm glad you thought to put on your shoes," he said, trying to ease her alarm with practicality.

She stared wide-eyed at him, dressed in her nightcap and robe. "I heard glass shatter as the tree came down."

Wind and rain blew past the menacing branches, ruffling the hem of her robe. Her shoulders slumped with defeat, looking at the damage and all the work she would need to do to make it right. It wasn't only the broken window, but also the shattered containers and their contents; flour, sugar and other pantry supplies, all dumped across the white tiled floor.

John considered Elspeth's expression. They really needed to hire more servants. "We'll all pitch in," he assured her.

"Oh no, sir. You can't," she replied before she could stop herself. In her world, masters didn't help the servants.

"We will."

"John?" Evie called from the top of the back stairs.

The lights flickered and the room went black.

Elspeth yelped with surprise. Then, in a more steady voice, she said, "I know where the candles and matches are." He heard her shuffling and padding about, glass crunching underfoot.

"Be careful, Elspeth." He turned toward the stairs. "Stay there, Evie. I'll be right up."

After some muttering as Elspeth bumped into things, the zip and swish of a match lit up the room. She held out a lit candlestick for him while she got another for herself.

The kitchen wall clock lay face down on the floor. He squatted amidst the pieces of glass and turned it over. "It's just half-past two. We'll leave this for the morning. Not to worry."

In the morning the storm had long since moved on. He hastily washed and dressed, then had to push himself to keep up with Evie as she hurried down the back stairs. He knew her concern was for her garden, even more than the kitchen. Elspeth was already downstairs, sweeping. Beyond the windows and the lattice-like wall of leaves and branches, Thomas could be seen crawling among the debris, inspecting the damage and cursing.

"My boy!" Evie cried. She threw open the back door and nearly dived into the foliage. "My boy! Is my boy all right, Thomas?" Hoisting her skirts, she began scrambling over the large branches.

"Be careful, Evie," John called as he came through the door, though he knew she wasn't listening.

Her voice rose with panic. "Where is he? Where is he?"

Thomas bit his lip and met John's gaze, shaking his head.

She climbed determinedly through another leafy barrier then suddenly stopped. "Oh no! Oh no!" she wailed.

John rushed through as quickly as he could, ignoring the scratches to his cheek and ear. Evie had dropped to her knees next to the main trunk of the oak at the edge of the reflecting pool. The pedestal had been smashed beneath the trunk and the boy's head was not only separated from the body, but broken in two and half submerged in the murky water. John caught up and knelt beside her, wishing he could help as she picked up the pieces of the boy's face, then the rest of his head. She tried in vain to fit them together. Then, cradling the broken pieces to her breast, she wept.

John almost pointed out that it was only a statue, but caught himself in time. He stared at her as she curled desperately into herself, inconsolable. He was puzzled. Her pain seemed much deeper than was reasonable. She seemed to react with more passion lately, with more vehemence than would be considered usual, but John had thought nothing of it. A woman was entitled to emotional upheavals. Even a woman as practical as Evie. He glanced at Thomas, whose expression was also colored by disbelief at her hysterics, then it softened to compassion. John wrapped his arms around Evie's heaving shoulders and held her as she cried.

Chapter Twelve

Then the nightmares began.

The first episode woke John with a start as the mattress shook. He lurched out of bed to turn on the light, fearing another destructive storm. But the room was still. He turned to look at Evie, a sense of alarm coursing through his veins. She appeared to be having convulsions. Her heels, under the sheets, sporadically pummeled the bed. Her head, damp with perspiration, thrashed from side to side.

"No," she moaned. "No. No. I had to … I had to!" The restrained horror in her voice made John shiver. He placed his hands on her shoulders and gave a gentle shake.

"Evie! It's all right. It's me, dear. You're all right."

Her frame relaxed immediately, becoming limp. Her eyes flickered under her closed lids, as if her mind were taking stock of herself and the situation. Pent up air escaped her lips and she struggled to sit up.

"Was I dreaming?" she asked worriedly. "Did I say anything?"

He stroked the side of her face. "Don't worry about it, Evie. You're fine now. Just an uneasy sleep is all."

She flushed, clearly self-conscious. "It must have been more than an uneasy sleep for you to wake me. A nightmare, I suppose. I can't remember what it was about. Don't you hate that? Though perhaps it's a blessing. Just look at me. I'm soaked."

John went to the washstand and came back with a towel, then gently patted her brow and neck.

She seemed to regain her composure under his hands. "It must have been from the pâté and champagne last night." She smiled and got to her feet, heading to her dresser to get a clean nightdress. "Remind me not to mix the two before bed again."

The following evening brought on thoughts of the man Job, for Evie received news of another upset to her world. A call came through, to say her only living blood relative, her father, had died of heart failure.

John was surprised that there wasn't more to Lord Julian Grenville's estate. Not that he cared personally; his own family allowance was ample. Evidently the late Lord Grenville had generously given his only child, Evelyne, her inheritance already, as a wedding gift in Russia. The possessions of her dead husband had been confiscated by the Bolsheviks, but fortunately Evelyne had most of her own funds in French and British banks. She'd had a net worth of at least four hundred thousand pounds when they'd married, and she took care of her own assets.

John had always loved that about her: her independence and self-reliance, and how she could thumb her nose at many of society's unreasonable rules. He loved the frank way she looked at life; she had no pretensions at all. Evie was the most honest person he knew.

1920 - House Party in Sussex

Kirstead Court was George Ballantine's country estate. The same architect who had designed the Dutch House in London's Kew Gardens had built it in the seventeenth century.

"I like your Uncle George," Evie said, unpacking her things for their weekend stay. "I don't imagine he gets to enjoy this home very often since he has to live in London to run the plant. And it must get lonely with his wife and son gone." She shook out an evening gown before hanging it up. "I take it you didn't get on well with Basil."

"Not particularly, though I wouldn't want to go into detail and speak ill of the dead. I was quite fond of Aunt Grace. She was unpretentious, like you.

I love my Uncle George. Although he's my mother's brother, he reminds me of my father, which is no doubt why he so readily took Father's advice, as well as assistance, when he started up the company. Fortunately, the fact that he is not my father means he doesn't believe he has the right to live my life for me. Not that he doesn't have a paternally-inspired agenda for inviting us to this house party. I sensed something in his voice when we arrived. I imagine we'll find out as the weekend unfolds."

He sank onto one of the window seats. Three tall windows offered a view of the rear of the estate. He could see the stables, which were in excellent condition, and the meadows beyond. The view appealed to

John's weary spirit, a welcome break from the dirt and hubbub of London.

"Harold mentioned dinner will be at seven," Evie said, unclasping her necklace.

Shafts of hazy October sunlight formed patterns on the bed and floor. John glanced at his watch then caught the look in Evie's eye, soft with suggestion. He smiled, before crossing his legs to untie his shoe.

The sun sank behind Mount Benson as they dressed for dinner. After John helped fasten her into a sleek, floor-length red gown, she lifted a new red and black cocktail hat from its box and placed it on her head. The hat hugged her crown, coming to a point at her brow, and was adorned with black beaded appliqué. Her face flashed him a question, and he smiled his approval. He would be forever proud to have her on his arm when they made an entrance.

Their appearance however, went unnoticed due to an argument among some of the other guests as they'd gathered for drinks before dinner. One of the gentlemen wore a suit that looked a bit tired and his shoes needed polish. He was gesticulating in earnest to a portly fellow.

In the group stood an attractive platinum blonde holding a distinctive V-shaped glass in her slender fingers. Its contents must be that new sensation, the martini. John had only recently heard about this simple concoction that had taken New York City by storm. The woman's expression focused with interest on the interchange. She had the potential to be fascinating. Some of their fellow guests would be from the theater, Uncle George had said: a married couple who were actors and a man who was a playwright.

"I only meant that she could try to be more circumspect next time," the portly man insisted. "It would be more chilling were she to..."

John's uncle George Ballantine left his other guests and approached John and Evie, hands held out in greeting. "My dears, you both look charming." He spoke in a subdued tone, apparently not wanting to interrupt the "fun" his colorful guests were having. He shook John's hand firmly, then kissed Evie on the cheek and beamed at them in a fatherly fashion. "I'll make introductions after the smoke clears. What would you like to drink?"

"Whisky for me, please," John replied.

"I see there's coffee," Evie said, glancing at a table laid out with a coffee and tea service.

Uncle George nodded to the two servants standing within hearing distance. The footman went to get the decanter while the maid attended to the coffee service.

"Lily was spot on with the character," the tired suit was expounding. From the man's protective stance, John assumed he was Lily's husband, and Lily was the blonde. "She is the Lady Macbeth of the season—of the century!"

Lily stood slightly behind her husband, listening. Her expression vacillated between embarrassment and exhilaration at the attention.

"Eh-hem," George Ballantine said, interrupting. Hands dropped, mouths snapped shut. "I'd like to introduce my nephew John David Armitage and his lovely wife Evelyne Adeliah Armitage."

The course of conversation confirmed that Malcolm and Lily Fischer were the actors. The two played more East End than West and had just performed Macbeth. The portly man, a playwright with a cherubic face and mischievous glint in his eye, was introduced as Sid Newfield.

Seated in a wing chair was Lady Birnam, John's widowed Great Aunt Tilly. Her age gave her the patina of a past era, but her gaze revealed she was still "in the game". Since John had spent many years in America, then had gone to the war, he knew her only distantly, but well enough for a decent measure of fondness.

Bernadette, Uncle George's basset hound, stationed herself next to Lady Birnam, as if she, too, were a lady. Aunt Tilly did not care for dogs in the house. Bernadette seemed to sense this, and as a result relentlessly aimed to please the woman by sitting as close to her as possible. As Lady Birnam held up her champagne glass, saluting Evie, the Grand Dame's elegant foot was busy pushing away the affectionate pooch.

Lastly, the introductions included a young gentleman, stationed before the fireplace, who had been silent thus far. Lord Dunwoody was a country neighbor, in his late twenties, and the sole Dunwoody inhabitant of Parkfields. His impressive property lay on the other side of Mount Benson. John hadn't seen the man since childhood. He noted, however, that the man's engaging smile favored Evie as he approached to greet them.

As conversations resumed, Lady Birnam stood and walked toward a painting by J.M.W. Turner, which Grace had acquired before her death. It was a romantic landscape, richly framed and hanging between two bookcases. John thought he'd heard there were at least three of Turner's works at Kirstead Court.

"I do love this painting, George," she declared, not caring if anyone heard.

Harold, the butler, announced dinner and the party filed into the dining room. Lady Birnam took her place at the head of the table opposite her nephew-in-law, George. She seemed more fascinated by the theater guests than a lady of her position would usually show, and displayed no concern whatsoever regarding sitting at a table with the bohemians. She took in everything, and humor danced in her dove-gray eyes.

John watched her, realizing how little he knew of Aunt Tilly. He felt a slight pang of regret that, because of her advanced age, there would not be many more years which they could share. She sat with her back straight, wearing loops of pearls and white-gold accessories; fine gray, white, and silver silks draped elegantly about her. John knew little of women's fashions, but she certainly dressed in what he deemed as modern.

George had his nephew sit at his right and Lord Dunwoody at his left. Evelyne's shoulder brushed against John's and she smiled at George Ballantine. "Your place is lovely, dear Uncle," she said. A wave of warmth ran through John when he heard Evelyne embrace his favorite uncle as her own. "And such fine modern improvements for a historic country home."

George beamed. "The house has been in my family for years, but after John David's father got me into the world of business I became of more comfortable means and could then add the bathrooms, electricity and the telephone."

Evelyne leaned in. "And how brilliant to have radiators in the bathrooms. You must be the envy of many."

The servants performed their tasks smoothly and were scarcely noticeable. The wine and first course had been served before John had even become aware of their presence.

"One must be practical in our day and age," Lady Birnam concurred. Had she meant the well-placed radiators or that which it took to obtain the financial resources? From under the table near Lady

Birnam's ankles, Bernadette belched. The great lady ignored this indignity and turned to the thespians.

"I do hope that it might be possible sometime this weekend for you to demonstrate your talents. Is there something in your repertoire we might see?"

"Why, thank you, Lady Birnam," Mr. Fischer replied. Looking at their host, he said, "Possibly during one of our afternoons, if it pleases you."

George Ballantine said, "Absolutely. What a waste it would be to have such talent among us and not have the occasion to enjoy it. I think more than ever, after the dark days of the war, we need the arts to remind us we are human."

"The Fischers have much to offer for a soiree, if I may say so," Mr. Newfield, said. "I've enjoyed many such samplings." With a wry smile, he added, "Would you prefer murder, comedy or madness?"

"Murder is always interesting." Lady Birnam replied, returning his wry smile. "I prefer tragedies to comedy myself."

Lord Dunwoody said, "Murder certainly is a colorful bit of stagecraft. But, then again, so are mad scenes. I love how theater imitates life, sometimes with absurdity. My particular preference is when it makes us look into our own souls."

"I remember your father saying that very thing, Lord Dunwoody." George Ballantine nodded and gave his neighbor a significant glance.

Dunwoody appeared to consider this. He dabbed his lips with his napkin and replied, "I believe he did. Of course, many folks do. Quite common." He replaced the napkin to his lap and smiled. "And, as you so eloquently just said, the arts remind us that we are human." John thought he sensed an undercurrent here, but attributed it to Dunwoody's persona.

Evelyne said, "I saw a performance of *Lucia* in St. Petersburg when my father was stationed there. The soprano did a marvelous mad scene. London ladies might have found it too 'human,' but I loved it, and so did the Russians."

"Each character and situation has its challenges and its pleasantries," Lily supplied. "I have found, when an audience senses the element of risk—the risk of credibility, for example—that a greater reward ensues, a more intense satisfaction when it's pulled off well." She delicately cut, then speared, a piece of poached salmon. Her air of satisfaction betrayed that she felt pleased with the pithiness of her own words and sentiment.

John was more impressed, however, that any sense of accent in Lily's speech had been ironed out through much work on elocution. This was, to her credit. He couldn't imagine where she was from.

Each small light bulb in the wall sconces and chandelier was covered with individual black leather shades. The candelabras' glow enlivened crystal glassware and the ladies' jewels. John sipped an excellent Côtes du Rhône and felt himself relaxing. It was going to be an interesting weekend.

Harold, whose duties since the war had evidently diversified, carried in a large platter laden with a roast of beef. A footman whose head was hidden behind a mountain of sliced lamb followed him. George Ballantine was, after all, in the business of animal slaughter for consumption.

Hours later, John sat with his uncle in the library while the rest of the party gathered around Lord Dunwoody, who was telling stories of horse racing and illegal boxing matches.

John leaned in and said, "Bully for Britain," he was being good-naturedly tongue-in-cheek, "in even having a labor party." They'd been discussing the conditions of factory workers in America and Britain, and particularly, that of the family businesses. "But if we don't improve the conditions of workers, there could be a strike at the very least, a revolution at the very worst." He went on to explain why he hadn't been willing to be a part of Armitage Meats back in Chicago, how he and his father had gone round and round on the topic, to no avail.

John added, "Children were even used as workers. Some got hurt, were maimed, even eaten by rats!"

"Yes, yes. However, that bit about being eaten by rats is probably just fiction. But, let me say that I am aware of some lads not yet seventeen who are working for me, and it's a good thing for their families. I know one whose father is a drunk, another who has no father. These lads are the support of the family, making more than their exhausted mums could make."

"I'll grant you that point," John conceded.

"I appreciate your humanitarian spirit, my boy, but I must also answer to my shareholders. They got used to great profits during the war. I could never convince them to cut profits now by increasing costs. There isn't an industrialist out there that is paying more or offering more to workers than Ballantine Foods. I hope you'll reconsider, son. I have no heir. It's only Aunt Tilly, your mother and me left. I aim to leave some things to them, if I precede them in death. But most of my estate and my shares in the company I wish to leave to you. Having you on the board at the company would be a good thing."

John touched his uncle's sleeve. "I'm overwhelmed to hear this, Uncle. I'd never even given your financial affairs a thought—"

"I know that, son. That's one reason why I'm so fond of you, and of your delightful Evelyne. But may I ask, John, what are your political leanings?"

"Ha! None, sir. I take it you'd like me to assure you that I am not a member of the Fabian society or a Bolshevik. Let me put you at ease here. I loathe bureaucracy, be it in government or even in business. I've become much too independent, I'm afraid."

In the ensuing silence, images of street urchins arose, shivering with cold, some scared and rightfully wary. Gazing at the fire, John added, "The plight of children could make me political, though."

"As long as you don't take it all on your shoulders, young man."

John straightened, expelling a self-derisive laugh. "Okay. The board, you say? I will at least give it some thought. I love my father, but I could never work in the same business as he. You, on the other hand," John grinned, reached for his glass of port and said, "Well, perhaps. Yes, perhaps."

"Glad to hear it. Now, uh, forgive my impertinence, John David, but are you two planning a large family?"

"Uncle George, only you could ask me that, and I answer." A smile spread across John's face. "As many as we can manage."

For the next few hours, there were lots of light-hearted stories over port and brandy. A parlor maid kept Evie and Lady Birnam supplied with fresh pots of tea. The elderly lady was playing ruthless hands of German Whist with Mr. Newfield and winning every game. Uncle George and Lord Dunwoody reminisced for some time while sitting near the fire. They talked of the late Lord Dunwoody. George then talked at length about his memories of watching young Dunwoody playing sports with Basil and some of the servant boys.

Evie was accepting a fresh cup of tea when George and Dunwoody fell into a sudden silence, as if the two came up embarrassingly dry in their conversation. Uncle George looked as if he were struggling for something to add, when the Fischers stepped in and began asking Dunwoody about Parkfields.

John was content to remain by Evie, just within earshot of the lively foursome while also observing the merciless Lady Birnam at the game table. He sat back on the settee and leaned a little toward his wife, allowing his eyes to close just long enough to relax the muscles in his face. Evie offered a pleasant though mundane contribution to the group discussion out of courtesy. John breathed in her perfumed hair and yearned to fall asleep next to her in bed.

Toward the end of the evening, John's attention rallied when he heard Lily say something flirtatious to Dunwoody. However, Mr. Fischer was showing more interest in something Uncle George was saying. The actor was possibly taking issue with their host. Fischer's face flushed scarlet, looking more like anger than embarrassment. Maybe it was just inebriation and confusion, or perhaps a bit of bantering poorly taken. However, Lily Fischer calmed things down quickly enough and with more dramatic presence than John imagined she had ever mustered on stage.

After pulling his nightshirt over his head, John looked out the bedroom window at the quiet, moon-bathed grounds. A hint of motion in the shadows drew his attention down and to his right in the yard. A stable boy strode from the main house, returning to his quarters close by the horses. The moonlight turned the lad's blond hair white, as if he were an apparition. But with a quick turn of his head, a look over his shoulder, normalcy resumed. The young man ducked inside and the stable door closed.

Frost spread atop the outbuildings and lawns, glistening in the silence. All was right with the world as John got into bed next to Evie.

Chapter Thirteen

John and Evie were the first ones in the dining room the next morning. Recalling that the party had gone on into the wee hours, John was not surprised. Places were set on the table for all guests, substantiating the premise that no one had yet been down. At the sideboard, he lifted a silver dome and found barely-cooked rashers sloppily heaped on the platter. Under another was a tureen of watery porridge. He then felt the teapot; it was tepid, almost cold. Something was very wrong.

Evie's lips pressed in a tight line. "I hear crying in the kitchen." She pushed through the baize door and her heels tapped along the kitchen linoleum with determination. "What's going on here?" Her tone was not so much that of anger as it was authoritative. She would naturally be protective of Uncle George's reputation. Wailing and hysterics exploded in response.

Registering a foreign object stationed outside, just beyond the dining room windows, John turned and considered an unfamiliar black motorcar parked in the mews. He then entered the kitchen and saw most of the servants seated at the kitchen table, cheeks tear-stained, hands wringing. Harold sat limply in a chair backed against a wall, looking pale, possibly even in shock.

"Someone's killed the master!" Meg, the kitchen helper, cried. "Murdered in 'is own bed, he were."

Evie gasped, then stepped forward and took hold of Meg's arm. "It can't be. What happened?"

A hot wave of panic flashed up John's neck. "No!" he cried. Without thinking, John was upon Harold, grabbing the butler's lapels and jerking him up, as if ridding the suit, the man, of any possible lies. "What's going on?" Instead of indignation, the butler's face remained grief stricken.

John's peripheral vision darkened while distraught voices receded, echoing as if from a tunnel.

"Eh-hem," a stranger's voice came from the doorway, reining John back to attention. "I'm afraid it's true."

John turned to face the newcomer.

A young constable stood on shifting feet, a pad of paper and a pencil in hand. "We've called in an inspector and the police surgeon. Lord knows how long it'll take them to arrive."

"Surgeon? You mean my uncle's hurt but alive?" John asked in desperate hope.

"No, sir. 'e's quite gorn. 'is throat slit as 'e lay in 'is bed."

Cook and Meg wailed again. Even Evie looked about to faint; she sank on the chair next to Meg, looking wide-eyed with horror.

A nervous tic erupted under the constable's right eye as he realized his gaffe. He looked to be in his late twenties, a thin man with a large Adam's apple. This quiet, rural area would surely have seen few murders. He visibly struggled with whether he should be authoritative—as if he had intended to shock them all into confession—or apologetic. Then sadness clouded his features.

"Oi beg yur pardon," he apologized, then straightened up and added, "But tha's wha' we have to deal with here. Before the inspector arrives, oi have to keep all o' yurs here on the property, and Burnie—I mean, Constable Burns—is guardin' the master's room."

"I want to see my uncle."

"Yur can't now, sir. His room's off limits." The constable continued to shift from one foot to the other.

Cook, after clearing her throat and straightening her apron, nodded to the constable and said, "Ya must need a cuppa." Then to the group, she added, "We all of us need our strength. Come on, Meg. We'll get breakfast going. Sorry for the mess out on the sideboard." She nodded to John and Evie. "We was all besides ourselves when 'arold came down and told us wha' he found." She pulled out a chair at the servants' table and nodded to the constable. "Willie." Then she rolled her eyes, mocking herself and said, "I mean, *Constable*, take a seat here. We'll get yoo some tea and toast. 'arold, you can take up something to Burnie, and me and Meg will get things fixed right at the sideboard."

Cook shook her head at John. "Now, Mister Armitage. I knows you 'ad a terrible shock, but you mus' 'ave something in you. Please, go to table and we'll take care of yoo."

Evie was up, holding out her hand to him. Cold sweat prickled beneath his clothes, his thoughts suddenly muddled and clumsy, his neck stiff. But he took her hand and allowed her to lead him back into the dining room.

Sitting at the table, stiff and white faced, was Lady Birnam, apparently already informed of the tragedy.

It took about two hours for the inspector and surgeon to arrive. The Fischers and Newfield had cloistered themselves in their rooms. Lord Dunwoody came down late and took himself into the kitchen for tea and something to eat.

Lady Birnam then went and sat in the library in anticipation of the inspector's necessary questions.

For the time being, Evie made John lie down in their room. It was the first time he had ever wept in front of her. He couldn't stop, even when she cradled his head at her bosom.

It was mid-afternoon before Inspector Roberts asked to see John Armitage in the library. It had previously been made clear that John and Evelyne were to be questioned separately. Harold, who had relayed the request, still looked worse for wear, ashen-faced, slightly stooped and unfocused, as if his mind kept rehashing events. He could be reviewing the obvious—the horrific discovery of his master. But the very calmness that was cloaking the man made John wonder if he were not analyzing small facts and details that might have come his way over the past several hours. Or, was the butler shaken by his own interview with the inspector?

As John followed Harold down the hall, a nervous-looking Lily Fischer opened her bedroom door, stepped out, then promptly went back in, shutting the door with a soft click. Lady Birnam's personal maid was coming up the servants' stairs with a tray set for tea. She turned and headed for her mistress' room at the end of the hall, which was the farthest door from Uncle George's suite of rooms. John thought the maid's name was Dorothy, or Dorothea. In any case, before stopping to knock on her Lady's door, she turned and looked at him sternly. Or was he imagining her disapproval? He reached the main staircase, his hand damp as he took hold of the banister.

Once at the bottom, Harold bowed his head fractionally and parted company, leaving him to his fate.

John stopped at the library's pocket door. "Shall I pull the door to?"

The middle-aged man bending over notes arranged on the game table was sitting so far on the edge of his seat that John thought he might drop right to the floor. He slowly looked up in response and replied "Mr. Armitage?" His plain-featured face looked at John for what seemed like little more than confirmation. There was no courtesy in his expression and no keen-eyed, inspector-esque measuring of him either. At least not yet.

John nodded.

"Yes, then, if you would please, sir." The inspector swung his arm as if it were necessary to indicate to John which direction to close the door.

John pulled and slid it to and then approached the table.

The man finally stood but did not hold out his hand. "Inspector Roberts," he said by way of introduction. "Please sit there." He gestured vaguely to one of the three other chairs while gathering up some papers, as if to keep them from John's sight.

John sat on the chair opposite the man, which seemed the natural choice. "May I ask whether you've learned who killed my uncle, Inspector?"

"You may not…sir. No, it is I who'll ask the questions. But my having to ask you questions should answer *your* question, I should think." His smile was more of a quick grimace.

Roberts continued, "Please, Mr. Armitage, tell me what you can about the events of last evening before you retired to your room."

Having no idea who had been driven to murder, John vacillated between general observation and ridiculously minute details.

The inspector expounded, as if John were dim, "Everything and anything that you recall: what might now seem a bit odd, who was where when." He sat back, notebook and pencil poised.

John recounted the evening as best he could. Who sat where for drinks and the silly argument of the theater folks, who sat where for dinner and what conversations he could remember, the doings in the library afterward—all of which seemed absolutely normal. Lastly, he tried to recall the order in which everyone left for their beds. The image of Lily Fischer making her way up the stairs with her husband's assistance made him smile. Incongruent to her dramatic intervention just beforehand, she, at the end, played the role of the delicate wife.

Light patterings of rain marked time on the windows. Inspector Roberts was leafing through pages of notes noisily. John looked about the room for the first time. The fire was getting low. A tray of half-eaten lunch was still on the marble-topped tea table. Outside, he could see raindrops rippling puddles on the terrace tiles.

The grayness of the day lay heavily on John, and he became conscious of his own breathing.

Roberts looked up from his notes. "I have a note here that a member of the party, as well as one of the servants, overheard George Ballantine tell you of your financial prospects; that for all practical purposes, you are his sole heir."

Heat flashed up John's chest and back, and his pulse began beating like savage drummers in his head. He tried to ignore the inspector's incriminating tone and reply casually. "That's true, and, frankly, not especially surprising. His only son died last year, of the flu. Aunt Grace died before that. So, it's just Lady Birnam who, obviously, is well-along, and myself. And my mother, of course, in America. My father is what some might call an Industrial Baron, so leaving money to her would almost seem, well, at best, unnecessary."

Roberts eyed him for several moments. His expression read quite clearly that *money is a powerful motive for murder.*

The Inspector finally said, "I don't suppose there's anyone but your wife who can verify that you remained in your room after retiring?"

John must have looked incredulous.

Roberts' gaze intensified. "You didn't get up and, uh, visit with anyone else?"

John wanted to laugh but felt too much pain to release it. "My wife and I are perfectly happy, and, are ... very close. No need for nocturnal visits, sir." He tried to conceal a growing anger. His voice sounded strained as he said, "And I loved my uncle, Inspector, and would never have wished him any harm."

After another cold, relentless stare, Roberts said, "That will be all for now, sir. You can go—anywhere you please, I suppose, but within the Ballantine grounds. No one is allowed to leave the premises until I say so. Is that understood?"

"Yes, sir." John swallowed involuntarily, got up and left the room.

That evening, Cook was in a tizzy over the constables conducting business in her kitchen. All the servants were lined up, along with the guests, to be fingerprinted. John knew little of the arts of the practice, but he was doubtful that any dusting for prints—as they had called it—could be so readable. The constables had spent hours in his uncle's room for this purpose. He hoped it would lead to a quick arrest, but they would likely only find prints of the servants who had reason to have been there prior to the murder.

He was grateful that neither he nor Evie had been in the room.

The police surgeon had left hours ago, but John was not privy to what he might have accomplished. Other than time of death, what else could the doctor discover? Roberts would certainly not share any findings with him.

While dressing for dinner, John and Evie discussed their interviews.

"I don't suppose inspectors need to be especially courteous," Evie said while clasping on sapphire earrings. "They have a difficult job to do; you'll have to grant the man that."

"You are the most generous person I've ever known," he replied with a teasing lilt. "So Roberts didn't make you nervous?"

"Not at all. You shouldn't let his reference to your inheritance bother you. That's a natural matter to take into consideration."

John wished he could feel more certain that suspicion would cease to shroud him; it felt as impossible to overlook as would one's own public nakedness.

Chapter Fourteen

Dinner was later than usual, what with Cook's further protestations and the necessary tidying up of the counters. But she had fed the inspector before he left for the inn. And the constables had partaken of some apple pie before going to their homes.

Expectedly, a pall pervaded the dining room, though John's fellow guests, and fellow suspects, gave a good show of carrying on. This obdurate penchant for their stiff upper lip demeanor was something for which John had to credit the Brits.

"I washed and washed till my fingers were numb," Lily complained, addressing Lady Birnam about the fingerprinting, or was this a subliminal confession about blood on her hands? The actress then wiggled her 'numb' fingers dismissively at the footman, indicating that she would forgo the soup. She looked particularly smart, dressed in a silk gown of midnight blue, cut in the modern style and a jacket in the same color, which was designed to mostly cover her shoulders in a fashion similar to a stole. After examining her hands again, she picked up her wine glass and drank its contents in one go.

John's gaze swept across each face as he sipped his claret. He accepted the soup with a nod.

Harold and the footman looked more disturbed and somber over the dreadful event than the Fischers or Newfield, but of course the servants had been fond of their master, hadn't they? On the other hand, somber expressions were hard to read. John imagined guilt, or preoccupation with a scheme's details, could look the same as public grief.

Lady Birnam's years of discipline had her sitting straight, her expression ironed out, eyes hooded. Out of courtesy she replied to the actress, "I've found that a little lemon with the soap and water helps."

"You've been finger-printed before?" Newfield asked with good-natured humor.

Lady Birnam simply met this with a wan smile. Of course, no comment was necessary. John knew she was not easily offended or too critical of the gaffes of a social inferior.

Platters of roasts were now served, this time a wild turkey and a pheasant. Sadness draped over John; this reminded him of his uncle's business affairs with meats. It took an effort not to show emotion, and he could eat no more than one forkful of pheasant. Evie gave him an understanding smile.

From somewhere upstairs came the low, long howl of the grieving Bernadette.

Lord Dunwoody took a large portion of each roast. "I can't see why they refuse to let me return to my place. Surely, it must have been a servant or an intruder." He was oblivious of his own bad taste in discussing this at table, as well as of the silent disapproval that followed. "It's not as if I live abroad. They wouldn't even let me take one of the horses out for a ride earlier. Blast." He chewed his turkey with vehemence, then washed it down with his wine.

John found Dunwoody irritating, but the man's complaints conjured up a memory of the stable boy coming from the main house in the moonlight. A completely normal thing. The fair-haired lad had likely enjoyed a late dinner in Cook's kitchen. But something about the way the young man had moved about nagged at him now. He had looked over his shoulder before entering the stable.

By dessert, Dunwoody came to his social senses and apologized. His comments and charms, however, were mostly directed to the wives, neither of whom encouraged him.

Lady Birnam took control. "Lord Dunwoody, I have a fond memory of you as a boy. A cricket game in the meadow one fine summer day. You and a servant from Parkfields, one about your age, joined Basil, George's stable boys, and even Harold, I do recall." She shot the butler a pleasing smile while he and the footman stood next to the sideboard. The slightest grin crept across the man's face as he remained at attention.

She added, "Grace and some lady friends and I sat nearby in the shade, taking tea. It was awkward for you chaps, having such small teams, I'm sure. But you all played so brilliantly, and when your team lost, Lord Dunwoody, you were such a good sport." She looked off with the memory. "Those were such good times."

"Why, thank you, Lady Birnam, for having taken note of us at all, let alone recalling our childhood games. Yes, I remember the occasion well myself. But I was merely good at masking my feelings, I'm afraid. I confess now that I was dashed angry with Basil. But then again, I often was. It all seems so silly now."

The conversation followed the course of fond memories, a welcome relief from the matter at hand.

The rest of the evening had the guests coming to and from the library sporadically. No games of German Whist, no singing around the piano, not that John could imagine Lady Birnam belting out *Keep the Home Fires Burning*. Without Uncle George, there was little adhesiveness to the diverse group. John expected undercurrents of suspicion to be swarming about but saw little evidence of it, as though everyone wished to accept that the killer was either a servant or an intruder, as Lord Dunwoody had suggested.

The next morning, just after getting dressed for breakfast, John answered a knock on the bedroom door. The footman handed him a sealed envelope and nearly whispered his, "For you, sir." This was followed by a token bow and discreet descent down the servant's stairs.

"What is it?" Evie asked.

John tore it open and read it. "It's from Lady Birnam. She requests our presence in her rooms before breakfast. I wonder what this is about?"

Lady Birnam opened her door before John could raise his fist to knock. She hurried them inside. Her morning ensemble cloaked her in shades of dark lavender, but her eyes were fraught with anxiety, her skin papery.

"Someone is trying to poison me," she announced in a low voice.

John heard Evie's intake of breath.

He could only fumble out a question. "How do you know?"

"It isn't you, is it, John? Dear God, it can't be you." Her wide, troubled eyes darted back and forth, measuring his reaction. "No, I see it isn't." She sank on one of the boudoir chairs and gestured for them to sit, as well. She stared at the floor for seconds, apparently collecting her thoughts. He'd never before seen her so candidly alarmed.

"I always have a glass of water at my bedside each night. Thank Heaven I didn't sip it. After getting freshened and dressed this morning I thought I might have some water, but as I held the glass to my lips, I thought I smelled a slight odor. I don't know if my mind was playing tricks on me, but it smelled ever so slightly of almonds. I took it right to the sink in my bathroom but before pouring it out, I took the tiniest sip—and it was bitter. I spit and rinsed my mouth and poured the lot down the drain. And then I realized that I should have saved it for the inspector to have analyzed, but it was too late."

Evie reached out and touched her sleeve. "Is there any reason to suspect your maid?"

"Absolutely not. I'm sure of it. Dorothea is completely loyal. We get on well, and her references were impeccable." Looking more herself, she said in a dry tone, "She's been with me for four years; if she'd wanted to do me in, she could have, long before today."

John wanted to ask how sure she was of the taste and aroma, but thought it might sound demeaning, as if he suspected dementia.

She saw this in his expression. "I know you're thinking I am imagining this." She shook her head. "I even rinsed the glass, I don't know why. I've never lost my composure before—I should have thought to keep the water for analysis, to test it on the dog, if nothing else. But I'm sure my water was tainted with something. I suppose one could cook up all kinds of dreadful concoctions between the laundry, the potting room and the pantry." She searched each of their expressions. "I'm not losing my mind—of course," she added under her breath, "those who do never feel as if they are." She stomped her foot. "Oh, curses and damnation."

John got up and went to the dressing table. "Is this the glass?"

"Yes."

He lifted it to his nose and tried to catch any scent. He turned it, angled it. Maybe there was a slight scent, but could he be imagining it, too? "I suppose we could see if Scotland Yard could get anything from this in their laboratory. We'll report this to the inspector."

"Oh, do we have to?" Lady Birnam pleaded. "I mean, what will we learn? I mean, really. And now your prints would be on the glass, and that wouldn't do. Please let me decide whether to bring it up or not. I just had to speak with you two—at first to assure myself, and then to confide. I feel better, thank you."

She stood and squared her shoulders. "Now, let us go down to breakfast with our little secret between us. We won't allow anyone to think that we are in the least shaken."

The transformation of her features was like observing an actress slip into character. She took Evie's arm in hers and tilted her head for John to get the door. "Shall we go?"

Walking down the hall, she said under her breath, "I do think I'll ask Harold for a key to my room, so I can lock it while I'm out as well as in. Yes, we shall show our true mettle and get this all sorted out...Let's just hope we don't have a mad butler on the prowl." She led the way with determination, Evie trying to keep up, John in their wake.

If anyone had really poisoned Lady Birnam's drinking water, no one in the dining room seemed at all surprised or disappointed when she entered for breakfast with John and Evie. Lord Dunwoody barely rose out of his seat for the ladies, so intent was he in his conversation with Lily Fischer. Both Mr. Fischer and Mr. Newfield—who were competing in taking helpings of kippers at the sideboard—smiled upon Lady Birnam and the Armitages as if they were welcoming long-lost cousins. And Harold stood to attention, looking better—like his old, calm self.

Conversations and appetites were as natural as could be. John wondered momentarily whether they might be too natural, but honestly, each member of the party and staff carried on without offering one shred of doubt as to their character.

He could finally eat. The meats and kippers and the toast with marmalade were so delicious, John almost forgot that the crisis was yet recent. But the last swallow fought its way down.

He expected the constables, Willie and Burnie, or the good inspector himself, to show themselves on the property shortly with more questionings, more dustings, with repeated searches in all the rooms and whatever else there was to do.

There were funeral arrangements to be made, and eventually, legal and fiscal matters to be settled. If John was not mistaken, the family solicitor was in Bloomsbury, and likely he, Evie and Lady Birnam would—once they were allowed to leave the property—travel back to the city for the settlement of the estate. He could envision the three of them sitting opposite an aged attorney's desk. If the inspector only knew how little the three of them cared about money.

Harold poured John more coffee. The aroma lifted his spirits. He was about to take another sip when an odd expression on Lady Birnam's face caught his attention.

She said, "I know this sounds rather unorthodox, Harold, but could I please have some *almond* liqueur for my coffee? I have the oddest fancy for it just now." She smiled brilliantly, her eyes bright as her gaze swept across the different faces before her in quick analysis. The fool woman was going to get herself killed, broadcasting hint and suspicion before one and all. If anyone here had used one of those poisons that smell of almonds last night, they might have to act quickly to silence her.

He did admire her daring, though. Then, a cold feeling crept into him, as if a shadow had blocked the warmth of the sun. Could she be acting out a role on his account? If she were a mad murderer, playing the victim might deflect any suspicion from herself. But why not inform the inspector? She had not wanted him to know; she had tossed the evidence down the drain. Besides, what motive could she possibly have for killing George Ballantine? John's stomach knotted when one of her previous comments rose in his mind. Uncle George had been talking about taking entrepreneurial measures to shore up his fortune when she replied *One has to be practical in this day and age*. "Practical," as in augmenting her own fortune with an ill-begotten inheritance? Lady Birnam was such an odd duck, John wondered if she might kill simply to inherit Grace's collection of Turner landscapes? If John were to view her as a murderess; one willing to take drastic measures—this would be too chilling an idea to accept. For the moment, he tried to shake it off. He soon began to feel ridiculous for even thinking of it.

The only reaction to Lady Birnam's present charade that John noticed was a slight hesitation on Harold's part. The man had probably waited upon her his entire life in service and had most likely never heard the woman mention *almond anything* before. But he bowed to her wish and left in pursuit.

John sipped his coffee while feeling Evie's alert presence next to him.

It was taking the butler a bit more time than John expected. Instead of heading for the liquor cabinet in the library, Harold could be heard clinking in the kitchen or butler's pantry.

He reappeared finally with a cylindrical glass filled with a tawny liqueur. Lady Birnam nearly beamed at him as he placed it next to her coffee. Surely, she couldn't expect Harold to poison her in front of an audience. What was she thinking? She let the liqueur sit, however, and brought up the subject of Oscar Wilde.

Sid Newfield was, not surprisingly, the first to jump on this, which livened up the table. The conversation hummed.

Moments later, a slight movement caught John's eye. At first, he thought his mother's aunt was adjusting the hem of her dress. Then he realized with a jolt that she was testing out the amaretto on Bernadette. She caught John's gaze and straightened up while her lips did a quick bemused shuffle side to side. The now empty glass sat before her.

A heated discussion about the play *An Ideal Husband* was whirling around the table while the grand lady sat still, no one noticing the mischievous glint in her eyes. Lily pulled a locket from her décolletage. With the male guests' attention on the actress, Lady Birnam winked at John. Bernadette belched from under the table.

Chapter Fifteen

The sun came out on Tuesday for the first time that week. Small cloud shadows dappled the meadow and crept along toward the woods and Mount Benson. All of the guests were allowed to leave the estate to attend the funeral service at the village church. Lady Birnam had made the arrangements via George's new telephone.

Alighting from George's Rolls-Royce Silver Ghost aided by a footman, Lady Birnam stood and waited for John and Evie to take their places beside her. A black cloche with a simple black satin ribbon crowned her head.

"I was being undoubtedly silly yesterday, asking for amaretto," she said under her breath. "I mean, Harold would hardly poison me in front of everyone. Of course, he could have claimed that someone must have put poison in the liqueur bottle itself. That, too, is beyond imagination, unless someone here is mad. I wasn't thinking clearly, I admit, but I suppose in the back of my mind, I wanted to see whether the amaretto had been laced with poison."

John wanted to say something on Bernadette's behalf, but just shook his head. Was his great aunt the one going mad?

The October breeze felt fresh and blessedly warmed by the sun. The rest of the house guests were now arriving in the Fischer's motorcar. A few of the local people stood in the churchyard like gravestones.

Lady Birnam quickly added, "I'm normally quite collected, you know I am, John. But this mess has me singularly befuddled. I now recall the main motive for my charade: I wanted to try to read others' reactions, and I got absolutely nothing for my trouble." She gave an elegant shrug beneath her sable-trimmed black coat.

"At least Bernadette enjoyed it and had a nice nap that morning," he replied.

Evie took his arm and they followed his great aunt up the gravel path, into the church and along the aisle to the front pew.

The vicar's singsong voice vexed John, for the man seemed to be the last to know how insincere he sounded. But the service was surprisingly short. Lady Birnam must have insisted on as much.

In short order, they were standing in the cemetery for the interment. John noticed the inspector, dressed in a black suit and coat, standing next to a tree back near the gate. Willie and Bernie were among the mourners, as were most of George's servants. John didn't know any of the local people, having only been a guest at his uncle's home for week-long parties with his family. He noticed the stable boy but only after the lad removed his hat and revealed his fair hair in the sunlight. The young man was standing in close proximity to Lady Birnam's lady's maid, Dorothea. Cook and Meg had stayed home to prepare food. And Harold had stayed back to take care of his duties, as well.

John found the funeral luncheon back at the house more tedious than comforting. Many came to pay their respects. Most came out of curiosity. And always in the shadows were the constables and the inspector, and the mournful Bernadette.

People were still lingering in the house, primarily in the dining room where Cook, Meg and Harold kept the sideboard looking proud. Evie, who fortunately had brought along a black dinner dress ensemble, was standing at the end of the dining room, looking lovely, if a little flushed. John admired her style, preferring today's ropes of onyx beads over the exquisite Russian jewelry she seldom wore. She was talking with Lily and the vicar's wife. Feeling his duty had been amply served, John slipped from the main house and ambled toward the stables.

The quiet of the day outside felt soothing after all of the hubbub and protocol in the big house. A gray and white cat limped along the yard before ducking into some tall grass at the edge of the lawn. It looked as if it had lost a fight or two, yet when John saw it again emerge and continue its hunt, he felt a kind of comfort, a reminder to keep going despite difficulties.

The nearest door to the stables was ajar and he let himself in, immediately enjoying the bracing aroma of hay, warm horses and wood. The young man who managed most of the work in the stables was there, suit coat off, pitchfork in hand, apportioning some hay into one of the stalls. It was more like he was fussing over a beloved animal than doing actual work.

The animal in this particular stall was a handsome mare. John didn't know horse breeds, but he thought it might be an Arabian. Its rust-colored body ran to black at each of is extremities.

"Excuse me," John said to the stable boy. He didn't introduce himself, for the young man must have known who he was. The blond-haired lad politely acknowledged him with a nod before setting the pitchfork in a corner. He looked to be about twenty, lean and—from the look of his hands and shoulders—very strong, able to deal with any fiery colt that needed breaking. He was possibly only five or six years John's junior but he seemed younger—no doubt because of the likelihood that the man had never seen the horrific terrors of the Great War.

"I was wondering if we might have a chat," John continued, looking around for a place to sit.

"Yes, sir. Me name's Adam Beardsmore, sir. Over there will suit, won't it?" He pointed to some hay bales next to a tethered golden-hued colt. He led the way. John sat but Adam remained standing next to the colt. The young man's gaze filled with either anticipation or wonderment as to why this gentleman wanted to speak with him.

John began by complimenting him on the fine state of the stables and the horses, asked a few polite questions about the animals and thanked him for paying his respects at the funeral. Finally, he asked, "You've been here for some time, Adam. Do you have any idea who would've wanted to kill my uncle?"

Adam's brow knitted in what might be grief but his blue eyes held John's gaze while something kept him from answering.

"Did you get on with my uncle?" John asked, recalling the night of George's death and the sight of Adam moving stealthily from the main house in the moonlight. As John said this, he was aware of the pitchfork, not far from Adam's reach.

"Oh, yes, sir." The young man relaxed fractionally. "I got on wiff 'im. Not wiff 'is son, I'll say, but I did wiff the master."

"Was Basil difficult?"

Adam snorted like the Arabian mare. "One time, Master Basil came in 'ere and placed his hand on me like this." The stable boy put his hand on the colt's rump. "'e never did it again, I'll tell yer tha'. Woulda 'orse whipped him, if I coulda, but I did enough, as 'e never touched me like tha' again."

"Well, I never got on with Basil, either," John said, trying to gain Adam's trust for his next question. He added, dryly, "Anyway, Basil's dead."

Adam allowed a chuckle to escape, not out any of moral judgment, clearly from surprise at John's candid irreverence. Then, remembering the tone of the day, he resumed seriousness.

"On the night my uncle was killed, Adam, I happened to see you leaving the main house and nervously looking over your shoulder. I need to ask you what you had been doing that night." John felt his throat constrict and sensed his muscles tense in preparation for his reaction.

Adam stared back, perhaps with disbelief at the question, perhaps in fear of being found out or perhaps in anger at the insinuation.

In a quick puff, Adam expelled held-in anxiety, then shook his head. "Yer gotta believe me, sir. I only went to sort things out with—" He stopped himself, his lips became a thin line and he stood straighter. Then he made a decision. "Yer see, me and Meg sees each other every day, and I like 'er, and," he flushed in embarrassment, "and I've showed 'er 'ow much I like 'er—quite a lo', but I really prefers Dorothea, and I don't get ter see 'er but when the lady comes to visit." He shook his head at himself. "Mister Armitage, I jess got me some women trouble is all. Tha's all it is. I loved me master." Tears welled up in his eyes; one tear streamed down, then another. "He was a good man." He choked back a sob. "The p'lice been askin' all around. I don't 'ave any idear who'd want'a hurt 'im, I don't!" He sank on a bale and stared back at John without any shame in crying, as if he hoped John could come up with the answer.

John reached out and put his hand on his shoulder. No words were necessary. He got up to leave.

"Unless," Adam said, peering into some distant shadow just beyond John. "Unless, well, I 'ave no proof, yer see." John waited him out. "An' yer not suppose to rat on the gentry, like, bu' I've had me doubts about Lord Dunwoody, sir."

The last guest to leave the funeral luncheon later that day was Lord Dunwoody in handcuffs, escorted by the police.

John had immediately reported to Roberts what he had learned from the stable boy. The heated interrogation of Dunwoody, held in the butler's sitting room, rang throughout much of the first floor, allowing John to overhear the inspector use a bit of untruth that tricked Dunwoody into confession.

The untruth had to do with a witness coming forward about the murder of the real Lord Dunwoody seven years ago. The imposter in the pantry was Tommy Welch, the son of the previous cook at Parkfields and of the previous Lord Dunwoody, thus an illegitimate son and a very illegitimate heir.

Tommy had been tutored along with the master's son, Edgar, in the nursery. Lady Dunwoody had died at Edgar's birth. Her widowed husband found various ways to deal with his loneliness. No one but the living parents knew that the boys were half-brothers; no one acknowledged their similar features. Seven years ago, Tommy accompanied Edgar to London for the settling of affairs upon Lord Dunwoody's mysterious death. En route, Tommy killed the heir and dumped his body in Lake Mullens. He then dressed in Edgar's clothes, secured the inheritance with a splendid impersonation, and from London sent word that the entire staff—including his mum—was let go. He did, however, provide references for them.

Tommy enjoyed life in London for a year. He had sought out his new staff of maids from the city's after-dark street set, thereafter moving the whole lot back to Parkfields, without anyone being the wiser.

On the first night of the Kirstead Court house party, in Ballantine's library, George had begun to ask Dunwoody-the-impostor some questions. The gentle owner of Kirstead Court was merely in a mood to reminisce. Evidently, Tommy felt uneasy enough about such delving into his past that he took desperate measures to keep his secret safe.

John explained this to Evie in their room. He said in conclusion, "So Lord Dunwoody's title and wealth were all extorted."

Evie, sitting sideways on the bed, looked at John, her eyes wide in horror. Her gaze then clouded. She grew pale and fainted, limp on the bedcovers.

John dropped to his knees alongside her. "Evie," he called, taking her hand.

She moaned and moved her head, took a deep breath and opened her eyes.

"Did I faint?" She looked astonished at this. Slowly, she sat up. "Did I say anything?" Her face creased with anxiety.

John sat next to her and held her hand. "No. Are you all right?"

She looked down for a long moment, then met his eyes. "Yes, yes, I'm fine. John, we're finally going to have a baby."

John hooted with joy. As he pulled her to him, a shadow crossed her expression, the coloring of which may well have been unrelated to the seriousness of motherhood.

Chapter Sixteen

Two months later, Evie miscarried again.

As much as John felt like wallowing in misery, he mustered all the strength he could, to console Evie. He soon learned, however, that this had to be done mostly in silence. He took her for long walks, finding it agonizing to keep from talking. Sometimes, they found a little relief in watching sunlight on the river when it looked as if all the crown jewels were floating on top. Observing the occasional lark soaring above chimney tops brought a certain solace. How John wished they could rise above their dark world, to feel exhilaration again. But city noises often advanced without warning, strangulating John's nerves as he felt Evie's body stiffening next to his. And such noises—sounds of gaiety—practically filled London's lanes, coming from its pubs and parks; the onslaught of children's laughter struck at their hearts the most.

Even after a few weeks, Evie still perceived most of his comments as patronizing. However, before a month passed, normal conversation emerged, slowly, like the dawn, and their relationship felt closer than ever.

The estate of George Ballantine settled handsomely on John David Armitage, according to the will. Georgette Armitage, John's mother, had been bequeathed only articles of sentimental value. John arranged to have those shipped to Lake Forest. Lady Birnam received a few stock shares of Ballantine Foods and any artwork she fancied from George's two homes. She unabashedly took the J.M.W. Turner landscapes and a few other paintings, leaving the rest for John. She also adopted Bernadette.

Dearest John David and Evelyne,

I am excited to tell you that I will be taking the Aquitania across the pond for a visit. I am looking very much forward to meeting you, Evelyne—you've been a dear about correspondence, truly. And you, John—how long a time it has been since I've looked into your eyes.

John's mother elaborated on those sentiments, covered mundane news from home, and then she detailed her travel arrangements.

Additionally, I must see my Aunt Tilly. I've no doubt the grand lady soldiers on, but I am not unaware of her age and intend to spend some time with her while we can yet enjoy the things that ladies do in London.

It was the closing that bothered John.

Franklin sends his regrets about this trip. They are expanding their soap line, one that will revolutionize the market as it will be what we call a deodorant. Lord knows this will be a gift to mankind! Please consider a trip back home, you two. Father is anxious to see you and is very sorry about being tied up at the moment. He sends his love.

With all my heart,
Georgette Armitage

John had thought he had grown inured to feeling slighted by his father, but the vexation revisited with a sharpness that took more than a day to repress.

Since the war, he had been feeling idle, which he didn't care for. Perhaps word of his father's business made this concern surface. John was not a man for clubs. On many an afternoon, he paced in his study, wondering what he could do to give meaning to his life.

Evie had been volunteering at the London Jewish Hospital, which surprised him. Not for the nature of the work, recalling her self-sacrifice at the Front; and most certainly the surprise was not from any smatterings of anti-Semitism, for he had liked many of the Jewish people he'd met at Northwestern University and later at the Front. He simply wondered at the choice. With her maternal void, he would at least expect her to be nursing children at the hospital, but she only mentioned adults. After seven years of marriage, he still sometimes felt that his wife was an enigma. Surely, most husbands must feel this way.

The location of her charitable work, which had her crossing town to—of all places—Stepney, concerned him. John usually felt that he was a modern husband, allowing his wife her spirit and privacy. But he put his foot down where her safety was concerned. At first, she had countered that the East End was surely safer than the Western Front, which irked him to hear. He then felt crushed when she insinuated that he was acting like a pompous old man. But she finally acquiesced to his hiring a chauffeur for her commute. Of course, he made sure that the manservant he hired would make a good bodyguard, as well.

Gerard Jones was an ox of a man who had not been trained in the world of service but rather had driven delivery. Before the war, he had handled horse-drawn wagons, sometimes for moving furniture, sometimes for the Lambeth morgue. Later, he became a favorite driver of not a few British officers at the Front. John found him making a delivery at his neighbor's house. While standing in the mews the previous Thursday, he observed the arrival of a piano to the home of Lady Eleanor Blixen. It was the kindly manner the Cockney displayed which caught John's attention. Maneuvering a new upright rosewood piano up a flight of stairs was awkward enough. More so when your partner's stature and strength are inferior. But the larger man offered guidance and encouragement and only cursed once. After the task was completed, John engaged the men in conversation. He took to Gerard readily and hired him on the spot.

Tutoring Gerard on his manners and decorum became a high priority.

"Sorry, sir, but I can't do nuthin' wearin' these blasted gloves."

The attention to Gerard's "nuthin's" and "wearin's" John gratefully delegated to Lady Birnam. He helped the man with his dress and decorum. One morning, when guiding the East Ender on how and when to bow fractionally or fully, the seam at the large man's pants ripped loudly at the behind, and the two men collapsed with laughter on the hallway chairs, carrying on like schoolboys.

There was much to do before the arrival of Georgette Armitage.

As it stood, John's mother would undoubtedly be shocked at how few servants they kept.

A few weeks later, John came up with a solution to his idleness. It was at this time that he learned of Evie's real interest in the hospital. They were taking tea in the conservatory on a gray April afternoon, sitting in front of two potted palms, when he brought up the idea of starting an orphanage.

"I could sell my shares in Ballantine Foods and use a portion of the proceeds for this," he said.

Evie set her cup and saucer on the tea table. Her face lit up and her eyes glistened. "What a wonderful idea. I'm not going to be needed much longer at the hospital. Oh, John, I can't wait. What do we do?"

It was then that John pressed her for more information about her volunteer work.

"Well," she paused as if to collect her thoughts. "I met this kindly old man when I was seeking a jeweler to help me sell a few pieces. You know how I worry about those I met in St Petersburg. Well, uh, when I can, I make donations to an organization that tries to bring them out of harm's way. I didn't want to work with Sotheby's." Her expression and quick pace told him, *Don't ask me why.* "I learned of this Mr. Rubins in Stepney from Elspeth. The area where he has his shop, John, is really quite safe. Don't look at me like that. Anyway, he took sick just before finalizing a negotiation on Irina's tiara, which had been a gift, uh, some time ago. They only have volunteer help at the hospital. So I took care of him, and he plans to be back to his shop next week. Danger doesn't matter, because now we have Gerard," she said dismissively. With vigor, she added, "And more importantly, because now we can move on with a new venture!" She stood and took both his hands in hers. "I love the idea."

John's suggestion earned him a very pleasant afternoon.

Chapter Seventeen

The cacophonous arrival of Georgette Armitage gave the impression that the lady was commandeering festivity and fanfare throughout the entire process. One would not guess that this noble-looking woman's wealth came from slaughtered Mid-Western pigs and underpaid immigrant workers. Trunks and trunks of her trifles paraded past the docks of Southampton, along Victoria Station's platform, and through London's busy streets in hired motorcars to the Mayfair residence.

John met her in Southampton, made all of the transport arrangements and accompanied her each step of the way. She wore a black and tan cloche, adorned with so many coq feathers she could have glided into town. A fur boa was draped over her bosom. John didn't know his fur; he just knew it wasn't cow or pig hide. He'd guess it was mink.

By the dinner hour, most of the hoopla had ended and John's mother had settled into her usual frank though refined self. It shouldn't surprise him, but he hadn't thought of the aging affects time would impose on his parents. He had last seen them in 1915. His mother's hair was now running to white, which was rather striking. But despite the little sags and lines, Georgette effused just as much spirit as he remembered; and she was still lovely. She immediately took a liking to Evie, repeatedly saying how her daughter-in-law was every bit as charming in person as in her letters (Evie had been more dutiful in correspondence than John).

Gerard, the chauffeur, doubled as footman, butler or general dogsbody to assist with affairs during the visit of their special guest. John and Evie had spent hours trying to bring the East Ender up to speed on proper service. However, tonight the large man was so nervous that, as he was setting John's soup before him, the broth sloshed about like a troubled sea. Despite all their efforts, Gerard looked like a pugilist in livery. Tiny beads of perspiration dotted his brow and upper lip as he resumed his position next to the sideboard. John found the man's determination endearing.

Georgette talked of Chicago's up and coming developments. Her circle of friends quite naturally included industrialists and developers.

"There are so many wonderful buildings going up. The Palmolive family—they're soap people, dear—she explained to Evie—are soon to be putting up a marvelous skyscraper north of the city's Loop. I am so excited about the number of art deco structures in the make. Near the river—that's West Loop, John—we're finally getting a decent opera house. The back of it, facing the river, is going to look like a huge throne. Oh, it too is going to be several stories high. And the portico will appropriately be French Renaissance-Revival. I can't wait for it to open." Her eyes widened with delight. "And that Mr. Rosenwald is such an inspiration to us all. Chicago is so modern—such an exciting place to be today." She gave John a significant look that said he should be there; following this, she cast a winning smile his way and sipped her champagne.

After dinner, they sat in the drawing room where the ladies got into a discussion of opera. Lady Birnam, seated by the low-burning fire, tried valiantly to turn the discussion to the talents of J.M.W. Turner. She failed, Puccini prevailed, but through it all Uncle George came to mind. Not that John had had much of his uncle's company during his life, but he wished to heaven that he could be sipping port with him now. He ached for the kindly man's masculine company.

"We were so saddened when we heard of the death of Puccini that we held a dinner in his memory at the Palmer House," Georgette said with a sigh.

They discussed the composer's final work *Turandot*, and how at its premiere, Maestro Toscanini had set down his baton at the place where Puccini had written his final note. "I wish I could have been there for that," Georgette lamented.

Evie liked opera, and John knew he should be taking her to such things more often.

Spring rain pelted the windows, the sound muffled by the velvet curtains.

Perhaps it was the liberal servings of wine and port that left John suddenly and uncharacteristically unguarded. Or that unexplainable compunction, that galvanic compulsion, that a parent's mere presence could engender which loosened his lips. In any case, John surprised himself when he heard his own voice. "We want to open up and run an orphanage."

Georgette Armitage and Lady Birnam froze and sat still as statues. Evie looked at him as if she couldn't believe he would be so candid.

The fire hissed.

His mother's face then lifted with pleasure. "I'm so delighted to hear this, John. I was worried sick when you ran off to the war, then curious that you had appeared to be idle since—I'm not critical of the idle rich, for that is one's heritage. But you, I could not imagine you idle. And with your ideals about workers' rights." She looked to Lady Birnam. "Edwina had filled his mind with such nonsense after reading that trash by Upton Sinclair. I was grateful John hadn't become a socialist, or a communist." She turned back to John, after giving Evie a charming smile. "This sounds right for you, dear. You need a purpose. I hope someday you'll aspire to something grander—here, I just mean beyond the local—for you have it in you. But I applaud the move."

She was not ready to relinquish the floor. "You will find it challenging, even painful, but you both have my complete vote of confidence. You will make a difference in the lives of many."

An involuntary swallow helped John choke back tears; he was taken by surprise—never in his life could he recall a word of praise or a vote of confidence from anyone other than Edwina.

Evie stepped in. "Why, thank you. We've only just made the resolve. But we're anxious to get started."

The moment was all John needed to compose himself. "Yes, I've found a property that I want to show Evie. It's in Islington. From what the estate agent said, it seems most suitable."

"I'm sure there's no shortage of children in need, but where and how are you going to come by them?" Georgette asked, her interest sincere.

Evie replied, "We've discussed approaching existing homes for orphans, but when I was doing some volunteer work at London Jewish Hospital in Stepney, I came to learn of the countless children living on London's streets. I'm sorry to say that I had never really given this matter enough thought previously. I had been so caught up in my own life that I didn't even know there were so many homeless children." She looked at John. "So, I think we'd like to start something from scratch, right, John?"

"Yes. And I suppose if I made rounds to each of the police stations in London and let them know of our intentions—once we're set up—I think that should help get us started."

Lady Birnam's frame was ramrod straight, her hands folded daintily in her lap. "You'll have to teach them absolutely everything, dear." It took a moment for John to realize she was not being dismissive. "You'll have to teach them to blow their noses, let alone how to do so properly."

"And, we could have the servants help us. I was thinking that Cook and Meg could be brought in from Kirstead Court. Maybe even Harold and Gerard could help young boys with games of cricket and such." Evie grinned with delight.

"I don't mean to presume," Lady Birnam began—John expected her to discourage the idea now. "But if I could be of any use..." John blinked twice, analyzed her expression for sarcasm and saw only sincerity. "I mean," Lady Birnam continued, "after you get them all cleaned up, that is." She fanned her face with her elegant hand. "I know, I know, when it comes to children, I know precisely nothing. But I do know etiquette, and they could only benefit from understanding how to comport themselves. We could help them become of some use in society, in the working world, I mean." Her eyes were bright, almost dreamy.

"Well, Lady Birnam, that is wonderful," Evie said, reaching out to touch her.

"I'm afraid I'll have to insist they be clean, as I have just said, but before I go to the grave, I should like to be of some use, I think." She added, "Not *think*, I know I would." She beamed.

The departure of Georgette Armitage seemed more subdued somehow. Before leaving, she had signed over the house to John and Evie. Not with the intention, of course, of the home itself becoming an orphanage. The neighbors would never allow it. More importantly, grand as it was, it was not large enough for what they wanted to do. It was a gesture of her love for them, and her support.

Stepping out of the Silver Ghost, she smiled into Gerard's eyes as he stood to attention, holding open the car door. She said, "My congratulations to you, Gerard. You have learned and performed well. You instill me with hope that the children's venture will succeed. I only wish—" A dignified nod by way of salute was all she could manage.

Slowly, Georgette Armitage turned, took John's arm and walked, head high, with him into Victoria Station.

Later, at the Southampton dock, before walking up the ornate gangplank, Georgette looked earnestly into her son's face. "John, please take this check for your orphanage." She handed him an envelope. "I ask, not demand, but ask, that you name it Armitage House. I want your father to be a part of this. I'm sorry that he couldn't be here, and that—" She blinked back tears. "He is a good man, John. I can't tell you how many times he brings up your name, how often he laments not being part of your childhood. He may never say this to you, I'm afraid, for he is quite proud and old-fashioned, but please make us a part of your venture. I have all the confidence in the world that you will do well with your lives." She leaned in and kissed his damp cheek. "Please do come and see us someday." With that, she turned and walked somberly up to the waiting Aquitania.

Chapter Eighteen

The property for sale in Islington had been a nunnery, standing grandly three stories tall with a Spanish tile roof. Beneath the windows were intricate tile mosaics. Evie commented on the beauty of the building's symmetry while also acknowledging its practicality. The first floor could accommodate four classrooms, two parlors, two dining rooms, with a large kitchen wing in the back. And there were both front and back staircases within the central section.

"We'll have to segment the east wing from the west to separate the boys from the girls. Fortunately, there is a bathroom in each wing already," Evie said.

John led her around to the back of the property.

"Oh, a proper garden," Evie enthused.

John analyzed the walled plot, overgrown with weeds, pleased with her penchant for imagining possibilities.

He pointed to the stretch of lawn at the north of the property. "And there is even room there to accommodate some athletic activities.

They meandered around the area. Evie moved with lightness, her hand on his arm, her eyes beaming with pleasure.

She said. "Lady Birnam is right. We'll have to teach them absolutely everything, I suppose." The idea was daunting. "But it's important, and we'll help them become useful." She stopped and faced him. "Oh, John. Thank you." They kissed for some tender moments on the bricked terrace. A dog barked from a neighboring property and some gentle raindrops fell from the gauzy June sky.

Six months later, there were eighteen children in the Islington Armitage House. Part of the staff came from Kirstead Court: Adam, the stable boy, Cook and Meg. John had sold off the horses, and Adam chose to marry Meg. He was a practical lad; he and Meg could work at the orphanage as a couple, whereas had he married Dorothea, they would both end up looking for work (since Adam wouldn't dare work alongside Meg after marrying another). Harold stayed at the country home with the assistance of a footman, a groundskeeper and Muriel Welch, the mother of the late Tommy Welch. John had felt sorry for her and offered her work, bringing her back from dependence on her sister in Cardiff. Tommy, of course, had been hanged for his crimes. Heaven only knew what the new owner of Parkfields thought of his colorful staff.

The boys ranged in age from five to thirteen years old: Billie, Peter, Jedediah, Tom, Ewan, Ian, Jiggs—whom they were trying to rename as Geoffrey, but he was the rebellious one—Jonah, Peter, Thomas and Joe. The girls ranged in age from two to thirteen and were Sally, Helen, Jane, Miriam, Lillian, Eloise and Louise. Eloise and Louise often mistakenly responded to each other's name, or just replied together when one of them was called.

John and Evie had become attached to Gerard and chose to keep him as butler in their own home. Plus, he occasionally served as chauffeur and headwaiter at dinner parties. But Gerard did enjoy working with the children. So, as he could fit it in, he worked part-time, helping Adam with athletics coaching. John got wind that Gerard was giving boxing instructions to the boys and put a stop to that.

They also hired two maids-of-all work and a teacher by the name of Miss Bodenheimer. Lady Birnam held her classes in elocution and etiquette—mandatory for both boys and girls. Adam and Meg had the dastardly responsibility of keeping the children clean enough for the grand dame. Few children in London had daily baths as did those at Armitage House.

"Now, no need to feel embarrassed, dear," Lady Birnam said with reassurance. "I completely understand. All you've ever heard your entire life is the Cockney way." John's Aunt Tilly smiled warmly from her Chippendale chair in front of the class. Gerard had brought over a few of her things so she could teach in relative comfort. Next to her sat a tea table, which Meg oversaw. At each class hour, she brought in a fresh pot to keep the elderly teacher's throat lubricated. It's a wonder, John thought, that his auntie didn't float out into the hall at day's end.

Young Helen stood off to the side of Lady Birnam, her cheeks still flushed, despite the encouragement. Elocution exercises alternated between individual attention and classroom participation. Lady Birnam was bloody determined to assist each student to master the King's English. And while reading a passage, poor Helen had fallen back to saying *sumfink*.

John was enjoying today's lesson over all. About once per week, he would sit in to observe; Evie did so more frequently. Watching the humanitarian come out from behind his great aunt's previously austere façade brought him pure pleasure. The students loved her. He noticed that already Louise and Eloise were emulating the lady's delicate gestures and proper posture.

The classroom door opened and Adam stepped in quietly, walking toward the back as lightly as he would when hunting. John nodded acknowledgement as the young man slid into a desk seat next to him. The staff often sat in to improve their language skills, as well, Adam being the most earnest.

"Unless you travel to Holland," Lady Birnam said blithely, "you simply won't encounter that many occasions where your mouth needs to enunciate an *ink* at the end of a word. Well, of course, with the exception of *think* or *blink* or, hmm, *ink*, as in ink well."

"Or stink," Jiggs offered.

"Precisely, Jiggs," she replied without missing a beat.

"Why Holland?" Sally asked.

"Well, Holland is burgeoning with *ink*s, don't you know. You're certain to run into a Lord Van TeWinkledink or a Lady Hepperdink." She flicked her wrist, as if Dutch names were like so many varieties of gruel. Some of the girls giggled, catching the snobbish humor.

"It is absolutely crucial that we master the correct pronunciation of the *ing*. Now your ear begs you out of habit to say *somefink*. We will train both our ear and our speaking faculties to become at ease with *something*.

"Now, Louise, let me hear you say *ing* and we will exaggerate a tad and say *inge*."

Helen looked deeply into her teacher's expression, frowning in earnest, and enunciated, "*inge*."

"Marvelous, dear. Now we'll try the entire word a few times." And afterward they went through a few renditions of similar words and relative phrases.

❖

John and Evie managed affairs together, with one exception. When a constable would show up with a homeless juvenile delinquent "for approval," Evie could not be present, since she would take in anyone, and they just didn't have the room. She suffered such heartache after having to turn a child away that John couldn't bear to put her through it.

The sun had gone down, and John was still in his study at Armitage House when rapid staccato knocking at the main door startled him. He marched down the hall and opened it. Constable Grimes stood on the terrazzo stoop under the dome of light from above the door. Next to him, barely waist high, wiggled a lad in disheveled dirty clothing.

"Sorry, sir. I know we often call for an appointment, but I 'appen to know this tyke personal like, and I was passing by and saw your light on. Would ya 'ave a moment to spare the boy?" By the anxious look of the man's brow and the intensity of his gaze, John could see this was important to Grimes.

"All right. Let's go to my study and see what we have here." John led the way, after closing the door.

Once behind the office door, the constable said, "This 'ere's Bertie." Grimes' hand gently held the boy by his shoulder. There was more wiggle than resistance on Bertie's part. John could smell the stale dirtiness of the boy even across his desk.

"Go stand over there, lad," Grimes said, pointing at the far end of the room. The boy obeyed, and Grimes leaned over the desk. "'is mum were a woman o' the streets. A Jewess, expelled from 'er community. Died the other day of disease. The boy's healthy enough. Caught 'im stealing. Didn't wanna take 'im down to the station, seeing as 'e's starvin'. Can't blame 'im. I know'd 'is mum, like. She were nice, and I think 'e would do well at your place. I'm really 'opin' you can take 'im."

"Are you sure he has no family? Perhaps, now that his mother has died, her family will take him in," John said with more reasonableness than he really wanted.

"Oh, I tried that. You shoulda 'eard the awful things they called the lad. No mercy in that household. Even if they would, I'd 'ate to leave 'im there. But, no. They don't consider 'im theirs. There's nowhere else but the workhouse—they can call it the Poor Law Institution—but it's still the workhouse and is still a turrible place for Bertie to be. I'd really like to see 'im in 'ere, I would." The man's eyes pleaded.

John thought that Grimes would as soon take the boy into his own household, but realized that the constable was probably struggling with his own meager income, let alone the discord it would cause if his wife were dead set against it. Other thoughts came to mind, as well, as to why Mrs. Grimes might not want the boy.

Seeing John's hesitation in a positive light, Grimes continued, "Oi 'appen to 'ave the boy's birth certificate right 'ere." He pulled out a wrinkled envelope from one of his pockets and unfolded the paper. "Ya see there, 'e's six years old, 'e is. And I knows the magistrate will let us work this out. I already talked to 'im afore comin' 'ere." And he handed John another piece of paper.

John smiled at the man's compunction. He had no choice, really. He looked at Bertie and was taken with the boy's large brown eyes. Those big dark pools looked back at him, whether assessing him or pleading for mercy, he couldn't tell.

"Fine, constable." He took the papers. "We'll see how it goes." He nodded his head, indicating the interview was over. Grimes could now go home to his own family.

The constable walked up to the boy and gently put his hands on his shoulders. "You be good for these folks, Bertie. I can't tell ya 'ow important it is that you be good." Grimes straightened to go, a tear glistened in his eye. "I can let myself out, sir." He opened the door to the hall to leave. John cleared his throat and raised his hand to stop him.

"Oh, and, uh, thank you, Constable Grimes. Thank you."

Adam, who normally oversaw the boys' bathing, was in his rooms with Meg. John didn't want to disturb them, so he took Bertie upstairs to the boy's wing and sought some clothing. Evie had some clothes stored away in the linen closet, which was a room in itself. It took some time for John to find pants that would be short-legged enough. Bertie looked more like four years old, such a waif of a child. The boy just quietly followed John around. Once in the bathroom, Bertie ran to the toilet and urinated a steady stream that ran for minutes. No wonder the lad had been so wiggly. It took quite a bit of soap and scrubbing to get him properly clean, but Bertie was compliant enough. Afterward, John gently brushed through the boy's snarled hair, and eventually untangled most of it.

"How does that feel?" John asked.

Those huge brown eyes stared back at him. "Well enough, sir." His voice almost a squeak. But at least he spoke well. No trace of Cockney. Nor was there any foreign accent. Of course, it wasn't but three words. Nonetheless, it pleased John. Why? He knew why. It was too early to really be considering this, nonetheless he decided to take Bertie home to meet Evie. He couldn't wait.

John got him into the Silver Ghost and wished it weren't dark out; he would love to see those large eyes get larger at the sight of the fine automobile. The paperwork indicated that the boy was from Stepney, and there wouldn't be many Rolls-Royces motoring about there.

"Is this your first ride in a motorcar, Bertie?" he asked as the car began to purr forward.

"Yes, sir. It's amazing." John was surprised. Again, only a few words, but they indicated intelligence, unlike poor ten-year-old Jedediah, whose speaking had been unintelligible upon entering Armitage House and who clearly lacked imagination. John was sympathetic to the awful conditions many street children endured in their formative years. But how exciting to find a youth like this one. He hated to admit that he was hoping intensely that Bertie might fill the void he and Evie had been feeling. The orphanage, he sensed, was just not providing enough for his wife's maternal needs, although he could not see her admitting this. On many topics, they could talk into the wee hours of the morning. But some things were too personal, or too *something*. He now realized how he and Evie more often circumvented a number of such subjects, preferring to keep them vague, or denying their existence altogether.

You're an impetuous lad, Edwina's voice chided. He cast it off and turned toward Mayfair.

When his damp hands slipped a bit on the wheel, he realized his nerves were trying to get his attention. Was he insane? How could he be so impulsive, bringing this boy to meet Evie when he hadn't gotten more than a handful of words from him? What did he know of the lad's temperament? But having Bertie sitting in the car next to him in some visceral way soothed a pain John hardly ever acknowledged. He and Evie had just celebrated their eighth anniversary. How great it would be to share the world with a son, to help him experience life and develop character. John would be the father he never had.

What John couldn't see of the boy's expression in the dark car was made up for when he observed Bertie's demeanor while being led through the Mayfair house. Before now, John had taken for granted the grandness of the place. The foyer was marble, the staircase magnificent. John checked his watch, and realized for the first time, that he was late for dinner. Quite late. He quickly steered Bertie toward the dining room, the boy's eyes taking in as much opulence as he could digest. For a minute, John thought the child's expression was about to glaze over altogether with all the stimuli. But at that moment, those haunting eyes looked up at him, blinked twice, then brightened, filling John with warmth.

They continued into the dining room and John immediately met Evie's gaze. With pursed lips, perhaps poised for complaint, her impending speech was stifled once she noticed little Bertie hiding behind John's leg. Her face lit up; but for long minutes, she just took in the sight. She understood instantly. Evie stood, dropping her napkin on the floor, walked around the table and knelt in front of the child.

Bertie must have liked what he saw for he took the initiative and with a now beaming smile said, "My name's Bertie."

Evie simply held the boy to her breast while John stood there; his face ached from grinning.

They had Gerard ask Cook to make porridge and pudding. Bertie's dining capabilities were adequate. And he attacked his pudding methodically, savoring every bite.

For long into the night, Evie sat by the fire with Bertie on her lap and the two talked. His mother most certainly had read him stories by Beatrix Potter. He recited most of *The Tale of Peter Rabbit* quite admirably. John had never seen Evie look more radiant.

Part of John wanted to find out more about Bertie's mum—her life, how she had been educated, probably not how she worked and suffered on the streets—and part was afraid he would learn something that might lead to the boy being taken away from them.

Evie insisted that she sleep next to Bertie in one of the guest rooms. She feared he might wake in the night and become frightened. And, indeed, that night, he did call out for his mum and cry. John came up and stood outside the bedroom's door listening to Evie's calm murmurings to the child.

After a few days, Evie asked that Bertie stay at their home permanently but be educated with the children. The three of them fell in step together easily. But before pursuing adoption, John wanted to check a few things out more thoroughly.

On March 8th, 1928 Dorothea called John and Evelyne to report that Lady Birnam had passed away in her sleep.

The funeral for Lady Birnam was actually a memorial service comprised of art and music. Years ago, John's great aunt had taken issue with the minister of her Anglican church and had little to do with formal religion since. A lady of her age and station didn't have to worry about others' opinions.

Her will thus dictated that a memorial be held at The Abbot, an art gallery housed in a Highgate cathedral. An art dealer by the name of Wedford had bought the historic structure for a fine price when the post-war congregation began dwindling and was unable to care for its upkeep. Nicely refurbished, half of the pews had been replaced by walnut panels, displaying a fine collection of paintings. He even had a J.M.W. Turner, the possible cause for Lady Birnam's connection with the place, John thought. After seeing works of art by such ethereal light, a natural effect of towering clerestory windows, it was no wonder the man had made his offer. A number of pews remained toward the high altar, available for lectures and services at not-too-modest a price. His great aunt had established a trust in John's name for the rental of The Abbot, her florist of choice and the musicians. Fortunately, the singer Lady Birnam most favored for the inevitable occasion was available: the French mezzo Germaine Cernay.

The observance might not have had as big a turn out (most of her lady friends had died some time ago) had it not been for the school. All of the children were exceptionally well behaved as they sat together as one family with John, Evie and Bertie. Adam and Meg, Gerard, Cook and Miss Bodenheimer shared the last pew.

Mister Wedford got the pipe organ with the deal. The hired organist and Miss Cernay began with an operatic lament by Purcell, *"Thy Hand, Belinda."*

When I am laid in earth, may my wrongs create no trouble for thy breast.

Evie leaned in and whispered, "Aunt Tilly would not be disappointed with this, John. Such a beautifully somber ambience, lovely flowers. I like the music. You carried out her wishes well."

Germaine Cernay was not above milking a good line for all its worth. *Remember me … remember me!* Were it sung by a stone cold singer, the music and text would be nonetheless haunting. Cernay added a touch of desperation in her phrasing with chilling effect. A shiver went down John's spine. He turned and caught a fluttery flinching of Evie's eyes. Ian and Ewan had large tears trailing down their cheeks. Jiggs and little Bertie looked pained at heart. Eloise and Louise had poised postures, as if being lady-like were more important than ever. All of them sat as still and pale as the statues in the alcoves.

The composition and the performance of this aria filled John's senses with sadness.

"Beautiful, simply beautiful," Evie commented.

John cleared his throat and whispered, "I'm mostly glad Aunt Tilly lived to be part of the school. In such a short time, she touched the lives of the children, inspired them to improve themselves. She wanted purpose, to pass along something …"

"Yes." Evie rescued him.

After a few meditative organ solos, the next vocal piece brightened the atmosphere by means of its major key and theme: "The Meek Shall Inherit the Earth." Light and lilting, the music bounced along, supported by rich chord progressions. *They shall delight themselves in the abundance of peace.*

Evie said, "I haven't heard this before."

"She wrote it herself, a number of years ago." He unfolded the program that was crushed in his hands and pointed to the selection. "It is based on Psalm 37, it says. She was quite good at the piano."

"How I wish I'd known her better."

And they shall dwell therein forever … forever.

The joyous aria continued building, the supportive chords becoming more complex, Cernay's voice sailing atop. Like forces of nature, the duo released the last refrain at full throttle, and the music rose as if determined to lift the Gothic keel-shaped vaulting. Majestic tones of resolution reached the final chord, filling the place with presence, reverberating in John's breast. Then silence hung suspended like the last breath of ecstasy. Ultimately, however, making the weight of finality heavy.

Lady Birnam was gone.

Chapter Nineteen

Several days later, John and Evie were having coffee in their morning room.

"Do you think your Mr. Rubins might know something of the family of Bertie's mum?"

Evie started, her brows arching. "Do you know how many people live in Stepney?"

"It's a close community. We have her name. I'd like to pay him a visit."

"Oh, John. Do you have to? What if you opened a Pandora's Box? I couldn't bear to lose Bertie." She was leaning forward in the wing chair, her fingers clutching the upholstered arms.

"I really think it would be best. I'd like Gerard to drive us there this morning. Bertie will be fine at The Islington House."

With lips pressed firmly, she offered no further argument.

It was a sloppy spring day. Rain spattered down in erratic fits and starts. A lone drop splattered on John's brow as he got out of the Rolls. Evie led the way into a pleasant but modest looking storefront (modest for one selling Russian jewels to private clients).

The man coming from behind the counter to greet them was evidently Mr. Rubins, and he was delighted to see Evie, but of course he would be. He looked to be sixty-something, quite paunchy, and he waddled, wearing slippers that scuffed on the wooden floor. These were leather slippers with exotic pointed toes; they could very well have come from the Steppes. His small eyes were bright, and he gave the impression of unquestionable credibility. John found himself liking the man already.

"Berenice Marczak?" Mr. Rubens' mouth pronounced the name as if he were allowing wine to linger on his tongue. "Berenice." He relished dramatic enunciation. Aunt Tilly would've approved. "Yes. It must be the same. The Marczak's disowned the poor thing. She ran off with a man who'd been tutoring her in writing and journalism. He's a Gentile. I don't believe he married her. Well, I'm quite sure he never did for word came round about the kind of work she was forced to do. They gossip something terrible here. You want to know about this man, too? Yes? I couldn't tell you his whereabouts. Marczaks might know, but I doubt it." He shrugged, softening the lack of any real direction with a cherubic smile. "We haven't seen Berenice since. Sorry to hear that she passed on. Life can be Hell on the streets."

Riding back to The House, Evie said, "John, I don't want you trying to find out who that man was. There's no way of proving whether he was Bertie's father now. And where was he for Bertie? Certainly not providing anything for him or his mother. Please leave it."

"Everything will work out," John said, waiting for her rebuttal and grateful that she, at least for now, acquiesced. But he decided to talk with Constable Grimes. Perhaps he could let John know whether there had been a father in Bertie's life at one time. For all he knew, Grimes could be Bertie's papa, seeing how the policeman was more than a little familiar and concerned.

"Bertie was two by the time I became aware of 'im, and there was no man in the house; or I should say, in the rooms she rented, 'cept for business, like." The flush on Grimes' cheeks betrayed something. It could just be that he was simply embarrassed to discuss the trade. But, being a policeman, he should be well used to talking of it without any moral squeamishness. Grimes quickly added, "I can tell ya that you should 'ave no problem with the adoption. Like I said, I been talkin' to the magistrate meself. When do yer see 'im?" Something in Grimes' eyes told John that the policeman already knew.

"Day after tomorrow, as a matter of fact. Thanks again, Constable. Everything should be just fine. Bertie and Mrs. Armitage are very close. We all are." John grinned ridiculously and bid him Good Day.

The magistrate was indeed familiar with the case and was happy to see Bertie's welfare tidied up so well. The adoption went through, and the boy officially became Albert Jacob Armitage.

Gerard and Elspeth beamed their delight as they waited table that night at the Mayfair residence. The candelabra were lit. Cook made a Yorkshire pudding with the beef roast, and for dessert, a choice of blueberry pie or rice pudding. Bertie had both.

Despite the happy occasion, that night, Evie had another nightmare. Was it from having been at the Front? Something in her life before the war? Or was it to do with something current? At every turn, she dismissed John's concerns. Holding her afterward was all he could do.

John wrote to his parents with their happy news. He promised to send a photograph portrait of the three of them. And he promised to make a trip home with his family *right after we return from Paris. Evelyne has business to take care of there.*

Two weeks later, the headlines in all the papers were about the stock market crash. His father wrote to tell him that the trust fund that had been providing John's allowance was now worth half as much. He took credit for the fund's diversity and explained that many of their friends were now penniless. John's parents would always be secure enough with the business. Much of what John had inherited from Uncle George was intact. And Evelyne had her jewels.

Chapter Twenty

1930 Paris

They decided to leave Bertie in Gerard's care in Mayfair so he could keep up with his schooling at The House. Their trip to Paris was not going to take long.

"John, are you serious about wanting to go to Follies-Bergere tonight?" Evie said, while adjusting her fur jacket and buttoning it at the collar.

The morning breeze was cool enough to make their coffee all the more satisfying. It was their second day in Paris, and his wife had a fancy for sidewalk cafes. He once said that she would even dine al fresco in the snow. The November weather had greeted them comfortably enough.

He had wondered at her sense of urgency when she had asked to cross to France. She had long maintained her concern for those Russian acquaintances trapped behind its borders. However, this mission, apparently on their behalf, came about from something new, from an intensity coursing below the surface of her poise.

The two of them appreciated the strong coffee this morning, for Evie again had had a restless night. Today, they were going to look up a man named Zimsky—a man who ran an organization that tried to reach any aristocrats, those few still alive, with the aim of helping them escape from Russia.

Primarily, Evie hoped to discover whether Belovskaya's daughter was still alive and in a position to be helped.

"John? Did you hear me?"

"Oh, sorry. Well, I would like to see what all the fuss is about with this Josephine Baker and her "Danse Sauvage," wouldn't you?"

"Not particularly," she said dryly. "But if you really want to." She shrugged with an indulgent smile for him.

"I should think it would be nice to broaden our horizons a bit." He returned the smile in a self-mocking fashion. "She's referred to in the paper as 'The Creole Goddess' and they say her musical act should not be missed. Anyway, I hear she has a pet leopard."

"What does that have to do with anything?"

"Nothing and, um, everything. I suppose it indicates how exotic the evening experience might be, but if you think it might be too shocking—"

"Rubbish, and you're just baiting me. We'll go, if you like." She took another sip of coffee and squinted up at the sun. "What time is it?"

"Half-past ten. I guess you'd like to get going?"

They both enjoyed walking Paris, but to get to the Russian district, they first took the subway to Parc des Buttes-Chaumont, and after coming up to the Rue Botzaris, they turned down one of those ancient, winding lanes John loved. Footfalls on the cobbled ways mingled with the sound of fewer folks speaking French and more conversing in Russian and other languages that John did not recognize.

They had dressed modestly for their excursion. Various aromas met them on the narrow Rue des Chirac, which was almost an alley. At the next bend, a powerful and cloying odor assaulted him. John turned and looked right into the blank stare of a pig's head on a platter in an open shop window. Evie had her nose too buried in her notes to take notice.

"It says the place we want—a dealer in old books and manuscripts—is left around the corner from the flower shop."

In the next lane, two buildings down, there was a shop window with the name Zimsky in greenish-gold lettering.

"Well, hel-lo," Evie said to the building in her charming way. She smiled at John and led the way inside.

John entered and took a moment to enjoy the smell of a bookshop, that of hardwood shelves and old leather bindings, a scent accentuated by pungent ink, yet made heavy from human oils—some books having had many lovers.

An older pallid-faced man came from a back room. His eyes were such a light gray that they resembled pearl onions.

"Monsieur Zimsky?" Evie asked.

They then spoke in Russian. In short order, the shop owner ushered them to the back, which was actually the family kitchen and eating area. The three of them sat at the table while the man's wife went to tend to a customer in the shop.

As Evie and Zimsky talked, exchanging notes and other papers, John could do little but look around the room. It was immaculately clean, even smelling slightly of soap. On the walls were some lavishly framed portraits of what John imagined were different Russian families of noble birth. Stationed proudly on a marble-topped buffet sat a samovar, the little flame beneath winking.

Madame Zimsky came back from waiting on the customer and offered them tea. Instead of china teacups, she served the tea in short glasses each held within an ornate silver base. After noting that Evie was apparently "worth it", Madame Zimsky also set out some bread and butter for them. Not the black Russian bread that John expected, but white bread with a golden crust. It was fresh and delicious, and the tea had an essence of black currant that he found refreshing.

Before leaving, John saw Evie open her reticule and extract an emerald ring. Even from the slight distance, he could tell it must be worth a small fortune. Without hesitation, she gave it to Zimsky.

Beaming, she led the way back on to the narrow lane, her step light and girlish.

While passing the flower shop, she answered his question. "That was my donation to the effort. He knows where to sell it for what it's worth. As far as Marie Sergeyovna Belovskaya goes, he says I should come back in three or four days. He has a source that he thinks might know something of her welfare. Then we'll see what might be done." She took his arm and leaned her shoulder to his, slowing to a comfortable stroll, as if they were still newlyweds.

A group of men were doing some construction in the next block, one calling to the other. Evie stopped, as if interested in their project. Letting go of John's arm she took two steps forward and said, "Pavel, it's Pavel!"

It took only a moment for the realization to sink in. The happy spirit of the day dissipated, leaving him weak while his thoughts whirled and buzzed.

Evie ran up to the man standing by a wheelbarrow. John understood that Pavel must be about forty-five, but here he looked a decade older.

The legal husband and wife talked effusively in Russian as John stood at a distance. They embraced, Evie too excited to notice the dirt soiling her clothes. A few more words were exchanged.

As Evie was walking back to John, Pavel Dolgorukov stood planted and nodded at him from across the cobbled lane, a scant acknowledgement that John existed, and, perhaps, the total of his interest in social obligations. But in that instant, the two men took the measure of the other.

From down the alley, someone yelled in French, "Get back to work, Pavel."

Then the Russian nobleman dropped a sledgehammer into the wheelbarrow, turned, and began pushing it down the alley.

"Oh, John." Evie's eyes beamed. Her flushed expression was trying to evoke shared excitement from him. But John's stomach knotted and with effort he forced a smile. She enthused, "How amazing. It's absolutely amazing. We're going to meet later."

John wanted to say how rude it was that the man hadn't come over to meet him but held his tongue. And good thing, as he realized his own social failing. His fists clenched as anger inflamed his heart, his mind scrambling to justify his position: that common decency had held him back. It was only right to allow the reunited couple their privacy, which was quite different from Pavel's social neglect. The man must be adopting the manners of the commoner he had become.

As they were walking toward the underground, Evie read him accurately. She began setting the pace without another word; her heels clicked briskly, echoing off the brick and stone. John glanced toward his wife. They were each communicating their feelings as if they were screaming them aloud. A wall of defensiveness settled over her features, eyes stiffly focused ahead, lips pursed. He had no idea where this was going to lead.

Neither spoke until John shut the door to their hotel room.

Evie whirled around to face him. "Damn you, John. You're behaving like a child."

John's face went slack. Did he, their marriage and his feelings, mean so little to her? He walked around Evie to the window and stared out at the gloomy, dirty city.

"This matter is hugely important," she added. "We're dealing with a man's life, while you're giving in to schoolboy jealousy."

John wanted to say that the same accusation was true of the boorish Pavel, but instead said, "What are you going to do?"

"Oh, John." Every bit of her pulled tight with anger. "What do you think of me? If you can't believe in ..." She rushed into the bathroom and slammed the door. The lock clicked, and John felt as if he'd been punched in the gut.

He stood stationed at the window, looking out, his head pounding, as if Pavel were beating his mind with that sledgehammer. When John leaned forward, letting his forehead touch the glass pane, its coolness offered little solace. He admitted that he did feel like a schoolboy, a boy wondering whether his whole world was about to fall to pieces.

Down below, a few fluttering pigeons landed on the sidewalk across the street, pecking at some crumbs left by an old man, sitting on a bench.

John straightened and walked up to the bathroom door. "I'm going for a walk." He turned to leave, and then added, "Just know that I love you." She remained silent. He pulled their hotel room door shut and walked down the hall. He took the four flights down, not wanting to be confined in the lift with anyone. As he crossed the posh lobby, its animated cacophony grated on his nerves: excited tourists discussing their explorations, an arrogant American general berating his son and wife, the ring for a bellhop. John met the cool air with relief, turned right at random and distanced himself from the lot.

It wasn't more than a couple of blocks before he became satiated with remorse, feeling as though guilt could choke him. As he stepped off the curb, a whirring sound, followed by French cursing, jolted John to the present. He had almost walked into the path of a cyclist. What if it had been a lorry?

Large snowflakes began drifting down as he walked on, a few alighting on the back of his neck, seeping under his collar and trickling down his spine. It wasn't like him to be self-centered, consumed in his own feelings. Throughout his life, only his father had ever provoked his ire so powerfully. Evie was the last person on earth he wanted to carelessly offend or hurt. Wasn't it for this very reason that he had reacted so strongly? Their marriage meant everything to him.

He yearned to hold her and apologize. Turning back, his face was assaulted by the snow as it was now coming down fiercely, the flakes smaller and biting; and he deserved every sting. He had walked much farther than he realized. As he finally came up to the hotel, he smelled of damp wool but more repugnant was the smell of fault.

John opened his hotel room with both trepidation and enthusiasm. But Evie was gone. He rushed across to the note on the desktop. Her tone was considerate, thank goodness. She explained that she had gone to discuss matters with Pavel and Anna and might not be back until late. Not to worry, but to dine without her.

Anna? Was Pavel living with a woman? Or had he too entered into a bigamous marriage? Why hadn't Evie explained this on their way back to the hotel? Had she omitted this on purpose? Had she meant to make him feel jealous over Pavel? Again, his stomach knotted as he wondered about the real question: Did Evie want Pavel back?

His breath quivered as it escaped him. Then he realized the more likely reason for the discord: He had never given Evie a chance to explain anything.

Panic arose and surged through him. He was practically pushing Evie away with his stupidity. Taking deep breaths, he tried to steady himself.

While taking off his wet clothes, he poured himself the Napoleon brandy he had brought along. It wasn't until after downing a second glass that he went into the bathroom and dried himself off.

Dressed in his trousers and silk smoking jacket, he stretched out on the bed, stared at the ceiling and wondered how to avoid going mad while waiting.

A twilight state descended upon him and his mind began delivering arguments, reasonings about why Evie should stay with him. The beginning of each phrase was persuasive but soon sounded ridiculous. Of course she wanted to take Bertie to live with her and her legal husband, Pavel. She, Bertie and Pavel would move to Switzerland, after paying off poor Anna.

His heart beat wildly and a falling sensation jolted him awake.

"I'm sorry, John," Evie said, sitting on the bed, her faced creased with concern in the dim light.

He grappled for his senses as he sat up, his breathing still labored. "I, uh, ugh." He swallowed. "No, I'm sorry. What happened?"

"Everything will work out, dear. Pavel and I needed to discuss how to proceed. Not that I don't trust him, but I couldn't leave our resources and Bertie's inheritance at risk. What if Pavel, or his children, were to later try and prove I was his legal spouse. With the Imperial government dissolved and the chaotic state of things in Russia, the only thing for Pavel and me to do is apply for divorce here." She touched his arm in reassurance. "And I owe him something financially—he lost everything. We decided on a settlement of fifty thousand pounds. Well, he was against accepting anything, but time will come soon enough when he will not be able to work this hard, and his French was always dreadful and still is. With the settlement, he'll be able to set up a business in the Russian district and provide more security for his family."

Here, Evie was a modern woman, deciding financial matters herself, with her own money, of course. He accepted this with a grin, thinking she was the better person. After Evie leaned in and kissed him, it didn't take long for John to feel completely reassured.

"She's alive," Monsieur Zimsky announced proudly in Russian. John had to wait for Evie to translate. She looked oddly concerned but was soon smiling. This time the Zimskys brought out a bottle of vodka and cylindrical crystal glasses for the occasion. Madame then turned and began slicing freshly baked black bread. He was told a tradition was about to be observed.

With bright eyes, a lot of happy nodding and saluting ensued. And despite his scant understanding, John got into the festive spirit, helped by shots of vodka that went down with smoothness and pleasure. The Zimskys were well and truly pleased with the results of their efforts and especially with this underground rescue work that Evie had helped fund. At last, blue-blooded Russians who were eager to escape Stalin's regime had a ghost of a chance.

The Zimskys next fell into performing the celebratory ritual with the vodka. On the table were china plates with slices of black bread and pickle. Monsieur and Madame each held up a glass and bellowed *Vashe Zdorovie!* Then they took a whiff of a bit of black bread and said, *Nu.* This was followed by a deep breath, after which they drank down their vodka. Next they exhaled, sniffed the bread, took a bite of pickle, yelled *Oh Khorosho!* And had another shot. As John tried to imitate this, the Russians became even jollier

On the way back to the hotel, Evie explained that the sentiments of the ritual were jovial, toasting to one's health and then saying how good it all made them feel.

She then described how Marie Sergeyovna had made her way to Poland several months ago. It was now a matter of getting her across the German border, which was still fraught with danger. But, once in Germany, she would be provided with travel papers by a particular contact who had demonstrated a remarkable talent in documents and forgery.

With a free evening ahead of them, John again mentioned getting tickets to see Josephine Baker, but Evie said she had a headache and wished to stay in, her expression now serious.

When John closed the door after them, he realized that more than a headache was about to crest. Evie stood in the middle of the room and began to cry. He came up to her, placing his fingertips on that graceful neck he loved, a touch to console but one that was now feeling heat and pent-up energy. At first she resisted, shrugging off his hand. Was she angry with him? He waited.

"Oh, John, I've been keeping a terrible secret from you, and I'm so ashamed." Her emotions erupted before him, taking him by surprise. Tears flowed, her body trembled.

He carefully took hold of her delicate shoulders and directed her to the edge of the bed. Sitting by her side, holding her gently, he whispered a few soft words of reassurance.

She took a shaky breath and continued, "Irina never gave me any of her jewelry. I stole it. I loved her, but when her mind went, I simply helped myself to her fortune in jewels, art and money. There was no one to take the least notice. We were just guests at the Ritz. No one questioned what was hers or mine when the coroner came or even after they took her body. When I told them her only relative was in St. Petersburg, they just sighed, as if I'd just said Marie was dead too.

"I imagine the men who normally handled such official things were at the Front. Or everyone was just distracted with the war still raging on." She shrugged, and then looked at him, gazing through glistening tears, studying his features for reaction.

"I'm a thief, John. That's all there is to it."

A chill so cold as to numb all feeling spread through his body. His mind buzzed, and then screamed, "God in heaven, what to do?" A sinking sensation was followed by a flash of heat. He loosened his collar. Through the flurry of doubts and pain, a constant beam drew him along. He couldn't say whether minutes or hours had passed, but when the throbbing in his arteries subsided, he stroked her back. And with a steady, soft voice, he said, "We can work through this."

"How on earth could we possibly fix such a thing?" She pulled away. "How can you so calmly accept what I've done. Oh, if only …" She shook her head in self-disgust. "I couldn't bring myself to tell you before. I wanted to so badly, so… badly."

He held her. "Shh, it's okay." She flinched then relaxed a little.

"Just let me think," he said. A recurring drip from the bathroom sink marked time. Funny how such a sound could be there all the time and you finally notice it.

"Without question," he said, "we'll give Marie her mother's jewels when we can. If I'm not mistaken, you practically have a whole trunk load still, right?" She nodded, guilt still in her face. He added, "And, we can explain that we used some of the jewels to fund her escape; she can hardly complain about that. And if she's not satisfied, we can negotiate something."

"You make it sound so simple, but I feel terrible. And I don't see how practical measures fix guilt or pain." She turned to face him better. "But I, uh, I need to explain myself, explain—and don't think I'm trying to minimize anything."

"Wait." He got up and crossed to the credenza. "Let's talk about this over a drink. He opened his bottle of cognac, the sound of releasing suction, a gentle pop, already promising some consolation. He poured for them both and said, "Enjoy the bouquet and take a nice sip." He settled next to her and did the same.

"This takes me back to our first cognac together," she said, "at *The Black Swan.*" She stared at her glass. "I know it's foolish, but I want, I want so incredibly, to go back and undo my mistake. I've heard others say this kind of thing and thought it silly, never realizing how powerful such a yearning could be."

John settled back, leaning on his right elbow, encouraging her to talk.

"You see, at first, I just took one valuable piece of jewelry to help get Pavel into France—this was when I heard of the revolution and knew he was in even more danger. There was a man, someone like Zimsky, who was trying to form a network for this kind of thing. His name was Albrecht Ziemendorf. Some of these people were such mercenaries and opportunists. I knew Irina would be more than willing to help us, but her mind was becoming delirious. Anyway, I had no choice but to trust this man but he was expensive. I ended up giving him one of Irina's ruby rings. She had brought an absolute fortune out of Russia, John. There's even a Faberge egg and a few valuable paintings. When Irina had her mind, she was prudent. We knew of the rumblings of revolution, but most of Russian Society chose to ignore it, like Marie. Marie was being courted by a nobleman and wasn't about to leave St. Petersburg. But that's why Irina had brought along so much to her rooms here. And, well, my crime involves more than one ruby ring, as you know."

He sat up, close to her again.

"I can remember *the moment* clearly," she said. "Irina was babbling in her bed, speaking to the ceiling about card games with grand dukes during her youth. I was just in the next room when something made me open one of the wardrobes and then one of her special cases. I'm sure I was vaguely thinking about another effort to help Pavel. I lifted the top compartment and set it aside and then allowed my hands to hold and stroke exquisite strands of pearls. Next, I opened a drawer and took a very valuable ruby necklace. Holding it to the light, I stared at its beauty for I don't know how long. The realization was like a swollen river, unstoppable in its rushing flow. Paris was in chaos; I knew I could get away with it. And finding Marie, let alone getting her out of Russia seemed unlikely. And if she did get out, how would she be able to prove that her mother hadn't sold some items for the war effort? Despicable thought, I know. Those treacherous reasonings of the heart can be powerful, more than I'd ever thought possible. So," Evie's voice sounded weary, "in Irina's last days, while she was sleeping, little by little I moved her things into my room.

"I can only say, John, that those were desperate times, and that I wish I hadn't done it." She searched his eyes for understanding. "Now, I need you to say something."

"I think, uh, that was a courageous confession."

Evie sobbed in silence, as if holding in—hiding—the ugliness and shame. Then a cry escaped and she grabbed his arm. After some long minutes, she gained control.

He added, "Those *were* desperate times, and any of us could act uncharacteristically if pressed enough by circumstance. You've used Irina's fortune for helping others, and now you want to right the wrong. What more could I expect? I understand. And I love you."

"When you told me about Dunwoody—Tommy, was it? —the covering over of his, hmm, his ill-gotten wealth, I felt absolutely wretched." This brought on another wave of tears. After a short time, she leaned her head to his and spoke softly in his ear. "What I hate most is not confiding in you. John, please forgive me for not telling you this sooner. I just couldn't bear you knowing that I'd done such an awful thing."

"Okay, as to the theft, I understand completely and we'll fix the matter. As regards not confiding me, I forgive you."

"I don't deserve you."

He whispered, "Just let me love you."

Two days later, they walked into Zimsky's shop. Monsieur and Madame were flushed with excitement. Marie Sergeyovna was waiting for them in the kitchen. Evie and John followed the couple to the back living quarters, but when Evie entered the kitchen, she stopped and looked at the woman sitting at the table. The two stared at each other, and the silence between them became electric.

"That's not Princess Marie Sergeyovna Belovskaya," Evie announced.

Everyone looked at Evie as if she were crazy. Of course it was Marie Sergeyovna. That's the impression everyone else was giving. Even John thought Evie might be in denial or delusional over Marie, in view of the guilt she felt. But, of course, he had never seen Marie. No one had but Evie.

The woman stood and spoke. Something serious was being said. Cacophony ignited the room with everyone talking at once. The emotions of the Zimskys ran the gamut: disbelief, anger, understanding, sadness. The imposter remained serious. John watched in silence as Evie reached into her purse and handed out one hundred francs to the woman. She gave some instructions to Zimsky, still in Russian, then turned to John and said, "We can go now."

Evie kept a quick pace as they walked along the brick lane. "Marie Sergeyovna died of typhus. This woman pretended to be her when she thought she could get out of Russia. She had no expectations of any inheritance. She simply wanted freedom and a chance at a better life. We can understand desperation, can't we?" Evie looked straight ahead as she spoke. The tone of her words rang of irony, or maybe of self-mockery.

"I'm glad you gave her something to start her new life," John said, wishing he could help Evie feel better. Dare he try humor? "I guess I'm never going to see Josephine Baker." He hoped to heaven this would help and not make things worse.

Evie stopped in the middle of the Rue des Chirac, looked into his eyes, and broke out laughing. Her pitch rose, tears welled up.

It worked. Pleased, he took her hand and led her toward the subway.

"All right, let's try to get tickets," she conceded, trying to catch her breath.

"I say let's have a special quiet dinner instead. How 'bout at the Ritz, where we had our first decent meal together?"

"You're too good, John. Stop it." She laughed some more.

That evening they dined at the Ritz.

And from then on, nightmares no longer plagued his wife.

Chapter Twenty-One

June 1932

"How long before we get to America?" Bouncing on the balls of his happy feet, shaded by other passengers waiting to board, Bertie's eyes darted about the royal pier of Southampton.

"We get to enjoy the crossing for eight days," John replied, enjoying every minute of his son's enthrallment.

"I like those lions up there." Stationed on the highpoints of the ornate station, where the French might be tempted to put gargoyles, regal lions sat on their haunches sporting valorous shields. "And that's a smart looking clock tower."

"That's a cupola, actually," Evie explained. "And see how the top imitates a crown?"

Bertie's attention shifted to the brass band, which just struck up the strains of "Rule Britannia." Some of the more animated in the queue sang the anthem while others carried on their conversations. Seeing that Bertie's view was blocked by the shifting crowd, John hoisted him up to sit on his shoulders and turned to face the uniformed ensemble. Though nestled at the elbow of the curved pier, three tubas beamed like solar centers, baritones and trumpets like stars. Red tunics, gold braids, John could imagine his son's eyes riveted, hungry to take it all in.

"Oh look, over there," Bertie cried. Stacked, waiting to be loaded onto wagons, crates of bright bananas and, farther down, oranges, adorned the otherwise utilitarian docks. The Great Depression evidently passed over Southampton as had the angel of death just before the exodus from Egypt. Imports from the West Indies, the blood oranges most likely from Spain, shipped in abundantly while hordes of travelers shipped out.

Salty breezes began ruffling the sea of brimmed hats. Evie reached up and readjusted her hat pin with decision, her movements in sync with the next offering from the band.

"I love this song," Evie said as a Gilbert and Sullivan aria rode above the din.

The crowd began to move, boarding commenced, and John's chest endured the pummeling of his son's excited heels.

"Your grandmother sailed on this very ship," Evie said, holding down her hat despite its pin. John's stomach knotted at the reminder of the coming reunion.

Once on board, he felt he should indulge the boy. With Evie holding his arm and Bertie still on his shoulders, they negotiated their way to the railing to share in the obligatory celebration: well-wishers waving, passengers releasing colorful streamers—the air between brimming with goodwill. The ship's horn bellowed, more cheering ensued, and all that could be heard of the band was the beating of its drums.

"Let's find our rooms, shall we?" John suggested. "We'll get settled and then have a tour of the ship."

"Yippee!" cried Bertie.

John put his son down and led the way to the nearest entrance, his gaze seeking out a porter to assist them. They were jostled here and there, some folks excusing themselves, some not. It wasn't more than a few minutes, as they made slow progress along the deck, before John lost track of Bertie.

Evie realized it at that same moment. "Bertie! Bertie," she cried, looking about frantically.

Women waving, fat men standing about, everyone kept getting in their way, blocking their view. John would see a boy darting about, and then realize it wasn't Bertie.

"There he is," Evie cried and pointed.

Bertie was at the deck's railing, trying to climb up to see the activity on the docks again.

John dashed, pushed and scurried. A pompous-looking man became disgruntled and was taking a deep breath to chastise him, but John spied an opening in the crowd and leapt through; after which a large bosomy woman stepped in his way. Brushing past, he heard her gasp, as if she'd thought he pinched her behind. He made his way up to his son. Reaching out, he grabbed Bertie's arm and brought him on deck, his little shoes hitting with a thud.

"Yeow," Bertie cried. He looked up, startled.

John knelt down and held him. "Son, don't ever do that again."

Evie caught up, her eyes wild with worry and then relief.

John tried to be as calm as he could with his lecture. Evie wasn't the least bit calm, her voice high as she repeated everything John said, in case Bertie didn't get it the first time around.

Soon they were safe in their rooms, which were stately and comfortable, and blessedly quiet.

To help Bertie calm down (to help them all calm down), Evie began reading to him from John Milton's *Paradise Regained*. They were lying on the bed together, propped up on pillows while Bertie snuggled against her. She was reading: "*Well have we speeded, and o'er hill and dale, Forest, and field, and flood, temples and towers, Cut shorter many a league…There Babylon, the wonder of all tongues, As ancient, but rebuilt by him who twice Judah and all thy father David's house Led captive, and Jerusalem laid waste, Till Cyrus set them free.*"

In short order, Bertie's eyes closed. Evie shut the book and carefully got up from the bed, joining John in the small sitting area.

"John Milton for a child? He's not going to understand that."

Bertie mumbled in his pillow, "It's about restoring paradise, Father."

Evie gave John a cross look for waking up Bertie, but the boy was soon breathing loudly in a sleeping rhythm.

She whispered, "He likes the concept of the book, which I explained. He can pick up most of the imagery, but I was reading this to him, hoping to lull him to sleep."

"Ahh, well, I could use a nap, too." He smiled.

Sharing the dinner table with them that evening were the Richards, a middle-aged American couple who talked of their lumber business and their impressions of London, a Doctor Fielding, who taught physics at Columbia University, and who seemed mostly interested in the history of the Druids, of all things, and a wealthy widow from Aberdeen, who suddenly became an authority on Britain's early pagans.

The Armitages were looked askance upon, John felt, for having Bertie with them at table, although the boy was well-behaved. The others must have thought they couldn't afford a nanny. If they only knew they were dining with one of the wealthiest women in Europe. Both he and Evie wanted Bertie to be with them for the entire trip, not locked in their stateroom with a servant, as John had spent his transatlantic crossings as a boy.

Only once did Bertie transgress and that was when he began initiating conversation with the adults. Their son was used to talking freely with Harold and Adam and Meg, and, of course, he was excited. But John then observed Evie's approach to this. All she had to do was gently touch the top of the boy's hand with her fingertips. A sheepish smile spread across Bertie's face followed by a self-mocking shrug. He then became the picture of the submissive, retiring child.

When their waiter presented Cherries Jubilee, igniting the flame like a showman, John wouldn't have missed Bertie's expression for the world. The lad's face came alive, he even mouthed his "wow" silently in deference to the table guests. Evie was excellent at small-talk. By the end of dinner, she had charmed their table-mates, and so had Bertie.

John was awed by the approaching New York skyline, although he had seen the city before. When he glanced over at Evie and Bertie, his heart fluttered; their eyes, their entire faces, beamed with wonder.

"Would Monsieur and Madame care for a *snapshot*?"

John turned and looked into the smiling face of a mustachioed man, bearing photographer's equipment. He liked the way the man said *snapshot* as if each syllable were snapped from the air and captured in his black box of a camera. Money passed.

"Now, Madame, a little to your right. We want you in balance the Miss Liberty behind you—you being the much more striking. Oui, thaz good, Madame."

The flash blinded John momentarily. Bertie, giggling with glee, delighted in the equipment's 'poof' as if he'd just observed a Lilliputian fireworks display. The boy, with hand held fast in John's grip, could bounce on the balls of his feet with metronomic precision. John mindfully placed Bertie's hand in Evie's care and then arranged for the photographs (Mister Mustachio had taken two) and their trunks to be delivered to their hotel.

As they proceeded with fellow passengers, forming a phalanx at the gangplank, the air smelled of crude oil. A crew down below hollered and fussed, preparing to refuel the great Aquitania, which had been revamped from coal burning to oil a few years ago.

Docks, themselves, bore a harshness, like the workers servicing them. But rising above, multitudinous spires of architectural wonder beamed in the sun, awaiting the newcomers.

John ushered his family onto American soil, which at present consisted of concrete and planking, saturated with damp soot. The moment, however, brought a dryness to his throat. The reality of facing his father fatigued him.

"Taxicabs are rather big here," Bertie enthused as they stood yet again in a queue, a throng emitting, as throngs do, a blend of impatience, dignity and resignation.

A newsboy, about Bertie's age, bellowed out newsy tidbits, trying to sell his papers. Smudges of ink colored his cheeks, nose and hands.

Finally, they climbed into—Bertie dramatically collapsing into—a large Chevrolet cruiser. When the driver swung their door shut, the immediate sense of quiet and regained control eased all of John's muscles. As one, the three Armitages snuggled back into the upholstery, heads craned to peer out at the passing metropolis.

"How do these sidewalks get any sun?" Evie asked as their cab made slow but steady progress along manmade canyons. "And just look at all those people, moving like sardines, crammed on the walkways." She beamed at John. "How exciting."

Bertie had worked valiantly to keep his eyes open during the slow progress to the Plaza Hotel, but a few blocks into Manhattan, his head leaned against John's side. Child-pitched deep breathing arose from somnolence. All that bouncing about on deck must've been exhausting.

On their first morning at the Plaza, Evie read in the *Wall Street Journal* that there was going to be a luncheon that very day at the new Waldorf Astoria with former Russian dignitaries as special guests. She had John and Bertie dress their best, and they were soon back in one of those large American cabs, which nonetheless could only crawl through the traffic. At the Waldorf, Evie led them right up to the desk and asked for someone in charge of the guest list. A man with a goatee and his stout wife came up and after no more than a few sentences exchanged in Russian, the Armitages were escorted to a round table that could seat eight. The only other people at this table were a couple in their seventies who explained to Evie that they spoke only Russian. Bertie gave John a mischievous smile.

While Evie conversed in Russian, father and son worked at displaying the most polite demeanors though saying silly things to each other in English.

John made his face serious and said, "The cow jumped over the moon."

Bertie took his time spreading some butter on a slice of bread, then replied, "Peter Rabbit picked his nose."

And on and on it went, Bertie giggling only once.

As they were returning to the Plaza, Evie talked with exuberance about those she met while mingling about after dinner. Some knew people she had met in Russia; some even had known her father. Much of the conversations included the buzz about Anastasia surviving the revolution.

She then addressed their table antics.

"Mr. and Mrs. Markov were quite bemused over the conversation you two were having during luncheon. I told them that your mother tongue was Latvian and that you were practicing your English." She gave them a dazzling smile and kissed Bertie's forehead.

The train ride to Chicago seemed to take forever. On this leg of the trip, John and Evie took turns being irritable, and only for a dark ten minutes did they overlap. Bertie was too interested in the passing view of America to take much notice.

From Union Station, they took a cab to the Chicago Northwestern station, more due to transporting luggage than the few blocks walk.

"It's quite different from New York City," Evie said. "Oh, look, Bertie." She roused the boy from momentary stupor and pointed to the elevated tracks down the street. "There's the L Grandmama talked about." And just as Bertie turned to look, black and chrome train cars rattled along, shooing a flock of pigeons from underneath.

"That's the tops!"

"Bertie, please don't use slang, especially when we meet your grandparents," Evie said.

"I was trying to use a pun, Mum."

"Hmm." Evie patted his head.

John said, "Here's Chicago's opera house."

"An office building?—that's both strange and modern."

"Sadly, its premiere season opened to the market crash. Mother says the theater is practically in disuse."

Bertie was less impressed with the commuter train out of the city. For a young lad, he was already a world-traveling snob.

They disembarked at the Lake Forest station with their trunks and their fatigue.

"How lovely, a piazza and car park in one."

"They call it Market Square," John explained. He had forgotten how attractive the place was with its center fountain and flowers. Three sides of shops were either imitation Tudor or pillared Italian Renaissance. "It might be the first planned shopping center in America."

"I wasn't expecting to see brick streets and European style in a modern part of the world."

"Perhaps you mean near Chicago, famed for its smelly stockyards."

"Not at all." She looked at the awaiting Armitage chauffeur as if concerned he might take offense.

The Chicago Northwestern porter and the Armitage chauffeur, obviously familiar with each other, were busy taking matters in hand, loading the trunks in the boot of the huge Cadillac. John had never seen anything like it—a boat of a motorcar with rounded edges, shiny black with brilliant chrome. But as they took the winding sylvan lanes toward the estate, the new car on all accounts paled when compared with Uncle George's Rolls.

The chauffeur's name was Joe. As a kid on the streets of the city's north side, Joe and his pals sometimes carried messages for bootleggers and other "vermin", as he called them now. One day, his cousin got on the wrong side of Claude Maddox, ally to Al Capone. Not long after the famed St. Valentine's Massacre, his cousin disappeared. At least, his body was later retrieved from the Chicago River. Some folks disappeared altogether, now that the Mob ruled the city.

From Sheridan Road, the Cadillac passed the gatehouse and turned down the tree-lined drive. Bertie was sleeping, leaning against Evie. The house loomed in the distance, its limestone and brick evoking a stone-cold ache in John's chest.

"This is singularly impressive, John," Evie said with hushed enthusiasm. "Such symmetry—eight huge windows across the main house and, what? six across each wing."

Bertie came to, his lids fluttering. "Does the Queen keep a palace in America?"

John assumed his son was making another attempt at humor.

The front grounds drew John's attention, offering a bit of solace: grand oaks, Scottish pines and bright birch surrounded the lawn where he and Edwina had kicked the ball about on sunny afternoons.

You have to lean into it more, Master John David. Like this. He caught himself smiling and savored the brightness in his heart at the thought of seeing his Miss Eddie again.

Joe turned the Cadillac onto the circling drive-up and the pulse pounded in John's carotid arteries like an angry tympani player. When Georgette and Franklin came out and stood on the front terrace to welcome them, it caught him by surprise. He'd half expected his father to be in the city, working. And his father had aged. The pose of his parents, however, would make a great photograph; they looked so proper, dignified— and contained. The car came to a stop.

Franklin took one step forward, head high, lips tight, waiting. Georgette stayed just behind at his right. The Cadillac's interior door handle slipped at John's damp grasp. Joe came round and opened it. John stepped out, acknowledged his parents with a nod, and then helped his wife and son out of the car. He was about to make the introductions when he noticed his father's composure crack, then completely burst. Rivers of tears ran down his father's face. Breath caught in John's throat. Franklin rushed to him, embraced him and sobbed.

John's voice sounded loud, louder than intended, as he said, "It's good to see you, Father."

Dinner that night was peaceful and pleasant. Georgette asked to have Bertie sit next to her at table. She took pleasure in talking with him and showed him how to extract escargots from their shells. Bertie was fascinated with the snail and shell but didn't care for eating it. He did enjoy the pork roast, the mashed potatoes and the dessert: simple chocolate cake.

It was the best chocolate cake John could remember.

After dinner, Franklin lifted Bertie up on his lap while they sat on the back terrace. They settled in just as fireflies began to come out and dance above the lawn. Bertie watched with fascination. John expected him to jump up and run around in order to catch them, but the boy leaned against Franklin. The surf of Lake Michigan had a lulling rhythm, the adults chatted, and in short order Bertie was sleeping again, his head nuzzled against his grandfather's shoulder.

Evie beamed at the sight.

John said, "It must be a growth spurt; he slept on the train."

She clarified, "He knows he's safe and loved."

Two days later, John stood with Evie on the front terrace, awaiting the special guest of the day. The air smelled of alyssum and lemon oil, the latter from the ever-well-polished front entry. Bertie and Franklin volleyed a softball back and forth on the front grounds, a sight that brought both pain and pleasure to John. Franklin missed a catch and Bertie's giggling voice carried, echoing off the massive wall of crafted limestone that was Armitage House.

Evie murmured a sigh of contentment, sun on her wide-brimmed hat—purchased at Marshall Field's—her attention on the athletes. His wife's understanding and support of John's feelings about his father was as palpable as the warm afternoon sunshine. Just as evident was a niggling sense of pressure on him to forgive. John felt he had been more than generous already, but something in her determined demeanor radiated his way, poking him like an ox goad.

A glint of chrome shimmered through foliage. The Iooga horn sounded—Joe evidently couldn't resist. In a smooth, majestic approach, the Cadillac rounded the drive; its silver-haired passenger turned her regal head and clapped her gaze on her former charge. One would have thought that they *were* bringing the Queen here. But John well knew how un-monarchal the woman was.

The fine automobile sailed to a stop before them. True to her republican character, before Joe could come round to open her door, Edwina bolted out and came up to John, shoulders squared, and looked him in the eye. Despite the act she was putting on, he felt her excitement.

"I had to look deep inside those eyes to make sure it was my John David standing here bold as can be."

She flung her arms around him, a quick cry escaping her stubborn lips. He could feel her shivering, heard a quick sniff. She clung to him while reining in her composure.

She stood back, her face alight. Her inner glow outshone the webs of wrinkles and little sags.

She turned to Evie. "He's not a crybaby, is he? No, I taught him to be a man."

"My compliments," Evie replied. "He's a sensitive man, but strong of will."

Edwina nodded absently, not especially interested in whether or not John was sensitive. She looked over her shoulder and hollered out to Bertie, "Try releasing the ball a second earlier, lad. And then you'll hit the mark right enough. Good arm, though." She leaned forward and added, "For a little tyke."

Straightening up, she held out her hands to Evie. "You're every bit as lovely as I pictured you. And such a handsome son." Her eyes welled up again. "Oh, what a glorious day this is." She turned to the approaching ball players. Not the least intimidated by the great Franklin Armitage, she put her hands on her hips and said, "Well, let's get a move on. We've got lots to talk about." Turning back to John. "Yes, we do."

After interchanges with Franklin and Bertie, Edwina took John by the arm and led the party in to Georgette and the waiting staff of cooks and servers, ready for the luncheon.

After the meal, Edwina pulled John aside in a conspiratorial manner and said, "Tell me, you haven't become a capitalist, have you?" She scrutinized his reaction.

"Ha! No, not quite, well, not exactly. I'm, we're trying to be philanthropists. We started an orphanage in London."

She nodded. "There you go, then; 'use the world but not to the full.'" Her head tilted in thought. "There must be some way to help more than one household of orphans." She patted his arm. "I'm proud of you, my boy. But give that one some thought."

Later that day, Edwina corralled Bertie in the old nursery and began teaching him poker, of all things. John half expected to find them, later, smoking cigars. He left and took Evie for a stroll on the grounds.

The blue and green hues of Lake Michigan showed off their best. John enjoyed the warmth of the sun at the back of his neck. The lake looked inviting. "When I was a boy, I used to make my way down the bluff and go skinny-dipping. I usually had the beach pretty much to myself on any day that I ventured down there."

"That sounds rather nice, but it seems sad for a child to be so lonely," she said.

"Shall we?" John gave her his boyish grin, the thrill of the idea, taking him back to their wedding night. He tilted his head toward the water and hoped to coax her.

"Absolutely not," she protested, the prudish side of her rallying, a rare thing, but it was there. Then she smiled and amended, "At least not in the daylight."

Then John remembered that the lake would not be warm enough until August. His exciting image dissipated like the final shimmering trails of fireworks. But he shot her a wink.

They walked under the shade of some large cottonwood trees off to the north. "On Monday, I'm going down to the plant with Father. I think he still hopes I'll come back and take it over someday. Armitage Meats has become a household word in America. There's a union now—working conditions are better, in fact, much better than they were. But I just don't care to run a meatpacking plant."

A yellow finch scuttled in front of them, then flew to some shrubbery.

"It's so quiet and lovely here," Evie said, as they moved across the lawn. "It's hard to believe that the stockyards, the tenement housing and all those tall buildings made of brick and concrete are so close. I like Chicago. Well, thus far. But there's something in all the history of England and Europe that I like, too." She turned and gave him a significant look. "I suppose wherever you prefer to live, I'll be happy."

"What? What's this? I've said nothing about moving here. We have the orphanage and our life in London. And there's Kirstead Court."

"And you have family living here. They're all the family any of us have." She leaned in and with a conspiratorial tone, said, "I confess I was more fond of Lady Birnam and Uncle George, but they're dead. Your father has been very nice to us, and, well, there's only one Georgette Armitage in this world, and she lives here." She didn't add that Bertie should know what it's like to have grandparents fussing over him, but the thought was there.

The next morning was gray, a day of obligation. Joe drove father and son to Franklin's office in the city. The older man talked much of the way, and John felt as if he were still a teenager, bristling at any sense of parental propaganda. He knew he should be more generous, more adult, and take an active part in the conversation, but he couldn't muster up the interest.

While traffic along North Ravenswood Avenue came to a standstill, a number of children, mostly young boys, loitered in small packs around street corners and alleyways. Dirty, unhappy chaps, quite likely to find some trouble before day's end.

Joe turned from the wheel. "There's an accident ahead. We'll be here a bit."

A boy around Bertie's age and size watched them from the alley's end. John could look past the soiled face and disheveled clothing, imagining the lad all cleaned up, participating in a classroom, smiling. An older boy broke the spell by placing his hand on the child's shoulder and offering him a lit cigarette. What chance did boys like these have to make their way in the world? What chance did the world have when so many of its young never learned to interact with respect, to speak intelligently, to enjoy a symphony or a work of art?

The traffic cleared and they soon pulled into the front lot of Armitage Meats. The plant had grown into quite an operation in the sixteen years John had been away. Franklin had dressed up the place with opulent stone gateways, as if entering an estate, but the buildings were strictly utilitarian, as they should be, John supposed. The stench of the stockyards pervaded here.

Franklin took John around and introduced him to foremen, secretaries, almost anyone who could shake his hand and mumble things like *spittin' image* and *chip off the ol' block*. John was glad to make his father happy, and he had to admit that the orderliness of the operation was impressive. His father was quick to smile at any positive remark his son had to make. But John's soul was not in business.

The next night, Georgette arranged for the family to go to Orchestra Hall. They had their pre-concert dinner at an Italian restaurant in the Loop. When Joe dropped them off in front of

Orchestra Hall, Evie looked up and down Michigan Avenue and remarked on how impressed she was.

"And our conductor tonight is Maestro Toscanini," Georgette said, her tone effusive. They settled into their box seats.

With bright eyes, Bertie sat up straight, taking it all in. If his feet could touch the floor, they would be springing again with metronomic precision.

The first piece was Tchaikovsky's *Violin Concerto #1*. Toscanini impressed John as the most intense and brilliant conductor he had ever observed. He wouldn't mind seeing him again. John wasn't educated musically, but he sensed something special was being generated from the musicians by this conductor, as if Toscanini were eliminating sentimentality by means of clarity and tension. The soloist played remarkably well, especially the evocative second movement. Here, John realized for the first time that he favored melancholy in music.

All the way home, Bertie talked about the violin.

"We'll get you a violin before you leave," Georgette said, all too happy to please the boy.

John allowed Georgette the pleasure of generosity and encouragement.

Franklin offered, "There's a violin maker on Howard Street. I reckon he would have an instrument to fit a young man like you."

When the vacation came to an end, Franklin and Georgette accompanied John, Evie and Bertie to Union Station. To the casual observer, John thought, the family must look as if they had been close all along, with all the tears and hugging going on.

Before getting on the train, Bertie turned to his grandparents and announced, "We'll be back!"

John cringed and then smiled.

Chapter Twenty-Two

Between the dark and the daylight,
When the night is beginning to lower,
Comes a pause in the day's occupations,
That is known as the Children's Hour.

I hear in the chamber above me
The patter of little feet,
The sound of a door that is opened,
And voices soft and sweet.

From my study I see in the lamplight,
Descending the broad stair,
Grave Alice, and laughing Allegra,
And Edith with golden hair.

A whisper, and then a silence:
Yet I know by their merry eyes
They are plotting and planning together
To take me by surprise.

A sudden rush from the stairway,
A sudden raid from the hall!
By three doors left unguarded
They enter my castle wall!

They climb up into my turret
O'er the arms and back of my chair,
If I try to escape, they surround me;
They seem to be everywhere.

They almost devour me with kisses,
Their arms about me entwine,

Till I think of the Bishop of Bingen
In his Mouse-Tower on the Rhine!

Do you think, O blue-eyed banditi,
Because you have scaled the wall,
Such an old mustache as I am
Is not a match for you all.

I have you fast in my fortress,
And will not let you depart,
But put you down into the dungeon
In the round-tower of my heart.

And there will I keep you forever,
Yes, forever and a day,
Till the walls shall crumble in ruin,
And moulder in dust away.

--Henry Wadsworth Longfellow

John found everything at the Islington house running smoothly when he returned. Adam and Meg impressed him with their ability to relate to the children and keep things under control.

They were sitting around the kitchen table, having a staff meeting.

Adam said, looking more at Evelyne than John, "We need to find someone like Lady Birnam to help with elocution and etiquette."

John would have expected Meg to bring up such an idea rather than Adam. But he knew the former stable boy was proud of his progress in speaking "like the gentry."

Well, if he and Evie decided to move to America, Adam would be in charge, and it would serve him well to continue such classes.

The next morning John leaned back in his desk chair, feeling fresh for the day's work before him. Only a few things were required relative to the orphanage; he wanted to read over the progress of each student—he had been having Miss Bodenheimer keep a weekly report on this since Guy Fawkes Day. He had read that there'd been no serious behavioral problems of late. Jiggs usually challenged every command and house procedure, but there was an underlying kindness in the boy—something special hidden behind the cockiness.

The fireplace in the office burned at a low hiss. February's sunlight streamed through two large windows, doing a better job coaxing warmth in the room. It was a mild winter and one strangely prone to offering more sunny days than London was used to, engendering hope all 'round—at least in John's view.

He continued working on the letter he had been laboring over for several days. He hoped to be able to present it to their Member of Parliament shortly. The inept state of London's "poor laws" infuriated him, which was one reason why he labored so—he needed to hone his diplomacy. He troubled over how to tactfully say: *Those in workhouses should be nurtured rather than exploited with the sole aim of making the outfit self-sustaining.* Of course, this would include a major economic overhaul. John doubted that he would have much personal impact on this, but he had to try.

A knock at his door was followed by his wife's entrance. She approached, smiling. A black felt cloche crowned her page-boy hair and a practical black wool skirt hugged her hips with minimal flare draping down just below her knees. The matching wool top was cut in imitation of a naval jacket, its lapels framing the crisp white collar of her blouse. She settled in a wing chair, eyes brimming with intent.

"I've been thinking, John." He liked the way she began conversations. "About Eloise." Evie brushed at invisible lint on her skirt, as if shooing away inane impediments to a woman's esteem as a *thinker*. "Today at first-hours, she turned in a remarkable essay about the value of education. She's fifteen and sharp as a tack. I'm beginning to worry that we might have been a little short-sighted."

"About what?"

"Well, we got permission from the minister of education's office to run our home as a school, but we never pursued accreditation."

"Ah, so Eloise is thinking of continuing her education? Then, you're right, love. I've fallen prey to the same prejudice or mindset I'd like to see eradicated in society."

"Well, I'm guilty, too. I had only considered having the children learn how to interact with those of higher stations—thinking only that they might then obtain employment as clerks, head waiters or shop assistants and such. I'd never even thought that these children from the street, whom I have come to love dearly, could, let alone *would*, aspire to be doctors or solicitors or writers. If Eloise wishes to apply for one of the colleges, we are going to have to obtain credits recognition from the government."

When she left, John took off his jacket, rolled up his sleeves and reworked the presentation for his local M P.

He met with Mr. Albright in his Westminster office that Friday. The congenial older man suggested they talk over lunch at the *Boar and Crown*. John had heard good things about this Westminster favorite. And 'favorite' it was. If it hadn't been for the importance of his companion, he would have had to wait an hour or more for a table. As it was, a side room was reserved for MPs, magistrates, bankers and the more prestigious solicitors. It was almost a plebeian version of a gentlemen's club, affording those not necessarily titled some distinction—and all this glorious recognition from a pub called *The Boar and Crown*; that was London.

After settling down at a table near a window looking out on Bridge Street, John ordered a mince pie with pickle and a pot of tea. Mr. Albright ordered mutton and a pint.

"I wish London had more folks like you and your wife, Mr. Armitage. You are doing a nice thing for your charges."

John presented his letter. Mr. Albright accepted it graciously, though a hint of patronization hung between them, as if John should know better than to expect bureaucracy to affect much opportunity for the impoverished.

"As the Good Book says, my friend, *you will always have the poor with you*. But I will give your ideas consideration."

The publican's wife took it upon herself to serve the *high-office room* while the bosomy barmaids served the main pub. She reminded John of a dumpling, but she knew how to speak well and when to offer a familiar, humorous statement and when to be the invisible servant. She next brought them each a rice pudding and a fresh pot of tea.

A shiny Bentley rolled past their window, followed by a delivery cart pulled by an old dray horse. Low-lying clouds were creeping into town, and it looked as though a cold rain shower was sure to follow.

Finally, Albright leaned back, satisfied with the meal that had vanished from his plates and bowls and said, "As to accreditation, I will speak to the Minister of Education on your behalf. I would expect one of his assistants will be contacting you next week. You realize that your charges will have to pass stringent tests for what they've covered thus far; and your teachers will be examined, I'm afraid, more ruthlessly than any of the others in the city. But if all proves up and up, I'm certain you will be granted what you're looking for. It's a nice dream, that. Wouldn't it be something if at least some of our unfortunate urchins became men of learning. I don't understand what women want with higher learning, but there you have it. Why it's almost American." He laughed with disdain and picked at his teeth.

The man from the Minister of Education's office was a Mr. Weavel, a man of small build with a bald pate and a hesitant smile. He stood with John and Evie before the class.

"I am Mr. Weavel from the Minister of Education's office. I am entrusted with the responsibility of administering tests for all children and interviews with all instructors." He looked down his nose at the class and added, "I also am to report any and all behavioral problems. You will submit to my authority. If you do not, it will reflect badly on your school and may impair any chance of accreditation, but I can't assume that you know what I'm talking about, now can I? We will see."

John looked into the faces of each student and observed their wide-eyed acknowledgement. Even five-year-old Sally understood that somehow she needed to measure up. Bertie looked downright intimidated but eager to please. Each youthful face surreptitiously checked John's reaction, no doubt to monitor the gravity of the situation. Particularly concerned were the adolescent faces of Eloise, Louise and Jiggs. John realized how important education had become to them.

Mr. Weavel handed out a test relative to each age group that, accordingly, covered the basic subjects of arithmetic, reading comprehension, basic English history, a little geography and writing—printing for the very young, cursive for the rest. The children were taking the matter seriously. All John could hear was the scratching of pencils on paper and a nervous cough here and there. Mr. Weavel took it upon himself to watch for any cheating. After about forty minutes, the students began setting their pencils on their desktops. Sally was the last to finish, in spite of having the least to do. She was checking and rechecking. Her keen desire to perform well touched John. After she surrendered to the pressure and finally set down her pencil, she twiddled her thumbs.

The children were then placed in the care of Adam and Gerard for recreation.

John had Evie sit in on the interview Mr. Weavel held with Miss Bodenheimer. Currently, she was the only instructor. Not having Lady Birnam around for interviewing, or in other words, to question her abilities, was almost certainly a good thing.

It was an anxious two weeks, but John finally got word from Mr. Weavel that their school was granted accreditation.

The next night, Evie planned a celebratory dinner for everyone. Cook roasted chickens, made mince pies and three different desserts. John and Evie spent the day scurrying through Harrods, buying little gifts for each member of the house. During dinner it was apparent that Sally didn't understand what was going on.

"You see, Sally," Bertie said, bending low to meet her gaze, "If you want to be a teacher or a doctor, well, now you can."

Evie held back her smile while nodding in agreement.

Sally clapped her hands—her understanding, dubious.

When John and Evie distributed the surprise gifts after dessert, they received repeated hugs and kisses and "thank-you's" until the children were sent to their beds. The occasion was more satisfying than any holiday.

Next came the business of finding a violin instructor for Bertie. One morning, while crossing Covent Garden, John rounded a cart loaded with cabbages and practically fell over a busker, a homely man entertaining for tips with his violin, sitting between cabbages and cauliflower. With all of the haggling going on, it wasn't the best place for one to enjoy music. But from a starving-artist's point of view, this was where many a purse was already open.

"Pardon me," John said. He knew he hadn't harmed either man or instrument, but he asked, "Are you all right?"

The violinist nodded stiffly and resumed playing.

John glanced at the open instrument case and saw a mere handful of coins, a few farthings and one shilling. To John's ear, the young man played well. He looked around but saw no one taking much notice. When he dropped in a sovereign, the young man again stopped playing.

"Why, thank you, sir."

As John engaged him in conversation, the back of his mind repeatedly urged him to walk on and look for a teacher with real qualifications.

"Where did you study?"

"At Guildhall. Had my father not died at the Somme, I'd have finished." His thin shoulders shrugged with resignation, but his taut face indicated resentment over the evident plight of reduced circumstances. The man's name was Gleason Fitzgerald.

"And where do you stay, Mister Fitzgerald?"

Gleason hesitated. With defiant eyes, he replied, "Seven Dials."

Shame over his own social clumsiness flushed through John's veins. He had been merely thinking of logistics, in case he chose to offer the teaching position. Forcing a man with middleclass roots to admit before a gentleman that his rooms were in the seediest of slums was insensitive. Now John had no choice but to cast off the warning voice and do something about it.

John brought Gleason to Armitage House that afternoon. When Miss Bodenheimer finished with the children, he introduced the violin player to Bertie in one of the parlors. The boy, who had been so excited to begin, became uncharacteristically shy, and even a little frightened.

John had to admit Gleason did not have an inviting face. His nose—a bit crooked, as if he had been punched in a brawl—was narrow and weasel-like. Trying to see the man through his son's young perspective, John noticed for the first time how intense Gleason's eyes were, as if they could penetrate your thoughts. But complements began to enthuse from the violinist.

"Such a beautiful young son you have, Mister Armitage." He patted the top of Bertie's head. "Let me see your hands, lad."

Bertie's eyes checked with John's before holding them out.

"Go ahead, son."

"Ah, yes. These will serve you well." Gleason straightened and examined Bertie's violin. "And this is a more-than-suitable instrument, sir." He turned back to the boy. "You have good taste, young man."

Bertie finally smiled.

The lessons proceeded well. This led to the purchase of two pianos for accompaniment, one for Armitage House and one for the Mayfair house. Gleason even talked John into hiring him as a music teacher at the orphanage. And even a children's choir was formed.

From their drawing room, John and Evie could hear occasional scratchy strains of nursery rhyme melodies from upstairs.

"It's nice having music in the house," Evie said.

John mumbled his agreement into his whisky glass. After savoring the smooth taste and warming sensation, he smiled at her.

Light glinted off her tortoiseshell pen as she etched it about the pages of her diary. He never pried into her diary keeping, which is why she felt comfortable writing in it during some of their quieter evenings.

She added, "Mr. Fitzgerald is doing quite well. I'm glad you had a room made up for him over the Islington garage. I hated to think of him in Seven Dials."

In three months' time, Bertie was playing without any scratching noises. Rudimentary exercises became more intricate, melodies more sophisticated. The boy played with such feeling John and Evie didn't have to be told that their son had a special gift. But Mr. Fitzgerald went on and on about Bertie's potential when speaking out of the boy's hearing, careful not to create an unfortunate ego in his student. John wondered how the man failed to notice the lack of any arrogance in Bertie.

Chapter Twenty-Three

1933

Franklin and Georgette wrote to them, suggesting a family vacation on the Continent. Georgette had Vienna in mind, for Bertie's sake. She called it the "Musical Capital of the World."

John's parents arrived in Southampton that June and spent a week at Mayfair. John showed off Armitage House and was amused that the children and staff viewed his parents with near reverence, as if they were American royalty. Bowing and curtsying and practically mumbling, *Yes, m'Lord and m'Lady.* John enjoyed showing off his Islington family, his spirits only slightly darkened by the stress of not being able to read his father's expression.

The Armitages were sitting in the Islington parlor discussing the curriculum when John heard the front door open and close. Steady footsteps advanced, clicking on the terrazzo floor.

"Ah, here you are," Gleason said, dressed in his best black suit. He entered the room. Indignation flashed though John at the interruption, followed by a measure of awe. The man from Seven Dials had panache. Gleason approached the guests and handed Georgette a bouquet of flowers. His hands fluttered about before settling together at his chest. "I just ran to Covent Garden, thinking our guests might enjoy fresh flowers. He beamed at the Americans (not knowing Georgette was born and bred in Mayfair), "Covent Garden is the best place in all of London for flowers."

Franklin's sharp eyes appraised this character while Georgette gushed appreciative remarks.

Evie stood and took the flowers from Georgette. "That was very thoughtful, Gleason. Thank you. Would you be so kind as to put these in water for us?" She handed back the bouquet. His smile faltered but quickly recovered.

After clearing his throat, he said, "But, of course."

"Meg will let you know where to find a vase," Evie said with some charm, as if to soften the slight. Gleason's shifting eyes betrayed some offense at being discussed in the same breath with a "servant."

With a swell of his thin chest, he said, "I'll have the children ready for the recital shortly." He turned on his heel and left with as much grace as one possibly could.

To Gleason's accompaniment, Bertie performed a sonata by Mozart, showing how well two years of lessons had nurtured the eleven-year-old. Then the children's choir performed some pieces by Handel and Delius. Occasionally, Ewan's bleating voice surfaced—although instructed by Gleason to merely mouth the words, the tone-deaf boy repeatedly forgot himself and let loose. Each sour note raised a wicked gleefulness in John, who was more pleased by the youth's spirit than musical perfection.

At the post-recital party, the children beamed with exhilaration. Thinking of it raised a lump in John's throat. All children should know this feeling, and know it early in life.

John came up behind one of the settees occupied by Bertie and Jiggs. The boys had their heads together in conversation, oblivious of his presence.

Jiggs said, "It's rather fun watching ol' Fitzgerald strut about the room like a colorful cock."

Bertie leaned in. "More like the Belle of the Ball."

John stared at his son, amazed. Where had that come from? He almost spoke up to have a word with the two about respect. Seeing Bertie's cheeks still flushed from the days' excitement, he decided to do so at another time.

All seemed under control at Armitage House when the Armitages crossed the Channel for their summer holiday.

None of them had travelled by the Orient Express until now. They boarded the train in Paris with a high degree of interest.

Walking along the platform amidst spouting plumes of steam, Franklin held Bertie's hand and said, "I read that the man who started this business, a Mr. Magelbackers or Nagelmackers—Bertie giggled at the name—modeled his train-cars after the style of George Pullman's. So, you see, Bertie, we're having a little taste of Chicago as we cross Europe," Franklin said.

This little bit of propaganda—a subtle nudge to consider Chicago's assets, —had John recalling how he used to bristle at such things. Now, he simply smiled and shook his head.

Mahogany paneling surrounded the club car where the family settled after arranging personal things in their rooms. Glasses of Champagne clinked, glistening in the glow from the many brass light fixtures. Beyond spotless windows, French countryside rolled past. Stone cottages and fine chateaus, then lush vineyards, followed by cows in the fields. Franklin offered Bertie a sip of the bubbly. The boy hiccupped for the next fifteen minutes.

Later, in the dining car, they sat at two different tables due to narrow space. Bertie joined his grandparents, and again John's mother encouraged the boy to try escargot. This time, he liked them.

"It chews like a mushroom and tastes like garlic and butter, grandmother," he said, his face serious. "Ooh, I just had something crunchy, or more like snappy. Was it an eyeball?" Franklin released a robust laugh.

The din of conversation in the car hummed with the disjointed rhythm of different languages. John recognized French and German, which dominated the car, but there were others which, he did not know.

A platinum blonde dressed in a white silk gown that looked more like a negligee was leaning forward listening rapturously to a large man, speaking in German. Funny how German could sound aggressive, even when it's not. She looked as though he were reciting love poems to her.

While the Armitage family lingered over dessert, another attractive woman sashayed past their tables, accompanied by a young man. She was wearing a satin gown of the current French fashion, which revealed her fine shoulders and back. She carried a leopard-skin wrap and made her way to the head of the dining car. Her black hair, waved and curled, hugged her head. When she turned and sat, her African heritage was confirmed in her pleasantly exotic facial features. John heard a few whispers in the car; the name Josephine Baker was audible. Miss Baker nodded and smiled to an admirer before turning her entire attention to her young man across the white-linen-topped table.

As John and Evie were heading back to their sleeper room, their family behind them, he leaned in and said, "Well, I finally got to see Josephine Baker. Quite fetching. Too bad we couldn't see her dance in the follies."

"I'd say her walk is as much dance as I've ever seen. I think you've observed enough to be satisfied," Evie said in good-natured humor.

He looked at his wife. "Oh, I am satisfied, dear." He squeezed her hand.

Bertie slept with his grandparents that night.

On the third afternoon in Vienna, the Armitages were enjoying the pleasant environs of a beer garden. The women were shaded by an umbrella while the men enjoyed the sun on their faces.

"We're looking at expanding, adding another property—in Lambeth—to accommodate more children. But we can't possibly alleviate the suffering of even a fraction of the homeless children in London, let alone elsewhere," John said in response to his mother. She had been encouraging him to broaden his venture.

John realized that he and Evie had fallen into a comfortable spot with their own orphanage, as it provided for their own parental yearnings. They loved all the children and the staff. Of course there were difficulties, even a small uprising now and then, but not much more than a regular family would experience.

"How can anyone be a Messiah of this sort, Mother?" he asked. "There's no way we could have much impact on a problem of this scope."

"Not with that attitude," Franklin said. There it was at last—the criticism from the great Franklin Armitage.

John looked to his mother. "What do you have in mind, Mother."

Georgette's tall amber beer was garnished with a thin slice of lemon, the fine bubbles reminding one of champagne. She took a delicate sip and then smiled at her son.

"Incorporate and delegate," She said. "If you choose to broaden your scope, you'll need to attract contributors. And there is more contributor confidence when there's limited liability for your organization."

John's mouth dropped open, amazed at his mother's business savvy. Franklin smiled warmly at him, as if realizing he'd barked. No apology ensued. But John was just as glad neither of them spotlighted the ripple.

Georgette continued, "You can form committees for different areas of concern, such as one for institutionalized children, one for children in ghettos, one for orphans. Start in one place and then expand as you can. You'll obviously need someone to seek out financial support."

Franklin cut in here. "Yes, you need a Director of Development. He could approach businesses, even governments, as well as the wealthy."

Georgette corrected, "He *or she* could approach businesses." She gave Franklin a majestic smile and turned to John, "Your part, dear, will be in oversight and, as Franklin said, in delegating."

John grinned at her use of "will" verses "would" or "could."

"Oh, but we'd so miss actually working with the children," Evie said.

The light in his mother's eyes softened her pointed reply. "You'll have to decide whether you wish to help many or a few." With that, she backed off, flashed a brilliant—knowing—smile and sipped her beer.

Again, John marveled at Georgette. She had always seemed a little eccentric with her vanities. Perhaps all along she had been involved in more meaningful endeavors. Had he been too self-centered to have noticed, merely assuming that she had been focusing entirely on shallow social diversions? His face flushed with shame.

Franklin opened his mouth to speak but then shut it. His face creased. Then with decision he touched John's arm and said, "Son, I am proud of you. You have followed your heart, shown yourself courageous, served others while enjoying life. You have found your own niche. Whatever you choose to do from here, we are behind you all the way."

The sunburst in John's chest couldn't have been warmer or brighter than it was at hearing that. It crossed his mind to succumb to a bitter spirit for having to wait almost his whole life for commendation. But after only an instant he chose to be appreciative. It was the finest day he could remember. The beer was superb. He loved this convivial moment in Vienna. Only later would he realize that at that same moment, just to the north, a despot was framing trouble that would lead to the greatest crisis of all time for Europe's children.

Chapter Twenty-Four

Bertie

"I wonder what it would be like to live in Africa," Eloise said, her face wistful as she ignored her helping of tapioca pudding.

Next to him at the table, Bertie heard an intake of breath from his friend, as if Jiggs had been waiting for the moment.

"Well, I heard," his eyes brightened, "that the women of Africa sometimes wear absolutely nothing above the waist." His elbow poked at Bertie's side.

"Oh, Jiggs, what a naughty thing to say," Louise scolded. "Especially in front of the little ones, and in front of us; we'll be ladies someday."

Eloise, Louise and Jiggs were about the same age. Jiggs, the realist, once explained how difficult it would be for them to get a gentrified job, despite the blessings of Armitage House. Bertie recalled the time, a year or so ago, when Jiggs confided how earnestly he hoped to become a solicitor, or even a magistrate, upon leaving the House. His friend's dreams rose and dashed. To Bertie's way of thinking, Jiggs could already be a solicitor, and if he ever needed one, he would surely go to him. He trusted his friend implicitly; he trusted him to be kind, to be a protector, if necessary. He also saw that despite Jiggs's love for the Armitage House family, he was usually sad. And so Bertie smiled at him a lot, thinking it might help.

Sometimes, melancholy overtook him, too. The most recurring memory was of walking down the hall to tell Madam that he thought his mum was dead. *I can't keep yur, poor Bertie. I'd love ter, but I can't.*

Bertie savored a spoonful of his pudding, its comfort coated his insides. He wondered what was planned for tonight. His new mum loved to read to him, which was fine by him. His dad always looked at him kindly. And, spending time with mates like Jiggs was even better than pudding.

Helen and Sally sat across from him, wide-eyed at the conversation. They were usually in awe of the bigness of Jiggs' personality.

Bertie turned and looked at Eloise and thought about African women, then felt ashamed. He hoped no one noticed his face burning; quickly, he sipped his tea and inadvertently drew attention with a loud slurp.

Louise ignored that and said, "Well, what I think I would like about Africa is that it is sunny and warm most the time. I get so tired of gray skies." Louise tended to exaggerate her elocution.

"Well, what you wouldn't like is all the bugs and snakes," Jiggs said, tucking into his tapioca.

Louise was undeterred. "I would like to be a teacher, like Miss Bodenheimer, only in Africa."

Eloise said, "I'd like to become a writer like Beatrix Potter, but I'd also like to become a lady like Lady Birnam. She had so much confidence."

Jiggs said, "Eloise, we will none of us be part of Society that way."

Bertie could tell Jiggs wasn't trying to hurt her feelings. The older girls, while looking grown up, were all dreamy-eyed half the time. Jiggs knew what he was talking about, just like he did when mentioning African women, or life on the streets, or anything else.

Jiggs leaned Bertie's way and said, "How 'bout if we go outside and kick around the ball?"

Bertie nodded, thrilled at the idea.

"That will have to wait, I'm afraid." The voice came from the doorway behind them. It was Gleason Fitzgerald. "It's time for our fiddle lesson, old boy."

"Oh, blackness and death!" Bertie cried. He had heard Jiggs say this before.

"Come, come," Gleason said, unimpressed. "If Jiggs really wants to play with you, he'll be willing to wait until after your lesson. Don't dilly dally." He turned and disappeared, his footsteps clicking toward the parlor.

Jiggs smiled. "I'll be happy to wait. Maybe Adam will join us then."

That afternoon Bertie kicked the football to Jiggs, making him dash to the right. Jiggs stopped it mid-shin, quickly dropped his left foot on it and then sent back a high one. Bertie jumped, his brow rebounded the ball down before him. As his foot swung back for the kick, a commotion of voices and laughter made him stop. He teetered but righted himself admirably.

"What's that about?" Bertie asked his interest piqued. "Look," he pointed to the back of the Islington house. "They're gathering around Gleason." He took off to investigate the laughter. The younger children were fidgeting or jumping with glee. Jiggs' footfalls were gaining on Bertie.

"Hey, old boy," Gleason said to Bertie as he joined the group. "I've caught a wee mascot for your team." He looked pleased with himself, eyes shining, chest puffed out, which was his usual demeanor when he became the center of attention. "Takes a mighty quick hand to catch a wild rabbit." Gleason was holding the scared little thing by the scruff of its neck.

"Can I touch him?" Helen asked, already reaching out to it.

"What's going on here?" The stern voice belonged to Adam as he stepped out of the house.

Sally, oblivious to Adam's tone, jumped up and down and said, "Gleason caught a rabbit for us. I want to name it Peter."

Adam advanced and faced Gleason. "What do you think you're doing with that? Don't you know they carry vermin? Do you have any idea how hard it is to get vermin out of a house? Meg and I have enough work here as it is."

Helen said, "Come, girls." She directed the younger ones away from the tension surrounding Gleason's humiliation.

Gleason just glared angrily back at Adam. Bertie stood transfixed by the showdown, as did Jiggs.

Adam continued, "Fleas, lice and the like. I'd think a chap from Seven Dials would know all about vermin infestation."

Bertie heard something snap and then looked with horror at the bunny in Gleason's grip. The man had just broken its neck. Gleason threw the dead rabbit at Adam, turned on his heel and walked away.

Bertie didn't know what was said behind his father's office door that afternoon. All he knew was that Gleason left with a smile and Adam, a scowl.

As the weeks progressed, John noticed how well Bertie was advancing, musically.

He said to Evie, "I think our son is ready for a teacher with better qualifications."

She agreed and offered to pursue the matter.

Gleason got wind of it, approached Evie, and offered to assist, but his assistance only served to exhaust her. She would mention a Professor So-and-So. Fitzgerald would frown and shake his head and say *I've heard he has unsavory appetites, if you know what I mean.* His eyebrows danced at this. She would move on and finally find another possible teacher, and he would laugh and say *He got booed off the stage at his last recital.* The next one, *He's been known to beat his students in fits of temper.* Later, after hearing about a few *idiots,* Evie suggested that they offer Fitzgerald a promotion—to get him out of her hair. Gleason became the overseer of the new-to-open Lambeth house, in addition to conducting music classes in both orphanages.

"That ought to keep him busy," she said, grinning at John before turning out her bedside light.

Evie soon found a Professor McGrosso who had excellent credentials. The man was a graduate of the Royal School of Music in Manchester and had two students who now enjoyed good concert careers. Bertie liked the older man, and in one month, his technique noticeably improved.

The Lambeth property had previously been a small boarding school for boys and had apparently run out of financial support during the war. The place came at a very reasonable price. The former Islington nunnery had a capacity for twenty children while the Lambeth home could accommodate thirty.

In view of these limitations, his parents' advice replayed often in his mind.

Chapter Twenty-Five

November 1938

John took a slice of toast from the rack before him and was soon smearing it with a generous layer of orange marmalade. For a moment, he was five-year-old Master John David in his nursery. Edwina had generally directed his development with a firm hand, but occasionally she would indulge him. Allowing his love of marmalade to go unimpeded was one such extravagance. Her eyes would well with pleasure as she watched him ascend to Seventh Heaven each time he bit into this ambrosia. Quiet moments without cares. The marmalade tasted just as good this morning, the main difference being that he wiped his own lips afterward.

Muted light filled the linen-topped breadth between John and Evie. It was a pleasant, though gray, November morning. With adulthood, however, such quiet moments were usually accompanied by the constant presence of solemnity, that nagging by-product of responsibility and awareness of world conditions.

Evie crinkled the newspaper. "What awful news, John."

He had merely to stop chewing for her to continue.

"Hitler's Nazi-goons set upon Jewish-run businesses last night, smashing shop windows, breaking down doors. Reportedly, it's a wide-spread campaign. Many of the shops were looted. What is this world coming to?"

"I'd say the Great War pushed everyone over the edge into madness." Despite the lightness of John's tone, he often wondered whether this notion weren't in some fashion true. "Somehow 'man's inhumanity to man' has taken off like...like the Influenza, infecting millions."

"Where will it stop?"

"I believe you mean, where will it lead?"

She gave him a frank look and then a wry smile. "You're right."

The fear that another war could plague the world lay almost tangibly between them.

John heard Gerard down the main hall, answering the door. In short order, he stepped into the dining room.

"There's a man to see, um, the both of you." He looked to Evelyne and then back to John. Catching that Gerard said a "man" instead of a gentleman indicated that the East Ender's social discrimination was sharpening. Was Gerard becoming a snob?

He finally clarified, "A Mister Rubens, sir." Or did he fancy a touch of suspense?

"Ah, yes, show him in."

Gerard retreated. For such a large man, he could walk as quietly as a barefoot ballerina could along the marble-tiled hall. John reached and touched the side of the silver pot and found the coffee unsuitably tepid to offer their guest.

The old jeweler's slippered feet—for he would wear no other footwear—scuffed ever closer.

John stood and turned to greet him. "Mister Rubens. Please sit with us here." So convincing was his welcome, the old jeweler didn't demur as John held out a chair, placing him at his end of the table. "Gerard, would you please have Cook bring in a fresh pot of coffee?"

Once the niceties and fresh coffee were dealt with, the jeweler rested his cup on the shelf of his round belly. "I see you have the paper, Madame Armitage. You've read the bad news?"

"Yes." Their expressions cut through all other options, communicating by their shared concerns.

"One of our committees," by that John understood Rubens to mean one of the lobbying groups for the concerns of Britain's Jewish population, "is scrambling to put together a plea to Mister Chamberlain. But for good measure we also aim to solicit the aid of the Home Secretary. It's unreasonable to expect His Majesty's government to sanction a mass immigration of all Jews threatened in Europe, but with the escalation of danger being as it is, we must do something about the children. And we have to do so with alacrity."

He went on to explain various proposals for executing such a rescue, how they might best broadcast the need for sponsors, foster homes and contributors. "I'm hoping Sir Samuel Hoare might help us expedite arrangements for travel documents, as there's no time to lose. But first we must get this measure approved. Already we know that to get government backing, there'll have to be funds for the children, providing for their return to the Continent," he gave into an involuntary swallow, "afterward." The haunted look in the old man's eyes foretold horrific scenarios. The man had himself survived isolated pogroms. What was happening under Hitler's direction was growing in scope at every turn.

"We will obviously give this venture our full support, Mister Rubens," Evie said. "How can we best be of service?" Observing his wife's ability to sit in calm, duchess-like repose while exhibiting the conviction and compassion of a zealot thrilled John every time.

Visibly relieved, Mister Rubens set his cup on the saucer before him and leaned as far forward as his girth would allow. "The word on the street is that the Home Secretary is uncertain whether he should support this. Oy! Sir Samuel is quite full of air, indeed." He shook his head. "Our representatives had a preliminary meeting with him first thing this morning. The man can issue forth assurances that are almost histrionic. But, as I said, my sources on the street say he's struggling to see what effect his backing this might have on his political career before he actually takes it before the cabinet."

"But just—what?—four years ago, as Foreign Secretary," Evie's brows arched, "Sir Samuel was all for this kind of operation."

"Yes, yes, but now as Home Secretary things are getting complicated for him, as the government has to make quick decisions on immigration policies and procedures."

John said, "So, you're thinking that we might ask to have an audience with him? To indicate the kind of support we can offer?"

"Oh, no, not quite, Mister Armitage." He turned to Evelyne. "I was thinking that a more prudent tactic might involve Madame Armitage." He sent her a warm smile. "I thought you might be the best candidate to approach Lady Maud."

Evelyne's eyes narrowed as she worked out the connection.

Rubins said, "Nothing can inspire a political animal as expertly as the man's wife; that is, were she to have a certain, hmm, power over him. And I've heard that the Lady indeed does."

A coyness lit Evie's eyes. "And how has my favorite jeweler in Stepney come to know of this?"

"From the street, you see."

Evelyne looked out the beveled glass panes onto Wigmore Street. She had one of the few tables at the front window. They had arranged to meet at the *Penguin Café* to discuss a *charitable matter of the highest importance*—over tea, of course.

And Lady Maud was late.

In fact, she was twenty minutes late. Evie's fingers picked at her linen napkin; she was actually feeling something close to shame. Perhaps the wife of the Home Secretary would decide after all that the engagement would be slumming it; would Lady Maud simply write her off? Might this respected daughter of an earl question the social and political wisdom of associating with a woman whose father had been a mere baron, the bottom of the peerage system? Being wealthy didn't cut it here. She was no doubt aware that Armitage money was trade money. And if she only knew of Evie's expropriated wealth…

The respectable public strolled or paraded on the walkways. A smartly dressed mother and daughter, the girl looking about ten, stopped to consider whether they should take their tea here. They stood side by side, dressed in matching coats with velvet lapels, pondering the place. It seemed as though the mother, noticing Evie's stare, frowned and led the girl along. She knew she was being ridiculously self-conscious but couldn't will herself to stop it. She reasoned that she'd been trained to converse with Russia's Grand Duchesses. Didn't help. More than her ego was at stake this time—the lives of countless children could well depend on Evie's diplomacy.

The sky was dull gray, as were the street and walks, and the stone of the buildings. Only the doors and window sashes brightened the scene with vibrant red or shiny black. So neat and proper and British. A stunning green Bentley, its chrome almost blinding, was parked along the curb just down the street. Of course, some of the parading fashionable coats and hats offered respite from the grayness. The Bentley drew her eye again. Its uniformed driver was now opening the rear door and extending his gloved hand to its passenger. In one smooth motion, a lady came to stand on the sidewalk. She nodded and said something no doubt mundane to her driver and then remained for a moment after he got back behind the wheel. She stood like a statue, as if striking a pose, as if all should notice her in her fur trimmed dark blue coat, the material of which had an almost metallic sheen to it, and the cut of which had to be by Elsa Schiaparelli. The sweeping brim of her hat turned to the café, and Evie saw that Lady Maud had kept her appointment.

For all her posing on the walk, she swept into the café and up to Evelyne, who barely had to time to stand. Evie well knew not to initiate a handshake with a higher ranking peeress but Lady Maud was quick to do so, and with surprising firmness, as if she were a business woman. The cordiality in the lady's eyes cut Evelyne's anxiety by half.

Nonetheless, Evie found herself slightly breathless now that they were seated across from each other. She would place the Lady's age at ten years her senior.

A middle-aged, tuxedoed man came up to their table to speak to Lady Maud. After being introduced to the *Penguin's* owner, Monsieur Du Bois, Evie had little to do but look around the place while Du Bois gushed a volley of enthusiastic remarks to the café's celebrity. Five waiters stood along the far wall, all exceptionally handsome young men wearing uniforms that imitated tuxedos. How could she not have noticed them before? Her mind must surely be frazzled over the urgency of her mission. When the conversation came to a congenial conclusion, Du Bois signaled the head waiter to approach. As a quick, indulgent thought, Evie admitted that Du Bois certainly displayed business acumen, knowing how to attract the high-tea ladies crowd.

The headwaiter looked young for the position, twenty-something, but he was an Adonis: smooth olive complexion, eyelashes Evie envied, and black wavy hair. Were he to allow his mane to grow out, he could undoubtedly rival the Biblical Absalom.

Lady Maud broke into her thoughts. "I admire your work, Mrs. Armitage. And I gather we'll be discussing my husband's presentation to the cabinet of some form of rescue operation for Jewish children on the Continent."

The dashing waiter brightened at hearing this as he stood, ready to attend to them. Evie again considered his features and wondered whether the business at hand colored her impression that these appeared undoubtedly Semitic.

"But I'm sorry to tell you that I never interfere with my husband's work."

The young man appeared crestfallen, his eyes almost pleading with Evie to come up with the right reply. Was she losing her grip on reality? She could swear this young man was communicating with her. He stood erect, silent, yet his interest in the topic was palpable.

Her mind grappled for a line of argument. "Oh, Lady Maud, you shouldn't tease me like that. You, the Dame Commander of the Order of the British Empire? The first woman to arrive in India by aeroplane?" The Home Secretary's wife sat straighter, then gave the young man a quick glance (Was she basking in this bit of praise before him? Did she just bat her eyes?). The face turned stiff again as she returned her attention. Evie's mind wrested out a supportive illustration. "A husband may be a lady's head, but we can agreeably be the neck that turns it." Evie sported a winning smile.

The waiter practically nodded his approval. The hands that held pad and pen tightened, as if having to restrain them from applauding.

Lady Maud took control. "We should order and not keep this young man standing."

The order was taken, and the waiter disappeared.

The Lady's lips pursed and then said, "I support my husband's work, which is quite different. Accompanying him in his travels and—" With a swift change to candor, she leaned forward, eyes flashing bright like an excited child's. "Well, I have to confess, however, that the aeroplane ride was the best travel experience I've ever had. You cannot imagine—" She stopped, flicked her napkin on her lap, and said, "But I do not interfere."

Evie backed off, her thoughts racing as she carried on with lighter though current issues. The waiter brought out tiered plates of sandwiches and cakes and then poured their tea. He did so with such efficient movement, emotions erased from his face, that she wondered if she'd only imagined his interest.

Lady Maud did enjoy discussing her travels, allowing Evie to nod while taking delicate bites of a curried egg sandwich while she mentally sought for something convincing to say.

At one point, Lady Maud seemed about to dismiss Evie, but the next thing Evie knew, the young man appeared before them with a tray of even finer looking cakes. He announced, "This one, My Lady, is His Majesty's favorite." His inflections and animated face coaxed Lady Maud into trying what looked like a rum cake. He then brought a fresh pot of tea, and Evelyne was sure he was trying to buy her time for a last ditch effort.

"Hmm, I do like this rum cake," Lady Maud said, as if she had never tasted cake before.

The waiter was standing behind the politician's wife, trying to catch Evie's eye. In this short interlude, she was feeling as though he was becoming her partner in crime—for indeed, he was trying to assist her. A hint of drama even emanated from him after their gazes met: he raised his lively eyes to the ceiling and held his hands together at his chest. Evie tried not to draw Lady Maud's attention, but she struggled to read his pantomime. He repeated it, adding a cherubic expression. Messiah? What else could be behind his charade, considering the topic?

Evie relaxed in her chair. "People love humanitarian heroes, Lady Maud."

The Home Secretary's wife stopped mid-chew and tilted her head.

"While the Jewish population awaits their Messiah, Sir Samuel could take this crisis by the horns and become a humanitarian Messiah. I can only imagine the number of books that will be written about our time, its struggles … and its heroes."

The waiter beamed brighter than the Bentley's chrome.

Lady Maud patted her lips with her napkin and leaned back in her chair. "Point taken, Mrs. Armitage. I'll see what I can do."

Evelyne looked out onto Wigmore Street. She hadn't noticed until now that snow had begun falling. A thin layer brightened architectural reliefs. As she watched Lady Maud walk back to the Bentley, large, fluffy snowflakes danced about in the breeze; the whole area looked cheery.

Evie paid the bill and left a more than generous tip for the waiter.

The damp air smelled of coal soot, the kind of London night that made you wish you could wash everything once you got home. John squelched the self-indulgent thought; the mission at hand was monumental and worth the inconvenience of waiting in the cold and feeling the press of the crowd. The first *Refugee Children's Movement* train was about to reach Liverpool Station any moment.

"They must be so terrified," Evie said, a small vapor cloud wisped from her face. Her features could be lovely even when creased with concern.

"The trauma of leaving their parents behind has probably fallen by the wayside to some degree, I imagine," John said. "Most parents would've likely assured their young that this would be a temporary parting, like a holiday, some masking their feelings better than others."

"Could you imagine sending off Bertie, if he were still of a tender age? I would try to be cheery—I honestly don't know if I could pull it off." Her gaze drifted beyond the crowded platform. "Once the train would pull away and be out of sight…and afterward, returning home, the place deadly quiet…"

He tried to lift her spirits. "I would guess these tykes will feel excitement more than sadness, with the distractions of landing in a new country."

Finally, the train whistle could be heard on the December air. The fog was light, almost a fine mist, and getting home would simply be a matter of struggling through the congestion. John could now see and hear the locomotive approaching from down the line. The crowd packed together tighter. As a single entity, the throng surrounding John began breathing shallow breaths, high with anticipation, quick and rhythmic, parallel to the sounds of the chugging train that was now pulling up along the platform.

Porters and policemen attempted to maintain order. And, surprisingly, people complied; a stillness settled as the last groans of the train came to a stop. Volunteer foster families, boarding school personnel and news photographers—and the odd dignitary or two—united in purpose, waited. As the train began to disgorge the young passengers, everyone got down to the business of sorting. Each child had a large tag fastened to their coat. Volunteers from various groups shuttled the human cargo.

"Ah, here we go," John said, recognizing the volunteer matron from the Refugee Children's Movement.

The stout woman handed over two boys. "Mr. and Mrs. Armitage. These lads are to go with you."

John thanked her.

"Let's see," Evie said, kneeling and looking from tag to face. "Mortimer and Hector, brothers, I take it?"

The two boys, wide eyed and pink-cheeked each smiled their reply, which was evidently just an acknowledgment of kindness.

"Oh, yes; bruder?" Evie clarified. Heads nodded vigorously. "Mortimer and Hector Silverman."

John noticed the older one, Mortimer, taking his brother's hand. Their eyes remained fastened onto Evie and her reassuring manner.

Their coats and shoes were quality as was each leather suitcase. The boys shifted from foot to foot, lightly colliding shoulders, as if needing some added acknowledgement of the other's presence.

Like a fat goose swimming up river, the matron was parting the crowd, approaching them again. "Mister and Missus Armitage," she huffed. "For you, as well." She deposited two girls, quite a bit younger than the boys. The eldest was carrying a suitcase between them; the youngest was clinging to a doll.

"Lucy Baras." Evie read aloud, down on both knees. Evie's smiling gaze worked wonders on children in need. Young Lucy beamed back with what might be relief.

"And this is my sister, Miriam. She ate one of my sandwiches, but that's okay," Lucy said with well-enunciated seriousness; her accent slight.

"You both speak English?"

"Yes," Miriam replied, giggling at Lucy, as if she were pleased to share her sister's charm with them.

"I've got the last one for this trip." The voice of Gleason Fitzgerald from behind John's shoulder surprised him.

Gleason entered the circle of Armitage charges, carrying a boy with tear-streaked cheeks, whose breathing was yet jagged as if he had only just stopped crying. "Found him in the men's room. I don't know how he got away from the RCM folks, but he did.

John took out his handkerchief and wiped the boy's tears and then his nose.

"I better take him," Evie said, arms outstretched. The child calmed down as Evie held him. "Thank you, Gleason. How nice of you to come." Her tone indicated she too had not expected him here.

"This is a moment in history. Wouldn't miss it for the world." He smiled.

Bertie, March 1939

"You wouldn't," Bertie said, aghast.

"I just might," replied Jiggs. "Opera is boring. I mean it was nice of your mum and dad to have taken us to *La Bohème*. But if Mimi hadn't been a beauty, I would have been snoring away, and the guys will tell you readily enough that I snore like an old bear. If she had looked like a dog, I would have drowned her out royally."

"And gotten thrown out. Now you're playing with me, aren't you? You wouldn't pull such a diabolical prank tonight, not really."

"Why would I pull your leg, old thing?" Jiggs looked dead serious.

Though Bertie was now seventeen, the superiority of those few years Jiggs had over him still dominated their relationship. But for the first time, Bertie became incensed with him. And inklings of doubt over the near-perfection of his "older brother" were becoming uncomfortable. "How can you even think of being so, so—"

"So what? Impertinent, rowdy, ungrateful? I don't think your folks would view it as anything but a little mischief. You can see they have a sense of humor. And I bet they were each of them rather spirited in their youth. We need to have our fun now and then."

Bertie couldn't believe it. "You're trying to wind me up. You can't be serious."

"You'll just have to wait to see what I do or don't do, old thing." Jiggs's smile was as ambiguous as his stated intention. He got up and left the parlor with a book on London's poor laws tucked under his arm. He was now reading law at the University of London.

Jiggs, Eloise and Louise were now of the age that any other orphanage would have set them out on their own. But John and Evie saw their academic potential and allowed them to stay until they obtained their degrees.

The Armitage family had taken the oldest children to *La Bohème* earlier in the season. As much as Bertie loved music, he had again fallen asleep mid-way through the opera. Tonight, Evie was also including Ian and Ewan. Bertie had overheard his mum say to his father: *The children need to be exposed to culture; it's an important part of education.* Bertie had no idea how expensive opera tickets were, but after he had seen the opulence of the Royal Opera House in Covent Garden, he bet his parents were being very generous. This made him all the angrier with Jiggs for even thinking of pulling a prank during *Tristan und Isolde.*

Jiggs returned to the parlor, making a great show of having Eloise on his arm. The two were pretending to be toffs walking into the opera house.

"Oh, Mister Albert Armitage," Eloise said in an affected exaggeration. "How delightful to see you again at the Royal Opera."

Jiggs played along, "Didn't see you at Ascot last year, old chap. You missed a bloody good season."

Eloise elbowed Jiggs. "Don't say *bloody*, Jiggs. It makes you sound common and vulgar."

Bertie was feeling cool toward Jiggs. He was just realizing how people could have a complexity of layers. Gleason had been the impetus for this lesson. The man had too many sides to him. Nonetheless, Bertie tried to warm to his classmates' antics.

"I'm allergic to horses, don't you know," Bertie imitated their inflections. "And I *bloody* well sneezed my nose off the year before." He grinned at Eloise as she gave him an icy glare for his errant adjective.

Meg had always treated her charges very kindly, if not indulgently. After noticing their conversation in the parlor, she brought in to them the tea she had been preparing. "Tea, ladies and gentlemen?"

The three young people settled into regular conversation, and Bertie soon forgot Jiggs's rowdy intentions for the evening.

Eloise said, "I'm surprised they are doing Wagner. Londoners were just about ready to forgive the Germans, well, Wagner, at least, but now with all this talk of aggression in Europe and Neville Chamberlain's unfortunate attempt at appeasement, I wonder if there might not be a little trouble at tonight's performance." Eloise loved to talk as if she were already an adult. Well, theoretically, she was. And Bertie sadly admitted that it would not be long before his "older sister" would be striking out on her own. But she was not as worldly wise as she thought. She had hopes of becoming a journalist. Bertie had recently overheard Jiggs tell her that no newspaper would take her seriously. Jiggs then showed remorse and said that he would help her prepare for any coming interviews.

At Eloise's mention of trouble, Jiggs's eyes brightened. "Trouble, you say? Like a demonstration in Covent Garden? Hmm."

That was when Bertie knew there was no knowing what Jiggs would come up with next.

Jiggs's conversation returned to world news. "Everybody's talking about how wrong Chamberlain has been. Appeasement was a bloody failure. And now look at the mess in Czechoslovakia." A mischievous glint returned to Jiggs's eyes. "Do you really think people will be picketing at Covent Garden?"

"Well, they were doing so outside the *London Times* when I walked past," Eloise said. She had been scoping out the newspaper district on a weekly basis, trying to get up the nerve to walk in and apply for a job. "I guess it's because the *London Times* was favorable toward Chamberlain's position on the matter. Anyway, the conductor tonight is Maestro Bruno von Schweinfurt and I think some of the singers are German, as well."

One of the things Jiggs had hinted at doing tonight was raising a false fire alarm during Act III; then he said he had a better idea. Bertie could only shake his head and hope that his friend would not create any embarrassment for his parents.

After tea, Jiggs and Bertie started poking fun at the name von Schweinfurt with various alternatives and sound effects, chasing Eloise from the room.

It took both the Silver Ghost and the Bentley to transport the Armitage 'family' to Covent Garden. When Bertie alighted along the pillars, he drank in the night air, noticing an energy that refused to be weighted by dampness. Feeling this alive late at night was a not a common experience. He paused to watch posh-looking folks promenading about, cabs and cars lining up. He then heard rhythmic chanting and looked toward the sound. Stationed where the cabbages would be each morning was a handful of people holding up signs, ugly with derogatory slogans about Germans. The little band of demonstrators was making an attempt to dissuade people from going into the performance. Soon, some constables arrived. The chanting subsided. But Bertie was glad he had gotten to see the event. For the first time, he felt as if he were a part of an historic moment.

Jiggs shifted back and forth next to him, his pent-up energy palpable—galvanizing Bertie's thoughts. He vacillated between pressing Jiggs to reveal his supposed plans and simply ignoring him so he could enjoy the show.

"Come, come," said his mother.

Eloise held her head high and looked as snobbish as he had ever seen her. Louise joined her, and they linked arms as they strode in together. Jiggs held out his arm to Bertie and Bertie cuffed him on the shoulder since he couldn't reach his friend's head. Ian and Ewan followed them, and John and Evie coaxed quietly from the rear.

Bertie had seen the world, to a degree, since his first visit with his grandparents, so he could understand how big this first impression could be on Ian and Ewan. Once inside, he turned to see their expressions.

"Ian," Bertie called out in a whispering tone. "Ewan, close your mouths and try to blend in." Bertie smiled at them knowingly. The two boys were hopelessly agog at the marble, gilt and glitter. The boys responded with quick compliance and sheepish grins.

Mortimer Silverman moved about the theater much more comfortably, pleased but accustomed to concert halls.

"Your mum and dad look beautiful tonight," Louise leaned in to Bertie and said. "Such lovely pearls. It's as though they were made for royalty."

Bertie felt proud. His folks did look as though they were on top of the world.

"Where's Gleason?" Eloise asked. "I'd have thought he would have wanted to come to this."

Bertie bristled at the idea. He, for one, was glad Gleason had said he had other plans. "He's at one of his clubs." Bertie knew that they were not the kind of gentleman's clubs that his father would consider. But, of course, Gleason was not a gentleman.

A man dressed like an important member of society said to another, "I wonder what the great Maestro von Schweinfurt thinks of Herr Hitler?"

"No doubt he has performed for him. He conducted at Bayreuth earlier in the season, I know that."

The two men were oblivious of Bertie's presence.

"Ah, but that was before the invasion of Czechoslovakia."

"Do you want me to take you back after the performance to meet him? You can bloody well ask him then."

"Oh, I don't think so."

John and Evie began guiding the children into the auditorium. Ian and Ewan had their mouths open again. Bertie looked around appreciatively, feeling he was an old hand at concert halls and opera houses. The red velvet and gold satin were impressive. Maybe it was because he had been young, but he felt that nothing could compare to Chicago's Orchestra Hall. The group were finally situated in their seats. As the lights were beginning to dim, Bertie looked down the row and locked eyes with Jiggs. His friend's eyebrows danced up and down communicating mischief. *What on earth did Jiggs have in mind?* Or was it all a ruse to trouble him?

Hours later, Bertie could not believe that he stayed awake all the way up to the Liebestode. And he admitted that he was glad his mum had made him study the libretto last week. Isolde was now singing over the corpse of her lover.

How softly and gently he smiles, how sweetly his eyes open.

The poor woman was losing her sense of reality. But Bertie was enjoying the music. Wagner gave such attention to the orchestra, as if it were singing the haunting aria and Isolde were its accompaniment. But her voice was beautiful, so full and rich. Bertie suddenly realized with some shock and admiration that the poor soprano had been singing for five hours and was still going strong.

Do you not feel and see it? Do I alone hear this melody so wondrously…

Bertie was impressed. He looked down the row and saw that the girls were in awe. They had on their romantic eyes, their faces like beaming moons. Ian and Ewan had fallen asleep an hour ago. His mum and dad were holding hands while a tear was streaming down his mum's cheek. And then Bertie noticed Jiggs. He was in love with Eloise! The young man's eyes were fixed on her, the emotion naked on his face.

Afterward, in the lobby, Bertie's siblings were standing together off to the side, allowing John and Evie to chat with acquaintances while a stream of others were working their way out of the building and into their waiting vehicles. Bertie then noticed that Jiggs had Eloise off from the group just enough to be out of hearing distance. He was saying something serious to her. Bertie turned his back on them but little by little edged his way in their direction.

" …It's not that I'm saying no," Eloise said, her pitch higher than usual. "It's just that we both of us need more education. We couldn't support ourselves now. And, well, there's so much to experience. Wouldn't you rather travel first?"

"I want to travel with you at my side."

"It's just not possible now. I'm sorry."

Bertie's face burned with shame and he inched his way back to his family as quickly and as inconspicuously as he could.

He cleared his throat and tried to think of what to say to somebody, to appear as if he were engaged in conversation already.

"So, Ian. What did you think?"

Ian yawned. "It was, uh, amazing and exhausting. I'm ready to go to me bed, I'll tell you that. But I'm glad to have been included. I'll tell you that, too." A lazy smile spread across his freckly face.

Jiggs's disappointment was as evident as Ian's freckles when he returned. Bertie felt sorry for him. Eloise looked pale as she went to Louise and took her arm, replying softly to her question.

Bertie stood next to Jiggs, hoping he could help somehow.

Ewan surprised them all when he said, "I found it interesting that Isolde could just lie down and die of a broken heart like that. Do people really do that?"

Jiggs groaned and made for outside.

Bertie turned at his mother's inquiring look and said, "Jiggs and I'll meet you right outside, mum." And he went after him, dodging and bobbing in the crowd until he came up to Jiggs in the portico.

Bertie simply stood next to him. Their friendship was close enough that no words were necessary. Jiggs put a hand on Bertie's shoulder while wiping away a tear with his other. He sniffed violently and got his breathing under control just as the family was coming through the doors.

"You realize," Jiggs said sardonically, "that you could fit all of *Bohème* in the first act of this thing?" Jiggs's façade was back in place.

Spring in Sussex 1940

"I'm beginning to worry that this was a mistake, John," Evie said. She was leaning forward on the bench, her hands absently flexing and twisting a pair of cotton garden gloves.

The sun-baked earth felt good crumbling between John's fingers and under his knees. It had been blessedly warm for April and the day was beautiful. "There. That's right. Well done, Lucy."

"Ew!" Lucy exclaimed, jerking back from her row of cabbage planting. "A worm!"

"They are a friendly sort, child. Good for the soil." Nonetheless, John picked up the worm in question and placed it in the lawn just outside the newly tilled plot. Lucy eyed it suspiciously for a moment before returning to her work.

After they had moved the children from London, heeding the call to evacuate the young from the city, the Armitages had chosen out of necessity to convert a good portion of the rear lawn at Kirstead Court into a vegetable garden. Cook had her own kitchen garden, one that had served the family for generations, but it was not going to produce enough to feed fifty-two adolescent mouths.

Operation Pied Piper had commenced at the end of last summer. Fearing air attacks by the Germans, the government had arranged this massive endeavor, calling it the "biggest exodus since Moses." They had shifted almost two million children from London as well as from five other major cities. Sadly, the lower classes had been transported like cattle to the country. John and Evie had managed to squeeze all their charges, which they had gathered from both London orphanages, including the Kindertransport children, into the manor home John had inherited from his Uncle George.

The high-pitched voices of Mortimer and Hector rose from under an apple tree and Bernadette the basset hound trudged toward them, her expression resigned, as if she were well aware it was her duty to restore peace. The old dog had returned to Kirstead Court after the death of Aunt Tilly and was lovingly cared for by the staff. Once Bernadette reached the apple tree she sprawled under it, allowing the two boys to forget their differences and give their beloved pet plenty of belly patting and ear scratching.

"I'm sorry. What was that, dear?" John asked.

Evie nodded toward the far corner where Louise and Eloise were planting tomato seedlings Thomas had nurtured in the conservatory. "Lucy, why don't you help Eloise over there?"

Lucy scrambled to her feet and tottered off, tumbling over a row of planted potatoes.

"I was asking," Evie continued, "what if there's a land invasion? We're not all that far from the Channel coast."

It wasn't as if they hadn't talked about this before. In fact, they had been over it many times. But Evie was beginning to worry and fret more than ever. She had nearly gone into a paroxysm when Bertie announced he was going to remain in London and continue his education while volunteering for the Red Cross as a surgeon. John had overheard her giving Gerard impassioned instructions about keeping an eye on their son.

"Early days yet." John stood and stretched, hearing his back pop with the effort. "We are, on the other hand, not all that close to the coast. We're practically in Surrey."

"I'm wondering whether we shouldn't be looking for a place in Scotland."

"For this household?" He slid next to her on the bench and placed his arm around her tensed shoulders. "Don't worry, love. The Hun has all he can handle on the continent at the moment."

He stroked her hair and slid his fingers down the back of her lovely neck, hoping she couldn't sense the tension deep inside him. Her concerns, he was afraid, were legitimate. News of the collapsing French defenses continued to come over the wireless.

Chapter Twenty-Six

1940 Bertie

This wasn't how Bertie had expected to spend the nineteenth year of his life. Instead of enjoying complete immersion in the college experience, his routine and curriculum had exploded into dire fragments. Emergency medical training had replaced his music and psychology classes, and much of what had been allocated as social time was now occupied with shifts at the Red Cross emergency centers. All of this was due to the inconvenient occurrence of Hitler's Blitz.

"You think Gleason finagled his way out of London and into Kirstead Court?" Helen asked. They sat in the dim light of Ink's, a dingy coffee house near Kings College. "I don't see a problem. After all, he is their music teacher."

"He's in charge of Lambeth House and is also fiscal overseer of both properties. For months he's been talking as if he owns them both." Bertie's feet tapped under the table like rain on a tin roof. "All of a sudden his talents are needed more in Sussex?"

"But Lambeth House is all closed up for now. It's only natural he should go with your family and the children out of London."

The two light bulbs that hadn't yet burned out sent all their dim luminance toward the smooth blonde waves of Helen's hair, spotlighting her as if she were the only ornament in Ink's Café. Bertie had always viewed Helen Lennox as a sibling, the same as all the other Armitage House children, but moments of breathless excitement were arising of late. He wasn't unaware of his bloom into masculinity. In the past year, he had both worked out and filled out, growing two inches taller, and although his voice had changed a few years ago, he was now a definite baritone.

Bertie gathered their books and his thoughts, then rose with an effort. "We'd better start heading back or we'll be late for class."

The sky had been a relentless stretch of dreary gray of late. Even so, Bertie had to squint, adjusting to the comparative brightness after Ink's. The air constantly smelled of smoke these days, occasionally acrid, and it was highly noticeable as they walked past what had once been a fashionable row of terrace flats. Every one of them had been destroyed in the last raid.

Helen tucked her arm in his. "How are we ever going to put London back together again?"

"We are not 'all the king's men'." He saw her smile, which pleased him. Recalling the history behind the age-old nursery rhyme, he added, "Though all this is immeasurably worse than the war between royalists and parliamentarians."

The school loomed up ahead, bringing his mind back to the earlier conversation regarding Gleason. "Adam and Meg are from Kirstead Court. They wanted to go back in the worst way. On the other hand, Gleason's not a family man. He may never be. He should have stayed back to watch over Islington."

"Well, seeing how he's not your favorite, and you're here—"

"To the consternation of Mother," he interjected.

"Hmm. Well … I, for one, am glad you stayed." She gave him a sidelong glance. "But you might be more critical of Gleason than he deserves. And you get on so well with Adam."

Bertie shrugged it off and opened the south entrance door of their school for her. They had made it halfway down the hall before a familiar, horrific wail from outside froze them in their tracks. The urgent release of the air raid siren sliced through the area, jarring Bertie's senses, as did the resulting pandemonium in the hallway. Students and teachers flooded from classrooms, heading for the shelter.

Bertie pulled Helen along the wall, out of the rushing flow. "Do you want to go for shelter, or go out and watch?" he asked, reading her eyes.

She grinned conspiratorially. "Let's go watch."

Before they could get to the exit, a heavy drone growled through the sky, angrier with every breath until it was so loud it drowned out the siren. As Bertie stepped into the courtyard, the drone turned into a roar, taking his breath away. He looked up and watched wave after wave of Dorniers and Heinkels fly past, along with buzzing clouds of Messerschmitts. Like many young Britons, Bertie had learned about German planes early in the Blitz. If this had been merely an air show, it would have been exhilarating. It was even now, though it was a display heavy with dread. He grabbed Helen's hand, tugging her just inside the door.

Then came the awful screams of bombs hurtling down in their vicinity, followed by explosions. Clouds of debris and black smoke shot up to the east and the blare of the siren shrieked on.

"We'd better get to Lambeth," he said.

Bertie needed to be at the emergency shelter, ready to receive the injured. Helen would run ambulance routes once she signed in at the same center. They ran down the street and hopped into his parked Morris. Bertie slammed his foot on the accelerator, but when he rounded a corner he had to swerve to avoid a bomb crater. Auxiliary Fire Service vehicles, formerly London taxis, raced past them in the other direction, heading toward the burning buildings.

As they drew close to the medical center they could see people were already bringing in the injured, the walking wounded leaning on friends, family, and strangers. A man, eyes wide with desperation, carried a child in his arms, the little body mottled with blood and dirt. Without a word, Bertie and Helen hopped out of the car and headed in.

After a quick count of the medics on hand, Bertie ran down the hall and into the locker room. He threw open his locker and donned the surgical smock over his clothes, scrubbed his hands, and headed for the surgery rooms. As a student and volunteer, only the minor burn cases and patients with broken limbs were channeled to him, but there were always plenty of those after a raid like today's.

His first casualty was a frail old woman with a broken arm. "I tried to make it to the shelter," she said, her voice croaking with effort. "I'm just too slow. The explosion was a street or two over, but it lifted me up and threw me down."

The little lady, her French accent evident, tried to roll up her sleeve, but Bertie gently took charge and began his inspection. She smiled in a grandmotherly way at him between winces of pain.

"I'm sorry to put you through such trouble, mon ami."

Bertie puffed out his chest and gave her a boyish grin. "I'm at your service, mademoiselle. No trouble at all. Now, let's put this right, shall we?"

Her pale complexion reddened slightly at the term mademoiselle. She seemed delighted to be seen as something other than just a bothersome old woman. Another volunteer held her in place while Bertie snapped her brittle bone back in place, but she remained conscious and let out a shaky breath as he worked with the splint and bandages.

He straightened and smiled again. "There you are."

She blinked prettily through rheumy eyes and he wondered if at one point she might have been beautiful. "Thank you, young man," she said. With help from the volunteer she walked out, her pace slow but steady.

Several cases later he stood at a sink, torn between fascination and horror as water ran over his bloodied hands. He supposed he should be relieved. He hadn't lost a patient this time, but it had been close. The last head wound had been a bloody mess.

After his hands and arms were clean he stripped to the waist and sponged himself, wiping off his own drying sweat as well as the blood that had seeped through his apron. After dressing, he stepped out of the locker room and was pleased to see Helen was there, leaning against the opposite wall.

"The sun's going down soon," she said.

"Do you want to survey the damage?"

She nodded. They left the medical center and headed for Lambeth Armitage House, which had a well-situated roof top. The area outside was coming back to life with subdued activity. Some residents stepped out and stood warily in shadows while others shuffled, heavy-footed, through the devastated streets, offering neither a word nor a gesture.

"We'll leave the car here for now," he said. "Who knows if the next few blocks are even passable."

Bertie tried to drink in the coolness of the evening air, but when he inhaled he choked on drifting smoke and dust. They walked down the brick lane, past the cobbler shop, and Bertie felt a pang of sadness when he heard children whimpering in the back garden of a nearby house. Their little sounds were answered by the voice of their mother, gently shushing and reassuring them.

At the closed up orphanage, Bertie unlocked the main door and ushered Helen into the hall, then turned and locked it behind them before climbing the stairs. Once they were on the top floor they walked through the boys' dormitory, the leather soles of their shoes loud on the wooden floor. He lifted one of the dark curtains and opened the large window, then crawled out onto a stretch of flat roof, followed by Helen.

Bertie, under his father's oversight, had installed the railings himself when an adolescent. He gestured for Helen to sit next to him. His right shoulder pushed against the wrought iron when Helen settled close, her shapely body leaning against his. Ripples of exhilaration subsided, however, as he looked out over the devastation.

From there they could see the four huge chimneys of Battersea Power Station, the railway lines and goods yards of Vauxhall, all huddling under an umbrella of black smoke. In the pink light of the setting sun, the grays of the vista darkened, looking mournful. The docks, tar distilleries, and warehouses were frequent targets of these attacks and a number of historic gems throughout the city had been lost as well. Nothing was sacred or safe.

"Father is going to let the Joint War Organization use this building soon. They'll be needing more space to house the injured."

"I thought he was going to let the Red Cross use the building," Helen said, watching his expression.

"Well, that's what it is, actually. The Red Cross and the Order of St John combined their efforts for the war, hence their name: the Joint War Organization."

"Oh." She smiled at him, her expression saying he was the most brilliant of men. She lifted her hand and rested it on his knee, surprising Bertie. Excitement flooded his senses, leaving him unexpectedly breathless.

Bertie suddenly tensed for another reason. A set of slow, steady footsteps advanced in the dorm room behind the curtain. Alarm replaced enthrallment. Helen's eyes widened at hearing the approach. He was sure he had locked the door. He was about to get up when the curtain lifted. Gerard poked his large head through the window and smiled.

"Should be getting back, Master Bertie," the butler said, his words brightened by barely disguised mirth.

Bertie felt like a child caught out rather than a medical man who had just treated the injured. He could only shrug before Gerard's pointed stare. His mum's servant of choice was doing his job well.

"Yes, of course," Bertie said, his words slightly hollow. "We were just looking at the view."

He hadn't intended any designs on the fair maid at his side, despite what Gerard's attentions intimated. But when he glanced at Helen and read her disappointed expression, he realized she'd had her own plans.

This knowledge both excited and concerned him. His face burning and his mind awhirl, he turned toward Gerard and bowed his head, following the butler through the open window.

Bringing up the rear, Helen murmured, "Yep. Just looking at the view."

Chapter Twenty-Seven

Bertie sat alone in the large, empty dining room. Dust motes drifted in shafts of light before the large windows, their golden hues brightening as the sky finally cleared. He was absently tucking into his porridge when Gerard appeared.

"Excuse me, Master Bertie." The butler's sudden arrival jarred him completely awake, as usual. "Did I startle yer—I mean, you, Master Bertie? I apologize. My new shoes are so fine, I feel like I'm walkin' on air." He smiled with a mischievous glint, his eyes clearly referencing the episode at the orphanage from the night before.

Bertie touched the napkin to his lips, masking his smile. "Good morning, Gerard."

"Adam called before breakfast. He asked me to send you—I mean, if you'd be so kind—to see if you might meet him at Kensington Gardens at half-past eleven. I only need to inform him if you are unable to meet him."

"It's a fine day for the gardens. No need, Gerard. I'll see him."

Strolling toward Knightsbridge, Bertie breathed in fragrant summer flowers, enjoying the long absent warmth of the sun. The sunshine seemed incongruous in view of the sandbags piled at doorways, and windows taped against bomb blasts, but how nice to feel it again. He removed his hat and walked the rest of the way, enjoying the warm breeze as it tickled his scalp.

At Hyde Park, he turned left, eventually passing Royal Albert Hall. When he reached Kensington Gardens, he noticed Adam waiting for him. Fortunately, they both viewed this entrance as the main gate, even though others seemed more imposing. In days past, the whole Islington House group occasionally had made a day of it at the gardens. Those were happy times. Safe times.

"Hail to the chief," Bertie called, saluting Adam.

Adam thanked him for being both obliging and prompt. They fell into step, the sounds of London dulled by lawn and shrubbery until it dropped to a hum. The familiar avenues of trees and wide-open lawns were comforting, as was the sight of the small, brick palace of Kensington.

Adam broke into his thoughts. "I'll be frank, Bertie." His tone was good-natured, but it took a few more steps before Bertie's older brother figure said anything further, let alone got to the point. Bertie was content to wait.

"When I was your age," Adam finally said, "I hadn't always handled well the matter of women." Bertie was aware of the effort Adam put into speaking and grammar. The man's shortcomings somehow made him more human, more approachable. "I just need to say to you, uh, as a brother would," he continued, though stalling badly, "that you simply can't underestimate the visceral power that can arise between a man and a woman."

Bernie stifled both a smile and the impulse to compliment Adam's vocabulary. "I'm listening," he said.

Surprise lightened Adam's features, as if he had expected resistance. The men walked on, reminded of the war by the appearance of an anti-aircraft gun and some trenches dug here and there. It hardly seemed possible that all this violence and destruction had occurred here in London, the Throne of the Empire.

"Whether you are interested in Helen or not," Adam said, taking a few more steps and carefully considering each word, "or just women in general, I want to give you a bit of advice."

Bertie felt sorry for Adam, seeing him struggle to discuss such a delicate subject. "You don't have to worry about careful wording for me, Adam. I won't get offended."

Adam came to a standstill, his stern features creased with concentration. He stood in front of the Peter Pan statue, arms raised as he sought his words, creating the illusion that Pan was the man's shadow. "Bertie," he finally declared, "you have to know that when you start with hand-holding and kissing women, something takes over. It's a power like you'd never know otherwise."

Slightly embarrassed at the topic, Bertie only chuckled.

But Adam wasn't joking around. "Please take me seriously, Bertie. The point is you have to save yourself for your future wife. Now, I'm not a religious man, but I have learned a few things from experience. You'll be a happier man if you wait."

Bertie nodded. "I think you're right, Adam. And I would never want to disappoint my parents, or you, or Gerard. I have no intentions—"

"I'm not saying you have bad intentions. The thing is, you don't need any intentions. Things can just escalate when you're not looking."

They walked into Hyde Park and talked the matter to completion. Bertie thanked Adam and offered to take him out for a pint at the *Bull and Rose*. Adam, apparently satisfied his message had been sufficiently delivered, accepted the invitation.

That night the hateful wailing of the sirens woke Bertie, chilling him through. He leaped out of bed and ran toward the stairs, almost colliding with Gerard, who was bounding up, moving like a locomotive.

"Come, Master Bertie."

They proceeded downstairs and into the butler's pantry below the servants' stairs. Cook huddled on the floor in the corner, faded housecoat over her nightgown, cap on her head, wringing her hands with dismay.

"Oh, Master Bertie, this is bloody awful, if you'll pardon me for saying so." She had the light on, since the room had no window which might risk their exposure. Her eyes were wide with worry. "Bloody awful," she repeated with relish. "Those blasted Germans."

Bertie slid down the wall and sat beside her, taking her hand in his. Gerard squatted, then settled on the floor nearby, his fingers drumming a tattoo on his crossed arms while they waited for the planes to disappear into the night. The drone, the whistling screams of bombs raining on London, and the crashing explosions went on and on. This time nothing sounded too close, thank heaven. As the drone of engines diminished, Gerard got up and unlocked the servants' liquor cabinet, then poured a stiff brandy for each of them.

Bertie took a long sip and leaned against the wall. He thought about the buildings around the city, collapsing under the onslaught, pinning and killing innocent people. He reflected on the people in his life: Helen, Adam, Gerard, and now Cook, among others, and felt grateful for their presence, realizing how important people were to him. After his second brandy, he surprised Cook and Gerard by giving each a kiss on the cheek before he wandered back up to bed.

Chapter Twenty-Eight

1948 Armitage House, Inc.

Chicago looked as if it would make a fine headquarters for their company. At the age of fifty-three, John and Evie, along with Bertie, moved to America. Having Franklin on hand to establish all the legal rigmarole was helpful.

Since the Stock Market Crash of '29, John had been reluctant to sell any of his real estate. He felt the Mayfair House was a secure asset for the time being. They kept Kirstead Court because they loved it. And of course they kept both Islington and Lambeth Armitage House Orphanages. In Chicago, they bought a brownstone on Elm Street. The leafy Gold Coast neighborhood sat attractively near the lakefront and Lincoln Park, allowing John a pleasant stroll along Michigan Avenue to his office at 322 West Erie Street.

The charitable organization, Armitage House, Inc., occupied the top five stories of the property. The liquidation of the last of Irina Belovskaya's jewels covered much of the purchase price of the twenty-story office building. Who would ever have imagined that this art deco Midwestern building would have a link to Czarist Russia?

"There's a letter from Eloise on the sideboard," Evie told John when he got home. "I'll get it for you."

She handed it to him then proceeded to tell him all that was in the letter: Eloise was working on a novel; Louise was enjoying her teaching position in the East End; Mortimer and Hector had been allowed British citizenship; Helen was engaged to a Belgian with a medical practice in Soho—"I wonder what Bertie will say?"; Jiggs was enjoying teaching law at London University and he was finally going by the name of Geoffrey, at least on campus.

"But the most exciting news is that Eloise and Jiggs are getting married next week. I wish we could go, but the timing is bad."

The next day, just before luncheon, another envelope arrived, this time from Meg and Adam. Evie brought it to the dining table to share it with John and opened it with her usual eagerness. But, her smile faded quickly.

"Oh, no," she said, reading rapidly down the page. She tugged a handkerchief from her dress pocket and dabbed at her eyes. "They got word about Ian confirming their worst fears: he was killed in action at the end of the war."

"Oh, poor lad." John's stomach knotted. He felt suddenly weary. "I will always remember him, with his lazy smile and freckles. What an awful shame. I'll break the news to Bertie."

That evening John, Evie, and Bertie toasted the life of Ian Scroggins. After dinner, they talked and reminisced late into the night.

Chapter Twenty-Nine

1950 Chicago

"Thank you, Mr. Arwardy. This is great. I've been so busy setting up my practice I haven't had a chance to get to know the city well enough."

Melvin Arwardy gave Bertie a kind smile. "Your mother said as much. It's no trouble at all," he said. "Glad to show off my hometown when I can. The missus is playing bridge tonight and I thought, 'We can't have a young man move into town without a proper introduction to the Loop.'"

Bertie nodded. "Well, I sure am grateful, Mr. Arwardy."

"Please. Call me Melvin."

Mr. Arwardy, one of the middle-aged executives of his parents' company, still kept his hair cut in military style. He was a kindly man with old-fashioned manners, which helped Bertie feel at home.

A breeze chilled Bertie's face as the two men, each in cashmere topcoats, strolled amongst window shoppers and theatergoers under glittering marquees and city lights. Despite the chill, it was a lovely evening. Arwardy puffed on a fine Cuban cigar while Bertie sized up skyscrapers and busy side streets.

"Everything is so much bigger and newer here. Somehow, it's more vibrant than London. Your Windy City definitely has *la joie de vivre*."

Arwardy gave a cheerful nod. "Over there you can see the Chicago Theater." He pointed to its brilliant marquee, though he didn't need to, since it was larger than life. "*Killer Diller*. Now that's a fun film. The King Cole Trio plays in that."

Bertie lifted his brow in question and the older man frowned. "Nat King Cole? Never heard of him?"

"No. Must be good, eh?"

"A real class act. Hey, if you'd like to try real Chicago blues we could take in *Big Time Betty's*, about a mile down. Great nightclub."

"Sounds like fun. If you're game so am I."

Once they were south of Marshall Field's, the crowd and its accompanying noise diminished enough that they could talk without raising their voices. Only the intermittent clankings and rumblings of the L intruded on their conversation.

"I hear you're moving into Lincoln Park," Arwardy said pleasantly. His weighted tone suggested he had some knowledge of Evie's feelings on the matter.

"Ah, yes."

They stopped at Adams Street, waiting for the traffic light to change. A number of people stood at their elbows and more came up from behind. As if drawn by a magnetic force, Bertie's attention was pulled to his right where he noticed two young women, decked out for nightlife. They were talking in low tones and instead of facing the crosswalk, their eyes were locked on him. He glanced at Arwardy, who gave him a knowing smile. Acknowledging this shared bit of nothing with his companion, Bertie shifted his gaze so that it took in the traffic down State Street. He could see blazing neon lights ahead. If they belonged to *Big Time Betty's*, he figured they had a block and a half to go.

The light changed, but the Adams Street traffic was not ready to relinquish right-of-way. Horns blared, traffic snarled to a stop and the waiting pedestrians stepped off the curb, weaving their way through the fuming mayhem. Bertie and Melvin were herded and jostled for half a block before the crowd thinned to a more comfortable number again.

Arwardy slid Bertie a sideways glance. "Made any new friends here yet?" His implication was as clear as *Big Betty's* neon. Arwardy released a pleasant puff from his cigar, letting its vapor hang just above in the crisp, still air.

"I'm afraid in some arenas, Mr. Arwardy—I mean, Melvin, I am rather a perfectionist." After a few silent steps, he added amicably, "But I hear 'hope is an anchor for the soul.'"

The men entered *Betty's*, and Bertie needed a moment to make sense of everything going on around him. Though undeniably catering to the city's black inhabitants, *Betty's* apparently welcomed all races and social levels. The real diversity, however, was in the dressing of the place, including the *maître d'*, a large Latin-blooded man with a gleaming smile and a bloody awful French accent.

"Welcome, welcome, messieurs!" The man's hands, huge and hairy, gestured with flamboyance. "I am Alfonso and I am at your service. Welcome to *Madame Betty's*. Shirley here will check in your coats, yes?" He directed them toward a cute, redheaded girl behind the coat-check

Dutch door. While Bertie slipped out of his topcoat, a rush of night air ushered in four businessmen and prompted Alfonso to start up again. *Ah, welcome, welcome, messieurs …*

As the redhead handed Bertie his coat-check tag, she leant over the half door and whispered, "My name's Lucille. He can't keep us straight, that Alfonso." She winked at Bertie then took Arwardy's coat.

As the businessmen behind them dealt with Lucille, Alfonso's paw swept around and touched the back of Bertie's shoulder. "This way, *mon ami*," he said, including Arwardy with a nod, and guided them into the main room.

Passing through the dim light and smoky haze, they walked past Grecian urns, an Italianate mural, and a magnificent bar frame lit up by Christmas lights. The front of the bar had its own decorations: a line of women perched on barstools along its length, all of them rouged and of dubious character. Bertie and Arwardy followed Alfonso through an archway and into the main room.

A sea of candlelit tables, most of which appeared to be occupied, formed a semicircle to the stage. A hazy spotlight shone upon a woman giving what Bertie considered to be a fair Irish Billie Holiday impersonation. Her red hair, adorned with a white gardenia, was even brighter than Lucille's, startlingly vivid against the bosomy lass' black gown. *Lover man, oh where can you be?* The men at the piano, bass, and drums were black, and were doing a first-rate job with the song.

"Here we go, messieurs, our last table at the moment. Near the stage, all for you." Alfonso waited while Bertie and Arwardy slid into a tufted naugahyde booth, then gently draped a linen napkin over each lap. "Lucille, she will wait on you momentarily. *Bon appetit.*"

Bertie perused the mixed crowd, commenting on how pleasant the atmosphere was.

Arwardy leaned in and said discreetly, "Chicago is a very segregated city. But here at *Betty's*, and in a few other clubs, no one cares. They barely even notice. Blues is for everyone."

A middle-aged waitress approached the table and smiled blandly at them. "Good evening, gentlemen. My name is Shirley. Are we having dinner or just drinks tonight?"

Bertie wanted to laugh at Alfonso's consistency in mixing up the women's names, but he stifled the urge. Arwardy answered for them, asking Shirley for a bowl of nuts to go with their drinks.

"I'll start with a Coca-Cola," Bertie put in.

After she left for the bar, he leaned back to savor the music. The vocalist, her voice like velvet, looked as if she were singing just to him. *The night is cold and I'm so alone. I'd give my soul just to call you my own. Got a moon above me. But no one to love me.*

Bertie tried to ignore the burning sensation rising rapidly up his neck and into his face, but couldn't help confessing to Arwardy. "I don't know what it is, but there's something about Chicago that's making me feel ... I don't know. As if everyone wishes to marry me off or something." He was relieved to see understanding in Arwardy's eyes.

"Perhaps America is just a bit more forward than Britain is." Arwardy shrugged. "Or, maybe being new in a town, instead of where we have roots, it makes us more aware of this kind of thing."

Shirley returned, served their drinks and discreetly moved on.

Bertie raised his Coke in salute. "You're a sage man, Melvin."

For a moment Bertie considered explaining to Arwardy how university, a world war, more education, then a trans-Atlantic move had all played a hand in delaying his love life. Instead, he quashed his self-consciousness and made a determined effort to be a good companion to his host.

"Tell me about how you came to work at Armitage House," he said.

Arwardy downplayed anything to his credit and mostly discussed how the company had grown, how it was now ranking along with Community Chest and even UNICEF, in accomplishing fine things for disadvantaged children.

"What I like about your mother, Bertie, is how she seems to flit from one department to another in a way that's never intrusive."

Bertie took a sip of his drink, then smiled wryly. "Mother is never, or at least rarely, dogmatic, unless she's talking to me. Bless her. I can just imagine her in my father's office: 'Dear, don't you think it might be advantageous if Mr. A were to assist Mr. B here? Darling, what do you think about ...' So you see, Melvin, I feel especially victorious having won the war over getting my own place. And there were no casualties whatever."

Arwardy chuckled. "Your mother is adored by executive vice presidents and office staff alike. So is your father."

The information Arwardy went on to share over the next couple of hours cleared up some of the questions Bertie'd had about the company's latest ventures. He knew they were planning to establish themselves in war-ravaged Europe, as UNICEF had initiated, but he hadn't been aware of the possible goals, such as expanding into Africa, India and Mexico.

Bertie, now comfortably settled and sipping a decent brandy, enjoyed Arwardy's conversation while a solo guitarist performed Spanish songs in the background. At the end of the evening Arwardy left a tip on the table for Shirley while Bertie peered through the archway. He could see a ruckus had broken out in the lobby and discovered Alfonso, apparently doubling as the bouncer. The *maître d'* had no trouble removing the soused and rowdy customer, efficiently accompanying him out onto State Street. Bertie and Arwardy crossed the main floor, zigzagging around occupied tables and listening to a jazz quartet blare a fast, rhythmic piece behind them. When they stepped into the relatively peaceful lobby, Alfonso was dusting off his hands.

Arwardy conversed with the *maître d'* while Bertie went to get their coats, winking at Lucille as he placed her tip on top of the Dutch door ledge. He handed Arwardy his coat then struggled with his own. Alfonso nimbly leapt to aid Bertie, holding the cashmere collar, straightening the shoulders.

"Ah, there you go, *mon ami*. Perhaps you'll visit us again at *Madame Betty's*."

Bertie thanked him and stepped into the night air with Arwardy.

Alfonso's large head followed them around the door. "Oh, and *mon ami*, *Madame Betty's* is a good place to find love. Maybe next time, eh? Good night."

Arwardy laughed out loud, clapping Bertie on the shoulder, and opened the door to a waiting cab.

The next morning over coffee, Bertie reviewed some of his conversation with Arwardy. *A place like Betty's,* he had said, *can be better than a session with a shrink. Somehow, it takes you outside of yourself and lifts you up. It's interesting, considering the blues is...about the blues. I don't know. Somehow when I leave there, my future looks brighter.*

He had to admit that was how he felt as well. It wasn't just the music, it was the whole package. Even, if not primarily, the encounter with a character like Alfonso.

Bertie had purposely avoided one topic over the duration of the evening: Gleason Fitzgerald. To Bertie's annoyance, Gleason had convinced his parents to sponsor him into the country and allow him to join the firm. The man had always been too ambitious for Bertie's liking. No one could ever accuse Gleason of being lazy. His mind was in a constant whirl, creating and executing his own agendas. Many would defend Gleason, Bertie knew, saying he was only intent on doing his part in improving the charitable organization.

But he made Bertie uneasy.

As Gleason settled in, he often succeeded in worming his way into the family's circle, as well as into anyone's company who had position or pull in Armitage House, Inc. At fundraising dinners and galas, Gleason's constant attempts at being cynosure reminded Bertie of the first recital at Islington Armitage House, when his father had afterward chastised him for referring to Gleason as "the belle of the ball."

The hum of the kitchen clock reined Bertie back to the present. He was late for his job at the Skokie Clinic. Gobbling some toast on his way out, he smiled. He could forget all about Gleason. The walk-in patients from the area almost always made his work a pleasure.

He ran out the front door and into the morning air, breathing in the freshness of Lake Michigan, then hopped into his '48 Nash, parked at the curb.

Getting his first American car had been an experience. He was used to his little Morris, left at the Mayfair house. The car, with its 121-inch wheelbase and unbelievable width, had him initially feeling like a boy maneuvering a tank. After he'd bought it and pulled off the lot, he could hardly tell whether he was within his own lane of traffic. By the end of the day though, he'd gotten familiar with the car's dimensions and took great pleasure in cruising about, exploring Chicago.

Chapter Thirty

1952

State Street's bright lights were great for a night time outing, but walking along Maxwell Street on a Sunday afternoon held equal appeal. Bertie often drove his Nash to the west side then enjoyed a stroll through the Maxwell Street Market. Located in the shadows just southwest of the Loop's skyscrapers, the place drew vendors who sold anything from chopsticks to silver, from shoestrings to men's suits. On the weekends, particularly on Sundays, Maxwell Street and Jefferson Street were lined with folding tables, kiosks, even blankets on the ground, all displaying goods tended and perused by folks of varied ethnic backgrounds. It was a regular United Nations. When he had first discovered the place, he sensed he was looking into the soul of Chicago.

The west side had initially been populated with Russians, and Bertie understood the language. His first mother had been bilingual, and of course Evie was, too. Both had encouraged him to keep up his Russian. His pronunciation was sloppy, he knew. A Russian-born girl in Skokie had once said his accent was dreadful. But he managed to negotiate purchases and ask girls out in either language.

Bertie stepped out of the Nash and shut the door behind him, tugging up his collar for added warmth. For the middle of May, the temperatures were cool. He'd seen the first few tables on this stretch of Maxwell Street before and knew they were always run by the same Russian families. At the second table Bertie decided to buy a Star of David pendant on a gold chain, though he hadn't been raised with religion. Years before, Evie had read Milton's Paradise Regained to him, and that had been his only brush with anything spiritual.

His Jewish birthmother could have factored into his buying decision, but it didn't hurt that the seller of the pendant was an attractive young woman. She had nice eyes and when their gaze locked he knew he couldn't leave her table without buying something. Assuming she was a Russian Jew, he asked in Russian how much the pendant cost. She answered, apparently amused by him, and he handed over the cash.

Bertie stood in the shade of the building just off the sidewalk, purposely fumbling with the clasp, and eliciting the response for which he had hoped. She came from behind the table, took the clasp in her hand and draped the pendant and chain around his neck. Soon she was just behind him, fastening it just beneath his hairline. Her fingertips felt cool and soft.

"Thank you," he said in Russian as she returned to her place behind the table. "You have nice hands."

She laughed, slightly self-conscious. In English she said, "Your Russian is terrible. I mean…I mean your accent is."

He was relieved to switch back to English. "My friends call me Bertie. What's your name?"

"It doesn't matter, Dr. Armitage." She tilted her head, her eyes alight with laughter. "Bertie is a nice name, but I'm already married."

How did she know his name? He frowned. "Have you been to the Skokie Clinic?" He wanted to keep her talking. While she might think his accent was bad, he found her accent charming.

"My brother works there. He's an orderly." She shrugged, again self-conscious. "I've been there to see him."

"I see. Well, in any case, madam, thank you for your assistance." He touched the chain around his neck and gave her a small smile. "It was nice meeting you …"

"Mrs. Levin," she said finally, the curl of her smile slightly apologetic.

He bowed his head slightly and gave her an answering smile. "It was nice meeting you, Mrs. Levin."

He continued down Maxwell Street, trying to ignore the pang of disappointment eating away at him. He walked from the shade into the sun, but loneliness clung to him like a shirt in the rain. With a sigh he scanned the bustling market area, trying to cheer himself with the knowledge that he was alive and enjoying the diversity of this American city. He'd find a girl soon enough.

Bertie strode past a cluster of pudgy men puffing on cigars and selling various tobacco products. Once he had left their stall behind and the air was clear, he enjoyed a different aroma wafting from a place called *Guido's Eats*. Not an extremely imaginative advertiser, Bertie thought, but with location and good cooking, who needed advertising?

The tantalizing aromas of Italian beef sandwiches and other Italian-American delectables almost seduced him, but he kept on despite his growling stomach.

A little farther on Bertie heard what he deduced were three different languages coming from between two kiosks, then smiled, watching the handful of folks haranguing with aggressive gestures. One kiosk sold leather goods; the other was a newsstand. But the tenor of the babble seemed jovial enough.

From farther ahead he could hear music and when he listened harder he recognized the blues. A sign out front declared The Creole Four were performing in the shade of *Gabel's*, a store that sold whatever they could get a deal on by the truckload, which made for interesting shopping. The musicians were quite good. Odd, he thought, how even melancholy music could offer a festive air to the market.

He scanned the table of a group of Lithuanians selling books, but since he didn't speak Lithuanian there didn't seem much point in stopping. They weren't getting much action at the moment.

Bertie opened his collar and slipped his new pendant under his shirt. For some reason he wanted to wear it next to his skin.

After passing a bar with a sign advertising Canadian Ace Beer—a beer which he'd nearly spat from his mouth after he'd tasted it last year—he saw a young woman tending a card table of women's hair accessories. She smiled boldly at him, openly flirting, but she wasn't his type. He nodded politely and turned back toward his Nash.

Instead of eating at *Guido's*, he stopped by Armitage House to see if his folks would be interested in joining him at a nice pub on Sedgwick where they sold real beer and British fare. They readily agreed.

Sedgwick Pub was owned by a middle-aged woman named Madge Thompkins, whose figure was similar in shape to a dumpling. It was true that she offered decent British fare and Guinness on tap, but her penchant for playing melancholy songs on her jukebox almost had Bertie drinking whisky and singing the blues. He ordered a Guinness and watched Madge wipe down the bar, singing along with Russ Morgan and his orchestra, *You're nobody till somebody loves you. You're nobody till somebody cares.*

Bertie stared into his dark beer. How could he be in one of America's major cities and not find a girlfriend? What was wrong with him?

Evie poured a cup of tea and broke into his thoughts. "Jiggs sent you a letter, dear. He doesn't have your new address. Here's a picture of Eloise and him from their wedding." She reached across the table and handed Bertie the photo, a little curled around the edges since the wedding had occurred two years previous. Jiggs and Bertie had both been negligent about keeping in touch.

"I'm happy for him. Jiggs pined over her for a long time." He studied the snapshot, his smile curving up on one side as he regarded his old friend. "Just look at that scoundrel's smile. They both look really happy."

"Here's the letter that came with it," Evie said, passing it to him.

Reading Jiggs' letter should have brightened his mood. His friend was planning on running for MP for his constituency. Eloise and he were hoping to start a family soon. It was all great news. Bertie pocketed the letter and tucked into his fish and chips, hoping to mask his loneliness with a feigned appetite. He really was happy for Jiggs and Eloise. As he ate, Bertie resolved to keep up better correspondence with his old friends. He also decided to circulate more and make new friends here in America. Hopefully, through doing both of those, he'd find the right girl.

He pushed away his empty plate and stared at his beer glass, drained for the third time. If he had one more beer, he might just break out in song. At the moment Madge was crooning along with Ella, *Blue moon, you saw me standin' alone … without a love of my own.*

Bertie stared at his beer glass a moment longer, then poured himself a cup of tepid tea.

Chapter Thirty-One

John Armitage had always hated bureaucracy. Oftentimes, having to lead his growing charitable organization felt more tedious than fulfilling. While some of his VPs lived and breathed for their next promotion, he had never cared about position. Burton Jones, one of his most effective officers and a man to whom John had often gone for support, had tendered his resignation the other day so that he could jump ship and work for Community Chest. They had offered him higher pay and a clearer chance for advancement. With him gone, the position for Executive Vice President for Media and Public Relations was vacant.

John's choice for Burton's replacement rested between two men. The first was Melvin Arwardy, the soft-spoken VP assistant with two degrees, seven years of teaching in Chicago's public school system and three years of handling public relations for Community Chest. The other man was Gleason Fitzgerald. Gleason had no education other than what he had gotten at his British grammar school, but he did have twenty years of loyal service to Armitage House. John didn't know of any other man with as much dynamism and ambition as Gleason.

But ambition wasn't necessarily a good thing for this position. Gleason's predisposition for dishing out flattery was becoming a little too transparent. At one of the fundraisers the previous year the treasurer for Armitage House, Inc. had given a short speech. Afterward, while refilling the man's champagne glass, John heard Gleason praise the treasurer's speech up and down, telling the man's wife how proud she should be of him. At a private dinner the following week, the man's wife said in confidence to John, "I love my husband very much, but you and I both know he's not a public speaker."

Evie was often in Gleason's court, but this time she seemed indifferent to whichever choice John might make. Her current preoccupation was with opening the new Birnam Learning Center near 79th and Ashland. She spent a lot of time at the center, helping its managing director, Alan Machevich. John was well aware that Evie was determined to make sure no child fell through the cracks. The purpose of these centers was for each student to get the attention needed in order to achieve their potential. For the past two years she had spent one day each week working directly with children, trying to understand those with learning difficulties and finding out how best to offset the different types of handicaps she was discovering.

John called Bertie and asked to meet him at the Tip Top Tap, for a drink after work.

"We can watch the sun go down while we enjoy a whisky," he said, then patted Bertie companionably on the back as they headed to the top of the Allerton Hotel for cocktails. "Gerard is driving Mother up from the south side. She said she'd try to join us in time for dinner."

"How is Gerard? Has he talked about retiring at all?"

"Heavens, no, son. He still sees well and drives well. He only went down the wrong side of the street twice when we first brought him over." John chuckled. "I wish I'd been in the car to see his reaction. Mother said he forgot himself and broke into Cockney, cursing all the drivers who had right-of-way."

They chose a linen-topped table next to a window with a view looking south and west over the city.

John took a sip of his Glenfiddich. "Have you made any trips to Maxwell Street lately?"

"Last week. Great place. It's like a drug I need once a month."

Bertie's hand drifted impulsively to his chest, making a natural movement as if he were going to adjust his tie. Bertie seemed to be stroking something that was hanging under his shirt. John wondered if it was some kind of medical pendant, but he didn't ask. Instead, he asked Bertie about his work then leaned back and drank in everything: the sun setting over the city, the aroma and taste of his whisky, and the sight of his healthy, handsome son talking about his medical practice. Gratitude for life's blessings draped over John. Relaxed and content, he was now ready to bring up the question with which he hoped Bertie could help him.

"I'm wrestling with something, son."

Bertie frowned and focused on his father, looking attentive.

"If you had to choose between Gleason Fitzgerald and Melvin Arwardy for EVP of Media and Public Relations, which would you pick and why?"

Bertie replied without hesitation. "Mr. Arwardy has better qualifications. He's genuine and of unquestionably high moral character. Those characteristics are vital for that position."

"That's all?" John pressed.

"Anything further would be redundant or personal. If you want to know how I feel on a personal level, I respect Mr. Arwardy. I like him much better than Gleason. Hands down."

High heels clicked rapidly on the floor, capturing John's attention. He turned to see Evie entering the lounge, looking chic and youthful in her spring dress suit and pillbox hat. After kissing them both, she took her seat and ordered a gin and tonic. Both men sat back and listened as she enthused about her progress with the learning center and Mr. Machevich.

On the other side of the window city lights sprang to life as the sun's descent quickened. The family finished their cocktails then rode the elevator down, coming out onto Michigan Avenue. They decided to take advantage of the beautiful evening and strolled to *Johnny Nuccio's* for a pleasant dining experience on the town.

Before John Armitage could announce his decision, Gleason held a dinner party at his spacious apartment. He had recently moved to the best part of Ravenswood, which was only blocks away from Bertie's flat. Besides the Armitage family, the only other guests were Mr. and Mrs. Burton Jones, the departing VP, and his wife. When the three Armitages arrived, Gleason explained that the dinner was sort of a goodwill send off.

"To show them we have no ill feelings." A bit too profound, Bertie thought, but that was Gleason. "Besides, in this world of corporate movement, we may get him back someday."

The Burtons arrived and the conversation was polite and airy. The phonograph played various string quartet pieces before the meal and during dinner, offering respite when conversation became awkward. Gleason had made a beautiful duck *à l'orange* along with several side dishes. The host was generous with his libations; they went through three bottles of wine with dinner. For dessert, he was up and about, fussing over a chocolate mousse and snifters of cognac.

At one point, Bertie said, "Nice boots, Gleason."

In reality, he felt embarrassed for Gleason and his odd sense of fashion, but he tried to seem genuinely interested out of good manners. There wasn't a lot he felt comfortable discussing with his former violin teacher. Boots seemed as good a topic for the evening as anything else.

Gleason stood at the kitchen door, looking sheepish. "I couldn't help myself. I have taken a fancy to American cowboy boots. This is alligator skin from the Everglades. I hope to get to sunny Florida someday."

"Well, if and when I marry, I've often thought Florida might make a good honeymoon spot," Bertie said. "You know, Gleason, I've often enjoyed the beach just east of you. Have you tried an evening stroll down there? Few people think to enjoy it except on sunny afternoons, but on a summer's night it's very peaceful. You could almost swear you're in Florida. If it weren't for the lack of palm trees, it would look like a postcard from Miami." Finding himself suddenly the center of attention, Bertie told the group about the old pier he frequented. "Finding places for solitude in a major city is important, I think."

"You've got that right, old boy," Gleason enthused, scurrying around the table with snifters. While serving Evie her cognac, he gushed, "Evie, you are doing such an excellent job with the Birnam Learning Centers. And who is that overseeing 79th and Ashland? A Mr. Machevich? Good fellow."

Before the night was out, Bertie heard Gleason say something to John out of earshot of Burton, about a media idea he had, having something to do with symphony programs.

Two days later John made the announcement that Melvin Arwardy was the new Executive Vice President of Media and Public Relations. Bertie heard that Fitzgerald left the office with a migraine that day and stayed away from work for another day and a half.

Chapter Thirty-Two

1954

"I interviewed a nice teacher today," Evie said.

She and Bertie were enjoying a quiet moment over martinis at the Elm Street brownstone, sitting on the back patio. The early evening June sky was yet a vibrant blue. The breeze smelled of early roses and warmed earth. Even the slight edginess of tar wafting from some distant building site provided a pleasant composite summer sensation.

The patio provided a congenial setting, consisting of herringbone-pattern brick edged with moss, plenty of ivy and a few roses, and all of it surrounded by a tall brick garden wall. The garden had a southern exposure, so it enjoyed sunlight for most of the day. From there they could see the impressive cityscape backdrop, including the top of the Palmolive Building. But at present, Bertie was more intent on reading about yesterday's win by the Cubs.

"Hmm?" Bertie lowered his section of the Tribune's sports section and smiled at his mother. "Uh, that's nice, Mother."

Evie's gaze travelled over the flowers. "She is quite adorable, I think, and intelligent. A committed teacher. She looks like an Italian Audrey Hepburn. And she's about your age." She smiled and sipped her Beefeater and twist.

Bertie set his paper down and leaned forward. "All right, Mother. You have my attention."

"Well, I just thought you might like to meet her." Evie shrugged slightly and flashed him an innocent, wide-eyed smile.

"Lovely and intelligent, you say?"

"A gentle girl. I like her a lot."

He eyed her skeptically. "Well, Mother, from what I understand, men don't usually agree with their mothers on qualifications." Keeping his eyes on Evie, Bertie settled back and sipped his chilled gin. He cleared his throat and tried not to grin, but failed. "How do you propose I meet her?"

"I was thinking of holding a dinner for all our teachers and center managers. In fact, I have one planned for next Friday evening."

Bertie nodded, then shook his head, marveling at his mother's expertise. He crossed his legs and held up his glass in salutation. "You win."

Bertie's parents were always careful not to flaunt their wealth. It was one thing when they were entertaining possible corporate sponsors and friends of their own social class. For these they hosted lavish dinner parties at Elm Street or in Lake Forest with Franklin and Georgette.

However, when they entertained employees, the Armitages tried to show consideration and tact. For that reason the Birnam Learning Center party was held in the Banquet room of *Johnny Nuccio's* on East Delaware Place.

Lately Bertie had noticed Gleason becoming chummy with the EVP of Strategy and Marketing, Reginald Blumenthal, as well as with Blumenthal's assistant, the dour and inappropriately named Miss Lovejoy. As the party ensued, Bertie observed the trio huddling at a corner table and watched as Michael Robinson, a striking but arrogant man who worked in community leadership, joined the group. Bertie sighed, watching Gleason take charge in his ingratiating manner, pouring wine and steering the conversation.

A more festive trio was camped in another corner. This one had been hired by Evie to entertain. The happy ensemble was, at the moment, playing a rhythmic piece that evoked images of the vivacious Carmen Miranda. Conversations and samba beats buzzed around the room and Bertie was almost tempted to turn in his Côtes du Rhône for a fruity rum concoction. He tapped his toes and sipped his wine while waiting for the new teacher, Sofia Gualiardo, to arrive.

Eight teachers and three center managers were present, along with many of the officers and staff of Armitage House, Inc. When Sofia entered the restaurant, Bertie knew it was she. The world could not possibly be fortunate enough to be graced by more than one Italianized Audrey Hepburn. Her dark hair was cut short, in the fashion the actress was wearing this year. Her eyes were even larger and more striking than those of the movie star, something one would not think possible. Her nose was somewhat pronounced, adding an agreeable dramatic flair. Apparently she knew him by sight, for her eyes quickly settled on him and her face lit up with a dazzling smile. She approached.

"Bertie?" she asked. The subtle scent of her perfume and the intensity of her attention almost made him dizzy. "Bertie?" she tried again, looking as if she were trying not to laugh.

He panicked, feeling ridiculous and dimwitted. Bertie cleared his throat and tried to rebound, but could think of nothing to say but, "Sofia."

She nodded patiently, waiting for him to speak.

"Um, well, let's see …" In the back of his mind he heard other people laughing amongst themselves, enjoying the wine and the evening. He spoke on impulse. "How about if I get you a drink and we sit and have a chat? What can I get for you?"

"A Coca-Cola, please."

He swallowed. "Oh, uh, does it bother you if I have a …?" He held up his wine glass, feeling lame.

"Of course not, silly. I'll have wine with dinner. For now I'd just like a Coke."

The musicians were playing a rendition of Mr. Sandman. He headed for the bar and the Chordettes' lyrics sang in Bertie's mind where they pleaded to be sent "a dream". Waiting in line, his face ached from smiling.

He then led Sophia to a table by the window facing Rush Street, and held out her chair. Rain had begun sometime just after Sofia's arrival and the glass pane was dotted with diamond-like drops. Outside, the downpour pelted the sidewalk and street and thunder rumbled, echoing against the downtown buildings.

When Sofia was settled, he sat across from her, then made the mistake of looking into her eyes, thereby losing the ability to think clearly, again. He grinned sheepishly, making jest of his clumsy social skills. She laughed with him and the tension soon eased.

She asked him about growing up in London and about living through the Blitz. He asked her about her college days and first years of teaching. She was more interested in his music than his medical practice. And she seemed completely indifferent to his family's reputation and wealth.

At one point during the evening, Gleason approached the musicians with a request. Soon he stood in front of the band, singing *When Smoke Gets in Your Eyes.* All attention was on the man from Seven

Dials. In the second verse his voice slipped into falsetto as if he were imitating Rosemary Clooney and his audience loved it. He had them all captivated. At the melody's resolution, Bertie felt he was the only one who cringed when Gleason hit a sour note.

Chapter Thirty-Three

John Armitage walked down Michigan Avenue after a quick but delectable Chicago Dog from *Hedda's Hotdogs*, a favorite sidewalk vendor of his, stationed across from Seneca Park. This was Hedda's first year doing business outside of the Loop district, and from what John could see—after waiting in line for several minutes—she would be serving the Gold Coast for many summers to come. Showing a bit of consideration for his fellow board members, he had declined onions, but despite that sacrifice he felt he had enjoyed the best lunch of his week.

He entered the Erie Ave building lobby, feeling at peace with the world. His mother had encouraged him to buy this building because of its elaborate art deco details; she was still agog with the style. Personally, he liked the location.

As always, the elevator attendant took John up to the twentieth floor with quiet dignity. John thanked him, and after leaving the lift he went first to his office to collect his folio, then marched directly down the hall, past the reception desk to the board room.

From outside the frosted glass door he could hear voices raised cheerfully. When he stepped inside, the congenial commotion stopped, but he noticed suppressed excitement on the faces of many of the members. He walked around the large table to sit at its head, aware that people were still smiling, filling the room with positive energy.

Georgette and Evie came in after him. Franklin was not expected to attend. His doctor had encouraged him to avoid all unnecessary stress since diagnosing his heart condition. Both ladies wore Baker Boy berets, dress suits and high heels. His mother had a recent thing for sky blue, while Evie had stuck with her basic black and white. Despite their not having heard the prior commotion, they glanced around curiously, seeking the source of all the smiles. While waiting for the last two members to join them, John noticed that Gleason now wore glasses. The pallid man sported an exaggerated pair with the brow-line in black plastic, flaring out like butterfly wings. Unfortunately, Gleason's eyes were not the sort John cared to see magnified. Before the glasses, they had seemed merely penetrating. Now they looked wild and almost frightening, clearly revealing that he was not among the happy people in the room. Looking around the table again, John noticed the only other dour expressions belonged to Miss Lovejoy, Reginald Blumenthal and Michael Robertson.

John leaned back in his chair, smiling as well, and thinking this would undoubtedly be an interesting afternoon.

The secretary and treasurer scurried in at the last minute and John called the meeting to order. The minutes were read by the breathless secretary, then John asked about any new business. The first hand up was that of Edna Perry, the assistant to the new Executive Vice President of Media and Public Relations. She was a likable older woman who also was sporting new eyewear. She looked almost comical with her Edith Head glasses and jowly jaw. John smiled and called on her.

Miss Perry perched on the end of her chair. "Mr. Arwardy has accomplished something special for Armitage House, Inc.," she announced, playing the role of a fanfare trumpeter, "and for the children it serves."

Her magnified eyes gestured that John should call on Arwardy to elaborate. When he did, the soft-spoken gentleman explained how he had visited the radio booth at Wrigley Field after the last home game. He had met with Jack Brickhouse and later with Cubs manager, Phil Cavarretta, and asked whether they might consider donating free airtime. It took only a day for those two to talk with the owners and get final approval.

Edna Perry was practically in tears as she interjected. "Now tens of thousands will hear about the work Armitage House, Inc. is doing for kids. The common man as well as the big wigs. They'll all be asked to give their support. Just think what this might generate."

She snatched a tissue from her purse and blew her nose loudly while the other board members broke into applause. Evie fished for tissue in her own bottomless purse but Edna came to her rescue and passed out more to any who were softhearted enough to require one. This did not include the moody foursome, who merely applauded politely.

Chapter Thirty-Four

Frank Sinatra's velvet voice crooned from the Nash's radio. *I stand at your gate and the song that I sing is of moonlight. I stand and I wait for the touch of your hand in the June night.* Driving west down Harrison Street, Bertie reached over and held Sofia's hand. He didn't need Frank's encouragement to do this, but the music added the right touch of romance for their evening in Little Italy.

Bertie found a parking spot on Taylor Street in front of a café whose neon sign informed passersby that inside they would find Spaghetti Ravioli Budweiser. He came round the car, opened Sofia's door and held out his hand to assist her, then started to lock the Nash.

"You don't have to worry about that here," she said. "There's more than enough protection here."

He understood she was talking about the Outfit. Although Little Italy was not the base of their operations, this part of town had nurtured many a member in prior decades. Thus the old neighborhood was kept in good order.

And safe it seemed. Sofia was perfectly at ease, saying she wanted to take Bertie on a tour. She took his hand and they turned down a side street lined with narrow homes, row-houses and small apartment buildings, all of which had their windows wide open. Inside the buildings record players churned out Sinatra, Dean Martin or Mario Lanza. Small clusters of women in house dresses sat on the steps of each dwelling, gossiping in low tones. Bertie and Sofia passed a home where a young man, his dark hair slicked back, nuzzled his well-proportioned wife. She wore a dark polka-dotted housedress, her feet and legs were bare. Children played on the street, calling to others at the far end. Bertie thought this was probably the safest street in Chicago.

Perhaps to prove her point, Sofia led him back to Taylor Street via an alley. The setting sun cast a crimson glow across the darkening area, but Bertie could still make out the neatly kept gardens in each backyard. A dog barked and a man yelled at it from inside a house, silencing the sound. Only their footfalls on the concrete and sounds of distant traffic could be heard. Heady aromas of garlic and sauces began to work on his appetite.

Back on Taylor Street, life pulsed with noise and neon lights. Some folks lingered as if they'd already eaten, while others bustled about, seeming anxious to get a good table at their favorite place. Freshly washed cars cruised past, their chrome shining, radios playing softly, and couples inside sitting close to each other.

"Which is your favorite restaurant?" he asked, eager to sit across from her by candlelight. He also didn't think he could ignore the delicious aromas much longer.

She pointed down the street. "Let's try *De Legge's*."

When they entered the dimly lit establishment, it quickly became apparent that Sofia was well known there. She hadn't made reservations, but they were ushered to one of the best tables along the front window. The *maître d'* was a large man with white teeth who smiled a lot. He glanced from Sofia to Bertie with a sense of family connection Bertie was beginning to notice.

Sofia told Bertie she would like a bottle of Chianti. When the waiter appeared and Bertie mentioned this, Sofia interjected in Italian. The waiter nodded slightly, then promptly disappeared on his mission.

Bertie looked into her lovely eyes inquiringly.

She shrugged. "I just asked for a certain brand and year."

Dinner was delicious, every detail cared for as if the whole establishment had gone out of its way to make everything extra special. Sofia carried much of the conversation, he being happy just to watch her. Before dessert, an Italian girl in a short skirt and fancy blouse approached, asking if they would like their picture taken. Sofia beamed her assent. He leaned against her for the pose, his elation as bright as the flash.

After dinner, Sofia led him on another night stroll before taking him to the Italian ice stand. From the alley, the fringes of Taylor Street's colorful neon lighting reflected dimly off garages and trees, turning the alley into a kind of tunnel.

The night was perfect, as was the moment. Frank Sinatra returned to the scene, his voice sailing over the clotheslines from an open window somewhere. Bertie stopped and faced Sofia, admiring how the soft lighting made her features just visible enough to know he'd made the right choice. He put his arms around her waist and bent to kiss her, then lost himself in her warm response. Her arms came up around his neck and her soft fingertips stroked him just below his ear.

The kiss rose to a point of passion and Bertie felt as if he couldn't quench his thirst for her. Then the image of Adam standing in front of the Peter Pan statue at Kensington Gardens came back to him, his 'big brother' lecture echoed in Bertie's mind. Fortunately, he didn't have to take the initiative to slow things down because Sofia's lips pulled from his.

She took a deep breath and smiled. "I'm a good girl," she whispered. Her hand pushed against his chest just enough to indicate the need to break the spell.

"That's one of the reasons I'm in love with you." His words came easily.

Her eyes lit up and her lips brushed his cheek. "We'd better get that Italian ice," she suggested.

"We'd better."

Chapter Thirty-Five

John knew Gleason was enraged over Arwardy's appointment. It would not be an easy meeting. John had almost come to enjoy conducting board meetings, as if he were the captain of a ship with a loyal crew. But nowadays tension filled the room at every turn. Ideas proposed by anyone close to John and Evie were voted down by those in Gleason's camp, and that camp seemed to be growing. Gleason, Michael Robertson, Miss Lovejoy, and Alan Blumenthal had been joined by board members Mr. and Mrs. Innitzer and Grace Andrews.

A number of things about Gleason had been concerning John lately. For one, he'd heard that Gleason had been giving dinner parties, and John sensed these had a mutinous air about them. So when Edna Perry asked to talk privately with John, he was not surprised to hear her say that it was about a confidential but alarming matter. Before Edna closed his office door, she glanced down the hall like a nervous hen, and practically tiptoed to the chair across from his desk.

She leaned forward, her eyes wide and concerned. She was so nervous a tic had developed at the corner of her mouth. "There is something I have to tell you, Mr. Armitage."

He tried to remain as calm as he could to help her, though his heart had picked up speed. "Yes, Miss Perry. What is it?"

"Well, I, uh …" Her glasses slid down her nose and she pushed them back up. "There are some rumors being spread, and … well, they hurt my heart. I'll say that. They hurt my heart."

"Rumors can be nasty business, Miss Perry. Are you sure we should be discussing them?"

"Well, I'd rather not," she replied, her hands fidgeting on her lap. "But they're about you and your wife, and I think you should know about them."

John knew, of course, that humanity could beget pettiness, and the idea of people talking behind others' backs was something he detested. But in running an organization, such things were bound to occur to some degree.

"I suppose, then, that you should tell me about it," he said.

"Well, yes. Uh, well, first of all, I don't know how much word has spread, but some are saying that…that Mrs. Armitage has been too chummy with Mr. Machevich down at the new learning center. I don't believe it, of course, but someone is planting doubt about her character. And it hurts my heart."

John's stomach knotted. It was an ugly thing to suggest and he didn't know what to say. He had no doubts about Evie. In her enthusiasm to get the center up and running, he knew she was giving up hours of her time and energy.

"Uh, that's not the worst of it, I'm afraid," Edna said, pushing her glasses up the bridge of her nose again. "They're saying something about you, too. Oh, it's awful. I hate to say it, but you should know. There is the darkest suggestion about your orphanages in London. Something to the effect that when individuals open up homes for children, well, that their motive could secretly be something sordid." She sat back and let out a long, shaky breath. "I'm so sorry, Mr. Armitage, and I feel just sick that I had to tell you all that. It's disgusting to even put those thoughts out there, but somebody is doing this, Mr. Armitage, and … and it hurts my heart!"

It hurt John's heart, too. He tried desperately to get mastery over his anger, for he had no doubt as to the source of the slander. And he had a few other suspicions as well. After Miss Perry left his office, John went through his Rolodex and searched for a card he had inserted months before. He dialed the number and made arrangements to meet with Mr. Jack Tubbs.

Chapter Thirty-Six

The relationship between Bertie and Sofia progressed so well that one hot July afternoon he took her to Lake Forest and introduced her to his grandparents. Georgette's cook served lunch: a cool gazpacho, cucumber sandwiches, a salad, fresh fruit, and iced tea. They dined with leisure and both Franklin and Georgette appeared enchanted by the fine manners and gracious personality of their guest. Franklin even gave Bertie an approving wink at one point.

After another hour of conversation, Bertie invited Sofia to go for a bicycle ride.

"It's awfully hot, Bertie," Georgette said. "Do be careful. You don't want your girl getting heat stroke."

Because of the heat and their plans to ride to a beach, the couple changed into bathing suits. Sofia added a short gingham skirt over hers and wore tennis shoes. Bertie donned a light, short-sleeved shirt, swimming shorts, and yachting moccasins.

The winding sylvan lanes of the north shore were mostly shaded and a mild breeze lifted off the lake. Their bicycles glided through copses of trees along the serpentine route, past gated driveways and grand homes. Queen Anne's Lace and ferns carpeted the foreground and the air was alive with butterflies. When they were south of Lake Forest, they entered a small suburban village and rode past little stucco homes surrounded by fenced yards, their gardens filled with hostas and peonies. A pair of Carmelite nuns strolled through a small park of flowers, their wing-like sleeves waving to and fro, catching the breeze.

"There's a bubbler," he said, pointing at a water fountain which was artistically framed by benches and a berm of daisies.

They approached the unexpected haven and dismounted. As Sofia bent to drink, he stepped to the berm and picked a daisy. She straightened, her lips moist from the fountain, and he held out the flower.

"For your hair," he said.

Her eyes shone as she secured the daisy behind her ear.

"The public beach is just a bit farther along Sheridan Road," he said. "Come. The lakefront awaits."

After a few shaded, winding bends, Bertie signaled to turn east and the road made a straight shot to the bluff's view of Lake Michigan. They crossed a small stone bridge over a ravine and entered the park where they secured their bikes, gathered their few items and took the descending path to the beach.

The bright reflection off sand and water shimmered, inviting them down. Clusters of young people and families scattered along the shore, some laughing, some limp in sun-drenched comas. A few young men were showing off their athleticism, performing handstands and noisy imitations of football plays, even going so far as to have outright flexing exhibitions.

As Bertie and Sofia ambled farther down the shore, the breeze dried the sweat on Bertie's brow and neck. They spread out their blanket then deposited their shoes, towels, and sundries, and walked together to the water. At first they just waded in the shallows, holding hands, but the heat was too much and the urge too great. They took a quick dip and splashed around a bit before returning to their blanket.

While the remaining drops of water evaporated off their skin, Sofia asked, "Bertie, your family isn't Jewish, yet you're wearing a Star of David pendant. Why?"

He wasn't sure how to answer. "Well, I was adopted when I was just a little tyke. My birth mother was Jewish."

Her eyes were kind. "And your father wasn't?"

"I don't know who my real father is."

"Are you religious?" she asked.

"No. My family isn't, not really."

"Then why the Jewish pendant?"

"Does it bother you?" He touched the pendant, feeling slightly anxious, but she smiled warmly and he relaxed.

"Not in the least.

"Are you religious?" he asked.

"My mother is. For me, Catholicism is a matter of culture. I love my parish family and all my relatives but I cannot believe it to be..." She frowned, at a loss. "I don't know what to say. I suppose I'm bothered. Have you read Churchill's The Gathering Storm?"

"Hmm. No, but I've heard it contained, uh, an exposé of sorts. Something about Franz von Papen, a Cardinal Inni-Something-or-Other. And even the pope, and collusion with the Nazis. Is that what you mean?"

"Yes, mostly."

"You know what I like about you? I mean one of the many things I like?"

She smiled brilliantly. "What?"

"You're so honest. Honest with yourself and about life around you. You're not afraid to express yourself on personal matters like this, but you don't become defensive either."

"Do you think two people can truly love each other despite different religious opinions?" she asked, her eyes searching his.

"I don't know about other people, but I know I can."

Chapter Thirty-Seven

The August night felt balmy, as if Bertie and Sofia were strolling the beaches of the Caribbean rather than walking along Chicago's Oak Street lakefront. Here stood the old concrete pier Bertie had adopted as his quiet spot for solace. It was an induction of sorts, introducing Sofia to the place.

When they arrived, she breathed in deeply, smiling with pleasure. "I love it. City lights beyond Lake Shore Drive add a bit of dazzle while the lake gently laps around us."

"It's private."

"Yes."

He held her gently and savored her kisses. The soft drone of traffic beyond the sands came in and out of his awareness. They then sat, removed their shoes and dangled their feet in the water.

"When you first came from London, what did you think of Chicago?"

He placed his arm around her. "I was a wee lad for my first trip. We came to visit my grandparents. I thought Chicago was the best place on earth."

"I like thinking about that. About you as a little boy," she said. "I hope you have some photographs."

"Mother does. When I came here to live, well, I still thought Chicago was the best place on earth." He chuckled. "And I know the people are friendlier."

"That's how I feel," she said, nodding. "I mean, I've lived here all my life, but my family and I have traveled to New York and throughout Italy, and while most of those places have their charms, I like it here best—especially the food. We have Greek Town, Chinatown, ethnic nooks with Scandinavians, Poles, Russians, and," she said, smiling, "we have great British pubs."

"We need to go to a Cubs game," he suggested.

"Absolutely. I'm a diehard Cubs fan. And, as they say, once that's in your blood, there's nothing you can do about it."

"Do you believe in Billy Goat's Curse?" he asked, referring to when a Greek tavern owner had proclaimed a curse on the Chicago Cubs for asking him and his pet goat to leave Wrigley Field.

"We'll have to see," she replied with a chuckle. "The tavern sure is a lively place, and full of stories."

"How about a nice pint of Guinness at O'Neil's before we call it a night?"

She squeezed his hand. "Sounds great."

They meandered back to Lincoln Park, encountering only one other young couple walking hand in hand, and a lone man taking in the shoreline.

"Doctor Armitage?" Nurse Jacobson asked. "Uh, doctor?"

Her tentative question roused Bertie from his daze. "Oh, hullo, Miss Jacobson. Caught me right out, you did." He smiled somewhat sheepishly at her. "Did you happen to get the name of that jeweler on Wabash?"

"Yes, sir. My mother said you'll want to go to Silverman's. It's between Madison and Monroe. The jeweler there is the best expert on diamonds she knows."

"Thank you, Miss Jacobson." He couldn't help grinning. "Thank you."

Bertie's Mother was an expert on diamonds, of course, but he wasn't ready to discuss this with her. Not quite yet.

Chapter Thirty-Eight

"This is terrible," Evie said, looking utterly devastated.

Fortunately, John had suggested she sit while he told her what was going around the offices of Armitage House, Inc. She stared at him, looking forlorn. She set her coffee on the garden table and clutched her hands together under her chin.

He'd hoped the better part of human nature would squelch the slander naturally. The members of the board, EVPs, and office workers knew John and Evie fairly well. They had worked shoulder to shoulder toward the same charitable aims and some had even dined at the Armitages' table.

As a man of fifty-eight, John had been around long enough to know that envy nudges some down a slippery slope. It was envy, ambition, and something else John couldn't quite identify that was goading Gleason. It was hard to remember, to think he had almost stepped on Gleason—literally—that morning in Covent Garden. Gleason had been just a skinny man from Seven Dials, playing violin for tips before he'd been welcomed into the Armitage embrace, where he'd been promoted from mere tutor to Lambeth House overseer. The man's begging had prompted John to sponsor him so he could enter America. Gleason had convinced him that in America, he could better utilize his talents and energies for the benefit of the organization.

John berated himself for his own naïveté. He should have suspected the man's blind ambition. Especially since he had been repeatedly subjected to hearing Gleason sell his own abilities.

Evie dabbed a tear from her cheek with her linen napkin. "How can anyone respond to such an ugly accusation? To deny it only makes one look guiltier. You certainly can't go around drawing attention to your noble efforts and calling out your good motives. There's no defense." She wiped another tear. "Perhaps Gleason is having psychological problems."

John clicked his tongue. "Evie, you are too blasted generous. The man has become evil. His ego has destroyed any good sense he might have had."

John wasn't quite ready to tell her about his dealings with private investigator, Jack Tubbs. However, his suspicions had proven accurate, and the work of Mr. Tubbs was yielding fruit. Rotten fruit, but vital.

She sipped her coffee and released a shaky breath. It was a warm, lovely September day and a mourning dove cooed in the shade of a neighbor's garden wall. Evie tried to smile, as if the sound had cheered her. "Well, on a brighter note, I get the feeling Bertie and Sofia may be announcing their engagement soon." She sighed. "My little Bertie has matured into such a fine man. I'm going to miss being the only woman in his life. I love Sofia, though. It's only been a few months, but, well, if I'm right, I won't doubt their decision in the least. In fact, I'm hoping for it. We'll have beautiful grandchildren, John."

John crossed Oak Street, his lips tight with temper. Mounting tensions in the organization had him almost regretting his move to America. As he passed by the solitary stone structure of the landmark water tower on Michigan Avenue, he remembered the story of its survival during the great fire. He saw the tower as a symbol, and took in a deep breath of September air so that he felt strong enough to face his coming trial by fire. Due to Gleason's underhanded work, John expected the board might question whether he should continue as CEO in view of the assassination of his character. The board meeting was set for next Tuesday.

John entered the grand lobby of the Erie Street building and found the elevator for the twentieth floor already waiting for him. He greeted the attendant as he entered but noticed the man averted his eyes and could barely utter a reply. Had Gleason spread his slander even to this man, or was John becoming paranoid? Nonetheless, he thanked the man upon exiting then walked past the main reception desk where even young Miss Verstrati couldn't meet his eyes. She mumbled a weak "Good morning, sir," keeping her eyes on the desk.

John felt like going into Gleason's office and beating the skinny, bespectacled, balding man to a pulp. But he realized strategy would be his best recourse. It wasn't exactly the "high road," but John felt it was the only road he could take. If he hadn't, months ago, been sitting in Gleason's office and seen what had been in the man's trashcan, John would have had no recourse at all. For this small favor he was grateful.

As he closed the door to his office, he checked his briefcase to make sure the large brown envelope was still there.

It was.

After an hour of reviewing the scholastic improvements of the learning centers, which were coming along nicely, John heard a knock at his door. His Executive Vice President for Strategies and Marketing, Reginald Blumenthal, peered around the door. "Uh, Mr. Armitage? Might I have a word with you?"

Blumenthal had been the first one to join Gleason's court, and if John read him right, the look in his eyes was now sheepish. Then again, it might be a cover. John invited him in but didn't indicate a chair.

"I owe you a big apology, sir. A big apology."

John wanted to warm to his words, but experience made him tentative. He nodded for the man to continue.

"I feel I've been used. Manipulated would be a better term for it." He took a deep breath. "I see in hindsight that Gleason is driven by something disturbing. Up close it was difficult to see, sir, and I really apologize. It's just that he can be very convincing. I'm ashamed to admit I enjoyed his ability to nurture a person's ego, mine in particular. Before then, I'd never thought I was one to crave importance, but he saw it readily enough and took advantage of it."

John showed no expression on his face, determined not to make it easy on Blumenthal. Why should he?

"Anyway, I'm rambling. I want to apologize, sir, for listening to unsubstantiated gossip about you and your wife. Worse than that, I held gatherings at Gleason's insistence, discussing with others whether you and your wife had the proper characters to lead this organization involving children's welfare. I'm so sorry for this. I wanted to warn you that this will be brought up at Tuesday's meeting."

Blumenthal rolled his shoulders back, standing a little straighter, and cleared his throat. His eyes were red-rimmed but he held himself together as he sincerely met John's gaze. "I'm more than willing to do anything I possibly can to help. And if you feel that I should, I will offer my resignation. Sir, I can't apologize enough. I'm so ashamed."

"A resignation won't be necessary, Reggie." John hoped the use of the man's first name would imply some added reassurance. "And thank you, but I think I'm ready for Tuesday."

"Thank you, sir. I don't know what good I'll be in helping you thwart this mutiny, since it seems as soon as I began showing I was switching sides, Gleason started discrediting me as well. I won't repeat to you what he's been saying about me to everyone. All the man needs is a smattering of knowledge which he ferrets out early in the game when he's posing as your friend. He saves it in his arsenal and when he deems it necessary and useful, he twists it into a deadly attack. I don't think his mind ever rests. It wasn't until I became a target myself that I began to understand everything he'd done." Blumenthal cleared his throat and added, "I want you to know that I believe in you, sir."

John sighed deeply and stared at his hands, folded on the desk. Then he looked up and met Blumenthal's eyes. "I don't think anyone on the board will come off feeling unscathed in some way after Tuesday, Reggie. That's the problem with this sort of thing. Thank you for your apology, and—" He felt awkward but chose sincerity over formality, "and for your vote of confidence. I look forward to seeing you Tuesday."

That Sunday John, Evie, Bertie and Sofia spent the afternoon in Lake Forest with Franklin and Georgette. Their dinner included a beef goulash with egg noodles, since the current cook was Hungarian, along with steamed asparagus with Hollandaise, and honeyed carrots. For dessert, they enjoyed a lemon meringue pie.

The late day sun was pleasantly warm, casting long shadows toward the lake. The terrace was shaded and Franklin, looking a bit fragile, wore a light coat while he had his after-dinner port. Georgette sat next to him while Bertie and Sofia strolled at the bluff's edge. Occasionally either Bertie or Sofia laughed, their conversation floating across the yard with muted ardor.

John could remember clearly their first visit here as a family, and he felt a wave of nostalgia pass through him. Bertie had been only a waif, sitting on Franklin's lap on this terrace. John sipped a whisky on the rocks and gave Evie a smile. The day was a welcome reprieve from the hurt and stress at work.

Later that evening John paused at the entrance to the library and motioned to his mother. Frowning, she joined him in front of the drinks cabinet. John had chosen this vantage point so he could easily change the subject were Franklin to come into the room.

"It could become a maelstrom of ugliness, an Armageddon, tomorrow. Have you thought of how you might keep Father from coming to the meeting?"

"Yes," she said resolutely. His mother was still beautiful and regal, despite the lines of age and anxiety life had etched on her face. "Would you be so kind as to pour me some gin? Straight gin will do."

Suppressing a smile, he complied.

She took two determined sips, as if they were all etiquette would allow for her fortification, then replied, her whisper intense. "I have found that directness and honesty work best with Franklin. Well, honesty to a degree, at least. I couldn't bear to tell him the nature of the accusations, or even the fact that accusations are being spread. I simply stated that there has arisen a grappling for control of the company. He's experienced enough to understand these things."

"And he just accepted that?"

She touched his arm. "He has such confidence in you, John. He knows the state of his health and doesn't want to add anything to our troubles were he to …" She shrugged. "He said he'll sit at home and pray. John, I have to tell you, never in our married lives have I heard him make such a statement. One's final years does that to some people, apparently. He certainly has become more contemplative."

Evie's heels tapped down the hallway, then she popped her head around the mahogany frame of the archway. Recognizing their conspiratorial stances, she smiled and left.

"Frankly," John said, "I'd very much prefer for you and Evie to stay away as well, and not subject yourselves to all the mess that's sure to fly."

Happy banter, then laughter between Sofia and Franklin, trickled down the corridor from the parlor.

Georgette stood straighter and set her tumbler down with a clink on the marble-topped cabinet. "The Armitage name is at stake here. Nothing would keep me away."

John kissed her cheek.

In the night air out on the drive, they all lingered over their goodbyes. For a moment, John imagined Gleason cooped up in his Ravenswood apartment, slouched over his typewriter and planning his destructive dissertation. Then John looked out over the serene Lake Forest grounds, listening to birds exchange their end-of-day chirpings.

He noticed a few starlings as they soared in the azure sky, and he wondered what life would be like after Tuesday.

Chapter Thirty-Nine

John strode into the meeting room Tuesday morning and was practically smothered by the tension in the room. Those who supported Gleason were sitting on his side of the table; those loyal to the Armitages sat on the other. Gleason's clique had two more members than John's party. John took his seat, barely able to breathe, but kept command of himself and maintained an authoritative air.

Edna Perry fluttered in, closing the door noisily before taking her seat near Evie. She peered through her broad glasses at John, giving him a look that wished him well.

Gleason's stare, penetrating through Coke-bottle lenses, defied John.

Earlier, John had wrestled with whether or not to allow Gleason the floor. The agenda did indeed include a discussion of the qualifications of the current CEO. Did he want to allow the tension to build, then bring out the envelope? Or should he go for the jugular at the outset?

Evie, Georgette, Edna, Reginald Blumenthal, Melvin Arwardy and two others on John's side of the table turned to him. Gleason's side either averted their eyes altogether, looked to Gleason, or mimicked the man's defiant stare.

"Minutes, please," John said.

The secretary's voice quivered. Gleason and his camp were giving off such palpable negative energy John could barely concentrate on what she was saying.

After a long silence, John realized the secretary had finished. He cleared his throat and called upon CFO Jack Wood to run through the financials. While Wood droned on interminably, John made his decision. Wood finished and again John was caught off guard by the long silence. He stood, suddenly feeling stiff and old. He took a deep breath and then let it out, relieved to hear it didn't shake.

"As you see on the agenda, we are to include a discussion regarding my position. I should like to make it clear that I have absolutely no problem having my qualifications reviewed from time to time. In fact, I feel this is important in keeping the organization healthy." Despite the pressure in his chest, his voice rang with strength. He strolled around his side of the table and stood behind Evie. "And good moral character is essential for officers and board members of an organization that is here to help children. However, this discussion has been preceded by slander against my name and that of my good wife."

Gleason glared at John.

"Character assassination is an ugly, cheap ploy, and following our vote today I'd like it to be decided upon that we will never, ever allow this kind of tactic to arise again at Armitage House. We will adopt a procedure. Step one: if anyone in the future questions an officer's actions or character, that person must first discuss the matter privately with the officer. This step could squelch many a misunderstanding, while affording dignity. If the problem is still of concern, we will henceforth have an advisory board set up to privately hear such matters. We will not allow our organization to be subjected to underhanded tactics again."

The air was electric. John returned to the table's head and saw his wife's admiring eyes, shining with tears. His mother's lips were pressed together, a facial trait he recognized as her trying to contain her anger toward the dissenters. Reginald and Edna breathed in unison, their brows raised. Seeing their expressions, John gained momentum and reached for the brown envelope.

When he held it to his chest, John noticed Gleason's confidence ebbing. The man's eyes, magnified through his lenses, darted to the side then back again.

"Much of what has been going around by way of gossip and conjecture has been driven by one man's ambition. And this man has no proof whatsoever." He looked Gleason's camp up and down. "Some of you have been wined and dined and cajoled. I ask you now to question yourselves, to analyze how we've come to this point.

"Now, permit me to digress for a moment. I would like to say that it has been my oversight, my mistake, not having in place a more active procedure with which to recognize achievement. This will be rectified. I do apologize. But perhaps others have been similarly beguiled for the underhanded purpose of persuasion and manipulation. It is important for the balance of this meeting that we look into ourselves before taking a vote."

Miss Lovejoy's lips puckered with sour distaste. Michael Robertson sat back, stiff with arrogance. Clearly, they weren't ready to surrender.

John opened the envelope and poured the contents into his hand. "It is important, ladies and gentlemen, that I share with you evidence justifying my claim. We have an unprecedented problem on the table this morning. So without further ado, I will present evidence against Gleason Fitzgerald, and this on the matter of moral character."

John handed out 8 x 11 photographs, one to every two or three people. Gleason got up to leave but John was quick to call him back.

"Sit down, Gleason," he barked. "Ladies and gentlemen, here we are considering real evidence. Anyone can make conjecture, innuendo or twist facts. That kind of thing brings Othello's ambitious Iago to mind, does it not? Here you'll see that the man who has been talking about other people's characters has his own moral deficiencies. It occurred to me early on in the matter that it usually takes a sordid mind to imagine weakness and vice in others. Apparently this is the case."

John's eyes drifted over the expressions of everyone at the table, then rested on Gleason's sweating face. "Before you, are photographs that came into my possession from a reputable private investigator. They show our Mr. Fitzgerald enjoying himself in Calumet City, in the vice district. This area is run, as most of you know, by the Outfit. Clubs like the *Tom Cat*, *Boys Town* and *Cheat-ahs* are just a few places along the strip where Mr. Fitzgerald was caught on a number of occasions. Notice, on this last point, how he is dressed differently in different photographs along Calumet's State Street. In this one he's wearing short sleeves. And here, see the snow outside of Cheat-ahs? As I said, these were taken on a number of occasions over a period of time."

John took out more photographs. "Now these are taken inside one of the clubs, though I had to destroy some of the photographs for the sake of decency. I'm sure I don't need to elaborate on what takes place in these establishments; such things are unmentionable."

The meeting adjourned later than usual. Gleason left before it ended, humiliated and voted out of the company. Miss Lovejoy and Michael Robertson also fled, handing in their resignations as they left. Many others were contrite. As John had foreseen, no one left unscathed. Armitage House, Inc. had endured its trial, but not without cost.

After seeing Georgette off to her limousine, John and Evie trudged up State Street toward their home, feeling silent, weary, and victorious.

Chapter Forty

That night Bertie strolled restlessly along the lakefront, a velveteen box protruding from his left shirt pocket. He'd arrived an hour earlier than they'd planned to meet, and he walked the promenade, almost skipping with excitement. Being the prudent professional man he was, he buttoned down the pocket's flap before barreling out onto the sand, yipping like a wild dog in the night air, not caring if passersby thought he was crazy. After completing a series of cartwheels, of which he felt absurdly proud, he began walking toward the cement pier to wait for Sofia.

He had the beach to himself, a sensation that always filled him with awe. He gazed toward the skyline of apartment houses, noticing how the gunmetal gray sky was darker over the lake and vibrant over the city. The moon was just coming up in the southeast, its light dappling the water. The few stars twinkling overhead seemed determined to compete with the city lights.

From the corner of his eye, he noticed three young men walking toward him and his euphoria evaporated. Something shone ominously in one of their hands and Bertie suddenly became aware of how vulnerable he was. The quixotic might walk the beach, but so could thugs. Who would hear cries for help against the pounding of the surf, the sound-absorbing stretches of sand, and beyond that, Lake Shore Drive and city noise? They'd get Sofia's ring.

Bertie's heart began pounding in his throat and ears as he stood frozen, watching the three men continue toward him. He wanted to run, but for some reason he couldn't move. He assumed part of this was morbid fascination, a strange disbelief that such dreadful things really happened. He glanced around to see if any other people were near but only a vague silhouette moved far down the shore. The voices of the approaching men were distinguishable enough for Bertie to recognize a foreign tongue. His feet sank in the sand and his muscles tensed in preparation.

One of the men raised his hand. "Buenos noches, señor," he hailed good-naturedly.

Bertie, feeling slightly ridiculous, breathed a sigh of relief. The glinting object was a beer can. The three passed by, wishing him a good night. Bertie watched them meander up the shoreline, and with the release of tension came elation. He raised his eyes and counted a few more stars before continuing up to "his" pier. He was so absorbed in his thoughts that the sound of footsteps coming from behind him on the concrete pier took him completely by surprise. He turned, hoping it was Sofia. It wasn't.

Gleason.

"I thought I might find you out here, Bertie," Gleason said, speaking bluntly and standing about twenty paces away. "You did say you liked coming to this place."

"What are you doing here, Gleason? I thought—" He stopped short. He'd been about to say he thought the man had gotten fired today, but that would be thoughtless. Politeness was so deeply ingrained in Bertie's character it even applied to Gleason.

Then Bertie noticed the gun in his hand. He frowned. "What's going on?"

"You'll find out, old boy."

Bertie involuntarily took a few steps back. The end of the pier was only two yards behind him.

Gleason cleared his throat. "If you haven't heard about this morning, well, it doesn't much matter. Let me just say that I came up with a great idea today. The perfect way to inflict the most pain on the high and mighty John Armitage." With a twisted smile, he aimed directly at Bertie with his gun and took a step forward, then another. The heels of his alligator boots clicked on the concrete as he advanced.

Bertie was torn between terror and anger. "It takes a coward to shoot an unarmed man, Gleason, just like it takes a coward to slander folks for your own gain. You may kill me but you'll still have to live with yourself."

Gleason nodded, his smile dark. "I like my company. And after I do away with you, I'm leaving town. I'll find something better to do than hand out diplomas to *orphans*. Do you have anything else to taunt me with before I pull the trigger?"

Bertie looked beyond Gleason, hoping to see help of any kind. Then he thought of Sofia and prayed she wouldn't come while Gleason was there, armed and murderous.

Bertie heard the crack of the gun as he fell back, the impact as strong as if he'd been struck by a speeding semi. His head hit the concrete, shooting a jolt of agony through his brain like lightning. But he was conscious, down on his back and struggling for breath. He thought the bullet must have gone through his lung and he might survive, if only Gleason would assume he was dying and leave. But those clicking footsteps came closer.

Bertie gulped for air and was enfolded by a strange calm. He heard the surf, saw the stars.

Then he saw Gleason's face, the moonlight catching the man's smile as it spread in evil delight. Gleason aimed directly at his face.

Bertie heard himself whimper. "Please—"

This time he didn't hear the cracking noise of the gun. He didn't hear the water lapping or see the stars. Everything became nothing.

Cook and Part-time Staff—1985 Lake Forest

"She told me," Margaret said to Robin, "that Gleason Fitzgerald was caught at Midway airport that night by the police. He was wearin' a wig and sunglasses and was tryin' to get to Jamaica."

Robin had only been working under Margaret's authority for a month, but it had taken no time at all to become fascinated with this interesting family.

The young woman couldn't take her eyes off the framed, black and white photograph of Bertie, the beautiful man with the large, haunting eyes. When she did, it was only to look at another of the man as a boy, standing on the deck of a large ship, looking excited and gleeful. Then, one of an adolescent cradling his violin. The third-floor room had at least a hundred photographs of the cherished son of John and Evie Armitage, all framed and hung artfully. His violin hung on the wall, too. The room had an easterly view, overlooking the lake and daily sunrises.

Robin spoke her thoughts. "I'm kind of surprised that she chose a room with a lake view, considering."

"Oh, the missus suffered somethin' turrible, she did. I came here after he was gorn for 'bout four years, and when she got around to opening her heart to me 'bout him, she still sobbed through her words." Margaret shook her head. "I kinda wished I'd known him, but if I did, then it would hurt me, too, more than it does just knowin' about it. But she said they had him cremated because his face was so damaged. Sometime after his funeral, she and the mister chartered a yacht and scattered his ashes out there."

Robin looked out the window and stared at a myriad of winking, undulating glimmers, as if the mid-day sun shattered into countless pieces on the lake.

Margaret had caught her red-handed, snooping around where she shouldn't be, but the old cook understood. With the Armitages away for a gala with UNICEF, United Way and Armitage House, Inc., Robin had felt she could get away with a little poking around.

The photo-filled room was set up for contemplation and tears. Margaret allowed Robin time to look around and take it in. A gold-chintz chaise lounge was situated to look out the window. A wing chair faced a corner full of photographs. There was also a desk and chair. Shelves held an array of books, many for children and young men. There was *Peter Rabbit,* then one called *Paradise Regained;* there was also a series by Edgar Rice Burroughs about Tarzan. She could almost imagine a youthful Bertie devouring those. She estimated about thirty books altogether. Then she turned and spotted a photograph of Bertie and Sofia sitting in a restaurant.

"You'd mentioned Sofia. She was Bertie's fiancé, right? What happened to her?" Robin asked, still looking at photographs.

"Well, poor thing. She was the one that found him out there. And thank the Lord, she didn't come up on them and get killed herself. But, in time she married. She worked at the learning center till she started havin' childr'n of her own. I hear she brought her childr'n along to see Evie, but it got too painful for the missus. I can understand that. But Sofia still sends her cards now and then, sometimes with pictures of the kids. And the missus, she looks at 'em, sometimes for long periods, just starin' and thinkin' 'bout what mighta been, I suppose. But, listen to me. It ain't all sadness with them 'round here. They moved on as best they could. Got a lot of love, those two, for a pair o' ninety-year-olds." She chuckled.

Robin wasn't ready to brighten up. "So, is Gleason still locked up, I hope?"

"Now there's a story I kinda wish I knew more of, and then again, I guess I'm glad I don't. I hear they found him one day strung up in his cell. And, from what I hear, it wasn't necessarily by his own hand.

People love the Armitages, even some shady folks, like maybe the Mob and all that. So I reckon someone in there thought justice wasn't bein' served quite right. But now all that's over." She said this, as if the tour were over, too.

Robin drank in one more sight of handsome Bertie, whispered goodbye and followed Margaret out the door, closing it quietly.

Chapter Forty-One

1954 Elm Street and Erie Street

John Armitage stood at the window of his office, which looked out over the city to the north. He could see the shoreline that ran along Lincoln Park, knowing that his eyes were taking in the scene where his son …

If John had a telescope, he would be able to clearly see the concrete pier.

He had walked out to it once, saw his son's blood, now an eternal stain on the cement. How many storms would it take to wash it out of the miniscule crevices? How many sunny days to bleach it out completely? Part of him hoped it would take many years. But John would never go back.

He had taken a six-month hiatus from work. Afterward, the members of the board were more than eager to have him back as their CEO. All of the remaining officers shared the grief of the Armitage family. First the tragic loss of Bertie, then the passing of seventy-nine-year-old Franklin, who died of a heart attack three days after the funeral. Then, almost immediately afterwards, Edwina passed away.

Franklin had a typical funeral at the Presbyterian Church, entombed in the mausoleum he had built at an Evanston cemetery. The formal funeral supper was held at the house.

Edwina had dictated simple cremation. John asked his mother if he could scatter her ashes along the front grounds where they'd played together in his childhood years; she agreed.

When news of Gleason Fitzgerald's death had arrived, there was no satisfaction for John. At least the man's demise had not been his doing. He shook off a chill at the thought—he could have so easily taken matters into his own angry hands had the timing and opportunity come together.

Justice had been served. Justice felt empty.

Afterward, Evie took most of his attention. He feared that her breakdown would leave her emotionally, if not mentally, disabled. But she was rallying. Mostly, it left her often forgetful of little things while her mind went into occasional ramblings, as if it couldn't handle all of the emotional distractions.

For three months, they could not bring themselves to be intimate with each other despite their desperate need for consolation. There was too much awareness of the fact that their son would never have this kind of happiness. And when they finally did come together, they wept afterward.

Immediately after Bertie's funeral, Evie had to take a room at the Drake Hotel. She said she couldn't be in either home since they reminded her of Bertie. But, as if picking at a scab, she requested a room with a north shore view, and for days she just stared out at the scene of tragedy.

One day, John entered the hotel room and found her listening to a radio broadcast of *Tristan und Isolde*. When it ended, she stared out the window. Her words haunted him. *That's sometimes how I wish to be, John. Like Isolde, so that I could have just laid down near my son and died with him.* And then, *I don't mean to be so selfish, John, I'm sorry … but that's how I feel.*

After a week at the Drake, Evie went back to Elm Street. And after a few more days, returned to work.

"Uh, Mister Armitage?" Edna Perry's head came around the office door after John responded from his desk to her knock. A quiver of her jowl and the tentative tone of voice caused John's stomach to tighten and twist. She nearly whispered, "Uh, may I have a little word with you?"

A little word? She must be upset over something, again. And that something would have to do with him in some fashion. Most likely about Evie this time.

"Yes, Edna. Come in, close the door and sit down." His teeth were clenching despite his attempt at a calming smile. He set aside the report he'd been reading and folded his hands on his desk.

Her movements were jerky: a quick pull at her skirt before she sat; a fluttering of her fingers before the habitual pushing back of her eyeglasses. Even the gaze of her magnified eyes jiggled, as if she were repeatedly comparing his right eye with his left, unsure whether they matched.

"I, uh, hm." She cleared her throat. "I have two things I should mention to you." Apparently, she was wrestling with which "thing" to begin. She expelled a puff of air, breathed in and said, "Well, first of all, well, you probably have noticed this, but, I, uh, found Evie, uh, Missus Armitage mumbling to herself in her office." She looked to him for some confirmation. He nodded. She continued, "Unusual mumbling, as though she were conversing with Bertie. Not as if he were before her in her office, but, from what I could make out, it was like she were in another world with him. Something to do with planting flowers."

John swallowed. "Thank you, Edna. I have, as you thought, noticed this before. Of course I'm concerned, and I'm trying to find help." His stomach knotted tighter. "Fortunately, these, eh, interludes are short spells, sort of like daydreaming but a little harder for her to come out of. Try not to let it worry you too much." *Easier said than done.*

Edna's faced filled with compassion and then the nervous tics returned. "I'm afraid I upset her, sir. I surely didn't mean to. I pulled up a chair and sat with her, and in no time we were talking comfortably. She was her normal self. But I'm afraid I said something that upset her. I don't know how I could've been so stupid. I was trying to be helpful. Well, I said something about filling the void and she instantly became livid. She pushed away from me, began throwing papers around. The strangest thing is that she didn't say a thing, just stifled cries and grunts before she stormed out. I feel awful, sir. I'm so sorry."

His heart was pounding rapidly, but he said, "That was very brave of you to come and tell me. I know you meant well, Edna." He was standing, thinking of where he might find Evie.

As if seeing his thoughts, she said, "The receptionist told me that before getting into the elevator, Evie told her that she was going home for the day."

Edna repeated her apologies as he was running to the elevator.

John stepped into his front foyer and called to his wife, but his voice fell dead against upholstered chairs and Persian carpets. He stepped forward, looking right and then left into the front rooms and called again. Nothing. Craning his neck back, he called up the nautilus-spiraling banisters, this time producing an echo, which returned empty-handed from the four stories. A flash of heat followed by prickling cold sweat compelled him to call even louder.

Muffled footsteps from the back of the house brought on a wave of relief. The green baize door opened. "Oh, Mr. Armitage," Cook said." I am so glad to see you home. I called your office." She stood, a tea towel scrunched between her damp hands.

"Is it Evie? I mean, Mrs. Armitage?"

Cook's pale face creased with anxiety answering his fears. She nodded. "I saw her from upstairs." Her eyes went wide and bright with worry. "I mean, I was bringing up a tray for the missus, but she wasn't in her room. She'd come home all upset and went to her room. Well, when I got there, I heard the back gate slam, and when I came up to the window, I just caught a glimpse of her heading down the alley toward State Street. She didn't even have her purse. And she didn't look right, sir. You know? Not right. So glad you're here for me to tell yer. I called the office—"

"How long ago?"

"Bit more than ten minutes, maybe fifteen." The tea towel was now quivering along with the old woman.

He cursed the traffic that had held him up en route home.

"Please inform the police, will you? Report a missing person. I'll go in search."

He heard her *Yes, sir* behind him as he flung wide the front door and bounded for the city sidewalk. His left foot pivoted him west and he ran as fast as he could toward State Street, where he hoped to heaven someone would have seen which way Evie had gone. Panic rose up his throat as he realized the enormity of the city, the hopelessness of the task.

As quiet, leafy East Elm Street met with State, his path became blocked by a sudden flow of pedestrians, milling north or south. He looked into their self-contained faces, strangers in motion, moving like a river. Not one of them could be expected to have noticed his wife entering their ranks. A few walked in groups, conversing and laughing, grating his taut nerves.

Then, over the crowd, he noticed the newspaper kiosk in front of the Cedar Hotel. He darted through slow-moving traffic, crossing State, almost leaping around a group of shopgirls, who were suddenly looking at him with alarm.

His hands clapped down on the kiosk counter. "Oh, Maisie. I'm so glad you're here." He couldn't help the panic in his voice. "Have you seen Mrs. Armitage this afternoon?"

"Oh, yes, sir, I did." Immediate understanding filled her eyes. "The Missus, she were talkin' to herself and she went that way." Maisie pointed south, in the direction of the Loop.

He grasped her hands. "Thank you." And he ran off. The sidewalk narrowed at Rush Street, and when pedestrian traffic was thick, he darted around parked cars and ran along and against traffic. He was almost hit by a truck while crossing Chicago Avenue. Farther on, a police siren began whirring from the next block, fading in and out of buildings. What if Evie had been run over? Was she suicidal? His side began to ache as he kept running, looking down side streets, feeling helpless. After losing Bertie, if he lost Evie …

With feet and ankles that felt weighted down by cement, he slowed to a stop. His lungs burned and his spirit sank at seeing the hopelessness of finding one person in a metropolis. He stood trying to catch his breath and then he realized he was right in front of his office building. He bounded through the main door, tempted to slip into one of the phone booths just off the lobby and check in with Cook or the police. But what if Evie had gone up to their offices? He caught the first elevator. Still breathing heavily, he asked the attendant, "Have you seen Mrs. Armitage return today, Joe?"

"No, sir." John could see that the man was wrestling with how he should comport himself. The fact that something was decidedly wrong was evident. The ride up was taking forever. Joe finally ventured, "Um, is something wrong, sir?"

John cringed and wished there was an expedient way to check with the other two attendants. But if Evie did come here, they would know at the office. "Yes. If you see Mrs. Armitage, ask her to wait in my office for me, will you?"

"Yes, sir." The man shifted from one foot to the next, and, at last, the door slid open. John was through it and his heels thudded ominously as he approached reception. The new girl looked up with trepidation.

But nobody had seen Evie. He then went to his office and called the North Halsted Street Station. The desk sergeant's reply was so quick he'd cut off John's question.

Evie was all right.

The cab dropped John off at Adams Street and Michigan Avenue.

Sitting on the steps of the Art Institute, just behind the south green copper lion, huddled millionaire-philanthropist Evelyne Armitage. The afternoon sun, now low over the Loop, was blocked by the buildings. As he was waiting to cross Michigan Avenue, John's relief was dampened by concern that she might be cold sitting in the shade. The police officer who had reported in with Evie's whereabouts was sitting in his car, parked at the curb, keeping watch. As the crossing light changed and John stepped onto the street, the policeman offered John a smile that was knowing and empathetic. He saluted.. Recognizing either Armitage was not unusual since their pictures had often been in the Chicago papers at each school opening. John acknowledged him with a wave, and the officer began speaking into his police radio, evidently reporting that the matter was now in hand.

None of the visitors going up or down the steps seemed to notice Evie, however; a passerby could just as easily have taken her for a city bag lady, only she had no bags. Her blonde chignon had become disheveled in her trek, her green silk suit, wrinkled.

"Hi, love," John said softly, as if nothing were out of the ordinary; it took an immense amount of control to pull this off for her benefit. Her gaze had been riveted to something southwest from her vantage point. She turned slowly in his direction and an easy, girlish smile spread across her face. He slid down next to her and stretched his arm around her shoulders. It felt indescribably good to hold her after his fright. Still, he tried not to overreact.

She parroted his tone, "Hi, love," patted his knee, leaned against him and looked off again.

He tried to follow her gaze, and then realized the object was Orchestra Hall, the first Chicago venue they had taken young Bertie to when visiting Franklin and Georgette. After some minutes, he asked, "Are you cold?"

"Cold?" she repeated, distractedly. He coaxed her attention with his gaze. She turned to him, again, blinked, and returned from her lost world. Leaning in closer, she kissed his cheek, then looked around as if getting her bearings. "I belong here, I think." A southern breeze brought some warmth, carrying the scent of the flowers planted along the institute's south terrace. Traffic hummed, coughed and occasionally beeped. Snippets of conversations passed by, accompanying the many footsteps. "I don't belong," she looked into his face, "*We* don't belong in the modern Chicago…but here, by Mister Lion, oh, and his cousin over there," she pointed across the steps. "Remind me to introduce you later." Her tone was half-self-mocking, as if knowing her behavior had been odd, but John felt her love for him just beneath the surface of her words. Their bond, at least, was apparently helping her maintain some grip—he'd swear he could sense that; their love, an anchor: she may drift a bit here and there, but never too far—he hoped upon hope she would find complete recovery soon. He held her closer.

The officer in the police car remained at the curb, occasionally looking their way, a courtesy, it seemed.

Evie didn't notice. She patted John's knee and said with an air of self-deprecation, "I guess I was finding solace in what was old. You know, this museum, these buildings…they were all here when I was presented to the Imperial court in St Petersburg." She laughed, a giggly laugh, her eyes assessing her disheveled clothing. "Just look at me. Who'd ever believe me if I were to tell them I interacted with the Czars daughters? The grand duchesses—Olga and I were the same age, you know." She sat straight. "I could out-stifle a yawn with the best of them—such an era of decorum, it was...yes, it was." Her hand caressed the nearest paw of the Bronze lion. "So old. When we married—we believed we were invincible. Did you realize that? We survived the Great War, the epidemic…and years later, when we came here…with Bertie." She looked back toward Orchestra Hall. "Perhaps I was thinking that if I looked there, and if I thought hard enough, I could go back in time." She shook her head. And soon her breathing became quick and shallow. Her delicate frame began shivering. "I ache for our Bertie. Oh, John, I ache so strongly." Tears began flowing down her cheeks.

John realized his were damp, as well. He sat there holding her. They held each other and cried together, ignoring the crowds completely. Afterward, they were both damp, breathless and a little dazed, as if they'd just finished making passionate love.

The next thing John knew the city around them was alive with lights. He stood up, his hips and ankles stiff. "Come." He took her hand.

1962 Evie

This was Evie's third visit to Green Bay School in North Chicago. The winter season had been relentlessly gray and cold, infecting many with lethargy. However, hearing her own steps clicking and echoing down the hall with fresh verve brought cheerful Caribbean music to her mind. She was looking forward to working with a particular second-grader, the one Mrs. Clayton had said was a real worry because of his constant daydreaming. The teacher had explained that she would attract the boy's attention, but within minutes, his eyes were again on the snowy scene beyond the windows.

Mrs. Clayton said with concern, "The poor boy can't concentrate on a thing for more than two minutes."

Evie appreciated her dedication.

The boy's name was Brandon Stewart. One of the things that had attracted her was that he had a slight British accent. His mother was British, having married an American serviceman after the war. And the Stewarts lived down the street from the school.

Brandon was small like Bertie had been at his age. And like Bertie, Brandon had head and eyes that were disproportionately larger than his frame. Coloring was an immediate difference. Whereas Bertie's look was dark and dramatic, Brandon's was softer, his hair a lighter brown, almost a burnished auburn and quite wavy. He had a handsome brow and a sweet disposition. Bertie had had those haunting, intelligent eyes that pulled you in. Brandon Stewart's expression, quixotic and dreamy, inadvertently excluded you. Yet, in talking with him, Evie noted sparks of life and interest within his eyes. Her heart went out to him, fearing he might unwittingly distrust reality. Or, perhaps it was simply some cognitive handicap that they only needed to discover and then address.

Today, they were going to work on reading.

While the class was studying Dick, Jane and Sally, Evie took Brandon down the hall to the library where she could sit in a corner and work with him.

"There we go," she said invitingly. She pulled two easy chairs closer together and sat at his right, slightly angled. "Comfy?"

He nodded, his eyes happy at the attention.

"I'll just close the blinds a bit." She reached for the Venetian blind wand and turned it. She liked the snowy view of the hill but realized she had to limit distractions. However, she believed that a snack might serve as a help and not a distraction. In her opinion, atmosphere, attitude and interest were key.

"I am going to see if Mrs. Pulaski will let us have tea with our reading lessons. Would you like that?"

He nodded, somewhat in awe at the idea.

"Your mum is English. Does she make you tea?"

Another nod.

She was going to have to get into a viewpoint question here. "What do you like best with your tea?"

"Bread and orange marmalade," he responded quickly.

"Well, I'll see what I can do." She looked around at the shelves and said, "Why don't you pick a book and we'll get started."

"I'd like to do *Peter Rabbit*," he said, sitting there.

Evie felt pang of pleasure and pain, confusing her for a moment. "I'm sorry, *Peter Rabbit*, was it?"

"Yes, and they don't have it here. My mum reads it to me, and I know some by heart, but I want to learn to read it myself." He then proceeded to recite the first few pages. Evie was not prepared for this moment. About the third line on, she burst into tears while laughing at herself, completely befuddling the boy. Most likely, he had never had a hysterical woman sit across from him before. Evie pulled herself together and explained that she was just happy with his choice. It took all of her self-control not to pick him up and hold him on her lap; for she was at that moment recalling Bertie's first night at Mayfair. She saw Bertie sitting, snuggled on her lap, as they sat near the fire while he proudly recited the tale. She could even feel John's happy gaze on them. But she had to come back to the present, to Brandon. She smiled at him.

"That was wonderful. Tell me some more. You left off with uh, *Flopsy* and something-er-other, I'm sorry. Let's have a go at it from the top."

He got to what she thought was about page four, before he lost track.

"I will get that book, and tomorrow we'll begin working on reading the words together."

"With tea and marmalade," he cried.

She wiped a tear from her cheek.

Chapter Forty-Two

John took Evie out to dinner at the Pump Room. He felt celebratory. A candle in a hurricane lamp made flickering light patterns on the table and reflected off her jewelry. She was wearing jewelry again. She hadn't done so for some time.

"Brandon has done well on all of his assignments and tests, except for arithmetic. I much prefer working on reading with him, but we will buckle down and get that right side of his brain going."

Evie was always reading up on this and that about education. It was just recently that she'd learned about the right and left brain. She was thinking of writing a book about helping those with limited attention spans, much of this no doubt spawned by her work in North Chicago.

But she wasn't all work lately. She was also more attuned to John. Their intimacy had improved so much that he sometimes felt as if he were a twenty-one-year-old bridegroom again. And she had been ordering fresh flowers for their home, which, in this drab winter, really brightened things up.

"But I realize I have to be careful, John. I won't get carried away. I won't become Brandon's special friend; I won't let myself become possessive. Still, it feels so good watching him mentally grab onto things—things I fear he might otherwise miss were he not getting the attention. I really believe he is concentrating for longer periods oftentimes. But he can still succumb to daydreaming too readily. I've found that gentle reminders work most times, but only if I somehow convey my confidence in him. And, perhaps because of our rapport, just a touch of my hand on his has brought Brandon back—his attention back, I mean." She cleared her throat and looked over his shoulder for long minutes. She caught herself. "Oh, I'm sorry. I am rattling on. Thank you for being such a prince. You've been very understanding, and this," she looked around the famed restaurant, "was a very nice idea." Her smile was dazzling.

After dinner, he took Evie out dancing at Coco's Club on Rush. The entire evening was a great success.

On March 4th, 1962, the high-spirited-London-Socialite-Cum-Industrial-Baroness-Cum-Philanthropist Georgette Armitage died in her sleep. With John already working as a philanthropist, most of the Armitage holdings were entrusted to him. The reading of the will was a small affair, held in the offices of Ribich, Howard and Dirks on LaSalle Street. It was a bittersweet experience for John as memories flooded in and emotions came to the surface. And it was a lonely feeling as he realized that there were no more parents, aunts, uncles or even cousins left. He could not even allow himself to think of either Evie or himself dying and leaving the other behind, all alone. This thought brought on a new wave of grief over Bertie's death.

Chapter Forty-Three

"Brandon?" Evie said with gentle coaxing. She had just caught him looking out of the window, daydreaming. Instead of showing exasperation, since it was the third time his attention had drifted from the *Weekly Reader* today, she merely touched him. She had recently taken to placing her fingertips on the top of his hand whenever she needed to draw him to the present. He responded well to touch. She asked, "What were you thinking about?"

His eyes dropped to the floor, as they did when he believed he'd disappointed her. She had thought working through the student reader was a brilliant idea, filled as it was with short articles on childhood interests. But honeybees were just not holding the interest of the eight year old.

She and Brandon had worked together twice a week since last year. Evie felt triumphant at teaching him how to read. When reading aloud, the boy had inadvertently picked up her proper and precise enunciation, even her modulation—he was a candidate for dramatic reading. She could even imagine him as an adult, giving an inspirational speech. But maybe the idea of the "inspirational" surfaced because of President Kennedy's inaugural address, which was still echoing in her heart: *Ask not what your country can do for you; ask what you can do for your country.* Having lived a life of philanthropy herself, she loved the sentiment. Its oratorical spark could ignite millions to realize their potential for increased purpose and generosity.

Brandon stumbled over a word, and she was pulled back to their humble setting and endeavor. The determination in Brandon's face while reading aloud brought a lump to her throat. With suppressed anxiety, she hoped she would never again be deprived of such a child, that she could enjoy coaching this boy all the way to adulthood. For now, though, she was determined to find a way to stretch his attention span.

"It's all right, Brandon," she assured him after his mental lapse. "I want to know what you were thinking about."

"Um, well, I was thinking about pirates." His gaze was still on the floor. He'd evidently been conditioned by other teachers to feel ashamed over his daydreaming.

"Pirates. That's interesting. How did that happen to come up?" She kept her tone positive. Paging through the reader, she couldn't find anything that could have caused a leap to pirates.

"I don't know." He shrugged. "It just did."

"Are they scary pirates?"

"Hmm, not really. They try to be scary, but they're really nice deep down inside."

"Do you know any pirates?"

He looked up, incredulous, and chuckled. "No. I'm just making it up."

"Have you read about pirates?"

"No, just cartoons."

"Would you like to?"

His face brightened. "Yeah."

For the next several weeks, they read *Peter Pan*, then *Treasure Island.* Brandon's reading had now overtaken that of his classmates. But Evie still noted that if a subject was not of immediate interest to him, he'd daydream himself away to one that was.

During the winter months, she tried different things to help with this. The most effective was demonstrating how reality offered pleasant surprises. As an object lesson, she got permission from his parents to take him to the city. They got on the "L" and went to Chinatown. He especially enjoyed the shops of trinkets—she thought of them as junk shops but nonetheless indulged him with money to buy a few of the items that he was most drawn to. One was a small pottery statue of a Chinese nobleman. While sitting in a restaurant over chop suey, tea and fortune cookies, she asked him to make up a story about the statue. He did reasonably well for one not knowing Chinese history. She then discussed the value of knowledge to good storytelling. Brandon began talking through another story idea. Evie leaned forward with interest, her elbows on the cleared-off table. She realized her little protégé was becoming too dear, too important. But she cast off the nagging notion as she would flick her bejeweled wrist at a fly.

Gerard finally retired. The old chauffeur's eyes were beginning to bother him, particularly for night driving. After finding a nice, robust Irish woman in Cicero, he decided to get married at the age of sixty-seven.

For the occasion, they held a sumptuous reception for the happy couple at *Nuccio's*.

Evie was driving home from a day at Green Bay School in her new Buick. It swept so smoothly down Skokie Valley Road that she almost got pulled over for speeding. The sun was beginning to set over the western suburbs, so she turned on her headlights. Before her session with Brandon, she'd spent time at the Lake Forest home, helping the staff sort through the affairs of the late Georgette Armitage. She and John were taking their time deciding what to do about the staff, as well as with their various real estate properties: Lake Forest, Mayfair, Elm Street.

The Camelot Years with John Fitzgerald Kennedy in office were doing fine things for the economy. But Evie found herself having a hard time not flinching at hearing the president's middle name every time it was mentioned. The Kennedys looked like a charming family. She liked Jackie's style. But Evie was especially drawn to little John-John, who reminded her slightly of Brandon Stewart, despite the few years age difference.

Now and then she wondered why she had never pursued adopting a daughter. The desire had evidently never been strong enough; or maybe the right little girl had never come into her world; or maybe it was that Bertie had been so perfect, there was simply no need to think of adding a daughter to the family. And now, she and John were too old.

From the highway, Evie took North Avenue east, stopping at every red light and stop sign before finally getting to the Gold Coast neighborhood and Elm Street.

The light in the alleyway that led to their garage must have gone out. She drove slowly in case any pet dogs were around. The garage door had been left open for her and she pulled in and turned off the car. After gathering her purse, she opened her door, got out, straightened her skirt, slammed the Buick's heavy door shut and turned. The dark silhouette of a man stood in the open door, coming from the alley.

"Your purse, or I'll shoot."

John came home and found his wife on the sofa, mumbling nonsense and crying while clutching a blanket to her breast. He dropped on his knees next to her, held her and repeated reassuring words on into the night. He'd been called by Maria, one of their cooks, to come home immediately. Maria's Italian accent was so thick and she talked so quickly, he had struggled to understand everything on the phone.

Mrs. Fishbein, a neighbor, had seen a suspicious man leaving Armitages' garage, compelling her to cross the alley and check things out. She found Evie on the cement floor next to the car.

Evie had been fragile enough before this incident, though making great progress. Since the mugging, she now often receded into herself, losing touch, or semi-losing touch, with reality. Some time passed but she remained the same. John decided he couldn't tell her for some time that President Kennedy had been assassinated.

He thought of Brandon Stewart. He went to North Chicago, sought out Brandon's teacher and explained to her what had happened to his wife. He then got permission to take Brandon to the library. Sitting across from the boy, John gently told him that Evie would not be able to see him for a while. As Brandon sobbed, John could well imagine Evie's attraction to the child. He understood their bond. He assured Brandon that her absence wasn't the boy's fault in any way and that Evie still cared for him and was expecting him to do well in school.

It was a miserable drive back to Elm Street.

The next day, John began giving more attention to the matter of their residence. He loved living downtown. Their neighborhood was as safe as any good city neighborhood could be. Patrol cars had a regular presence in the Gold Coast district. But John could not chance having his wife be put in such a vulnerable position again. He could only imagine what had gone through her mind at seeing a man brandishing a gun. Knowing her, the loving mother, she no doubt was imagining Bertie's final feelings of fear and panic the night *he'd* seen a pointed gun. She had experienced several nightmares since the mugging. She never described them, but John wondered whether Gleason's ghoulish face was haunting her nights. He decided to sell the Elm Street brownstone and move into the Lake Forest residence.

He also called his solicitors in London and arranged for them to oversee the selling of the Mayfair home and Kirstead Court. Part of him wanted to have one last look at Bertie's rooms there. He couldn't see how it would help Evie in her current state. Then again, would she hate him for not allowing her the opportunity to decide for herself? He called London again and put the matter on hold.

1964 Lake Forest

"John come here, come here," Evie cried.

John ran down the hall toward her voice and entered the drawing room. She was standing by the large window that overlooked the rose garden to the south, her gray-white hair slightly askew.

"Listen, dear. Shh. Listen." She smiled like a young girl, looking at him in anticipation.

With his heart pounding, a flurry of emotions tried to settle inside him: relief that she was alright, sadness that she was still out of touch and curiosity over what she wanted him to experience. He walked up to her, touched her arm and smiled into her eyes.

"It's that piece, playing on the radio. Come. Sit and listen." She guided him to a sofa. They sat together as the late-day sun streamed around them. He'd come to recognize this music of Delius, realizing more and more its significance to Evie. Bertie had once performed it with a youth symphony in London. John believed it was entitled, "The Walk to the Paradise Garden." The serene beauty of it inspired images of a pastoral journey with promise of some pleasant idyll.

The final cadence hung suspended, filling the room and its garden view with dreaminess. Afterward, Evie leaned her head on his shoulder. "That was lovely, wasn't it? I, hm … I don't know what I'd do if you weren't here to share it with me," she said, her voice tremulous and child-like. When she retreated in this fashion, John had to fight back panic, fearing she might one day not return to reality.

"Promise me, John. Promise you'll never leave me." She faced him and searched his eyes, deeply, as if she could draw up hope from the well of his being. Tiny lines etched as a fan along her temples; but inside her eyes—the spirit within—John found his wife. And he could imagine her as she was at the Paris Ritz in 1917.

"I promise."

She turned back to the view, her gaze earnest; moments lingered.

In a low voice, she finally said, "When I listen to the Delius." She stopped, her breaths shallow but slow. After several moments, he wondered if she would continue. "I, hm, I picture us walking in a lovely garden, but not an English garden. This one has great vistas of beauty and serenity. And Bertie is with us." Her voice took on added solemnity when she added, "Did not Job say he would answer the call from death?" Then, as if sharing a childish secret, she whispered, "'The meek shall inherit the earth.'" She straightened. "So, John, everything will come out fine in the end. You'll see."

"I'm sure you're right."

Looking fully convinced, she turned back to the windows and gazed off, spellbound by her consoling images. John held her, both of them silent, while the sun slowly sank behind the trees.

Chapter Forty-Four

1965 North Chicago

A month later, John had an idea and soon found himself driving up Green Bay Road again. Before reaching North Chicago, he almost turned back. How would Brandon be affected by seeing Evie in her condition? John had been thinking only of Evie's possible reaction, hoping that Brandon's company might somehow draw her back. When the Buckley Road intersection light turned green, he pressed the pedal with determination and continued north.

The boy was now ten and, despite his learning difficulties, John saw what Evie had from the beginning: This boy had a hidden but present brilliance; and, perhaps more importantly, Brandon had heart. John was grateful to find Mrs. Stewart supportive of his plan.

When John shut the door of his Lake Forest home, Brandon stood at his side in reverential silence. The boy appeared to be holding his breath while slowly drinking in the opulence. John's eyes involuntarily welled-up, his feet rooted to the spot. When he felt Brandon's hand gently take his, there came a shiver of surprise followed by a prickling of tears. For an instant, he was standing in his Mayfair house, bringing Bertie home for the first time.

Brandon looked up. "Why are you so sad?"

How could he explain this moment of déjà vu? John struggled to compose himself, failed, took out his handkerchief and tried again. "Uh, it's okay, Brandon." He wiped his eyes. "Really. I, uh, I so appreciate your coming to visit Mrs. Armitage. She's been missing you very much." He knelt down and adjusted his tone for the matter at hand. "She might very well seem different to you. But don't worry." John reached out and lightly squeezed Brandon's shoulders. "I need you to be strong for her. And, well, just be yourself. Just talk with her about your books, and, well, anything that you think might make her happy."

Brandon stood taller and straighter, as if he were a young soldier taking orders. "Yes, Mr. Armitage." Then, almost shocking John outright, Brandon said with surprising insight, "I understand."

After some time, they found Evie upstairs in the room dedicated to Bertie. She was in the chaise, facing the view, her veined hands gripping the chair's upholstered arms. The angle was enough for John to see that her eyes were closed as she hummed a vague melody. Her head quivered in a slow rhythm similar to that of a consummate cellist deep in the spell cast by revered music. Sunlight glinted off the silvery wisps of her hair. Brandon stood breathlessly at John's side.

"Evie?" John said softly. She hummed and twitched as though determined not to relinquish her euphoria. John worried that, in Brandon's eyes, she must seem absolutely mad. He made eye contact with the boy and nodded for him to approach her.

The boy crossed the room with the slightest whisk and scuff, coming up to her side, half facing her, half facing John. His fine brow knitted with what looked like compassion. Evie continued humming, her silk robe crinkled against the chintz as she swayed.

John thought that Brandon would look at him again for reassurance, but instead the boy lifted his hand like a pianist and gently placed his fingertips on top of hers. He held them there and after what must've been two heartbeats, Evie relaxed, stopping all movement and sound. A moment later, her eyelids fluttered open. Her watery gaze locked with Brandon's while a smile stretched across each face simultaneously.

The next thing John knew, Evie tucked her legs under, allowing Brandon to sit at the end of the chaise. She held his hands and they both chuckled. Brandon then initiated conversation. He talked about books, television shows, about having another pleasant go at chop suey—this time with his folks, at a local restaurant.

Evie sat straighter, smoothing her hair with her hands and looking bright, focused and happy.

Though much better, Evie's progress came slowly.

A week later, John returned to Green Bay School. As he pulled up, he watched the activity on the playing field. A physical education coach blew a shrill whistle after an aggressive tackle. John parked across the street and watched the football game, wondering whether he might see Brandon. A short quarterback threw the ball high and slightly wild. At the far end of the field, a brown haired boy hedged with outreached arms. He flinched just before the ball made contact. And, as John painfully anticipated, the boy fumbled it, to the loud chagrin of his classmates. The boy was Brandon.

The coach threw his arms up in disgust, calling Brandon a sissy—loud enough for his voice to carry across the field to John's car. The other kids chimed in and then turned their backs on him. John was glad he hadn't gotten out of the vehicle. He wouldn't want Brandon's humiliation to be made worse. Didn't coaches work with clumsy kids? John had never personally seen a coach slay a student's esteem so heartlessly before. He could barely make himself watch the rest of the session. Brandon hung back, detached and miserable. When the bell rang and the kids were ambling back into the school, no one took up Brandon's company. The boy brought up the rear with his head hanging.

"Oh, yes. I remember your wife. I think Armitage House is a wonderful organization." Mrs. Pulaski had been the new principal when Evie had entered her office three years ago. "I'm sorry to know your wife hasn't been well."

John politely changed the subject, informing her of what he observed on the playing field.

"That's very disturbing. But let me first discuss Brandon with you, and then we'll tackle Mr. Majchrzak. Uh, take that as a pun or not." After a short smile, she set her elbows on her desk and said, "Brandon has not been doing well academically for some time. He's even more withdrawn than before your wife worked with him. I'm afraid he's a very unhappy boy."

"Do you know much of his home life, Mrs. Pulaski?"

"Only that his father recently got out of the military and is now, apparently, married to his civilian job. I don't see him as the nurturing sort."

Still haunted by the football incident, he said, "I'd forgotten how cruel children can be. When my wife and I were running an orphanage in London, years ago, we were able to keep a tight lid on such behavior, but, of course, that was all under one roof, a bit more finite. From what I saw, and if this happens routinely, Brandon must surely have some serious emotional scarring."

"You're right about the cruelty of children. Brandon's father apparently never had the time to teach his son anything athletic, no tossing of the ball or anything. So, the boy had little opportunity to grow out of the clumsiness some children face in their formative years. I agree that schools need more athletic mentoring. Once boys are branded, not one of the other boys has the courage to befriend them; so the Brandons of this world never learn from their peers to overcome their ineptitude. I'm afraid it just gets worse. It pains me, but, well, I suppose we are the ones dropping the ball—that pun was intentional." John returned the wan smile. She continued, "You're right, of course. Mr. Majchrzak should be mentoring and not bullying our students. I'm going to send for him. Do you wish to be present?"

John considered it. "Well, on one hand, I'd like to give him a piece of my mind, but I should leave that up to you and not be presumptuous. But I am angry about what I'd witnessed, I'll tell you that." He made his decision. "I should think it best Brandon not know he had been observed. I won't see the boy today. I'll leave Mr. Majchrzak to your expertise. I realize you have no requirement to update me on whether things improve or not with the coaching here, but I should be appreciative, if you would."

"We share a common interest, Mr. Armitage. You understand how school districts are run, and thus, cannot expect a whole new order of things. Mr. Majchrzak has tenure." She shrugged. "But I will try to reach him as one human being to another." She leaned forward. "But, I'm afraid, off the record, that he's not reachable." She gave a pained smile.

John phoned Evie from the office at Country Day School in Lake Forest. "I wasn't able to talk with Brandon today. I talked with the principal, however. She feels he is still in need of attention… We'll talk about it tonight, okay? … Love you. See you tonight."

John had met the athletic coach at Country Day on several occasions. Chuck Rainert was an avid supporter of Armitage House, Inc., often volunteering his time at their fundraisers. The two sat in the teacher's lounge over some dreadful coffee.

"Evie has become keenly interested in helping a student in North Chicago. Obsessed is too strong a word for it, but somewhere between 'keenly interested' and 'obsessed' is where she is at the moment." John had explained Evie's breakdown although, through Chuck's on-going connection to the Armitage organization, he must have been somewhat aware of the situation. John realized well-meaning whisperings over the welfare of his wife, and even of himself, had been circulating since Bertie's murder.

John talked about what he saw at the ball field in North Chicago.

"I'm afraid it won't be an easy fix for the boy," Chuck replied. "You see, the school has the kids playing some kind of ball sport almost every day. Boys like Brandon have developed what I call the cringe syndrome. When a child is under par with the majority of the other children in something physical like this, he'll get heckled; it's a fact of life. It's almost like chickens pecking to death one of their own. And, as I said, this happens almost every day. When a child experiences this kind of anxiety as a daily thing—well, I haven't read up on it, but I believe that neurological change results. I might go so far as to say damage takes place. What I mean is that the brain then forever and involuntarily signals panic, inhibiting any development of eye and hand coordination."

"That sounds grim," John said. "About as grim as this awful coffee." An idea came to him. "If the teaching staff wanted better coffee here, they could do something about it, right? Get rid of the vending machine and get an A-1 coffee maker, buy good beans, make sure that only those who care about coffee make it. And, voila! You can be caffeinated all day long with pleasure. What I mean is, how can we get Brandon a new coffee maker?"

"Precisely," Chuck concurred. "It would be a big process but possible. You have to remove the irritant or catalyst to the cringe problem. In this case, what I think is that you'd not only have to set Brandon among nicer "chickens," and here it really means those who haven't already seen the repeated failures, because kids will be kids. So, a clean slate, if you will. But, additionally, I suggest he initially take up different types of ball playing than those that contributed to the cringe syndrome. The reflex will still be there, but not as intensely. They don't offer soccer in North Chicago. We do here. Also, he could take up tennis. If he can build confidence in himself in some of these areas, then he is more likely to succeed in others."

"So, in other words," John said, "the only salvation for this kid is to move him to a different school, like this, but here is where I need you, Chuck, with real mentoring. Would you be willing to give this kid extra attention, if we brought him here?"

"I would be honored, Mr. Armitage."

When John got home that evening, he was unprepared for the state Evie was in: the recovered state. She greeted him with her hair colored blonde, neat in a chignon. She was dressed in a smart black wool dress suit and heels, her gaze cheerful and focused.

"I'm so glad you're home, John. I was hoping we could dine out and talk about resuming my work with Brandon." It was the old Evie.

He swallowed a groan, tried to keep in control for her sake but then surrendered to the flood of relief. He had to sit on the foyer settee. She sank next to him. Before she could inquire, he said, "I—I, uh, let me catch my breath. I'm sorry, hon. I've been so worried about you, and, uh." He took in a deep breath and looked at her through his tears. "You look great."

"Oh," she said, relieved and girlish.

They began laughing, he, then she, allowing it to build to near deliriousness, after which, a curative warmth settled over John. He stood and brought her before him while apprising her. "You look marvelous. Where would you like to go?"

She was beaming. "I have a yen for something Greek."

"Greektown, it shall be."

There wasn't a Greek in the place that said their "Opas!" louder than John Armitage that evening. Evie was almost one hundred percent. She'd now and then repeat herself, oblivious that she'd just said the same thing before, but she had reentered his world.

"Would you come with me to talk with Brandon's family about the school?" she asked. "It would look better."

"Of course." He intended to anyway.

"And, I would like to see if I can tutor him again. I was thinking about asking whether he knows how to play chess. I imagine that might help improve his concentration—that is, if he takes an interest in it."

"Well, I can bet that if he's playing with you, he'll take an interest."

"I'd have to learn, too. Oh, that would be fun. We'll have to buy a book and study up on it."

The server brought and ignited their flaming cheese and all three of them yelled, "Opa!" Then John held up his glass of Roditis and clinked it against Evie's. "Cheers."

The small ranch home had a tidy appearance. John turned off the ignition. "Well, here goes," he said, tapping his hands on his cashmere topcoat. He got out, walked around the chrome tail fins of the car's boot, and opened Evie's door. All of the dwellings in this neighborhood were modest, well-kept and close together. He could almost feel several curious gazes from parted drapes and felt ridiculously self-conscious as he slammed the shiny Cadillac door. A twinge of guilt nudged him for not thinking of finding a less conspicuous vehicle for the occasion.

Behind him, the bang of a screen door indicated their reception. John turned and saw Brandon skip down his front steps and approach, the grin wide on his face. From inside the Stewart's home a woman's voice was calling for someone—the exact words were unclear but it seemed like she was calling her husband.

Evie held out her hand to the boy. "Hello, Brandon. I've missed you."

The boy's grin spread wider as he shook her hand. He was a handsome boy, especially when he smiled.

In the still September air, their voices and footfalls carried, as if to cater to the curious.

"Aren't you cold without a jacket?" Evie asked as they got to the steps.

Brandon shook his head. "I've really missed you, too." His voice was husky. They entered and Brandon backed a step away, keeping his eyes on them. "This is my mom, I mean Mrs. Stewart, ugh, well, you already know that." He shrugged, and though self-conscious or nervous, he could not stop grinning.

Mrs. Stewart's expression couldn't seem to settle on an emotion, as if pleasure, embarrassment and, perhaps, something else fought for the surface. "So pleased to meet you both." Her smile was sincere as she shook their hands, her breath jittery from nerves. "Excuse me while I call my husband to join us." She stepped over to an open door off the small kitchen. "Jack, they're here." Her voice was weighted with meaning. He replied.

"He works on model airplanes in the basement, as a hobby. He must be finishing a delicate procedure," she explained. "Please, sit down. Can I get you some coffee?" The living room had one sofa and two chairs. He and Evie sat on the sofa with Brandon joining them.

Evie looked at Brandon. "Do you help your father with his model planes?"

In a hushed voice and wide-open eyes, he replied. "Oh no. I might mess things up."

His reply struck a sad chord in John, followed by warmth as he observed Evie's reaction. Not wanting to validate the unasked question in Brandon's words—the boy doubting his worth in his father's eyes—she covered it over with reassuring small talk.

Mrs. Stewart wasn't as skilled in these matters. Her hands fluttered in her lap as she leaned forward. "Jack is very fussy about things being done just so. He takes his hobby seriously." She sat straighter, as if trying to appear relaxed as footsteps advanced on the stairs. "They're military planes," she added.

The man came through the door off the kitchen, stood for a moment to assess his visitors and then crossed the linoleum floor. "Sorry 'bout that. Glue, you know. Ya have to tidy up so it doesn't dry where it's not supposed to."

John and Evie stood. A second later, Brandon got to his feet in clumsy imitation.

Jack Stewart approached them and held out his hand to John. The grip was firm, the hand warm and calloused. When Mr. Stewart looked at Evie, he paused as if not knowing whether one in society shook a lady's hand. She reached out and got the business done.

"I'm so glad to meet you, Mr. Stewart," she said. There was a lot of charm in those few words.

For just a moment, Jack Stewart was caught off guard. "Uh, please sit, sit." He walked to what looked to be *his* chair and sank down. He was a stocky man, likely in his forties, with a buzz haircut.

As if unable to bear the awkward pause, Mrs. Stewart said, "I'm from Liverpool, you know. Like the Beatles," she laughed, and shook her pageboy-cut brown hair as if she were Paul McCartney. "I understand you're from..." then, as she didn't really know exactly, "London, right?"

"Yes, but a long time ago," Evie replied.

The atmosphere improved after a few pleasantries.

Then John launched into the matter at hand. "As I'd mentioned on the phone, Mr. and Mrs. Stewart, we'd like to do something to help Brandon's education. In no way do we wish to supplant your family relationship or authority. We have spent our lives fostering education, and doing so in consideration of children's various backgrounds." John was wording this carefully, avoiding "special needs" or "disadvantaged."

Mr. Stewart said, "I've read about the work of your organization, but isn't it unusual for you to show interest in one child, one who has parents and a local school?"

"I'll be frank, Mr. Stewart," John said. "We lost our son a decade ago under tragic circumstances."

"Oh, our sincere condolences," Mrs. Stewart said. Jack Stewart nodded, as though from social coercion rather than sincerity.

'Thank you," John replied. "Previously, well, let me go way back. Initially, we ran an orphanage," he met Mrs. Stewart's gaze, "in London. And, we rather ran it as if we had adopted all the children, even arranging for the higher education of those who were interested. So, we started with a hands-on approach. Then, we became a larger organization, thanks to the initial help of Armitage Meats, my family's business. But after losing our son, my wife wanted to resume interacting directly with children." Masking the fact that Brandon was the one and only, he was about to rush into another point.

"Oh," Mrs. Stewart jumped in. "And you've helped him so much, Mrs. Armitage. Really, you have."

"Thank you." Evie replied. "I, uh, I was unwell for a while, as you may have heard, but I never stopped thinking about your son and his abilities."

"Abilities?" Mr. Stewart caught himself too late. His lips pressed together, hoping he hadn't offended his son or his guests.

"We made great progress in our reading, as you know," Evie said.

John said, "We understand that Brandon is not especially happy at Green Bay School."

"No," Mrs. Stewart was quick to say. "No, he isn't." Hope filled her eyes. Mr. Stewart became stone-like.

"We are more than willing to see that the matter of tuition at Country Day School gets dispatched, if you'd allow him to make the change to that school ." The tenor of John's phrasing was intended to imply that they might have some pull to have it waved for Brandon, to soften the impact of charity. Whether they could see through this, he couldn't tell. "We feel the school would provide more effectively for his needs. But it would take commitment from all of us. The school is about a thirty-minute drive down Green Bay Road from here. We realize that would be an inconvenient change of routine for you. But the advantages for Brandon would far outweigh that."

Evie jumped in. "I could be available to help out when your schedule might make the commute too difficult for you."

"Or," John offered, "in time, we might be able to arrange for a bus to pick him up. There are no other Country Day students from this area, uh, currently." He could have kicked himself for not executing the phrase more delicately, "There isn't a bus coming this far north, but we might be able to deal with that. However, that might take some time."

Mr. Stewart said, "Well, of course you don't have any kids from North Chicago going to a private school like that. Don't you think there'll be other problems for Brandon to face, being among rich kids when he'll always be from an ordinary family?"

"That's a valid point, sir," John conceded. "Although everybody is learning to interact with people from different backgrounds today. We see more of it in the cities than here, but it can actually be a good experience, as long as Brandon's interests are with learning and not in being someone he's not. And, from what my wife and Mrs. Pulaski tell me, Brandon appreciates learning."

"I do, Dad. Please let me go. I really want to go there."

Mr. Stewart looked at his wife. "Well, it's up to you. You'll be the one who'll have to drive him back and forth."

"I'll be happy to do that," she said, her eyes intent on his.

"You'll be pulling up in your old VW while all those Society moms will be pulling up in new Cadillacs and such."

"I don't care about that one bit."

"Well, I guess it's decided then." Mr. Stewart stood up and pointed his finger at Brandon. "But if your grades don't improve, I'm going to pull you from that hoity-toity school. Is that understood?"

Brandon paled and swallowed but kept his gaze trained on his father and answered, "I won't let you down." He then looked at Evie. "And I won't let you down, Mrs. Armitage."

Evie placed her hand protectively on his shoulders, and with a slight edge to her voice, said for Mr. Stewart's benefit, "All *we* are asking is that you try your best. That's all any of us can do. And we can find joy in that."

She stood and faced Mr. Stewart. "I have confidence in this boy."

Brandon and John stood. The boy beamed.

Mr. Stewart shifted his stance. "Well, then. Now that that's settled, can I show you folks my model airplanes? They're beauts."

Long shadows crossed tree-lined Green Bay Road looking like zebra stripes. Evie finally said, "I have dealt with a lot of people for what? Sixty years? Oh, my lord. And, and I've never run across a man who, after a serious discussion, then skirts issues by asking if we would like to see his toys!"

"I'm thinking he just didn't have much social experience growing up. But, I am proud of Brandon. For a little tyke, he sure has gumption."

"Oh, I was proud, too, John."

"My father failed me. I see now that it wasn't intentional. But if I hadn't had Edwina Pitt around, I wonder how well I would have faced life."

"You, dear, are a fighter. A quiet fighter, but a fighter. I can still see you running around, searching for me at Ypres, smoke and chlorine gas vapors everywhere. But, you're right. Some are born with resilience, but others can learn it. I'm going to think about that.

October 1965 London

John decided to take Evie to London and then, together, they would come to a conclusion about their properties. The gamble, of course, was the affect placing her back in Mayfair, Bertie's "birthplace," might have on her.

This was the first time that they'd flown over the Atlantic. Sabena's new Boeing 707-320 was comfortable, and he was surprised when he heard that they were preparing to land so soon at Heathrow.

He had phoned ahead to the woman who cared for their home. When they entered the grand foyer, it smelled fresh and clean. But the feel of the place was amazing. He couldn't help but think that it was still 1948.

First Evie walked into the rear drawing room. "I have to sit in this chair," she said. This was the chair where she had sat with Bertie the waif and listened to him recite *Peter Rabbit*. She looked at the cold, empty fireplace, but seemed unaffected. She then turned to John who made it a point to sit in the same chair he'd been in that night. He felt relieved to see the clarity of her eyes as she smiled.

"Thank you for bringing me back before selling it," she said calmly.

Evie then sat at the dining table and remark about how the boy had polished off helpings of pudding.

John felt the highest level of anxiety as they were mounting the staircase en route to their son's room. She opened the door and stepped in. The autumnal sun filled the room with something joyous. She went and sat on his bed, no doubt recalling the times she had sat and read to him, and her hands ran across the pillows beneath the covers. Looking up at a bureau, she gasped in delight.

"John look! I'd forgotten this was here!" She got up and crossed to the chest of drawers. On its top sat a framed photograph of Bertie holding his violin, looking so proud. She kissed it and then held it to her breast.

They spent the rest of the day roaming, sitting, reminiscing.

Later, in the sunroom with a pot of tea, John watched the garden, enjoying its end-of-day change as its color changed to darker blue-gray hues. A golden leaf drifted down past their window, followed by another.

Evie set down her cup and said, "I'm just fine. I can do this." She turned to him and added, "I mean I can part with this home, John. I'm ready to move on." She lifted the framed picture of Bertie that had been resting on her lap, gazed at it and added. "This was worth the flight." She beamed, her smile for him, her lovely eyes graced with gratitude.

Before heading back to Heathrow, they phoned Adam and Meg, as well as Jiggs and Eloise and arranged to meet at Islington House for a visit. The new cook prepared light sandwiches and tea and cakes. In the parlor, Evie brought out her picture of Bertie, which brought up some pleasant reminiscences. John described their private service, and the scattering of Bertie's ashes on the lake.

"I can hardly believe it, but a kind of peace has overridden my bitterness—not the hurt, of course, or the void." The "family" dignified this with supportive silence. Evie added, "The lake as his grave is somehow better for me than a cold marble tomb. It's as though the lake is ours and in some abstract way, Bertie is still part of our lives."

1965 Country Day School

All the leaves are brown (the leaves are brown); and the sky is gray (and the sky is gray-hey). The radio at the concession stand blared out *California Dreamin'* by the Mamas and the Papas. Despite this fitting description of their day, the November air was filled with anticipation before the soccer match.

Coach Rainert waved from the team benches and trotted over. "Glad you could make it today, Mr. Armitage."

"Wouldn't miss it. How's Brandon coming along?"

"Well, I don't think he'll ever be able to catch a football without cringing, but with soccer, he's the man, you might say. And, we have him doing some weightlifting and cross country running. He's gaining confidence, and, I believe, having a good time at it."

"Thank you, Mr. Rainert." John slapped the man's back. They shared a smile of satisfaction and then looked out over the field, anticipating the game.

John then bought a hot chocolate for Evie and a coffee for himself and headed for the bleachers. This was the first time Brandon was playing as striker for his team. Little clouds of steam rose from the two cups. John came up to the bleachers and saw that Mrs. Stewart was sitting next to Evie.

"Well, hullo. The proud mother. Is Mr. Stewart here?" John asked as he handed Evie her drink.

"No. He's working, but at least things are good at home. He's no longer threatening to pull Brandon from Country Day at every turn." She looked as if she were wrestling with what she wanted to say next.

"I just can't thank you two enough. I can't believe my son even wanted to play on this team. And here he is a striker." She looked toward the team down front. Some were taking off their sweatshirts, other boys were running and bouncing in place, raring to go.

"Can I get you something to drink, Mrs. Stewart?" John offered, before sitting.

"Oh, thank you, no." She looked down and then toward the players as though she felt unworthy to be in their company. Trying to sound comfortable, she added, "Nice day for this."

John watched Brandon and his teammates spike their energy with preparatory jumping jacks. "The boy is filling out nicely. Doing some weight lifting, I understand."

"He's doing a lot of everything. Sometimes I worry he's taking on too much. But he loves it all. Well, not his math, I'm afraid. But he's great with words. Reads voraciously, writes nicely, I think. Have you seen his poetry?" She was too excited to wait for more than a nod. "I think playing chess has helped his concentration. That was a brilliant idea, Mrs. Armitage. He's even trying to teach me. And he's been practicing his cello." Despite herself, a tear escaped and trailed down her rosy cheek. "I can't believe he's gone from a lost boy to one who finds exhilaration in almost everything." She turned toward the field and wiped away a tear.

"We were pleased to see his grades coming along so nicely," Evie said. "He'll have no trouble getting into whichever university he chooses."

John said, "I'm sure he'll earn a scholarship, the way he's going." The thought that, if nothing else, Armitage money would address the need hung in the air.

"You two are angels from heaven, you are."

Early in the game, it was evident that the Country Day Upper School team had, clearly, been well trained. The midfielders showed a lot of spunk as each moved in concert with the other team members. Playing offense, a midfielder named Brown passed the ball to Brandon who kicked it just beyond the goalie's reach. First goal of the game. Brandon's back and bum got patted by most of his teammates.

After a few plays, St. John's Academy got ahead. Now Country Day had the ball back. Brandon and his midfielders were making their way toward the goal. Again, it was Brown who passed the ball to Brandon. Brandon's foot went back for the kick but his left foot slipped a fraction and his kick went wild, just tipping the ball. As St. John's got control, Country Day fans groaned and a few even booed. Mrs. Stewart and Evie gasped. John's hands became damp and his heart pounded his chest. How would Brandon take the crowd's reaction? The focus of those in the bleachers shifted to Country Day's zone defense, but John kept his eyes on Brandon. What he noticed changed the nature of his pulse from anxiety to excitement. The boy's countenance shone with a victor's determination: jaw set, gaze fixed, his body moving lithely. A Country Day boy named Baske snagged back the ball. Baske, Brandon and Brown worked it back up the field as if they were blood brothers, knowing every gesture and intention. As they neared the goal, Baske passed the ball to Brandon who kicked it hard and into the upper ninety, just out of reach of the goalie.

"Right in the sweet spot," John cried. "Way to go, Brandon!"

It was a good day for Lake Forest, but a great day for Brandon Stewart and his mentors.

1975 Armitage Global

Engagement and purpose—that was the difference John saw in his wife. Evie had returned, fully involved again at Armitage House, Incorporated. Like a religious zealot, she'd been immersing herself in preparation for something she'd wanted to do for many years: expand their efforts to developing countries.

UNICEF had been making decent headway, reaching the most desperate areas with basic help. *People don't want charity, they want opportunities,* Evie had said, justifying her wish to build upon UNICEF's progress. *With education, people can at least have a chance, or at the very least, self-respect.*

John held up his tall beer glass. Despite the passing of more than a decade since Evie's illness, occasional waves of euphoria refreshed him. He gazed through the beer's golden effervescence as if he could see into a brighter future. The clink of Evie's glass against his startled him, pulling him from his musing.

"Cheers," she said with a chuckle. With bright eyes, her expression offered: *a penny for your thoughts.*

"You look lovely," he said.

Her lips twitched. Her restrained mirth revealed acknowledgment. The two of them were playing atop good undercurrents, the type of game that engendered warmth, as if they were alone in the place rather than surrounded by the happy-hour crowd.

"How's the nose?" she asked, nodding toward his Weissbier.

"Huh? Oh, the nose." He took a whiff and then a slow sip. "Ah, nice, and this has a banana-clove-ness about it. A little spicy." He sipped again and savored. "And a pleasantly dry clove-like aftertaste. Marvelous."

After some companionable silence, they talked about setting up a committee to investigate the circumstances needed in order to achieve their international aims.

Evie suggested, "What about asking Brandon to serve on the committee?"

Brandon Stewart had graduated at the top of his class from Lake Forest College the year before, and was working on his MBA. Throughout his college years, he had worked in different supportive capacities at their company.

"Yes, of course, if he wishes. My thought would be to start with the countries that are the most stable, politically."

Evie countered, "But the places that aren't, need the most help to educate their young."

The cocktail waitress came up and asked if they needed fresh drinks, or if they cared to order any food. John thanked her and settled the tab. He'd made dinner reservations at a more celebratory place—Chez Paul. The waitress departed.

He continued, "Yes, but we can't set up schools, fill them with our teachers and administrators and then have the whole works jeopardized by revolutions or guerilla activities. We need to obtain a fair prediction of an area's political climate, then institute a pilot program, learn the ropes better, and see how we might expand."

And so it happened that as John and Evie became octogenarians, Armitage House Inc. began to spread its wings over far-flung locales.

Chapter Forty-Five

1976

To offset the fierceness of the winter storm raging outside, John, Evie and Brandon sat around the black and gild tea table in front of the library fireplace. They were talking of equatorial regions.

"Personally, I'd like to go to Kenya," Brandon said, now officially part of the Armitage House team. He was studying a map of the African continent. Notebooks of research were piled on his lap and around him on the settee. "But I was thinking of choosing a country that was less developed but not especially prone to droughts."

"Agreed," Evie said. She was dressed in a black wool pantsuit sporting black velvet lapels, brightened by her onyx and gold jewelry; she even added an African-styled copper bracelet for the occasion. Checking the teapot, she got up from her wing chair and gently tugged at the old-fashioned bell-pull for Margaret.

"So, as much as I'd love to be in Kenya," Brandon went on, "I was attracted to Madagascar for our first sub-Sahara school, for several reasons."

"Forgive the interruption." Evie resumed her seat. "But what is the airport situation there?"

"There's one just outside Toamasina, state owned but open."

"What are these reasons?" John asked, enjoying Brandon's healthy self-confidence.

Margaret entered, having made record time. "Yes, ma'am." The matronly cook still looked fresh and cheery despite the long day.

"Could we please have a fresh pot of tea?"

"I'll get right on it, ma'am." Margaret smiled, beaming most of it at their guest before turning to go.

"Oh, and—" Evie's features creased, her gaze on Brandon, as if trying to read his culinary yen. "And I think we'd like some of those molasses cookies I asked you to make this afternoon."

Brandon grinned. "Yes, Margaret. You make the best molasses cookies this side of Persia."

"You got it, honey." And off she went.

John enjoyed the current familial sense of his household. Margaret was not only the best cook they'd had in years, but she knew as if by instinct the right degree of, and the right time for, familiarity and formality.

The wind howled against the six large windows behind the heavy draperies and occasionally moaned down the chimney, teasing the crackling fire. The surf below the bluff had been roaring all day. Brandon was staying the night, partly because of the storm but mostly because they all enjoyed the house party camaraderie. Brandon now had a bungalow in east Evanston.

Brandon said, "What I like about Madagascar is the healthy state of their agriculture, the degree of need for education, especially in the villages, and the potential for higher learning in its largest cities. The government is as stable as the best of them. There was a coup a couple of years ago but things have stabilized since." He turned to Evie and added, "And the snakes there are not poisonous." He smiled.

"What languages are spoken there?" John asked. "And, is Madagascar considered part of Africa? Just curious."

"Ah, to your last question, it depends on who you ask. Geologists, anthropologists and historians often refer to the Big Red Island as part of Africa, but the inhabitants themselves usually don't. As to languages, here's an advantage: French is pretty widely spoken there—it belonged to France until 1958, but you likely know that. So, that's a good starting point—it's much easier to find teachers who speak the language. But as soon as possible, our teaching staff should be expected to learn Malagasy, which, thanks to some British missionaries, is now also a written language."

"And what is the disease situation?" Evie asked.

"That's also a point in its favor. The only malady that you might want to immunize against is malaria. I've read nothing of the other diseases that plague the continent, no dengue fever or that kind of thing. And some of the island is dry and of higher altitude, so the possibility for malaria would only exist in the more tropical parts of the country."

They each sat back and switched to lighter topics while anticipating Margaret's return. In short order, they heard her footsteps coming down the hall.

"I have a nice pot for y'all and a platter, not just a plate, mind you, but a platter of these cookies. Mr. Armitage, would you like me to bring the decanter over?"

"That would be nice, thank you, Margaret. Brandon, would you like a whisky?" John stood and took the decanter from her.

"Maybe later, thanks. Tea and Margaret's cookies go together mighty well."

Evie said, "Margaret, dear? I think I would like a shot of brandy in my tea. Would you, please?"

"Yes, ma'am. On a night like this, I'd say you got the right idea."

Margaret found the brandy in the cabinet and set it down next to Evie. "I'll be turnin' in now, if that's all right?" Margaret said before leaving.

With a mouth full of cookie, Brandon made moaning sounds of pleasure for Margaret's benefit.

Evie rolled her eyes at him and said, "Thank you, Margaret. Sleep well."

John sipped his whisky. Speaking partly into his glass, he said, "There was one other thing I happened to read about Madagascar's attributes, Brandon."

"What's that?"

John took another sip, met Brandon's gaze, and smiled. "With the synthesis of peoples from the Indian Ocean—African, Indian and Arab, with a bit of French thrown in—one could find some of the most beautiful women in the world."

Brandon held a cookie in mid-air and replied, "You caught me out, Mr. Armitage."

The three laughed and talked by the fire till the wee hours.

Chapter Forty-Six

1981 Madagascar

The Land Rover rocked and complained as its wheels continued to spin and kick up loose gravel. While the crest of the hill, only yards ahead, taunted Brandon, beads of sweat began to run down his brow, getting in his eyes and blurring his vision. After a slight turn to the left and with slow steady acceleration, his front tires finally got onto some scrub. Once he had all four back on hard-packed earth, his wheels got purchase and shot the vehicle down onto the ensuing plain.

"Yee-ha!" he cried. Brandon Stewart was having the time of his life in the wilds of Madagascar.

About a mile out along the sweeping view sat a cluster of shanties. He was canvassing the area, searching for outlying families. The Albert Armitage Learning Center, set up in village of Mahkar, had been up and running for four months, but still had room for more students.

As he approached the shanties, it became evident that only two were inhabitable; the roofs of the others had long since rotted and caved in. There was a large shed along which ran weathered corral fencing. A donkey sauntered up to the fence and gazed sadly at him. Beyond one of the dwellings lay a struggling garden in desperate need of weeding. He pulled up to that house and saw, parked at its far end, a very abused Renault with no windshield, dented and coated with dried mud. And sticking out from under it sprawled two muscular legs.

Surprised that this mechanic—who couldn't have failed to hear his arrival—was ignoring him, Brandon proceeded with caution. He first looked around for any evidence of a farm dog. Fairly satisfied, he got out and stepped toward the sandal-clad feet.

"Hullo," he cried. The legs didn't twitch. Was he dead? After two more steps, Brandon heard snoring come from under the car. Just off the sagging porch, empty beer cans lay strewn here and there with flies alighting and buzzing.

Brandon squatted in front of the Renault. "Hullo."

The snoring stopped, a leg twitched, and the prostrate man's voice began rumbling in Malagasy expletives.

Not especially confident in his Malagasy, Brandon tried, "Bonjour."

The cursing switched to French.

Carefully, the man edged from under the car, sat up, shielding his eyes from the sun with his hand. He was wearing grimy khaki shorts and a sweaty undershirt. Puffy, bloodshot eyes stared at the intruder. The body was athletic though small-boned, whereas the man's face had that wasted look of one who lived fast and hard, appearing almost middle-aged when he was probably still in his twenties. He spoke in French. "What the hell?"

Brandon apologized for disturbing him and explained the reason for his visit. Dawning interest filled the man's expression, but Brandon noticed the gaze was directed to something behind him. He turned but all he saw was his parked Rover and a molting chicken pecking the ground. The man got up without saying a word, walked to a rusty well pump and was soon splashing water on his face and over his head. Unconcerned about the rivulets that ran off his greasy black hair, he repeated, "What the hell?"

Brandon introduced himself and explained, "I run a school in Mahkar. We're inviting rural children to come, even if it's only for a Saturday. Do you know of any children in this area?"

His nose pinched in distaste. Then a twisted grin slowly stretched across his face. "Nice wheels."

"Ah, yes, thanks." Brandon waited for a more relative reply.

"Manek is out hunting. Been gone for, I don't know, a couple of days." Behind the blank expression, Brandon saw that the mind was busy.

"Manek is younger, then? School age?"

"My little brother. Maybe fourteen, but almost a man."

"I didn't catch your name."

The man shifted.

"His name is Tarek, my brother," a boy's voice said from the house. "I heard of your school." The boy came out onto the porch.

"Manek, get inside."

The boy ignored him and stayed put.

Tarek puffed out his chest while mischief glinted from his eyes. He strutted past to admire the Rover. His musty stench caught in Brandon's throat.

"I like these wheels, man." His hand ran along the front fender and up to the driver's door. "The white man has good taste. Ya gotta give them that." In a split-second, he had the door open and was up on the driver's seat, reaching for the ignition.

Brandon leapt and clamored, "What do you think you're doing?" He reached in and grabbed Tarek, neck and armpit, and with surprising strength, pulled him out and onto the ground.

Tarek was up, hands slapping, feet kicking. They were soon grappling for control. Hot, deadly breath belched out as he cried, "If I don't kill you now, I'll come lookin' for you at your sissy school!"

"Stop, Tarek, stop," Manek cried, running to intercede.

Tarek cried, "Get ba—" Brandon overpowered him, throwing him down again.

Tarek scrambled up and ran toward his own car. Brandon hopped in the Rover, slammed his door and started the engine. As he was backing to turn out, he saw Tarek coming round the Renault, shoving his brother out of the way and gaining ground. The man screamed like a banshee while brandishing a wrench. With pounding pulse and shaky hands, Brandon struggled to find the gear. Finally, his tires kicked up dust and took off. Tarek's cursing sailed over the ruckus. In the rearview mirror, the angry man flung his weapon. The rear window shattered with a startling crash; glassy bits sprayed the interior. As he gained more distance from the scene, Brandon reckoned that he'd likely run into Tarek again.

From the deck of the *Scheherazade*, a mid-size cruise ship, John and Evie caught sight of Brandon and a young woman waving to them from the docks of Toamasina.

At eighty-five years of age, John resented having to dress like an old man. His susceptibility to skin cancer had him wearing a wide-brimmed sun hat. He hated even more his wrap-around sunglasses and orthopedic walking shoes.

Evie looked great, although she was wearing the same type of hat.

"There they are!" Evie cried and waved.

The mid-day sun was hot, making the vista of the old port a shimmering mirage.

Coming off the gangplank, Evie ran up to Brandon with her arms out. "Oh, it's so good to see you. So good, so good." She hugged him tightly, pivoting back and forth. After she released him, Brandon introduced John and Evie to Zoila Charbonneau, one of the teachers he had hired soon after arriving last year.

"I answer to Zoila or Zoe," she said amiably.

She was French Polynesian and had been teaching in Toamasina before accepting a position at the Armitage Learning Center.

John took Zoe's hand in both of his. "Nice to meet you."

"My pleasure, Mr. Armitage."

"Oh, it's just John and Evie," he replied.

Evie put in, "Yes, by all means."

John reached to pat Brandon on the back and then embraced him instead.

"Ah, my boy," John added in sotto voce, "I see you discovered for yourself what I'd said about the women in this part of the world."

"Yes, sir."

After a round of polite chatter, Brandon gestured to the north. "Your hotel is just over there. If your sea legs are up to it, we can walk. Or, if you'd prefer, I can get either a taxi or a rickshaw for you two." Brandon's eyes were smartly shielded by a pair of Calvin Klein sunglasses that made John want to throw his wrap-arounds into the Indian Ocean. They decided to stroll to the Tsara Komba Hotel.

Three porters came up with their luggage on trolleys. All set out toward the nearby resort. The yellow scarf attached to Evie's sunhat rippled in the breeze like a banner blazing ahead of a caravan. She chatted excitedly with Zoe, holding her arm as they walked, with John, Brandon and the porters in tow.

The hotel was simple but clean and spacious. After freshening up, John and Evie took the stairs down to the lobby.

"We're up for anything," Evie said to the young couple.

John offered a smile, fairly certain he masked his weariness.

"I have a café in mind," Brandon said, his eyes beaming. "And we'll take a cab. I had to drop off the Land Rover for a new back window before we drive out of town."

"The view and the café make for a nice introduction to Toamasina," Zoe said, quick to contribute.

The taxi struggled along the broad boulevard, gears grinding, tailpipe polluting while making obscene noises.

Evie made a face that said *Oh my!*

Trying to be one of the fellows, John commented, "This cab ride will be something I'll long remember about our trip."

The café *La Louise* looked painfully ordinary, but its terrace view of the city and ocean were marvelous. They got a table partially shaded by an overhead trellis and settled in.

"Oh, look at that," Evie remarked as a little leaf-tailed gecko scurried over a low stone wall. "How charming," she said, "as long as he stays over there." She smiled. The featured beer came from India. A few of the menu items were French, as the name of the place implied, but most were curries of one sort or another and there were different rice dishes. They ordered a spinach and cheese appetizer, then a lamb vindaloo, a coconut curry tofu, a chicken tikka masala and a saffron rice dish, all to pass around and sample.

Evie sipped her beer and asked, "Brandon, how safe is it here? Is there much crime?"

"Oh, it's about as safe as anywhere." Brandon replied, a beat too quickly, his eyes locking with Zoila's, as if to warn her to tread carefully. She turned and gave a concurring smile.

With nonchalance that John recognized as feigned, Evie observed, "You said your back windshield is getting replaced. Funny, back home it's almost always the front that gets hit by stones and such."

"Yes, well, out in the wilds, all manner of things fly up, er, while you're off-roading. It's a blast," Brandon replied, his expression shadowed.

"Interesting." Evie sat back, her smile tentative.

The meal was delicious. They dined while the sun was setting behind the trees, casting muted pink and blue-gray hues over the ocean. John could have sat there for the rest of the evening, but prudence won out.

Standing at the curb in front of the hotel, Evie said, "I can't tell you how exciting it is to be here."

"Well," Brandon replied, "we'll meet you here bright and early tomorrow. Our main point of interest will be that bazaar we talked about."

In parting, Evie kissed their cheeks in European fashion.

Zoila held on to Evie's hand and said, "Brandon is dropping me off at Veera's place, another teacher who keeps a flat here."

At this, Brandon's face flushed scarlet. Zoila looked self-conscious. But Evie embraced her firmly. "Good night, dear. You're," she stepped back, smiling, "you're absolutely lovely."

The next morning, they took off for a day at the bazaar. This time, they took rickshaws to the open courtyard near the center of the city. Evie went with Brandon; Zoila with John. John asked about her life in Madagascar.

"My parents were teachers. We lived in Reunion before moving here. For university, I attended Strathmore in Nairobi. So, we were here as a family for four years. They returned to Reunion two years ago."

Rolling and bumping along the old streets, John observed people who seemed both primitive and cosmopolitan. From what he could see, many small businesses were operated by Chinese, by Arabs, and by people who were a blend of the Indian Ocean races, making them strikingly attractive. Life here appeared more simple, appealingly so.

The Toamasina Bazaar reminded him of a Peter O'Toole movie, narrow awning-clad aisles wound about, creating a labyrinth filled with cacophonous interchanges.

Evie and Brandon ambled away, oblivious. John had to catch up and arrange a time and place to meet.

Zoila then led John to her favorite part of the market. In short order, he lost all sense of direction as they wended their way through, eventually coming out into another sunny courtyard. Three rows of benches were set in a semi-circle, some shaded by vendor awnings. In the sunny center were eight young African boys dancing athletically to the beating of drums. John felt he was seeing the Madagascar version of Brooklyn Rock, but the dancers possessed more elegance of movement. Happy spectators cheered and clapped along. The music was atonal, rhythmic and distorted as it blared from damaged speakers.

Zoila lead John to a shaded bench. She excused herself and returned shortly with a paper cup containing a cool beverage that was milky, fruity and delicious. The boys finished, to much applause. This was followed by an ensemble: a man with a sitar, one with two drums and a woman wearing a sari. She sang in a nasally voice and moved gracefully to the music. The crowd loved her just as heartily.

John relaxed and marveled how the unhappy son of a Chicago meat packer could, in his old age, feel at one with this melting pot crowd in Madagascar. He began recounting life's blessings—thinking how he had no regrets about how he chose to live, how full it all had been—when the pain encroached, the reminder of his one big regret—encountering Gleason Fitzgerald.

As if to help rescue him from this shadow, Zoila nudged him and stood. "How would you like to see some local art?"

He thanked her with more enthusiasm than necessary. Perhaps it was a woman's instinct; she couldn't have known how grateful he would be that she'd pulled him from the memory of Gleason.

They came into an alley cooled by shade and containing fewer bodies. John soon realized it was an ancient street with shop windows and the occasional rickshaw rattling through. They passed a young boy, sitting on his haunches against a wall, methodically eating an orange. John smiled down on him and the lad nodded in acknowledgement, the orange kept at his lips.

They rounded a corner. A flutter of colors drew his attention upward. Between this set of two-story buildings, laundry billowed in the breeze; pinks, whites and yellows brightening the shadowed lane below.

Zoila walked into a shop and beckoned him to follow. When he stepped in, he was met with the pleasant aroma of cloves and something pleasantly pungent. The set-up of the place reminded him of an old-time American general store; it was run by an older man and woman with a little boy assisting. The Indian heritage and resemblance of the boy to those John imagined were the lad's grandparents was evident. They all smiled at him with gleaming white teeth. At one side of the shop sat barrels of spices. Above them, on shelves, stood glass containers with more spices. There were wood-framed glass counters displaying bright woven textiles, expert carvings, some in wood and some in what looked like ivory. Zoila explained that the latter was in some cases horn, in others, whales' teeth. There were shelves behind the counter, full of basic items; apparently, it was also a drug store.

On the far wall, muted sunlight from a side window cast its warmth on a few disc-shaped works displayed on shelves. He approached. One in particular held his attention, a large ebony plate. The scene etched on it was of a family: a man, a woman and two boys in a canoe-like craft. It was expertly done. A work of art, in fact. He lifted it and held it with a reverential feeling before taking it to the counter, where he paid in francs, and refused the change.

Broad smiles flashed back and forth, heads nodded with enthusiasm, as if they were all scientists congratulating each other on discovering the elixir of eternal youth. The older woman carefully wrapped the plate and even found a box in which to place it. As if that weren't enough, she set it in a burlap bag with entwined handles. Zoila looked pleased to have been party to the find. Everyone did.

John and Zoila were late for the rendezvous at the front of the bazaar.

"Sorry, you two," he said. "Been waiting long?"

"We've been entertained by the comings and goings."

Brandon next led them to a nearby café that had the look of an Italian piazza. After drinks were served and sipped, Evie brought out her treasures.

"I just couldn't make myself bargain for these," she said.

"That's nice of you, Mrs. Armitage," Brandon said. "You know, any reduction you get in price means that the seller has to work that many more hours to make up for it. Things are not overpriced here."

"I suppose if it becomes commercialized for tourists that will change," Zoila said, "but for now, things are simple."

"I hope you will find these more to your liking, John," Evie said.

She pulled from a bag a Khaki-colored safari type hat.

"I love it." He leaned in and kissed her cheek.

"You'll look just like Indiana Jones in that, dear. And then I found these," she continued. The next item was a pair of Calvin Klein sunglasses similar to Brandon's. "I caught your look of envy yesterday, even though half of your face was hidden by those wrap-arounds," she explained.

"Well, that Calvin gets around," John said with a chuckle.

Evie bought a colorful scarf for Zoila and two different curries in capped attractive glass vials for Brandon.

John lifted the box from the burlap bag. "And this, my dear, is for you. I hope you like it." He hoped to heaven she would, that it would not backfire and disturb her.

Evie opened and unwrapped the gift meticulously. When she held the plate before her, a slow gasp sounded from her lips. She pondered the piece, tracing the etchings with her fingertips.

"Oh…my." Her voice faltered. Finally, she turned the plate for the rest to see. "Never in my life has a gift meant more to me." She shook her head and pressed her lips together, her expression full of serious marvel, as if trying to assimilate all that was bound up with the image—as if wondering whether one could press so many memories together?

"Thank you, John."

They followed up the occasion with a fine bottle of wine and then a seafood salad made of crab and lobster infused with ginger-lime, resting on a bed of fresh greens, and a chicken dish prepared with rice and fresh coconut.

Mid-way through the meal, Evie proclaimed, "Get me a glass of vodka, please, John. I want to raise it high and say for all to hear *Oh Khorosho!* How good this all makes me feel!"

Chapter Forty-Seven

Early the next day, Brandon and Zoila pulled up in his Land Rover and collected John and Evie. They drove out of Toamasino to the north and west. Along the outskirts of the city small clusters of shabby homes clung together as if for support. At one point, a friendly dog ran alongside them to the end of the neighborhood.

In short order, the hilly terrain opened up to wider vistas. Towering baobabs majestically dotted the scene.

Evie said, "I love those trees with their thick trunks shooting up to heaven before finally spreading out their branches. They resemble people stretching their arms to one another for something festive . . . or to praise their maker."

John appreciated the moment of silence the kids afforded Evie's sentiments, dignifying her. After a while he said, "I read somewhere that the human body naturally relaxes as it takes in an open, natural view."

"As we drive on," Brandon said, "the land and sky remind me of central Montana." Brandon must've have seen an amused expression on Zoila's face in the rear mirror, John thought. Brandon amended, "I don't mean to sound like a travel guide."

Later, they stopped at a family-run petrol station. Brandon introduced them to the Ragvandjee family, all of whom gathered round the counter to meet the folks who were behind the emergence of their school. The father said something in Malagasy.

Brandon translated. "He said they are grateful to have the school nearby. Well, to them it's nearby. We have another hour to go. It's the first school Raimo and Veroniaina have been able to attend. They thank you."

Evie, using her practiced Malagsy, said, "You're very welcome." And then resorted to a bit of charade to indicate to the children how happy she was that they could attend.

Mrs. Ragvandjee scuttled to the back rooms. She returned with a bottle of wine and held it out to Evie.

"Thank you, dear."

The mother bowed numerous times, smiling.

After Raimo filled up the Rover's tank, Brandon led John and the women to rest under the large shade tree to the side of the business. The Ragvandjee children took turns peeking out the station window at them, all bright eyes and teeth.

"They're an upbeat bunch, the Ragvandjees," Brandon said as he sat.

"Yes," Eve said, "So I can see."

Zoila began handing out pita bread, napkins and cans of juice. She then opened a plastic container, filled with bits of goat cheese, a little olive oil and oregano.

John leaned his back against the tree, feeling as content as he could remember.

Shadows stretched long when they pulled up to the village of Mahkar. The modest homes were almost shanties, but most were neat in appearance.

"The Sihanak people who live here are very tidy and polite," Brandon said, a bit concerned over the fatigue on John's face.

Finally, he drove up to the school complex and stopped.

Evie said, "It looks smaller than the pictures indicated. But I am very pleased. Aren't you, John?"

He offered a weary, though agreeable, nod.

"Very pleased, indeed." Evie opened her door and stepped out, turning this way and that.

"I'm so glad you are," Zoila said, getting out.

"I must walk around it. Would you prefer to come along, John, or wait here?"

"Go on. I'm fine here, for now."

"I'll walk with you," Zoila offered.

Brandon stayed with John, hearing Evie's enthused voice rising above the building in occasional, echoing snippets.

"It's not Country Day School," Brandon said, enjoying John's familiar facial expressions as shared memories arose between them. "Though it's just cinder block walls and metal roofing, it's amazing what takes place inside. When a class of active children begins to quiet down and hang on your every word—or better yet, when they gaze at every visual aid, as if they were discovering Shangri-La, well," he grinned, "there's nothing like it."

"Proud of you, son." John's tired face was slow to register that he'd called Brandon "son." The gentle philanthropist let it go—no self-deprecating chuckle, no correcting the comment—as if he were comfortable to leave it. And the flood of warmth, the sense of parental approval, after several months' work and adventure here, caught Brandon by surprise. The old bond was there, and John's watery eyes said volumes. The two sat silent in early evening's golden light.

Zoila and Evie came around the back of the structure, Evie leaning slightly on Zoe's arm.

At the edge of the school yard, Brandon noticed a boy in a tree, watching them. He looked vaguely familiar. Yet the boy, maybe in his teens, didn't look like one of their students, all of whom he knew fairly well. But with the shadows and distance, he could be wrong; he shrugged it off.

Brandon pointed to the faculty and guest cottages and said, "During the first few months, we had to make do with the well pump. I'd say it was after, hmm, Day Three that the novelty began wearing off. We really appreciated getting running water."

There were ten cottages at present. Zoila shared her two-bedroom dwelling with a math teacher named Honorine DuBois, a middle-aged woman of Haitian descent who Brandon had hired in Chicago. Honorine had been educated at Hull House and was keen to carry on the tradition of reaching out to those in need.

After John and Evie unpacked and freshened up, they joined Brandon, Zoila and Honorine. John looked better and was happy to take a stroll of the premises this time.

John commented amiably on the cost of getting electricity to the complex.

Brandon said, "We really appreciate having lighting and ceiling fans, but the best thing about getting electricity here is that it allows us to have a movie night for the children and their parents. Once a week, we project a movie on the exterior east wall."

"I like that."

"I was concerned that films like *The Godfather* or *Cabaret* might be too shocking for this gentle, isolated group. So far, we've shown them a few Disney films dubbed in French and a few black and white classics. For some reason, the villagers found *The African Queen* hilarious."

That night Brandon and Zoila set up the patio in front of Brandon's cottage with chairs, lit a number of candles and, when joined by John and Evie, served cocktails. Honorine brought over a light dinner as a gesture of appreciation and then excused herself.

In the twilight, Marcus Vincent, one of the teachers, ambled in from the athletics field. He kept a respectful distance, allowing them privacy. In the hush of evening, he waved from across the grounds and then ducked into his cottage. The smell of baked earth rose from the ground around them, and a bird called out plaintively before flying off into the night.

"I almost feel as if I'm on safari," Evie said. "Well, I suppose," she raised her martini, "a rather grand safari."

Zoila replied, "Madagascar is known as The Naturalist's Promised Land."

"Yes," Brandon added. "It's incredibly rich in plant and animal life. There are over ten thousand species of flowering plants."

"How lovely," Evie said. "And how nice to be sitting here with you two, relaxing and feeling this marvelously comfortable night air."

After a dessert of flan, Brandon brought out the port. Candlelight glistened off glassware and smiles while they lingered comfortably. A discussion of the outlying areas was in progress when an eerie wailing cry came from a nearby copse.

"My goodness," Evie said.

"Oh, that's just a lemur," Zoe said with a reassuring smile.

"What's a lemur?" Evie asked, her expression visibly un-assured.

"Well," Brandon replied, "it's like a monkey, but not really. As opposed to lions, tigers and bears, suffice it to say, it's a monkey-like creature."

"Well, harmless as they may be, I'll use that as my signal to retire. John, did you wish to stay up or come with me?"

"I'm well and truly tired," John replied. "A delightful evening. We dined like royalty. Good night, you two, and thank you."

A teacher named Felix Narcisse made breakfast for the guests and the staff the next morning. Tables and chairs were set around the grounds near the cottages. He cooked up scrambled eggs, made pancakes and brewed pots of coffee. Honorine prepared a fresh fruit salad.

Brandon leaned toward John and said, "If you'll recall, I'd interviewed Felix in Chicago. He'd been teaching math in Lakeview. And," he nodded in the direction of another, "That's Gloria Kroehm, a science teacher from Park Ridge. Loves it here."

"I look forward to speaking with them."

"As you know, I hired Zoe, soon after arriving here. And Jim and Marilyn Protsman. They're over there. I'll introduce you. They'd been teaching American children at military bases in Europe when they read an article about Armitage House and this program. They got settled in here a month ago. Jim told me just the other day: *We feel a keener sense of purpose with this. And Marilyn is completely enchanted with the children of Mahkar.* They're fine folks."

While enjoying his last cup of coffee, Brandon added, "There are twenty-seven children in the village of Mahkar attending. On Saturdays, the teachers have a rotation schedule so that at least one of them is on hand to tutor students who come from outlying areas. So far, we have an average of twelve youngsters who come the distance for the one afternoon. They walk in groups, arriving in time for lunch."

Zoila added, "We can hear them approaching from far off because they sing along the way. Their voices are lovely. I'm amazed that they all have decent pitch."

As they were finishing breakfast, the village children were gathering at the school building. Marilyn Protsman left her table and began arranging them in a greeting line for their special guests.

Each child had been practicing an English expression for the occasion. Most said: *Welcome to our village.* But there were a few who tried to be original.

Saleh, a boy with a toothy smile, bowed and said with a near proper British accent: *M'Lord, M'Lady.* Evie giggled with pleasure and the boy looked pleased with himself.

A girl who Brandon knew to be six years old seemed to be wrestling with the issue of how to address the guests. Brandon noticed her when she was fifth back from the front of the line. The girl's beautiful dark eyes were fixed on Evie, as if she intrinsically knew

Evie's propensity to love and show kindness. When she finally stood in front of them, her lips went tight, as though she'd forgotten her words. A look of decision rose on her face and she threw her arms around Evie's waist and hugged her tightly.

"Oh, my. How dear." Evie bent down and in French asked, "And what's your name, young lady?"

"Moira." The girl's expression brightened.

"Are you working hard in the classroom?"

"Oui, Madame. Oui!"

"What is your favorite American movie?" Evie apparently didn't want the moment to end.

"The Love Bug," the girl answered without hesitation.

"Would you mind being my friend today? How about if you stand next to me while we meet the rest of the students?"

Moira fell in alongside her, beaming and surreptitiously looking up. She couldn't have been more impressed. She looked as if she'd found favor with the queen.

That night, the villagers began arriving, carrying picnic items and rolled up blankets for the weekly movie. A sense of peace settled on Brandon as his many plans for the special activities continued to delight John and Evie.

The Ragvandjee family pulled up,piled out of their truck, and offered John and Evie another gift—a small carving of horn that Mr. Ragvandjee had worked on. It was artistically done.

After proper acknowledgement to Mr. Ragvandjee, Evie turned to show it to Brandon and John. "This is a precious to me as a Fabergé egg."

The evening picnic preceded the movie. Brandon set out two folding chairs so John and Evie wouldn't have to struggle getting up later. Here, the villagers provided the meal.

Dishes of various rice varieties were passed around, and there were plenty of fresh vegetables and fruits, as well as a dish called Koba, a pâté of rice, banana and peanut.

As the sun hung low near the treetops off in the western field, Felix began to set up the projector, aiming it toward the school building, where the east wall was windowless, whitewashed, ideal for their purposes.

They'd all been mingling after the meal. Brandon had Evie at his arm when out on the eastern plain, a vehicle came in close, off-roading, fenders flapping, tailpipe roaring. It was Tarek's banged up Renault making a circuitous route, coming close enough for the two men to lock gazes. The muscles in Brandon's arm spasmed before he could mask any reaction.

"Is that someone you know, Brandon?"

Following its departing course for some moments, he turned back to her and said, "No, not really."

The offending noise diminished to a distant drone as the last of the fuchsia rays spotlighted it, transforming its appearance into some bizarre alien craft before the Renault disappeared behind a hill.

Once all were settled, Felix played the obligatory cartoon featuring Bugs Bunny, generating lots of excited laughter from the children. The main presentation was a French-dubbed version of *Damsel in Distress* with George Burns, Gracie Allen and Fred Astaire. Brandon's spirits momentarily lifted, pulling him from his thoughts of the menacing Tarek. Seeing these villagers, this isolated people, catching on to the humor of Burns and Allen was curative. After the movie, a few children tried to imitate Fred Astaire's dance moves but each in turn ended up tripping over themselves or one another.

If he could put Tarek out of his mind, he'd consider the evening a complete success.

Had they known earlier about the children who approached the school singing on Saturday afternoons, John and Evie would have planned their departure differently. But Saturday was the day they needed to drive back to board their ship.

In the early morning sun, the staff and some of the village families came to station themselves on the grounds as a send-off.

Before getting into Brandon's Rover, John signaled a thumb's up to Honorine as she sat in her VW. She was going to follow the group back to the city. She and Zoila planned to stay the weekend before returning for classes on Monday. Brandon had to drive straight back.

Once in the city, they hurried through a late meal before parting. At the gangplank, Evie amazed John.

She stood with stoic strength, looking up into Brandon's eyes. "I am so proud of you. So proud."

They shared a private smile.

"I can clearly recall our first session together at the school library," he said.

"Yes." She smiled sweetly.

"Thank you."

"Yes." She embraced him. "Thank *you*, dear."

The rest of the goodbyes went quickly. John and Evie were then bustled on board.

Evie never shed a tear.

Chapter Forty-Eight

"I've never before felt so comfortable, so at home with new acquaintances. The Armitages are wonderful," Zoe said softly, her face nearly touching Brandon's as they stood together, embracing.

The quiet on the garden terrace at Veera's place was well suited for parting lovers, hidden from the street by lattices lush with greenery and flowers. The late-day sun filtered through the trees, dappling the scene.

"You charmed them, I could see, but, of course, I think you're a charmer already, don't I?" He leaned in, kissed her forehead and then smiled at her. Her eyes searched his. He lifted her chin with his finger and kissed her mouth, enjoying the warm richness of her response.

He took a slow breath and said, "Yes, quite the charmer. It'll seem like ages before I see you again."

"Do they really need your help tomorrow?"

"I'd feel too selfish, too guilty. Jim and Felix need me. It'll take the three of us to work on those bleachers."

He wanted to say something about having the rest of their lives together but stopped himself. He decided to wait until he found a proper ring to present before broaching the subject.

After another lingering kiss and a quick good bye, he hopped into his Rover and headed out of town.

Brandon pulled up to the Ragvandjee petrol station and parked his Rover in front of the gas pump. Cloud shadows drifted lazily across the open terrain, evoking a sense of peace, as if fat sheep were happily grazing before him. When the different formations of shade hovered over a low-lying creek or a patch of wild flowers, he enjoyed the depth it gave the vista and how the hues changed. Since Raimo didn't come out running to do the honors, he inserted the petrol nozzle and the pump clinked and pulsed in even beats. His gaze drifted to a couple of chickens pecking and scratching at the ground at the far end of the family's property. The family's old truck stood just next to the building. Beyond that, another vehicle.

Brandon hung the nozzle back on the pump and twisted his gas cap on tightly. While walking up to the house, a warm wind rustled in the leaves of the trees.

He opened the front door to the sound of the jingling bell and stepped inside. A short man stood at the register.

It was Tarek.

An instant of peripheral movement was followed by Brandon's arms being grabbed from behind, thrusting them overhead. He was trapped in the hold of someone large and strong and smelling of cheap beer. Another man from just behind the door rushed down and grabbed Brandon's right leg, pulling it up and out, holding it so that all Brandon's weight was on his left.

A low, throaty chuckle came from Tarek, as he slowly walked toward him.

Finally, he said, "Every dog has its day." His eyes were bright, his gazed locked with Brandon's. As if tasting triumph, Tarek licked his upper lip. "For me, it's to beat you into a pulp, you privileged white boy." His grimy face glinted, as if considering sadistic options for inflicting pain. He stopped close enough that Brandon smelled the alcohol on his breath.

Brandon wanted to kick out in defense, but there was no way to get enough purchase. Tarek's fist rammed his gut. All breath heaved out in a rush and Brandon's head helplessly swung down.

"Oh, that was good, man. Hmm, how about this?" Tarek stepped closer and shot up his knee, smashing Brandon's face. Darkness, inner flashing sparks, then pain roared in, filling, now crowding, the space between his eyes.

"Yeah, that was good, that was good."

Fluid warmth, blood, ran down his face and then inside, filling his throat, gagging him.

"Now here's my favorite."

"Please—" A thrust in his groin released a scream that filled his body; agony consumed him—it was devouring him. His arms felt light and then he crashed to the floor. A boot rammed his side. Brandon struggled to take in breath, he couldn't, he couldn't, he couldn't.

Chapter Forty-Nine

"I won't feel truly relaxed until Brandon is safe at home." Evie fidgeted in her deck chair, neither noticing the print on the page of the book in her hands nor the beautiful Indian Ocean.

"He'll be fine, hon," John said. "He only plans to be there another month. Next thing you'll know, he'll be sitting on the terrace with us, and hopefully, with Miss Charbonneau at his side."

"Oh, I liked Zoe right away. If she wishes, I'd love to have her help at the Cabrini Green Center."

"Talk about danger," he replied in jest.

"Now, Jane Byrne felt the project was safe. And if the mayor can stay there overnight, I'm sure our teachers are safe during the day."

John was about to argue about Jane's body guards et al, but decided to let it pass. He knew "safe" translated to "close proximity" in Evie's mind, so that she could more readily check on things for her reassurance.

Zoila

"Are you sure he's going to ask you?" Honorine said while flipping through an issue of *Atlantic Monthly*. Honorine and Zoila were sitting at Veera's kitchen table.

"I feel he is. I mean, you've observed him day in and day out for the past several months. Do you think he's the type to toy with my affections?"

"No, but men might act differently when in a foreign land for a time versus when they're planning on returning home. Be careful; I'd hate to see you get hurt."

"It's too late. If he leaves for America without me, I'll be devastated."

Throbbing pain and cold sweat were Brandon's first sensations. He next realized that the prevailing blackness was merely night's darkness and not the grave. He'd been left on the floor in a small pool of blood. A shudder of pain passed through his lower back and on through his groin. An involuntary grimace stretched and pulled at some facial scabs, causing a warm trickle of blood to cross his dry, swollen lips.

Though he sat up carefully, the pulsation behind his headache went into double-time. His attempts to take slow, deep breaths were blocked by pain, possibly broken ribs. Surely his nose was broken by the feel of it. Eventually, he got to his feet, keeping a hand on the counter to steady himself. Where was the Ragvandjee family? He fumbled for and found the light switch. Stepping over his own slick of blood on the floor, he shuffled toward the back of the house, encouraged at hearing little thumping noises from the living quarters. He got to the door and opened it but the dim light from behind him revealed nothing. The thumping and sounds from gagged mouths was louder. He found and flipped the switch to his left and saw that the room had been ransacked. Walking through it, he opened another door and was thrilled to see the family of four alive and merely bound and gagged.

After getting his broken nose tended to at the village infirmary, Brandon wasted no time in proposing to Zoe. Life together became more important than fussing over a ring. Their civil wedding was held at the school complex with the entire village joining in the celebration.

When they arrived in Chicago, John and Evie threw an elaborate reception for them at the Drake Hotel. Brandon knew the sentiment was laced with bitter sweetness—this was the reception they had never been able to host for Bertie and Sofia. Somehow it didn't take anything away from the occasion; rather, it added to it. And Brandon enjoyed seeing his two sets of parents joyfully interact. The orchestra began playing the *Merry Widow Waltz* from the operetta that dramatized the glory of a second chance at love. It was a heady experience, waltzing with his bride, surrounded by a sea of beatific smiles.

Chapter Fifty

1990 Evie

Evie stood on the vast stage of the civic opera house, her eyes passing over the heads of the expectant crowd. She was one of the guest speakers at The Thinking Woman's Conference and though she felt slightly jittery, she stood straight as she confessed.

"I was a jewel thief and a polygamist." The immediate and unanimous intake of breath from the full house pleased her. "Were you to hear the particulars today, however, you might think me silly for being concerned over my transgressions. But you must realize: to a young woman born during the reign of Queen Victoria, I was riddled with guilt and strongly felt the need for redemption. It was this need that catapulted me into the lifelong pleasure of philanthropy."

Seeing how readily she was commanding their attention, Evie continued, feeling more in control, even exhilarated. "To quote UNICEF's international Goodwill Ambassador, the beloved Audrey Hepburn: What is more important than a child?"

She'd thought it would be difficult to follow keynote speaker Jane Pauley, who had discussed The Value of the Working Mother. Jane was a well-known television personality, a lovely lady, and an experienced orator. But a good opening line and a reference to Ms Hepburn proved to be as effective as Evie had hoped. She let her eyes rest on some of the faces before her and recognized an array of celebrities: mezzo Frederica von Stade; former Chicago mayor Jane Byrne; and the first lady of Arkansas, Hillary Rodham Clinton.

Evelyne braced herself, summoning courage until she could almost feel it racing through her veins. Aware of her occasional memory slips and the inadvertent habit she had of repeating herself, she concentrated especially hard on where her speech was heading.

"Armitage House began as a humble orphanage in Islington, London. That is where we took in children who had been living on its cold, dirty streets, with no future before them."

She walked the audience through how the organization had grown over the years, how its focus had adjusted with the times.

"Today I'd like to talk with you about the matter of resilience." She enunciated the topic with a weighted, low tone. "Some children might be born with a naturally resilient nature."

Backtracking to the twenties in Islington, she mentioned how one of her girls, Eloise Clark, had endured the loss of one parent, then the other, and how she had then suffered the indignity of the streets, how she had welcomed education and, lastly, how she had dealt with obstacles in her literary career.

"Yes, my Eloise was given a chance, a home with love and structure, an education, not only in academics but in comportment and social skills."

Evie elaborated on how the classes had been handled in those early days, eliciting appreciative smiles as she described Lady Birnam.

"My dear Eloise Clark," she reiterated heavily, "the first of my many children, passed away last week at the age of seventy-one. As a child and as an adult, she rebounded from her difficulties and enjoyed a fulfilling life. In an age when few women worked at the highest levels, Miss Clark excelled as a leading journalist in London and went on to write seven novels, all well received.

"Another of our charges was a boy by the name of Jiggs, a name he had been given on the streets. He was my rebellious one. But as a young man he saw the value of education, applied himself, and in his adult years became a Member of Parliament.

"However, not everyone is born with a resilient nature. In those early years we didn't know how to teach resilience; we simply provided opportunity. After decades of working with children I eventually realized how vital it is that we help them develop this trait. This realization came from my own experience as an adult. I had thought of myself as a fighter, a woman of strength. In 1915, I served at the Western Front as a nurse. I endured the results of my own poor judgment, corrected my mistakes and moved on. Then one night, my beautiful son, my dear Bertie, was murdered." Her breath quivered. "Brutally murdered."

She wasn't playing the words for effect, but the phrase hung suspended in the silence, regardless of her intent. "And ..." she said quietly, swallowing hard, "and I thought I'd never bounce back. At that critical time, I was also assaulted at gunpoint. I slipped even farther down into the slough of defeat. But John Armitage, that darling man, wouldn't let me go. In my most dilapidated state, he treated me with dignity, believing in me while he cared for me. And I came back.

"I then worked with children who had Attention Deficit Disorder before the phrase was coined or much technique known. One of my little protégés, Brandon Stewart, was so successful at working around this difficulty that he is now serving as CEO of our organization.

"I was privileged to have played a part in setting up schools in Africa and most recently in Eastern Europe. Armitage House, Incorporated has helped thousands of once underprivileged children, many of whom now contribute to society in meaningful ways."

She hesitated, battling a wave of panic. Suddenly she feared she'd strayed from the subject. After a near-frantic mental review of what she thought she'd already said, Evie began explaining how to develop resiliency in children through the example of planting a garden together.

"The garden begins to grow. And each day you see delight in your child's eyes when they go outside to inspect its progress. But one night the garden is assaulted by a horrific storm. And we come to face a moment of truth, a moment crucial to equipping our children for life. We must help that child see that not all is lost. Yes, there's sadness to deal with, but there is also opportunity. You plant another garden and you build a fence around it. If that fails to protect it the next time, you introduce them to making rock gardens." A murmur of laughter went through the auditorium and Evie waited for it to subside. "What you've accomplished by doing this is teach them that people cannot allow themselves to just fold up and wither. They move on, they become creative. They become resourceful."

Evie took a deep breath, nearing the close of her speech. Aware of the diminutive stature age had pressed upon her, she stood tall, squared her shoulders and, with a note of finality, concluded. "This is one of the finest lessons we can learn for ourselves, and what a gift it is when we pass can it on to our children."

At that, the soundman swooped in with Leonard Bernstein's "Make Our Garden Grow" and Evelyne Armitage earned the longest standing ovation of the entire conference. Feeling the vastness of the crowd's love enveloping her, Evelyne almost cried. To keep from breaking down, she kept herself from looking at John in the second row. She shifted her gaze instead to her household staff, seated next to him.

Margaret and Robin were practically jumping up and down, cheering for her.

Evie gazed out over the entire crowd. "I am proud to be here," she said to herself. "I have filled my life with engagement and purpose. My life has made a difference. I am proud of that."

September 11th, 2001 Evie

The room smelled of Vicks VapoRub. Ruth Jones, the hospice nurse, came into the bedroom to check on John and Evie, who were propped up on bed pillows next to each other. Evie had just turned 106. John would join her next month.

Ruth walked up to the television, her brow creased with sadness. "You folks gotta see what just happened. It's awful." She took a shaky breath. "A plane just flew into the World Trade Center." Her hand hovered over the power button. "Shall I turn it on?"

"I have the remote, Ruth, thank you, but go ahead," Evie said.

The fiery scene filled the screen. "Oh," Evie muttered, "how terrible."

Ruth stood transfixed for several minutes, watching the distraught anchorwoman repeat the most recent update.

"All those trapped people. Oh, John, how awful."

John was still but for a tear running down his cheek.

Ruth said, her voice husky, "I gotta get back to the kitchen. I'll watch it down there. You want me to leave this on?"

"I've got the remote," Evie repeated, offering Ruth an empathetic smile of shared concern.

"Oh, yeah." Ruth shook her head in amicable self-derision and left, closing the door behind her.

The commentator clutched her microphone tightly and announced that a second plane had just struck the other tower and that it was evident this was a terrorist attack.

The Armitages watched, horrified.

Several minutes later, Evie looked over at John.

"John?" She nudged him. "John?" Her fingertips trembled as she touched the side of his neck. There was no pulse. "Oh, John. No." As the towers began to collapse, she realized John was dead. She turned off the television and lay closer, draping her arm over him. "Oh, John." She kissed his cheek and let her mind drift to a safer place.

Quietly, gently, Isolde's Liebestode came from the recesses of her mind. Evie hummed into John's side, Brigit Nilsson singing to the dead Tristan. Her lips caressed John's cool face, wondering if the warmth of her breath could bring him back to life. Could the sound of her voice heal him?

Mild und leise wie er lachelt, wie das Auge hold er offnet, seht ihrs, Fruende?

Memories and melody swirled around her; the smell of Vicks became that of the trenches of Ypres, acrid in her throat. Yet her song soared, drowning out the guns, which barked in the distance. She could see John standing on the scarred Belgian field, the vision hazy with green, ghostly clouds. Men moved about, gasping, some falling. In the chaos, John's urgent eyes searched desperately for her. The hero of the Front wanted her. She sang out as though comforting the entire expanse.

Do you not see it? How he glows ever brighter?

When his gaze finally settled on her, relief flooded his face and she was falling into his arms.

Do you not see it? How he glows ever brighter, raising himself high amidst the stars? Do you not see it? How his heart swells with courage, gushing full and majestic in his breast?

The heady fragrance of roses in their honeymoon suite at the Ritz heightened her ecstasy. Her new husband's breath warm on her neck was alive with passionate kisses.

Do I alone hear this melody so wondrously? … Are they gentle aerial waves ringing out clearly, surging around me? Are they billows of blissful fragrance? As they seethe and roar about me, shall I breathe, shall I give ear? Shall I drink of them, plunge beneath them? Breathe my life away in sweet scents …

Epilogue

The temperature was mercifully cooler for their labors under the subequatorial sun. Their project involved a memorial of sorts, being built just beyond the new terrace at Armitage School-Madagascar. As the new teacher lifted the Italian Cypress, he grunted with effort. Its height and weight were the same, if not greater than his own. Sweat dripped down his brow, but with Lucinda Ragvandjee looking on, he managed enough strength to heave it to the freshly dug hole. He worried she would notice the quivering of his knees as straddled the pocket of earth. He was thirty-four, still in the prime of life, but he had never handled an Italian Cypress before. With a measured squat he manhandled the thing into its new home. Now the second and last planting was completed.

An hour later the man wiped his face, neck, and hands with a damp towel and eyed the two trees critically.

"They are fine," Lucinda said, arranging the picnic she'd brought. "Straight and lovely, like pillars."

She poured his tea in somber ceremony, but when she passed him his cup, her large amber eyes lit with pleasure. The sun hung nearer the horizon, stretching the shadows of the trees, the tops of which had, for the time being, merged, shading the spread blanket. The coolness refreshed them as much as the tea and treats.

He looked up with awe at the limitless blue dome above his work. It seemed only seconds later that their world was bathed in dusk's rose and rusty hues.

"Are you sure this is where you wish to teach?" she asked, sadness coloring her voice. "You're overqualified. Of course you know that already. Sorry."

He knew she wished he would teach at the city university while she attended med school, but he couldn't change his mind now. "Yes," he said, "but we'll be able to see each other on weekends."

The high-pitched, melodious call of a sunbird sang from the top of the left cypress, followed by the hush of the earth and grasses all around. The two young people savored the warmth of the fragrant land.

"When does your brother get out of prison?" she asked.

"He's got a few years yet. I think three."

They turned as soft footfalls came up behind them. "Great job, you two," Mr. Protsman said, smiling benevolently. The older teacher was dressed for the evening in pressed khakis, white shirt, and loafers.

"Thanks," the younger man said, getting to his feet. "I guess I'll need a wash and change. It sounds as if the entire village and more will show up for the service."

Mr. Protsman nodded and eyed the two trees as a slight breeze, rich and balmy, rippled through their branches. From a nearby copse came the lonely call of a lemur. "This was a great idea, kids," Protsman said. "I only wish Brandon and Zoe could be here but, of course, they'll be at the memorial in Chicago."

Lucinda stood with ease and brushed off her skirt. The young man enjoyed her graceful movements and admired the soft line of her neck as she looked heavenward. The rose-colored sky, arching above the twin cypress trees, peaked into incendiary colors. Bands of clouds swaddling the horizon deepened into lavender and indigo as crickets began their pulsating chirpings in the grass.

Mr. Protsman turned to leave, then stopped and smiled affectionately at the young teacher. "Oh, and let me officially welcome you on board here. We are all very proud of you, Manek."

###

Historical References

I incorporate two past public figures in this novel: Sir Samuel Hoare, 1st Viscount Templewood and Lady Maud Hoare, Dame Commander of the Order of the British Empire, Viscountess Templewood. I did so fictitiously and good-naturedly and hold them in very high regard. The humanitarian spirit they had demonstrated over the years is commendable and it echoes here.

I could not find any evidence that the Aquitania actually docked at the Royal Pier in Southampton, as it had other piers of this locale. So, it might be a liberty taken in using this particular pier in connection with the story. I had reason to select it over the other options.

The shores of Lake Michigan are dotted with concrete piers and breakwaters from past decades. However, to my knowledge, there is not one at Chicago's Oak Street Beach. This was a liberty taken for the sake of the story.

35919747R00164

Made in the USA
Lexington, KY
30 September 2014